DRAKE RESTRAINED
BOOK ONE OF THE DRAKE SERIES

S. E. LUND

ACADIAN PUBLISHING LIMITED

Copyright © 2017 by S. E. Lund

All rights reserved.

No part of this book may be reproduced in any form or by any electronic or mechanical means, including information storage and retrieval systems, without written permission from the author, except for the use of brief quotations in a book review.

❀ Created with Vellum

S. E. LUND'S NEWSLETTER

Sign up for S. E. Lund's newsletter and updates on her latest releases, sales and even free books!

http://eepurl.com/1Wcz5

Unsubscribe whenever you want – your email will never be shared!

CHAPTER 1

There are three things you should understand about neurosurgeons.

Huge balls. Laser-like focus. Hero Complex.

Cutting into the human skull to operate on the brain required nothing less.

I stood at the sinks in the anteroom outside the operating theater at New York Presbyterian, cleaning my knuckles with a scrub brush. My new neurosurgery resident, Stuart, stood beside me, the plain blue cap and scrubs, safety glasses and binoculars giving away little about his personality, but he was a neurosurgeon and that pretty much said it all.

This was our first real surgery together since he started and I was interested in watching him perform. He would do all the grunt work – the incision, sawing the bone to remove a piece of the skull, then sewing up after. I'd do the parts requiring greater finesse – mapping the location in the brain using the CT scanner, threading the electrode into the brain and adjusting the voltage, ensuring we had it in exactly the right place. I'd oversee it all to ensure he did it properly.

I turned to him and watched as he scrubbed in.

"My nurses tell me you're one of the youngest neurosurgery residents at NYP."

"Besides you, you mean?" he said and gave me a smile, which was visible only as a narrowing of his eyes over his surgical mask. "You were even younger than me when you did your residency."

I nodded. "I graduated high school early and finished my undergrad in two and a half years."

"You were one of the youngest medical students at Columbia ever. Even more ambitious than me."

I laughed. "From the looks of your CV, you're no slouch."

I felt Stuart's eyes on me. "You know the nurses call you Dr. D."

I raised my eyebrows. After being at NYP for only a few days, Stuart felt secure enough in his status to bring up the OR nursing staff's pet name for me.

"Dr. Delish, right?" I said, grinning. "I've heard it all."

"Dr. *Dangerous*."

I laughed at that. "I'm surprised its not Dr. *Demon*. You must have been talking to my ex-wife's friends. They hate me."

"Oh, take my word for it – these nurses did *not* seem to hate you. Not at all," Stuart said, the corners of his eyes crinkling. "They seemed to see the *dangerous* moniker as a definite plus. There was a lot of snickering going on." Stuart shook his head. "The ladies do love a bad boy."

I shook my head. "That they do. But you know, bad boys are just really *really* good at making women feel a little wild."

"Your dad was a legendary bad boy," Stuart said as he ran clear water over his soapy arms. "Flying planes, playing in a band, parachuting. Shock-trauma surgeon at U of Maryland. You're a lot like your father. The acorn really doesn't fall far from the tree…"

"I'm *not* like my father," I said, a bit too firmly. "And I'm not a bad boy. I'm a very *good* boy. Trust me. That's just their very active imaginations." I gave him a grin, holding up my hands and backing through the doors into the operating theatre.

Once inside, I was pleased that my favorite circulating nurse, Ellen, had my sixties music mix playing over the sound system. The nurses and technicians were moving their heads to the backbeat, which was such an important part of the British Invasion era music.

"On top of things, as usual," I said to Ellen and saw her brown eyes widen behind her surgical mask.

"Was there ever any doubt? " She handed me a sterile towel. "You have me well trained."

"There was never any doubt," I replied. "And it's the other way around, Ellen. You have *me* well trained."

She laughed at that. "Whatever you say, *Dr. D...*"

Dr. D...

I was used to the friendly ribbing from the OR nurses I worked with on a regular basis. I never knew which moniker they meant by it. I *hoped* it was Delish. She winked at me, obviously having overheard Stuart and not Demon, but you never knew.

Inside the OR and in the halls of NYP, I was Dr. D, but outside, I was someone else entirely. Master D, to those who knew my secret life, a Dominant in Manhattan's BDSM community, specializing in B&D – bondage and dominance. I made the mistake of becoming involved in a BDSM relationship with a nurse when I first entered the lifestyle five years earlier, and that had almost ended in disaster.

Never again.

From then on, I kept my two personas separate, never letting them meet. My career in neurosurgery at NYP relied on it.

A FEW SELECTIONS from the Rolling Stones played over the

speakers. I developed a love of all things 60s from my father, who was perhaps the biggest influence on my life despite the fact he did everything he could to avoid being a father. He died as he lived – fast and loose, his private plane crashing in the wilds of Africa while on a trip to Somalia doing work with Doctors Without Borders.

Everything I was I attributed to my father's influence. No matter how I tried to escape him, I wasn't successful but for one exception. My father thrived in chaos – first in a battlefield ER and then in a shock trauma ward back home. In contrast, I needed – *demanded* – complete calm and total control.

That need for control extended to all aspects of my life – my work, my home and sex. The only place I allowed less than perfect control was my choice of music, which was always loose and wild. Psychedelic rock. Jazz. Vintage Punk. Grunge Metal. Everything else in my life had to be precise, planned, laid out in writing and in triplicate, if possible.

Control was my thing. Dominance during sex was my kink.

My bondage closet would fascinate a shrink.

WHILE UNDER MY THUMB by the Stones played over the speakers, I considered Richard Graham, my patient with Parkinson's Disease. My team and I would implant electrodes deep in his brain that sent out pulses of electricity to very specific structures responsible for motor control. The operation would require total concentration on my part and that of my team of surgeons and nurses, but it was that control and focus that I loved.

With Jagger singing in the background, my scrub nurse helped me gown and glove up. Once Stuart finished with his portion of the surgery, I approached the patient, examining the incisions before placing the electrodes.

"How are you, Mr. Graham?" I said, keeping my voice firm

but warm to reassure him. He was sedated, semi-reclining, but conscious and responsive so we could make sure we didn't damage any key areas of his brain.

"Great tunes," Mr. Graham said. "You came through with the Stones."

"Music relaxes patients. We do what we can to make this as stress-free as possible, considering that we have to keep you awake during the procedure."

I consulted the CT images and checked to make sure everything was in proper alignment before threading the electrode into precise position, guided by a CT-generated image of the man's brain on a screen beside the operating table. Stuart stood beside me, watching my every move.

When I stimulated the section of the brain where the electrode has been placed, Mr. Graham's hand stopped shaking completely. His head was imprisoned in a metal cage designed to keep him still, so he could barely see his hand, but he could feel it and his response was why I did my job.

"*Holy Mary*," he said, his voice filled with awe. "Would you look at that..."

I smiled to myself, but didn't allow too much time for celebration. One moment where I lost focus and Mr. Graham could bleed or lose function. The success of the procedure was all down to how much skill I had guiding the electrode into the very specific part of Mr. Graham's brain that was responsible for motor movement. Even given my skill, there were still risks.

Fortunately, my concentration was above average and the electrode was in proper place. The pulses of electricity would stop the errant movement in Mr. Graham's limbs. He'd be able to hold his own cup of coffee again, use his own spoon, fork and knife.

When Mr. Graham's surgery was finished, I bent down to look him in the eye.

"Everything went really well," I said, squeezing his shoulder. "As we discussed, you'll still have the tremor until your surgical wound has healed, but once it has, you'll come back in and we'll activate the electrodes. You should be completely free of your tremor."

"Thank you, Doctor," Mr. Graham said, tears in his eyes. "Thank you."

I left the OR, removed my mask and gown and went directly to the waiting room to tell his wife and children about his surgery.

His wife cried when I delivered the news that the operation was successful. When she held her arms out, I allowed her to hug me briefly. She was probably afraid she'd have to start feeding him herself, wiping his ass and changing his diaper.

I loved my job. I'd do it for free.

AFTER I FINISHED DICTATING my report, I left the hospital and drove to my apartment in Chelsea.

Driving in Manhattan taught you two things: patience and ingenuity. When traffic was backed up, as it was that night, you had to either wait it out or find an alternate route. I decided to wait because, sometimes, a shortcut really did turn out to be a long journey, especially when everyone else had the same idea and the streets became one traffic jam after another.

That evening, I was tired after a long day of teaching and surgery, so I was anxious to get to my apartment as soon as I could for a shower and bite to eat. As I waited for a tow truck to remove a car that had been involved in an accident on 57th Street, my cell chimed.

ALERT: Appointment with Allie – MR.

Allie was my current submissive. I went to her apartment three times a week, on Tuesdays, Thursdays and Saturdays, ten o'clock sharp, for a ninety-minute session of bondage and dominance.

Tonight's appointment wasn't our usual scene where I tied her up, blindfolded her and tortured her with pleasure. MR meant 'mock rape'.

Mock rape wasn't my personal preference. I didn't respond to a woman's fear or inflicting pain – quite the opposite. I responded to a woman's trust to let me tie her up and blindfold her. I responded to her cries of pleasure. I chose my submissives carefully to ensure that they didn't have inclinations for pain or humiliation. Although Allie and I had been together for eight months and I thought I knew her desires inside and out, I'd been wrong.

I thought we had explored every kink we both had, so when she asked me to fulfill her secret fantasy after months of silence about it, I agreed because we were otherwise very compatible. Once every week or two, as a treat for being especially obedient the rest of our time together, I'd sneak into her apartment at a random time, chase her around, force her onto the bed, tie her up while talking dirty to her, and pretend to rape her. When I did, her orgasm would be explosive and that always made my own so much better.

Before the light changed, I saw a text from Ken, my band mate and the best man at my wedding. He'd arranged an extra gig at O'Riley's, his family's Irish Pub, for later that night, before our Friday gig at The Front. We had added some new songs to the usual sets we played. Playing at O'Riley's would give us the extra practice.

I considered – it would mean either canceling my appointment with Allie or seeing her earlier than 10:00, and I knew she'd be disappointed if I did. Still, my band came first and so I would have to postpone to another night or come by at 9:00 for a short scene. I texted her to let her know.

CHANGE IN PLANS. *Have another last-minute appointment at 10:00 and have only an hour. Will be by at 9:00 for a brief B&D session. Be ready.*

NEXT, I texted Ken that I'd be at O'Riley's, 10:00 PM sharp. Enough time to get home, eat a light meal, take a shower, and head off to Allie's place for a quick scene. Mock rape was off the agenda for the night. I knew Allie would be disappointed, but events were out of my control.

AT 8:30, I received a text from Allie as I was finishing a bowl of leftover pasta and tomato sauce I warmed up in the microwave.

I'M at a restaurant with my friends. Can we make it 9:30 instead of 9:00? I wasn't expecting you until after 10:00...

I NOTED with some irritation that she didn't use the proper form of address. If I didn't go until 9:30, I would have barely any time before heading out to O'Riley's.

NO TIME for anything but vanilla, then. I want to find you kneeling by the front door, in your hose and garters, in proper position. Quick and dirty against the wall.

She wasn't pleased.

What's the rush? You know what I wanted...

I did know what she wanted. But I couldn't do a proper MR scene in less than half an hour. They always required greater aftercare and that took time to do properly.

Allie, do I have to remind you about the terms of our contract? I have to come by early, or not at all.

I waited for her response, but it didn't come for a few moments.

All right, Sir. I'll be waiting.

I texted right back.

In proper position.

She replied.

In proper position, Sir.

I exhaled, glad that she'd submitted despite her disappointment. I didn't need the trouble.

Good girl. *See you then. Be ready for me.*

I finished my pasta, had a quick shower, and dressed in jeans and a white linen button-down shirt. I stowed both my guitars in the back of my Mercedes GL450 SUV before driving to her apartment.

I had a bad feeling about the night as I drove away. There was nothing I could do but face it.

CHAPTER 2

WHEN I ARRIVED at her tiny apartment in an old brownstone in the Upper East Side, she wasn't in proper position, on her knees by the entrance. Instead, she was in the kitchen pouring herself a shot of vodka, and talking on her cell. She was wearing street clothes – a black skirt and white blouse instead of her heels, garter belt and hose.

She looked every inch the law clerk with her platinum blonde hair pulled back in a bun and wearing a pair of black horn rimmed glasses. In fact, she looked very much like Lara and I wondered if that wasn't why Lara chose her for me.

Allie wasn't ready for me.

I stopped in the hallway of the dingy little apartment with its dark parquet floors and tiny window letting in barely any ambient light. After putting my key to her apartment into my pocket, I shucked off my shoes and jacket. Then, I entered the cramped living room.

Allie was a law student and there were books and papers and legal briefs all over her coffee table and sofa. Empty energy drink cans littered the windowsill. The room smelled of old coffee grounds.

When Allie saw me, a moment passed between us and I knew what she wanted.

Despite what we had agreed to earlier, quick and dirty against the wall, she wanted me to force her. Or punish her.

I didn't like administering punishment. It did nothing for me, but I knew it did something for a lot of subs. I made it clear to Lara that I did *not* want to become involved with painsluts, for neither of us would be happy in the long run. I could administer a hard spanking when necessary, I knew how to use a flogger and cane, but doing so did nothing for me sexually or emotionally. Truthfully, it went against my oath as a physician – do no harm.

I had *planned* on getting my shot of vodka while she knelt by the door waiting. I planned on standing in front of a kneeling Allie, her eyes downcast, her hands clasped behind her back so that her breasts jutted forward. Just the way I liked her to be.

I wanted to order her to take me in her mouth and suck me into hardness while I held her hair in my hand, guiding her mouth. She'd let me, like a good submissive. I wanted to fuck her from behind, fast and hard until she came. Then, I wanted her to finish me in her mouth. It would be pure vanilla, but I only had fifteen minutes to get both of us off, which was far too quick for what I usually liked.

She should have been waiting for me the way I liked. Instead, she was challenging me to make a choice: leave in anger, punish her immediately over my knee, or chase her into the bedroom and rip off her clothes before taking her hard and fast.

I considered.

If I left, I'd make it to the gig on time, with some time to spare, but it would be pretty much over between us. Despite being together for eight months with few bumps, insubordination like that, with me leaving, was not survivable.

If I decided to punish her immediately for disobedience, I'd have to sit on the couch and demand that she present herself to me so I could spank her over my knee. I could then fuck her on the couch. She'd come very quickly if so, for she was always worked up after a spanking. She'd need a lot of aftercare, for she'd be fragile after my punishment, so I might be pushing the window in terms of time to do it all properly and would be late for the gig.

If I decided to chase her and force her the way she wanted, I'd probably have enough time, but it would mean that I would be giving in to her instead of the other way around.

She whispered something into her phone and put it on the island. She removed her glasses, her eyes on me, waiting. In an instant, I decided.

I started towards her, my brow furrowed. Usually in a mock rape scene, I had to be a good actor, putting on an angry demeanor to keep in the role. Tonight, I really was angry and had to exert even more control over myself so the scene didn't become real. She anticipated my response, running to the back of the apartment before I was able to get to her. She made a half-hearted attempt to close the door to her bedroom, but I was faster and managed to wedge my knee in between the door and the jamb.

She squealed a bit in fear, although this was exactly what she wanted.

I didn't say anything. Instead, I used my greater body weight and strength to push the door open, careful all the same not to hurt her. She ran to the other side of her queen-sized bed, effectively trapping herself in the corner. I went to her, now totally calm, unfastening my belt, and then the buttons on my jeans.

She glanced hungrily at my groin, hoping to see an erection, but I wasn't hard – *yet*. By the time I reached her, she stood against the wall in the corner, her back to me, breathing fast. I placed my hands on either side of her on the wall, trapping her with my body. I leaned in, my mouth next to her ear. I was breathing fast as well, but part of my arousal was due to anger rather than lust. She was pushing things farther than I wanted to take them.

"What the *fuck* do you think you're doing, trying to escape me?" I said, my voice low, my body pressed against hers.

"*Please*," she whispered, her voice breathy with desire. "Please don't hurt me…"

"Don't *hurt* you?" I growled. "You're lucky I don't take off my belt and smack that pretty little ass of yours."

Except, I was beginning to suspect that's what she really wanted. I wouldn't give in and provide it for that was topping from the bottom.

Instead, I turned her to face me.

"You were very bad," I said and grabbed her hair, twisting it in my hand so that her head tipped back. "I have to punish you."

I kissed her harshly, my mouth claiming hers, tongue finding hers, sucking it. With my other hand, I grabbed a breast and squeezed. She moaned into my mouth, her eyes pressed shut.

That aroused me. Not merely the feel of her breast in my hand, the soft swell of it inviting. It was the sound of her desire that finally ignited mine.

I pulled away and turned her back so that she faced the wall, my hips pressed against her butt, one hand slipping around her body to rip open her blouse, grab her breast beneath the fabric of her bra, squeezing it, tweaking her nipple hard between my thumb and forefinger. She moaned at that, pushing her butt against me.

I pressed my erection between the cheeks of her round ass, shutting off my mind so that I responded to her body, to her arousal, my hand slipping down her belly to her groin. I ran my hands over her thighs, then hiked up her skirt roughly, my fingers finding her thong. She was wet, her panties damp, her body ready for me.

I wrenched it aside so I could slip my fingers between her shaven folds to find her hard clit, which I teased with long slow strokes. When she moaned once more, I grabbed her skirt, pulling it up to bare her ass. She leaned forward, her arms on the wall while I ripped one side of her thong, sliding the remaining fabric down her thighs so that she was completely exposed. I knocked her legs apart with a knee and removed my erection from my boxer briefs before sliding it between her legs and over her pussy from behind.

She gasped as I stroked the tip over her clit again and again, pressing her body back to meet me. I knew she was aching to feel me inside of her, but I'd deny her for as long as I could.

We were exclusive, had both been tested and so there was no need for a condom, which I used only with new subs until I knew they were healthy. It was a risk, and as a physician, I understood the risk, but I preferred it that way. I loved the feel of a woman's pussy around my dick.

Nothing in the world felt as good, as exquisite, as mind-blowingly ecstatic as coming bareback inside a woman's body.

I gripped her hips and pulled her into position so that she fell forward, her forearms on the wall, her thighs spread wide.

"Now I'm going to fuck you," I whispered in her ear, the tip of my erection teasing the entrance to her body. "But you're not going to come. Do you understand?"

"Please..." she whispered, her voice a whimper of need. "Please, Sir, let me come. I *need* to come."

"Why should you come, Allie? You deliberately disobeyed me."

"I was late getting home, *Sir*." Her voice was still a bit petulant. She hadn't submitted emotionally yet. I could feel it, a small bit of defiance making her less pliant than she should have been.

"No excuse," I said, knowing that we were at a crossroads. She would either start to obey in mind and body or she resist. If she complied immediately, I'd let her come. If she resisted, I'd punish her with orgasm denial.

If she did resist, it was more proof there was something seriously wrong with our relationship and that I could no longer deny it. She wasn't satisfied with the arrangement we had and we either had to renegotiate our terms or end things.

"You were talking on the phone when you could have been undressing and preparing yourself for me. Now, *I'm* going to be late."

"Why do you have to go?" Allie whined, craning her head back to me. "You promised me Thursday nights…"

I grabbed her hips and entered her with a single hard thrust. Despite her unwillingness to submit, I was still going to get an orgasm out of this mess so I began thrusting in earnest, focusing on my own pleasure, intent on coming as fast as I could with the least amount of effort to please her. I knew that she was pushing things as far as she could to get me to submit to *her* wishes when it should be the other way around.

She was more like Lara than I realized…

She was not going to top me from the bottom. I should have dragged her over to the bed and pushed her down over my knee, spanking her ass to drive home my disappointment in her disobedience, but I didn't have time. Denying her an orgasm would have to be punishment enough.

As if she finally understood, she said and did nothing while I thrust inside her. I didn't attempt to pleasure her at all, my hands gripping her hips, my focus on my orgasm.

I didn't enjoy straight fucking like that, usually preferring that I had completely spent my sub's need first, but I knew there would be no recovering from this – not tonight. Not without me being late for the gig. I didn't want to be late, so I thrust intently until I came, white-hot pleasure exploding through me, but my orgasm was less than satisfactory. A hollow knot of disappointment in the pit of my stomach prevented me from truly enjoying myself.

Allie was left unfulfilled, which was my intent, but it didn't feel like much of a victory nor did I think the lesson would be effective. Instead, it felt like total failure.

I had failed to acknowledge and deal with the signs that she wanted more from me than I wanted to give. I hadn't taken the time to sit with her and figure things out, get back on the right track and salvage the evening – and the relationship. When it came down to it, I was more intent on getting to O'Riley's on time than fixing things with Allie.

That alone was a revelation.

I pulled out of her body, pressing my hand against her back to stop her from moving, and sat on the bed across from her. I watched for a moment while I caught my breath. She stood with her thighs spread wide, my semen dripping out of her pussy but even that didn't satisfy me as it usually would.

I exhaled heavily. "You can get up now."

She stood up and pulled her skirt down as if embarrassed. Then she went to the ensuite bathroom and I heard the water running as she tried to clean up. I followed, providing her with some aftercare, thinking as I held her in my arms and stroked her cheek, that things had fallen to far apart to recover. Instead of being my submissive, obedient to my wishes, unquestioning about my orders and plans, she had instead tried to be my girlfriend.

She *wasn't*.

She couldn't be. I didn't do girlfriends.

Finally, I helped clean her thighs, wiping away my semen carefully with a wet cloth, no words being spoken between us. Once I was done, we stood side by side at the vanity. While I washed myself off, she watched me in the mirror. I could feel her gaze on me, and when our eyes met, she made a face of remorse, her brow creasing, the corners of her mouth turned down.

"I'm sorry. I was a bad sub, wasn't I?"

"You were. I'm sorry, too," I said while I tucked myself in and buttoned my jeans. "I'm sorry you disobeyed me. Now, I have to run or I'll be late."

"Where are you going in such a rush?"

I splashed water on my face and then ran my hands through my hair. She had no right to know where I was going. That wasn't part of our arrangement. When we signed our contract, we agreed not to poke our noses into each other's personal lives. She wouldn't try to learn more about me and my life outside of our sessions, and I would do the same.

I felt bad that things had gone wrong that night – I should have just cancelled the session entirely, given the gig, but I was too focused on trying to fit everything in. It was my fault for being preoccupied.

"My band's playing at O'Riley's at ten."

I left the washroom and she followed me to the front entrance, where I slipped on my shoes.

"Your band's more important than me?"

"*Allie...*" I said, my voice low. I shook my head but said nothing more. She knew my private life was not her concern.

"Don't be mad at me." She leaned on the wall, watching me as I slipped on my jacket. "I can't help it if I'm disappointed. I was looking forward to tonight."

"I'm not mad," I said, but it was a lie. "I'm disappointed. You know the rules. You agreed to our terms. We're going to have a little talk on Saturday night about what happened and what to do about it."

"I'll come to O'Riley's and we can talk after. I've never heard your band play."

I shook my head. "No, Allie. You know the rules."

She exhaled with barely-contained frustration. "Come back

after your gig," she said. "We can talk then. I don't want to wait until Saturday."

I shook my head. "I have early surgery tomorrow."

"What about tomorrow night?"

"We're playing at The Front."

"Come by after. We can do a scene. I promise I'll be a perfect sub. We can talk then." She said nothing for a moment while I slipped on my jacket. "You could stay the night," she said softly. "You have no surgery on Saturday so it doesn't matter how late we are. We could have breakfast."

I shook my head, exasperated with her but fighting my inclination to raise my voice.

"*Allie*," I said, my eyes meeting hers, trying to hold her gaze but she avoided me. I took her chin in my hand. "Why are you doing this? I don't sleep over. You *know* that. I don't do breakfast."

She pulled away and stood at the door, her eyes not meeting mine. "I deserve more."

There. She said it.

I stopped and inhaled deeply. "If you feel that way, then you do." I cupped her face with my hand, stroked her cheek. She couldn't avoid looking me in the eyes. "I can't give it to you. I'm sorry."

Her eyes brimmed but then she forced a smile. "Forget it. Just forget I said it. Let's go back to normal."

I hesitated, not sure if we could go back to 'normal' now that she admitted she wanted more.

"We'll talk more on Saturday night." I opened the door and then I turned back. "Be ready for me. In proper position." I leaned in and kissed her on the lips then I stroked her cheek briefly.

She forced another smile. "See you."

I left without looking back, my mind already focused on getting to O'Riley's in time for our gig.

Any endorphins from my recent orgasm quickly dissipated and I felt a sense of gloom that even the prospect of my band playing our new set couldn't dispel. I knew in my heart that Allie and I were probably over. Saturday night would be confirmation. I couldn't see my way to working things out with her. She'd be disappointed unless we moved the relationship beyond what I wanted and needed.

That wasn't going to happen.

CHAPTER 3

WHILE I DROVE to O'Riley's, I thought about Allie.

A law student Lara found for me when my previous submissive and I parted ways, Allie had initially ticked off all the boxes in my to-have list for submissives. Her body was fit from taking martial arts, she was attractive, and she was intelligent.

I wanted a strong woman, mentally and emotionally, who happened to get turned on by power exchange in the bedroom. Women who were professional, who were intelligent, and who had their own mind but chose to turn it off during sex so they could go places they couldn't on their own. Women with a kink for being tied up, helpless, and at my complete mercy for the hour or two we were together for mind-blowing sex.

It meant things were a bit more complicated for I had to manage their will, which occasionally broke through, asserting itself.

Like Allie's was.

When I first met her at the café where Lara and I went for coffee, Allie regarded me with a determination I found amusing. I knew she was the kind of submissive who had her own mind and will and strength, but wanted to give that up to me. Her bold gaze made me want to see her on her knees.

Sure enough, when we were alone that first time, she became completely submissive, as if her perfectly put together persona was a façade and she couldn't wait to turn over her power to me. I enjoyed our scenes for she loved being blindfolded, gagged and restrained while I tortured her with pleasure.

In the last couple of months, things had changed. Subtly at first. More episodes of deliberate disobedience when I would have to administer a spanking. Then, she confessed about her secret desire for mock rape.

When I told Lara of the developments, Lara warned me that Allie might be hiding more secrets and that I should be prepared. I *hoped* we had been open and honest with each other about our needs and desires. Up until the mock rape request, things between us had been comfortable, predictable, and satisfying.

So, despite how well we had done for the past eight months, her recent desire for mock rape and more punishment made me suspect that she was dissatisfied and that insurrection was brewing under the surface of her almost-perfect submissive posture. If so, we'd have to end the relationship. Although I'd grown fond of Allie, I didn't love her and couldn't commit to anything that involved pain or humiliation nor could we become emotionally involved. All I wanted was B&D sex three times a week – Tuesday, Thursday and Saturday.

I had a regular practice session with my band on Wednesdays and usually a gig on Friday nights at one of several venues that featured 60s music. Saturday afternoons I spent going over business at the Foundation my father started in order to donate equipment to hospitals in the developing world. I took Sunday off most weeks to decompress, and either went to my club to play racquetball with one of the other regulars or stayed at home drinking coffee and reading the Saturday *Times*. I had no pets, and every plant my housekeeper had brought over to brighten up the apartment died due to lack of attention and water.

Occasionally, I attended an event for Doctors Without Borders, and now and then, I met with my fellow surgeons at NYP for drinks and a meal, but otherwise my days and nights were taken up with surgery, music and sex.

I had little room in my life for anything or anyone else.

My fellow surgeons joked about me being a bachelor and tried to hook me up with their single friends, nurses at NYP, and female physicians, but I was not in the market for a partner. There were times I felt a sense that time was passing far too quickly. Despite the fact I was at the top of my game as a new neurosurgeon, that my body was fit and my reflexes and coordination sharp, that my life was missing something, and that I was running too fast from one part of my life to the next. Other than the occasional bout of excess when I drank a bit too much vodka, I didn't confront whatever it was that dogged my otherwise perfect life.

Now, things seemed like they were winding down between Allie and me and I felt a darkness in the back of my mind like a storm cloud on the distant horizon.

I ARRIVED at the pub with a few moments to spare. Once parked at the rear of the building, I removed my guitars from the back of the car, and entered through the alley, past the kitchen where cooks were busy cleaning up after dinner service. I took a dim corridor to the office where Margaret O'Riley, the O'Riley family matriarch, sat going over the evening's dinner receipts. A beautiful woman in her sixties with a greying bun and piercing blue eyes, she smiled when she saw me. I leaned in and kissed her on the cheek.

"There you are," she said, examining me over her reading glasses. "Ken's already on stage setting up. Did you come right over from surgery? Have you eaten? Ask the cooks for something if you want."

"I ate something," I said and gave her a smile. "Thanks anyway, Mom."

I took the hallway past the public washrooms to the bar and small stage on which we would play. Ken, Margaret's son, was the drummer in our band. The oldest of five children, he had his mothers blue eyes and his late father's bald head.

Ken always dreamed of being a rock musician, but in all likelihood would inherit the pub from his mother and become an owner instead of a musician. But we planned on playing as long as venues would book us. Heck, we'd pretty much play for free if that was all we could find.

We were all talented amateurs who never made a go of music but retained a love for it, especially music from the 60s and 70s. Mersey was a British Invasion cover band named after the river in Liverpool where so many great British rock bands originated. We played Irish pubs like O'Riley's and the occasional wedding. Now and then, we played Psychedelic Rock as well but our specialty was the Brit Invasion, The Rolling Stones, The Animals, The Yardbirds, and The Zombies.

The other two band members were Johnny Mears who played keyboards and Cliff Walters on lead guitar and vocals. I played acoustic guitar, bass guitar and sang. We met in college and had been playing together ever since. Sometimes, I thought it was merely so we could spend time together. None of us needed the paltry sum we earned each week.

We were pretty tight as a band, having played together on and off for ten years. But we'd recently added some new tunes to the repertoire and tonight was a chance to practice before our big gig at The Front on Friday.

I passed the dining room, which was almost empty, a few

patrons lingering behind at white cloth-covered tables to finish their coffee and desserts, the lights low, candles on every table giving the room a romantic glow. As usual, the lounge styled in dark woods and decorations taken from a pub Ireland was full, the dozen small tables and banquettes filled with regulars. In the old days, before the smoking ban, a thick pall of smoke would hang over the crowd, but in the new Manhattan, the air was clear.

Some canned music played over the sound system and the customers were busy talking and drinking while Colin O'Riley, Ken's younger brother, presided over the bar. The band would play on a small raised platform near the back of the lounge. Ken was there, finalizing the setup of a full drum kit. There were several amps in place, wires and electrical cords snaking through them.

I put down my guitar cases and clapped Ken on the back. We embraced briefly in greeting.

"How's it going?" Ken said as he lifted his top hat cymbal into place. A few years older than me, he was a tall lean man with a long face that seemed perpetually somber. "You had to tell your girl you'd make it another night, I take it?"

"Nope. We had a quickie."

"What?" Ken said and laughed. "You rogue. You know I live vicariously through you. I'm lucky if I get sex on the weekend when the kids are finally asleep."

I grinned, although the quickie was hardly satisfactory for me, but Ken didn't have to know it. He and the other guys had no idea about my preferences for kink. They only knew I had a series of girlfriends who I kept separate from the rest of my life.

Although they often pushed me to bring whomever I was with at the time to meals at their homes, I refused politely. I claimed that my girlfriends were busy with school, which they usually were since most of them were students, and that we spent most of our time together in bed when we had the chance to see each other. Which was also the truth, except of course, that they were usually tied to the bedposts, blindfolded and gagged.

I didn't tell them that fact either, although I was certain it would make their day. If I did, I knew I'd be the butt of endless jokes about kink, so honesty wasn't an option. My secret world remained just that – secret – from even my best friends.

"So, when am I finally going to meet this young woman of yours? What's her name? Alice?"

"Allie," I said. "Is the keyboard set up yet?" I glanced around the stage, trying to divert Ken from his well-intentioned attempts to meddle in my personal life.

"Quit trying to change the subject," Ken said, smiling. "You've been seeing her for what – a year?"

"Eight months."

"So? What the hell are you waiting for? Bring her by the bar some night. I know mom would love to meet her."

"We're not serious," I said. "Just fuck buddies."

"Fuck buddies for eight months?"

"She's a student and is too busy for a real relationship. I'm not looking for a girlfriend. It's just sex and it works out fine for us both."

"Mom worries about you. She thinks you still have a broken heart."

I laughed, but that thought bothered me. "My heart is made of stone," I said and pounded my chest, smiling in an attempt to lighten the mood. "Tell her she shouldn't worry. I'm *fine*."

"You have to get over Maureen, Drake. You need to find someone serious. No more fuck buddies, man. Find a woman you could love."

I didn't say anything in the hopes he'd stop with the advice. No luck.

"It's been five years and you still haven't had a steady

woman. You only ever have fuck buddies and none of us has met a single one of them. That's not healthy."

"Hey, I'm living the dream," I said, a little too angrily. "Sex with no strings. No emotion. Look, I'm not planning on getting married again, so let it drop, OK?"

Ken watched silently while I set up my bass guitar. I felt his disapproval, and finally met his gaze.

He shook his head. "Let's get the keyboard." Ken led me to the back of the bar and the door to the basement. We kept some equipment stored there, and so we went down to the room beside the wine cellar and carried up the keyboard. We spent the next quarter of an hour setting up, waiting for the other guys to arrive.

Thankfully, Ken dropped the subject of my personal life.

Once the other guys arrived, and we did a sound check, Colin took the mic at the front of the stage to announce us, not that the usual crowd wasn't already familiar with us and our music.

"And now, back by popular demand and with a new selection of Brit Invasion tunes, please give a round of applause for our own Ken O'Riley's Brit Invasion cover band *Mersey*."

Colin turned to us and bowed and we all bowed back, me standing to the left of the stage, Ken on drums, Johnny on keyboards and Cliff on lead to my right. We started with a series of Beatle's oldies, No Reply, And I Love Her, and then In My Life. Cliff took the lead on vocals since he was the closest in sound to John Lennon, but I did background vocals. As we played, I watched the patrons. They stopped talking and turned to listen, responding to the song and the Sixties sound. It was going to be a good crowd.

We'd added in a few new songs, most from the Stones, and playing at O'Riley's gave us a chance to perfect them. We'd performed once already on Wednesday at Mickey's, a small club in Chelsea, and had practiced the previous Sunday at O'Riley's during the day, so we weren't quite as tight as we would be with our usual playlist.

I took lead vocals on four new covers, Heart of Stone, Play With Fire, Under My Thumb and Paint It Black, all by The Rolling Stones. My voice was a bit lower in register and I more easily mimicked Jagger's saucy voice. I'd done a lot of role playing with my subs over the years and was more relaxed about performance. Plus, I enjoyed putting myself in Jagger's petulant bad-boy shoes.

I liked all four new songs, and enjoyed playing my Gibson bass – my father's old instrument. Cliff and Ken provided background vocals on Heart of Stone. The crowd really seemed into it, and gave us a rousing round of applause when we finished. We moved right into Play With Fire, and then Under My Thumb without stopping. I loved playing the bass line in Under my Thumb and because the bass was so important, it was one of my favorite new covers.

Our final song of the set was Paint It Black, also by the Stones. It was hard driving and had a great rhythm. We still needed work to tighten up a bit but luckily, the Stones were always a bit loose and so our lack of practice didn't really hurt too much.

Our sound was right.

We finished the set to a roar of applause and bowed before leaving the stage to go to the bar for a break. Our second set would be mostly The Yardbirds and The Animals – our usual repertoire.

I leaned against the bar and took the glass of water Colin poured for the four of us, and then the shots of tequila he also provided.

We passed around the salt shaker, shot back the tequila and bit the limes.

"Good set," Colin said after refilling the shot glasses. Then, he turned to me and pointed to the back of the lounge. "Your lady friend's here."

I frowned and turned to look where he pointed, thinking that maybe Lara had shown up. She occasionally came to our gigs to listen to us play, but it wasn't Lara.

It was Allie.

Allie showing up at O'Riley's was totally unacceptable.

For a moment, I saw her the way the guys would -- tall, athletic and with pretty features. She was beautiful. As if to please me and ward off my reprimand, she wore the black leather dress I liked and made her wear to dungeon parties. Her platinum blonde hair fell around her shoulders like satin and her makeup was perfect. Any man in the bar would have been pleased to have her at their beck and call.

She was also wearing leather wristbands that I used to restrain her during our scenes, as if to remind me who I was to her.

Her Master.

Ken dog-whistled and leaned in close. "Is that her?"

"It is," I said, not pleased to see her at O'Riley's. "Excuse me for a minute."

"She's stunning," Cliff said, his eyes wide. "We never get to meet your mysterious women. I was starting to think you were lying about having a girl. Introduce us."

"I don't think so," I said. "Maybe some other time."

I left the three of them at the bar, knowing they would be gossiping about Allie while I was gone. I could almost feel their eyes on me as I threaded my way through the tables. A few customers stopped me to tell me they enjoyed the show, and I nodded, offering a polite thank you.

When she saw me approaching the table, she forced a smile, but I could tell she knew I wouldn't be happy.

"Allie," I said and sat across from her. "You know this breaks the terms of our agreement."

"I wanted to talk to you tonight."

"We agreed to talk on Saturday night."

"I didn't want to wait that long." She reached across the table and took my hand. I wanted to pull my hand away, but didn't want to cause a scene.

"You shouldn't have come," I said.

"After all this time, you still don't want me to hear you play? Christ, Drake," she said, her voice filled with emotion. "It's been eight months. Don't I deserve some little scrap of humanity from you?"

I pulled my hand away. "You have my complete and total focus sexually. That's all I can give, Allie. You knew that when you signed the contract."

"The contract is just for show, Drake. You know it's unenforceable."

"It is. If you're not happy with the terms, you can leave at any time."

"Just like that?" She shook her head, her eyes bright but I could tell she was fighting her emotions. "You feel *nothing* for me beyond sex? I feel like you know me more deeply than anyone else has, *ever*."

I glanced around, trying to decide how to handle her. I took in a deep breath and then leaned closer, my voice low but loud enough for her to hear me over the buzz of conversations around us.

"Allie, I know you *sexually*. That's it. I don't know anything else besides the fact you're a law student. Nothing." I exhaled. "I don't know what color you like, or your favorite dessert, or what movie you watch over and over again when you're sick, or even what kind of music you like."

"I love *you*," she said, her eyes brimming. "Don't you love me, even a bit?"

"No you *don't* love me. Look, Allie," I said, trying not to be too harsh. "I've been married. I know what love is. You can't *love* me if you know nothing about me. I can't love you if I know nothing about you."

She forced a smile, as if to keep from crying.

"Don't you *want* to know me? God, Drake, I have sex with you three times a week. You know my secret desires. Are you so heartless that you don't care to know me more deeply?"

I sighed, exasperated. This was the talk I knew we'd have to have sooner or later. I hoped it would be later, because I still enjoyed Allie sexually, but she was transgressing the terms of our agreement. She was unable to keep it purely sexual.

"I know about you," she said and squeezed my hand once more.

"You weren't supposed to know anything about me. That was part of the contract. No asking questions, no doing research. No stalking."

"I'm not stalking you. For Christ's sake I fuck you three times a week. How can I stalk you?"

I shook my head, not sure of what to say.

"I asked around. I did some research. You're a neurosurgeon at NYP. You play in the band. You've been in the lifestyle for five years since your divorce from a nurse who used to work with you. Your father's dead. Drake," she said and leaned in closer. "I could love you, if you let me."

I shook my head. "Don't do this. I can't do more. I don't *want* to do more." I sat in silence and we stared into each other's eyes as if waiting to see if the other would relent.

Tears finally spilled out from her eyes.

"I'm sorry," I said, shaking my head in disappointment. "I can't give more. You knew that when you signed."

"If you can't give me more, then it's over."

"I can't." I sighed and pulled out my keys from my jacket pocket and removed my key to Allie's apartment from my keychain. I placed it down firmly on the table across from her. "I didn't want to end it this way, but you're right. I guess it's over."

I exhaled heavily as I slid it to her, exasperated that she was doing this now.

She stared at the key, her expression one of disbelief, her eyes wide. I could see that her cheeks were red even in the darkness of the room. She didn't really believe I'd break off the relationship, probably hoping that the mere threat of it would push me closer.

"Don't do that," she said, her voice wavering. She pushed the key back towards me with a trembling hand. "Give me another chance."

I shook my head. "I already gave you a second and third chance. You crossed the line too many times." I kept my voice firm, although I, too, was upset. I just couldn't see any way around it. "You know the rules."

"You broke a promise. You *promised* to spend every Tuesday, Thursday and Saturday evenings with me as long as we were together. I think I deserve to be upset."

I held up my hand. "I promised unless circumstances arose that were beyond my control. Mersey got an extra gig, and it was a chance to get more practice in before our big show on Friday. I had no choice."

"You *always* have a choice." Her voice broke and she brushed tears from her cheeks quickly. "You *choose* to put your band ahead of me. You *choose* to be unknowable, as if you can keep things all neat and tidy between us. All you want is a few good orgasms a week so that nothing like real emotion interferes with your perfect little *life*."

"You knew when you signed my contract that we would just be play partners, nothing more," I countered, but her assessment of me stung just a bit. "You told Lara and you told me you didn't *want* anything more."

"After all this time?" Her tears were flowing now. "You couldn't find it in your heart to let me come and listen to your band play? You *are* heartless."

I shook my head. Other men might give in, try to make things work, but I couldn't have her breaking the terms of our contract that way. If I let her, she'd try to break all the terms, and that wouldn't do.

Three times in the past month, she'd tried to go beyond the careful margins I'd drawn between my life as a Dominant and the rest of my life as a surgeon and musician.

She'd asked me to stay the night once after a very long session where I had tried some new rope tricks with her. I'd refused. I didn't stay with my submissives. It was a Tuesday and I had an early surgery scheduled the next day. Then, she'd asked me to come to her apartment early and have supper with her on a Saturday night. I refused once more, reminding her that I didn't do meals with my subs. The only thing I ate when we were together was her.

Finally, she'd asked earlier that night if she could come and listen to Mersey play at O'Riley's. I told her no. My music and my sex life did *not* mix.

"You know," she said finally, her voice breaking. "I listened to those songs you sang. That one – the one where you say you have a heart of stone?" She stood, pushing her chair back so hard, it fell over. "You don't even have a heart." Then she grabbed her bag off the table and stormed out without looking back, the key left on the table in front of me.

I stood and righted her chair then turned back to the bar, my friends staring at me, expressions of surprise and interest clear on their faces. Now, I'd have to tell them we broke up.

I checked my watch. Our next set was due to start in a few minutes. Luckily, there wasn't time for them to demand a full debrief.

I sighed and went to the stage, bypassing them so I could avoid even having to discuss what just happened, the key to her apartment left behind on the table.

CHAPTER 4

THE NEXT WEEK went as usual, except I didn't go to see Allie on the appointed nights. Each weekday morning, I woke to my alarm at six. Showered, grabbed a coffee and toast. Dressed. Drove to New York Presbyterian where I had a full slate of surgeries booked.

I purposely didn't think about Allie, immersing myself in my cases, consciously blocking out her words about me. I knew about denial, having studied psychoanalysis briefly during my undergrad. If I kept myself busy enough, I wouldn't have time to mourn the end of the relationship.

If my personal life had gone to shit, at least my work as a surgeon was going well.

After dictating my surgical reports and checking in on my patients, I left NYP and took my car to meet Lara for lunch at a café near the hospital. I knew she would have heard from Allie about our breakup and would want to interrogate me about it.

I arrived, still wearing my scrubs, and after placing my order at the counter, I went to the table. Lara looked impeccable, as usual, wearing an expensive suit, her hair tidy in a smooth updo. She had her usual salad and espresso. The café was busy at this time of day, so we sat in a corner for added privacy. The noise of patrons talking, the clink of glasses and cutlery, helped mask our discussion.

"Drake," she said before I even sat down, her voice sounding irritated. "I hear you and Allie ended it in a bad way. That's not like you. You should have called me sooner."

I sat across from her, surprised at her tone.

"She wanted more," I said plainly. "I can't give it."

Lara sighed and shook her head. "She told me you broke up with her in public."

"I had no choice," I said, feeling defensive. "She came to O'Riley's."

"So?" Lara said. "I've heard you play before."

"You're my friend."

"Can't you be friends with your subs?"

"I have all the friends I need. I need a fuck partner who likes a bit of kink. Look," I said, impatient with her. "I *told* Allie from the start that our relationship would be strictly sexual. Nothing more. She wanted to be my girlfriend, Lara. I don't do girlfriends. You know that."

"Poor Drake. Still hurting after all this time? Still have mommy issues?"

I frowned. "What are you talking about?"

She shook her head and said nothing but I knew damn well what she meant. She was referring to my divorce from Maureen and the loss of my mother when I was ten.

It was after my divorce that Lara and I became reacquainted after a decade being apart, each pursuing our own lives. We met in an abnormal psychology class when we both studied sexual perversions of the sadomasochistic variety. She took the class because she *was* a sadist and I did because I was fascinated with those who were obsessed with pain, giving it and receiving it.

I didn't want to give pain. I wanted to cure it.

We never crossed over into being sexual partners because both of us were too dominant in personality and she felt strange that I was so young, only eighteen when we met while she was a few years older. I knew she was kinky when we were friends before, but at that time, I resisted the notion that I was as well. When I was in trouble after my marriage failed and Maureen obtained a restraining order, I ran into Lara at a café and we caught up once more. It was then she diagnosed me as a sexual Dominant.

She urged me to take training from her so I could do it properly. At that point, broken as I was, confused and wounded, I agreed. For three months, I was her submissive, learning what it felt like to be tied up and helpless, how to be safe when using ropes and restraints, how to flog, whip and administer spankings. She even used a strap-on with me so I'd understand anal sex and how to do it properly.

Once Lara felt I had learned everything there was to learn about being a sub, explaining to me why she was doing everything, I graduated into being a novice Dom, and under her tutelage, had my first subs. It made us especially close, those months after Maureen and I separated and I began to explore the world of BDSM. She felt a certain ownership of me as a result, and I felt very indebted to her. She took me when I was broken and fucked up, and fixed me. Put me on the right path, and helped me learn who and what I was.

Because of that history, she couldn't help but interfere. If it had been anyone else, I would have not-so-politely told them to fuck off, but it was Lara. Allie was a favorite of Lara's because she was studying to be a lawyer. I knew she'd have received an earful from Allie about our breakup.

We sat in silence for a moment, the atmosphere chilly between us. I felt her disapproval from across the table.

"So you want me to find you someone new."

I nodded, glad she decided to move on and not belabor things.

"Experienced or novice?"

"A novice. I don't want to get anyone with bad habits or expectations I can't meet. I'd rather mold their expectations."

She raised her eyebrows at that. "Isn't it better to find someone who already knows what they want? You might get someone who needs more than you want to give. Like Allie."

The waitress came and brought my order – tomato soup and a toasted BLT. I waited for her to leave and then shook my head.

"If I do, I'll move on."

"Just like that? You'll move on."

"Yes. I like exploring with a new sub. I want someone pretty vanilla but with a need for domination. Someone into power exchange, but not pain. You know what I like."

"Yes, I do." Lara sat back in her chair and watched me dig in to my BLT. "I may have someone for you. Two students I met during a seminar I gave on finding a Dom. Neither of them are very extreme and have no real desire for pain, but both expect to be spanked, hair pulled, and one likes hot wax."

I considered. "Send me links to their photos and profiles on FetLife."

AFTER MY LAST surgery of the day was finished and I'd done rounds to check on how my patients were doing, I went directly to the health club a few blocks from the hospital, where I worked out several times a week.

While in the locker room, I saw Ethan McDermott, Justice of the Supreme Court of New York, and my father's oldest and best friend from Vietnam. After I finished tying my shoes, I went to where he sat with another man.

"Judge McDermott," I said, wanting to show him deference, despite being very familiar with him. "How are you?"

He turned to me and a wide smile broke out on his face.

"Well, young man, how are you?" He stood and held out a hand and we shook. He was shorter than me, greying with heavy jowls and bright blue eyes. He turned to the other man, who looked to be in his fifties as well. "George, this is Drake Morgan – *Doctor* Morgan, the son of my old buddy in the Marines. His dad and I were in 'Nam together at the tail end of the war. Drake, this is Justice George Smart, one of my colleagues."

A round of handshakes took place and then Ethan turned to me, eyeing me carefully.

"What have you been up to since I last saw you? Been keeping busy with surgery? Teaching any classes?"

I nodded. "Robotic surgery," I said. "I'm keeping out of trouble. How's everything with you? Your family doing well, I hope?"

"Just fine. Elaine is planning our vacation over Thanksgiving. I'm busy with campaign business, as you can imagine."

"Where are you going over Thanksgiving? I'm presenting a paper in the Bahamas at a convention."

"Elaine wants something tropical."

"The Bahamas are great. Keep it in mind. And how's Heath?"

Ethan's only son, Heath was a lawyer like his father, but specialized in corporate law. Rather quiet instead of outgoing like Ethan, but obviously on the same career path. "Heath's doing well. Been busy in Haiti on and off. Reconstruction work. That sort of thing."

"How's Katherine?" I said lightly. Katherine was the true apple of Ethan's eye. He always spoke about her with real fondness, but I still hadn't met her. She never attended any of her father's social functions or fundraisers.

Ethan had been adamant about internet security and refused to post pictures of his family online. Even though I had searched for info on Katherine, there was none to be had. Her Facebook page was friends only. I had the feeling she was still too fragile and he was protecting her from public scrutiny. There were no pictures of her online except when she was a small child in the obituary for her mother.

"She's doing well. Very well, in fact. Still working on her Masters."

"I read her work on Mangaize you sent me," I said, remembering the somber articles on Africa she wrote. "Really got me in the gut. Is she feeling better?"

Katherine had volunteered in the camps in West Africa and had been traumatized by her stay there. Her articles were published in a student-run magazine and she had won the Columbia Journalism prize for them. She'd also had a breakdown.

Ethan had spoken about her to me because of my interest in psychology and because I was a physician. I knew her history and had offered advice to him on how to handle his beloved daughter's emotional scars. Not only had her mother died the year before, but Katherine had gone to Africa during the worst days of the famine. It proved to be too soon after her mother's death and she hadn't really grieved fully. The two events combined led to her breakdown.

Ethan nodded, his face solemn. "She's pretty much recovered, but still laying low. Got another year of work before she's finished her degree."

I nodded. "Glad to hear she's doing better."

"Me as well," Ethan said and laid a hand on my shoulder. "Listen, I'm hosting a fundraiser for Doctors Without Borders on Friday night. You're welcome to come. I know your father's foundation did a lot with them and I'm sure you wouldn't mind forking over some of your dad's hard earned cash for a good cause."

"I'd be honored."

"Good. 6:30 until 8:00." He glanced at George. "Well, I guess I better get a move on. See you on Friday. You know the address."

"I do. See you then."

I left Ethan and went to the weight room for my workout.

THAT NIGHT, I tossed and turned in my bed, unable to get comfortable despite being exhausted. The discussion with Lara had raised all kinds of uncomfortable memories.

Her comment about why I needed dominance didn't help me fall asleep either. My mother was a sore spot in my life – a bad memory from my childhood, which had always been difficult, despite the wealth and privilege. I didn't remember any happy period when she lived with us, for she was never able to recover from the death of my brother Liam. She laid on the couch in her pajamas, watching soap operas all day or staring out the window at our back garden, her face pale, her hair a mess, the house a mess around her. My father was too busy with his career to notice, or too self-absorbed to intervene. In hindsight, it was clear that she had been depressed for years, and had neglected me, but knowing that did little to make me feel any better.

She left me when I was ten. I had a dozen nannies and babysitters in her absence, who all doted on me, but they also left. I had a string of failed relationships before I met Maureen, and maybe three years of happiness before I was swamped with work during my residency and our marriage started to suffer from neglect.

I never saw it coming when Maureen did leave me. Her

words that day wouldn't register. I heard the sounds they made, but it was like they didn't penetrate my brain.

I'm leaving you, Drake… I can't live with you any longer.
I don't love you any more and I'm damn sure you don't love me.
I don't think you ever did.
You don't know how to love anyone but yourself.

I spent the following month in a funk. Maureen moved out of our apartment and within a month, had moved in with Chris. She obtained a temporary restraining order to keep me from contacting her. I had to take time off from work because I couldn't concentrate. I spent days in my sweats, drinking myself into a stupor each night in order to fall asleep. I came really close to losing my privileges at New York Presbyterian, but luckily, had a sympathetic boss.

Lara saved me from total breakdown, helping me to see that my marriage was fated to fall apart because Maureen and I were not sexually compatible. That I was a Dominant, and wouldn't be happy unless I had someone sexually submissive as a partner.

I didn't look back. I didn't want to, for there was nothing I could do about the past. Now, my life was well-ordered, and everything was clear, delineated, predictable. I was in complete control of everything in my life. It was perfect.

Really.

CHAPTER 5

On Friday afternoon, once my last case of the day was done, I left the OR and spoke with the wife of my latest patient. After that, I dictated my notes on the procedure and looked over the cases on my slate for Monday. If I left right away, I'd get home just before seven, shower, eat a light meal, then I'd make my way to the fundraiser Ethan was hosting – one of the first Friday evenings I'd had off in … I didn't know how long.

A night off to mix and mingle with power elite in the philanthropic circles in Manhattan – maybe drum up some donations for my father's foundation. I'd leave the fundraiser, go home and change, and then we were scheduled to play at O'Riley's at ten. A busy day and night as usual.

I was meeting Brent Jameson, a colleague of mine in Neurosurgery, for a drink after work to discuss an upcoming convention where we would both be presenting papers. We usually met at The Horn and Crown, a brew house a few blocks from the hospital and so I drove home for a quick shower and to change clothes before the fundraiser. I'd grab something to eat at the bar and then make my way to Ethan's for the event.

The Horn and Crown was a regular haunt for staff at New

York Presbyterian and they had a bottle of my favorite brand of vodka – Russian, called Anisovaya. I picked up a taste for it from my father, a Sovietophile who loved all things Russian. A strident socialist, my father idealized the Soviet Union under Gorbachev, and I suspect he was actually sad when it collapsed, the Berlin Wall falling. He made dire predictions about lawlessness there, and his predictions came true.

We disagreed on most things political. As a teenager with a penchant for Libertarianism, I did not see eye to eye with him on the subject of Russia or politics in general. I was happy to see the crumble of the Soviet Union. He mourned it, spending even more time on his old Russian car, a Lada, which was held together with duck tape and love.

The night the Berlin Wall fell, he poured us each a glass of Anisovaya and we shot them back. I was only thirteen but it seemed as if I graduated to being a man in my father's eyes on that night. The anise-flavored alcohol had been my favorite ever since.

When I arrived at the bar, Brent was already there. The bartender recognized me and was on top of things, pushing a shot of Anisovaya towards me.

I shot it back and sighed. While I enjoyed tequila shots now and then, and a beer or two on occasion, vodka was my drink. I ordered a martini and Brent and I caught up on things, discussing cases, and then our papers. Finally, the bartender pushed an iced martini towards me, a twist of lime as garnish just the way I liked it. I checked my cell and before I knew it, it was almost time to go to the fundraiser.

I glanced around the bar and as my gaze moved over the crowd, I caught sight of a couple of attractive young women standing at a table along the periphery of the bar next to a small dance floor. One of the two I recognized from NYP – a pretty blonde nursing student that I'd seen around during her surgical rotation.

The woman with her was brunette and on the petite side, with a nice rack. Our eyes met momentarily, and I smiled. She wasn't my usual type, but there was something about her. An innocent look that was in direct contrast to the sexy little black dress she was wearing that barely held in her cleavage. I wondered if she was a nurse as well but I hadn't seen her around NYP.

Maybe a new nursing student. If I hadn't been in the lifestyle, I might be tempted to go over to the table, strike up a conversation with the blonde so I could meet the brunette, but that was out of the question.

Before I left the bar, I went to the washroom for a quick pit stop and bumped into the pretty brunette. She pushed the door open to the woman's washroom and knocked into me. I had to grab her to keep her from falling, because she was wearing ridiculously high leather heels and hadn't seemed to have mastered them.

"*Whoa*," I said, and caught her by the arms, pulling her against my body. "*Steady...*"

"Oh, so sorry," she said and grabbed onto my shoulders. She glanced up shyly, her cheeks reddening. "I'm not really used to these."

In that moment, I was struck by the soft warmth of her body, the scent from her hair, and the soft curve of her breasts pressed against my chest.

She was *delicious*.

I was probably half a foot taller than her and from my vantage point, I was able to peek down her dress and see the swell of her breasts pushed together by the tight bodice.

Now, I had admittedly fucked a lot of women in my time. Before I was married, I played around a lot, trying to figure out what sex was all about and what I liked and needed. I was married for five years and had a *lot* of sex, especially in the first few years we were together. Since I divorced, I had quite a few submissives, both as regular play partners and one-offs I topped at dungeon parties.

I wasn't an inexperienced teenager, but the way my body responded to her, you would have thought I hadn't had sex for months instead of a week and a half.

In that second or two I had her in my arms, her body pressed against mine, I imagined her naked, those breasts bound with thin leather straps, the leather wrapped around them so they protruded, her nipples hard and swollen. Her lips would be parted, she'd be blindfolded, and would gasp as I ran my teeth over the sensitive peaks, just a tiny bit of pain to make her aware of how soft and warm my tongue was afterwards.

God... She was lovely.

She smelled like shampoo and citrus. I wanted to bury my face in her groin and inhale deeply.

I finally pulled myself together enough to respond. "Trying to defy the laws of physics?" I said and smiled as I helped steady her. I glanced down at her shoes once more. "Nice shoes though. *Love* the leather straps..."

I would love to see her naked, *my* leather straps binding her body, looping around her tiny waist and over her hips, down between her thighs, splitting her labia...

"Thank you," she said, straightening up with my help.

At that moment, I wished she *were* a submissive. She had creamy white skin, and looked to be of Celtic background with green eyes and long golden brown hair. Her shyness suggested she might incline towards submission, especially with someone older, but there was no way of knowing from such a momentary meeting. It was wishful thinking on my part.

She smiled briefly and then turned back to the bar as if she couldn't wait to get away from me.

Despite my strong response to her, I knew she was right to do so for in that moment, I wanted her the way a wolf wants a doe, the need to possess her completely welling up inside of me more powerfully than it had in a long time.

Run away, little girl. You don't belong with someone like me.

I followed her back to the bar without using the washroom, forgetting completely why I went. At that moment, I wanted to go up to her and speak with her, but instead, I finished my martini with a gulp to help calm me. I said goodbye to Brent and made my way through the tables to the door. As I passed her table, I caught the brunette's eye and smiled. She smiled back, her expression shy.

She *was* submissive – I had no doubt of it. She'd never approach me herself. With her, I'd have to be the one to make the move, and I was upset that I didn't have more time or I would have, despite the fact I never approached women outside the lifestyle.

It would likely be a huge mistake so I tried to push the encounter out of my mind as I took the stairs leading out of the pub to the street where my car was parked.

I might have to ask the blonde about her if I saw her again at the hospital. I knew it was a mistake to do so, but there was something about the pretty brunette that attracted me.

In truth, I couldn't get her out of my mind.

I drove to Ethan's apartment on Park Avenue, taking the elevator to the penthouse suite where the fundraiser was being held and put on my best game face, prepared to raise money for my foundation and donate some to Doctors Without Borders so I could help make Ethan's event a success. After getting a drink from the bar in the living room, I stood at the edge of a group of people discussing the latest antics of some politician they all loved to hate.

"Oh, Drake, I want you to meet someone." Peter, one of Judge McDermott's lackeys, pulled me away from the group. "Has his own foundation. You might know him – Nigel Benson. Sir Nigel. Recently Knighted by her Majesty for his work on the West Africa famine."

Peter led me over to one of the tallest men in the room, a heavyset fellow with a smiling face and a shock of grey hair that seemed to fall perpetually into his eyes so that he was always brushing it back. He spoke with a thick British accent, which I could hear all the way across the room.

"Nigel, this is Drake Morgan. Chairman of the Liam Morgan Memorial Foundation. Careful with his hands," Peter joked. "Neurosurgeon."

Nigel extended a huge meaty hand to me and we shook, his grip crushing. "I've already had the pleasure," Nigel said, giving me a knowing smile. "Drake."

We'd met at a dungeon party he attended with his partner. It was only later, when we'd both been at a Doctors Without Borders fundraiser that we realized we shared a mutual friend in Ethan McDermott. I had to rely on his discretion not to out me to Ethan, but then again, that would out Nigel to him as well.

"Nigel," I said, smiling back. "Always good to see you."

"Good to see you again, as well," Nigel said, smiling distractedly. "How's brain surgery? Keeping you out of *trouble*, I presume…"

I laughed, knowing exactly what he meant by that. "Always," I said, noting the saucy twinkle in Nigel's eye. "I really enjoyed *Travels with Nigel*." Nigel's latest episode of his travel show had aired on PBS on one of the few nights I stayed awake long enough to watch a repeat.

"Oh, yes," Nigel said, turning away. "Oh, there's Elaine.

Excuse me," he said and nodded to me. "Nice talking to you again."

"You as well," I said, amused that Nigel had barely spoken more than two words to me. He was a social butterfly and flitted off to speak with Ethan's wife, Elaine.

I took the moment to find another group to join, listen in to what all the people were talking about. My world was so constrained – surgery, more surgery, playing with my cover band at small gigs, occasionally tying women up and fucking them senseless, more surgery. It was good to get out and mingle.

I put my drink on the table and made my way to the washroom. On my way out, I was shocked to encounter the pretty woman from the bar and for a moment, I was speechless. Before I could say something, she saw me and turned and tried to hop away, holding the pair of leather heels she'd been wearing at the bar in one hand while she steadied herself against the wall with the other. She'd obviously fallen, her knees scraped and bloody, her palms scuffed.

Her cheeks reddened when I approached her and I knew she was embarrassed that I found her in her current condition.

"You're *hurt*," I said as I went to her, looking at the heels she held. "Those shoes again?"

"Yes," she responded quietly. "I fell outside in the alley. The heel of my shoe broke."

"Here," I said and put my arm under hers so I could pick her up and carry her into the bedroom.

"*Whoa*," she said, her body resisting. "You don't have to pick me up."

"Don't worry. You're light as a feather." I glanced down her body to her feet. Her hose were ripped, her ankle and knees bloody as well, bits of dirt and gravel in the wound. "You've probably sprained your ankle."

Her hands went around my neck and I carried her down the

hall to a bedroom at the rear of the apartment. I placed her on the bed, and sat across from her. In the process, her dress had hiked up, the tops of her sheer black stockings and black lace garters on display. Despite the awkward situation, I couldn't help but respond to the sight of her sprawled on the bed, her legs slightly open. The vision sent a jolt to my dick, which throbbed in appreciation.

When she realized she was exposed, she quickly pulled her dress down to cover herself.

"Oh, I'm sorry…" she said, her cheeks blazing.

I smiled. "Don't worry." I took her injured foot and examined it, noting the abrasions to the skin. "I'm a doctor."

She removed her coat and covered her lap with it as if in protection from my gaze. "Still, you shouldn't have to see that."

"Oh, I don't mind." I grinned without meeting her eyes as I checked her ankle for dislocation but it looked fine. "I don't mind at *all*." Seeing her garters and the fact she wore stockings made me a little giddy. She was a little thing, but I suspected she was also adventurous, given her garters. I wondered if she would be adventurous enough to let me tie her up with my soft leather bindings and make her come three times in a row without stopping. At that moment, there was nothing else in the world I wanted more.

"Ouch!" she said when I moved her ankle to the left, testing to see if there was any tissue damage.

I glanced up at her. "That hurts?"

She nodded.

"What about this way?" I twisted it the other way, gently this time.

"Not as much."

Besides some abrasions on both her knees and palms, she was otherwise fine. "Don't think it's broken," I said and sat up. "You might as well take off those nylons. I'll have to treat those lacerations."

"Oh, yeah."

She hesitated for a moment and then I realized why. She didn't want me to watch her remove her nylons.

"*Oh.*" I glanced away, unable to stop from smiling guiltily.

I was a doctor, yes. Most of the time, when faced with a patient in distress, I was able to put on my doctor cap and stethoscope and be completely professional, even when dealing with a beautiful young woman. I was able to shut off the *man* almost completely.

But to her I was only a man claiming to be a doctor – a man who only seconds earlier had thought of her naked and helpless body in a scene that involved bondage and dominance…

I wondered what she would think if she knew my thoughts. Would she run away from me in horror? Would she be too curious and take a chance?

That way was dangerous, as I had learned with my ex-wife. It was very difficult to introduce the idea of kink to a woman you barely knew, let alone one you thought you knew inside and out.

I turned my head, folding my hands on my lap, trying to appear as harmless as possible while she unfastened the garters and rolled down the nylons. I watched her out of the corner of my eye, unable to resist peeking, but she caught me.

She cleared her throat. "Excuse me?"

"Sorry." I turned my head away again, grinning widely. "Just don't get to see real garters very often."

"My best friend made me wear them," she said, her voice amused. "Now she'll be pissed that I ruined her nylons."

"It's a shame they were destroyed," I said, trying to sound serious but failing utterly to hide my amusement. "I especially like the ones with the seam up the back. Really retro."

Once her nylons were off and she repositioned herself so that her thighs were covered by her coat and dress, I examined her calves, looking for any sign of a fracture. I checked her kneecaps, but they were fine was well.

"Calves and knees look *great*." I bit my lip to keep from grinning widely and left her on the bed, going to the en-suite bathroom to look for some supplies. I checked in the cabinets and drawers for something to clean her wounds and found a bottle of peroxide and some cotton balls, gauze and bandages. I wet a washcloth and brought everything back to the bed, using the cloth to clean off the dirt, the hydrogen peroxide to clean the wounds.

"What kind of doctor are you?" she asked, her voice light.

"Neurosurgeon."

"So you cut up brains?"

I laughed. "Something like that," I said, amused at the way the public thought of neurosurgeons. "I don't cut them up as much as fix them. Robotically-assisted electrophysiology is my specialty. Using electrodes to treat disorders like Parkinson's and epilepsy. You're thinking pathologist. But don't worry," I said as I washed her cuts. "We also learned to look after superficial wounds. And I have a truckload of insurance, just in case you're wondering…"

I finished tending her, conscious of her gaze on me, and when I glanced up, she looked away, her cheeks reddening once more. She was a shy little thing but so pretty with the soft golden brown hair, full lips, small youthful features. She bent forward to hold her dress and coat over her lap and I couldn't help but notice her ample cleavage once more.

Delicious.

I wished once more that she were submissive…

"You'll be fine," I said finally, as I finished taping up her cuts. "Don't need stitches. Just a bit of antibiotic ointment and a few bandages. But you should rest your ankle." I stood up and regarded her. "Are you going to stay or do you need a ride home?"

"I better stay," she said, her voice soft. "Do you know who Elaine is? Can you ask her to come and speak to me?"

I nodded. "Sure. If that ankle doesn't get markedly better in a couple of days, you might want to get an x-ray. Can't do anything for a broken bone in your foot but rest it. You could probably use some crutches."

I smiled and left her on the bed, but what I really wanted to do was push her down on it and run my hands over every inch of her from head to foot, slipping one beneath her skirt to feel the garters, and her panties. I wanted to pull down her bodice and push my face between her breasts, bite her nipples softly to hardness and suck on them until she moaned with delight.

But discretion is the better part of valor...

CHAPTER 6

I RAN a hand over my groin to ensure that my semi was flagging before returning to the party. I found Elaine, Ethan's wife, standing with a small group of donors by the huge window in the living room. She was a decade or more younger than Ethan and pretty in an elegant way, everything perfectly in place and expensive. Ethan was a lucky man.

"There's a young woman in the back bedroom who asked for you. She fell outside and hurt her knees."

"Who?" Elaine said, frowning.

"I didn't catch her name," I said. "Sorry."

I was surprised that I'd been so unprofessional, but I was caught between being a physician and a man and she was such a delicious morsel of a woman, I'd been thrown off my game. That was completely unlike me, but the compromising position I'd found her in and her obvious embarrassment made me reluctant to pry any deeper.

I found Dave Mills, the manager of my father's foundation, standing in the living room with a couple of men and joined his group. We shook hands and he introduced me to two donors from some tech company. I barely caught their names, still thinking of the pretty young woman with garters and nice breasts, wondering who she was.

When she entered the room, I was aware of her right away.

She stood just inside the doorway, her arm on Elaine's shoulder, as if she was reluctant to be there. Once more, I was struck with how pretty she was in an innocent way. Long straight golden brown hair. Light green eyes fringed with thick dark lashes. Clear fair skin. A little sleeveless black lace dress to her knee. She was wearing black slippers and bare legs, her bandages obvious.

"There you are my girl," Nigel said, his voice booming above the chatter, so that everyone in the room turned at the sound. He pushed through the people standing around him to get to her. She blushed, her cheeks reddening but she smiled when she saw him. She opened her arms wide and Nigel picked her up, holding her up in the air as if she were weightless.

The contrast between the two was amusing. Nigel was close to three hundred pounds and six foot six, and she was all of five foot three, and probably one hundred and twenty. He placed her back down on the ground and kissed both her cheeks in the Continental manner before putting a huge arm around her shoulder, escorting her into the crowd. I watched with envy as he introduced her to all the lawyer-types and businessmen in several-thousand dollar suits.

Dave stood beside me.

"Hey, Drake. Did you meet Nathaniel Graham?"

I was too busy watching Nigel with the pretty young woman to care.

"Who?"

"I told you about him. His agency works with relief organizations to outfit field hospitals in war zones. You should come over and say hello."

"Sure," I said, watching as Peter, Ethan McDermott's chief of staff pulled the pretty woman away from Nigel, escorting her around the room. She smiled at one of the men she was speaking to and her smile transformed her face from merely sweet to full out lovely. She looked wistful when she smiled like that.

Innocent.

That innocent look did something to me and inside of me, two forces collided. I loved how young she looked, how fresh. Part of me wanted to protect her. To be her champion. The other part of me – the darker part – longed to see her on her knees before me, waiting on my every word, completely under my control. How much I'd like to be the one to corrupt her and turn her into a wanton woman for my personal use. How much I'd love to see that sweet face filled with lust, her eyes heavy with desire.

Peter turned to us and brought her over before Dave could drag me away.

When Dave saw them approach, he stood straighter, adjusting his jacket.

I put my drink down and watched her expectantly. I was glad to meet her formally, having felt an immediate and intense attraction to her. There was just something in her bearing that brought out the Dom in me. Despite my usual reluctance to seduce a vanilla woman, I was already thinking of ways to approach her, become her lover, and then, when I felt secure in her openness to it, introduce her to D/s and bondage.

"Drake, Dave, may I introduce—"

Before Peter could introduce her, Dave stepped forward. "Ahh, the lovely Miss *Bennet*," he said in an affected British accent. "Um, I mean the lovely *Kate* needs no introduction."

Kate. The pretty young woman I wanted to eat like a delicacy finally had a name.

She glanced at Dave and then to me. When our eyes met briefly, she smiled. Then she turned back to Dave.

"It is a truth universally acknowledged that a man in possession of a good fortune must write out a check and make a donation to the cause," she said in an equally affected British accent, keeping with the *Pride and Prejudice* reference.

Dave laughed. "Well played, Ms. McDermott, well played."

It was then I made the connection. Kate.

Katherine...

A shock went through me. The pretty young woman I had imagined ravishing only moments earlier was none other than Ethan's beloved daughter.

"You're *Katherine*..." I blurted out like a smitten schoolboy.

"Oh, this is Kate McDermott," Dave said, gesturing to Kate. "Kate, this is Dr. Drake Morgan, brain surgeon, bass player, philanthropist. I assumed you already knew each other."

"I met, but didn't really formally *meet*, Ms. McDermott," I said, a surge of something indescribable flowing through me. "I've known you by reputation for years. My apologies for not introducing myself."

"By reputation?"

"Your father told me about you, and I read your articles on Mangaize."

She smiled briefly, and then turned away as if still embarrassed by our encounter.

Dave turned to her. "Dr. Morgan's father Liam fought with your father in Vietnam. Drake volunteers with Doctors Without Borders," he said, sounding officious. "I run his foundation, which donates surgical equipment. Drake goes to war zones where civilians have experienced brain trauma and fixes them up."

She turned to me and her pretty green eyes widened. "My father's spoken of you before. It was Dr. Morgan this, Dr. Morgan that. He thinks you're practically a saint."

I smiled, enjoying how easily she blushed. She couldn't hide her emotions and that was something I highly valued in a sexual partner. So Ethan thought I was a saint? Little did he know... And if he knew how I was lusting after his baby girl, how I wanted to blindfold and gag her, tie her up and fuck her over and over again, he'd probably hire a hit man to take me out.

"Sorry, I didn't introduce myself earlier," she said, her cheeks and neck covered in a flush. "I was in *kind of injured* mode."

"Nice to finally meet Ethan's beloved daughter." I extended my hand. "Your father told me so much about you. I should have known it was you by your eyes, but I was in *slightly caddish doctor with bad bedside manner* mode and not my *charming and gracious guest* mode."

I kissed her knuckles and glanced in her eyes as I did, noting how once more she blushed, her cheeks red.

I *had* to have her. It was that simple.

"I'll leave her with you then," Peter. Then, Dave stepped forward as if trying to get in between us.

"So, Ms. Bennet, how have you been since our last meeting?"

They made some small talk about Jane Austen, and I watched as Dave tried to push himself on her, standing very close to her, shaking her hand and smiling at her in an attempt to monopolize her. She smiled, but I could tell by how she stiffened that she didn't enjoy his overly-obvious attention. She pulled her hand out of his and stepped back.

"My father warned me about men like you, Mr. Mills," she said, sneaking a glance at me. "Suave. Charming. Devastatingly handsome..."

"Oh, that's *riiight*. Your father *The Hangin' Judge*... Does he keep a shotgun under his bed to keep away your suitors? I take it you only go for the nerds? The dorks? The ones who don't have a clue what to say or how to treat a woman? Some of us do know."

"I don't know why I'd be of much interest to you," she said, as if trying to change the subject. "I'm looking for donations. Care to donate to Nigel's foundation?"

Dave smiled at her and they locked eyes for a moment as if in battle.

She was shy, but she wasn't a pushover. She was just as witty as Dave and wasn't intimidated by him.

"Kate was with Nigel in West Africa during the famine," Dave said to me.

"I'm well aware of her work in Africa," I said, not taking my eyes off her. "The Judge talks about you a lot."

"He does?" Katherine frowned as if she was surprised.

"It was always, Katherine this and Katherine that. He's very proud but he's kept you pretty well hidden."

"I've been really busy with school and work..."

I nodded, aware of how she'd had a breakdown after returning from Africa. How concerned Ethan was about his beloved daughter. How fragile she had been for a while, but how she was coming back slowly.

"Your father told me you got a job with *Geist*. What are you writing about now?" I said, wanting to focus on her as a person rather than as a woman, the way Dave was.

"Philanthropy in the age of social media."

Dave turned to her when he heard that. "Drake's foundation funds a number of hospital projects in West Africa if you're interested in philanthropy. I'm his manager of fundraising."

"Yes, that's what my father told me." Kate smiled at Dave. "I'm doing an article for *Geist*," she said. "Maybe I could do an interview?"

Dave stepped closer to her and leaned in, not getting her obvious cues.

"I'd be only too happy to do an interview, Ms. McDermott. Your place or mine?"

She laughed but I could tell she was embarrassed at his suggestion.

"I think she meant she wanted to interview *me*," I said, irritation with Dave's cluelessness filling me.

Dave wouldn't let up, waving me off.

"You're *far* too busy with all your important breakthroughs in robotic brain surgery, your band and humanitarian projects, Drake. I'd be *more* than happy to oblige, take Ms. McDermott off your hands."

"Either one of you would do fine," Kate said and smiled. Just then, Peter came back and put a hand on her shoulder, scooping her up and away from us. Dave made a telephone sign with his hand and mouthed *call me*.

"Nice to meet you Dr. Morgan," she said and smiled at me, and it sent a little jolt to my groin. I wanted that smile all to myself. I wanted to see it in the morning when she woke up naked in the bed beside me, her hair all mussed, her cheeks warm.

"Please, call me Drake, considering," I said, pointing to her knees.

She gave me another quick smile and left, limping off with Peter to the next group of wealthy suits.

I felt an actual physical reaction to her leaving. Regret. Loss.

I rarely felt this way about a vanilla woman, but she... She wasn't just any women. She was different.

She was *Katherine*.

"So *that's* Ethan's daughter," I said, a bit breathless, my heart beating faster. "He calls her Katherine. I didn't connect the dots at first."

"Oh, I forgot," Dave says. "You and the Judge are on a first name basis. I'm surprised you haven't already met her."

"Other than at the health club or at a Doctors Without Borders event, I never see Ethan socially."

"Too bad she's his daughter. I'd like a piece of that," Dave said, wagging his eyebrows.

"Wouldn't we all," I said, bothered by his suggestive tone.

Dave laughed. "I offered but she's not biting."

I raised my eyebrows. "You actually hit on the Ethan's daughter?"

"Hey, she needs some dick, too," Dave said and laughed again. "Poor girl." He took a sip of his beer. "Must be hard to have a man like him as a father."

"I wish *I'd* had someone like him," I said and frowned, my irritation with Dave mounting.

Usually, I was amused by his antics. We met and became friends during several drunken parties in our undergrad years, and had seen each other at our worst, but just then, I wanted to tell him to get serious. Kate wasn't just some easy hookup. I could tell that just by meeting her. She was smart, talented, and fragile emotionally. Someone like Dave would use her and throw her away when someone new spread her legs.

I sipped my drink and watched as she was introduced around the room to various movers and shakers.

Judge McDermott's daughter wore black retro hose and garters? I felt a real affection for the old man, which fought with my desire for his daughter. He had been quick to befriend me when my father died and for that kindness he showed when he didn't have to, I was loyal to him for life.

I watched Kate as she limped beside Nigel Benson, leaning on his arm for support. She knew what it was like to have a famous and powerful father. To live in his shadow.

"So, how do you know Katherine?" I said, wanting to know more about her social life.

"I tried to get her drunk at a fundraiser a couple of years ago but she played hard to get."

"Maybe she wasn't attracted to you," I said, hoping Dave would get the hint.

"What? Not attracted to me? Never," Dave said, laughing. "She's no innocent. She dated some former Marine pilot who flies for Doctors Without Borders. I know because I checked up on her."

"She's not your type, Dave," I said, irritated at him.

"Every pretty woman is my type," Dave said and slapped me on the back. "Daughters of preachers, senators and judges are probably wilder underneath the formal exterior. You know, pretending to be a good girl, but underneath, nymphos. I bet she's hot."

I had to hold myself back. "She's doing her Masters of Journalism at Columbia and was in Africa with Nigel when he did his documentary on Mangaize. She's not a nympho." I was growing more angered with Dave by the moment, feeling more and more protective towards her the more he pushed. "She's a serious writer. You should read her work on the Mangaize camps. Really heartbreaking."

"She's got a nice rack," Dave said, grinning. "I had hopes she'd come home with me some night and ride me like a stallion."

I frowned, angry that he was being so carnal about her.

"She's not like that," I said, gritting my teeth. Of course, I had already thought of tying her up, blindfolding her, and eating her like an ice cream.

Dave held his beer up to his mouth for a sip. He grinned, wagging his eyebrows suggestively. "I haven't found a way between her thighs just yet, but I'm working on it. One of these days."

"She's not your usual type, Dave. She's smart," I said, trying to keep my anger in check. "Full scholarship at Columbia. She's really driven."

"Obviously too busy for men. Must be a lesbian," Dave said with a grin.

That really pissed me. "Maybe she's just *picky*."

"Must be if she turned me down," Dave said and laughed out loud.

"Maybe she's just not into you," I said, wanting him to get the hint.

"You're just jealous because she was having eye sex with me and not you. Apparently Ms. McDermott isn't impressed by your neurosurgical skills or the size of your wallet..."

No, she didn't appear to be, showing no particular interest in me at all other than to note that her father had spoken of me.

I had to admit I'd go vanilla for her, at least, for a while. But *to thine own self be true* was my motto. I'd want her on her knees to me and soon.

Then she was spirited away to another room and I stood there and watched her leave. I hadn't wanted to get to know a woman like that for some time. *Know* her. In every sense. Usually, I didn't want to know anything about women except their kinks around submission.

She was different. Unfortunately, she was Judge McDermott's daughter and so completely off limits. He was my father's oldest friend and she was not the kind of woman I needed.

Finally, someone joined Dave and me and the conversation turned to new regulations governing tax shelters. I couldn't pay any attention, my mind occupied thinking of Kate and how our fathers were best friends before my father's death. I was certain my father would be happy to know the two of us were together. But I was getting ahead of myself. I hadn't even asked her out for coffee.

A while later, I came upon a group containing Katherine and stood on the periphery to hear her talk about West Africa. She turned and spoke directly to me.

"People with influence have to step up to the plate and use their power to do good. Like Dr. Morgan, using his father's foundation to provide hospital equipment to Africa. Those who have the means should use them."

I was completely surprised that she referred to me and

bowed my head, touching my chest to show her words had affected me deeply.

"My father was committed to Africa," I said. "I'm just trying to fill his big shoes using whatever influence I have."

As that conversation ended, Nigel pulled Katherine away and once more, I felt a mix of emotions – pleased that she acknowledged me, and frustrated that I wanted her and knew I couldn't have her. I could never have her because of Ethan. He'd die if he ever learned of my lifestyle. I knew I'd lose his friendship if he found out. I felt such affection for him and such respect for Katherine that I couldn't do it despite how much I desired her at that moment.

I hated myself for being so principled and for once in my life, I wished I were more like Dave Mills, lacking any scruples when it came to women.

If I were, I wouldn't let her out of my sight.

But I wasn't like Dave and so for the next half-hour, I tagged along behind Dave as he made his way around the room, glad-handing the other big rollers who were here from Wall Street, thoughts of the delicious Ms. Bennet in her stockings and garters plaguing me. When I next saw her, she was standing surrounded by a herd of men who were all eagerly listening to her talk. I kept to the periphery of the group to see what they were discussing.

"So, I read your article last month in the newsletter on the need for direct action, and civil disobedience on the famine in West Africa," one of the Wall Street suits said.

She nodded, totally absorbed in the issue, unaware that most of her audience were barely listening, too busy imagining her naked, her limbs restrained with soft leather ties, her body in various lewd poses, an expression of pure ecstasy on her pretty face.

Or maybe that was just me.

ETHAN WAS LATE ARRIVING at the fundraiser, showing up just a few moments before it was over. I was getting ready to leave, having agreed to give Dave a ride home, when Ethan came over to me, pulling Katherine behind him.

"Drake, did you get a chance to meet my daughter, Katherine? I don't believe the two of you have met."

I held out my hand and Ethan and I shook as we usually did.

"Judge McDermott," I said. "Glad to see you. Yes, I did meet Katherine. *Finally*. You've kept her pretty well-hidden."

Katherine turned to Ethan. "Dr. Morgan used his medical skills on me, father. I fell in the alley and he patched me up." She pointed to her knees and Ethan made a show of inspecting her wounds. He turned and smiled at me.

"Well, that's just great," he said and shook my hand once more. "I knew you'd come in handy one day. Thank you for looking after my very tomboyish daughter, Drake. She has a tendency to take a bigger bite out of life than she can always chew." Ethan winked at Katherine. "Can't call her timid, at least. Maybe foolishly brave."

Katherine frowned. "How am I foolishly brave, Daddy?"

"All your life, you've been trying to keep up with the older kids, like your brother. Going to Africa with Nigel and staying in one of the camps is a perfect example. How many of your friends can say that?"

She shrugged. "Lots of us volunteer, Dad. We have to in order to stand out on college applications and for scholarships. Dawn went to India."

Ethan nodded. "Still, you have to admit it was pretty brave." Ethan turned to me. "Thanks for looking after my baby girl," he said to me.

"No, my pleasure," I said, happy that Ethan was finally willing to introduce me to his daughter. "Thank you for inviting me. I was pleased to finally meet the mysterious Katherine you've spoken so much about but kept well-hidden." I smiled at her.

"Not hidden," Ethan said. "Katherine's been very busy with school and the student paper, haven't you, sweetheart?" Katherine smiled, flushing a bit as if embarrassed at the attention.

"Of course," I said.

Ethan left with Peter and Dave, Katherine and I were alone by the front closet where our coats were hung. Katherine took her coat out and was just about to put it on when I stopped her.

"Here," I said. "Let me get that."

I took the coat and held it up for her.

"I can do that," she said, trying to take it from me as if she didn't want any help.

"Please, allow me."

I helped her on with the coat, and when she pulled her hair out from underneath the collar, I leaned forward and inhaled, enjoying the scent of shampoo and her perfume. I adjusted her collar and the shoulders. She turned around and smiled at me, a quizzical expression on her face.

"Thank you," she said and gathered up her bag before limping to where Ethan stood, speaking with Nigel. As I watched, she kissed him when he offered his cheek.

"Good night Daddy," she said.

"Good night, sweetheart." He glanced over at the door where Dave and I were standing. Then I went over and said goodbye to him. We shook hands once more and then Ethan turned to Katherine.

"Do you need to use the limo service?"

She shook her head. "I'll catch a cab."

I frowned, wondering why she'd turn down the use of the limo, not wanting her to have to take a cab. "Nonsense," I said. "Let me drop you off. Where do you live?"

Ethan rolled his eyes. "In a hovel of a rent-controlled apartment building in Harlem," he said, obviously in disapproval. I turned to Ethan for an explanation.

"Don't ask," he said. "She could live somewhere nice, but that's my Kate. Independent to a fault."

"*Daddy*," Katherine said, frowning. "I have a perfectly fine apartment." She turned to me. "I'm sure it's out of your way. I can catch a cab. But thank you."

"I insist," I said. "I won't take no for an answer."

She and Ethan said a final goodbye, this time Ethan kissed her cheek, and I felt a momentary twinge of envy for their relationship. My father and I weren't close in the last years of his life and I regretted it so much. It was nice to see that Ethan and Katherine were so close.

I opened the door and Dave escorted Katherine into the elevator. Dave offered her his arm at the same time I did and instead of taking one or the other, she leaned on both our shoulders.

"So, Katherine," I said, as the elevator went down to the garage level. "You should watch those cuts, make sure they don't become infected. If they do, you can go to a clinic to have them cleaned."

"Thank you," she said. "My best friend is a nurse, so I'll get her to check."

"Where does she work?"

"Harlem," she replied. "She's doing her Master's right now and only works part-time."

I nodded. That must be the friend I saw her with at the pub. The blonde nursing student I'd seen before.

When the elevator opened, I took her arm to help her walk. I felt her initial resistance but finally, she gave in when I kept hold of her. I held the door to my car open for her and helped her inside.

"Where do you live?" I asked once I got in the driver's seat.

She gave directions and I drove through the streets north

and west to Harlem. Dave turned and glanced back at her from the front seat.

"So Kate, do you feel like going out for a drink? I'm still up for some fun tonight."

When Katherine replied, her voice was hesitant. "I don't think so…"

"Come on, live a little," Dave said, pushing things as usual. "I've been trying to get you to go out with me for a long time. Why not tonight? *Muse* is just around the corner from your place. We could have a drink and something to eat."

I watched her in the rear view mirror. She shook her head and caught my eye.

"I don't think so," she said. "I have class tomorrow early…"

"Kate, you are just such a mean woman," Dave said, laughing. He turned to me. "See what I mean? Turned down again!"

"Maybe you should take a strong *hint*," I said, trying to give him the message that she didn't want his attention.

Dave made a face at me and turned back to her. "No offense meant, Kate."

She shook her head, and in the darkness, I could see her face was flushed. "No offense taken." She smiled but I could see it was forced.

Dave was never one to give up easily. "One of these days, you *will* have to go out with me, Kate. Live a little. Nigel told me you've been practically a hermit for the last two years."

"Final year of classes before I write my thesis," she said. "I've been working hard trying to keep my grades up."

We arrived at her apartment block and Dave hopped out as soon as the car stopped. He opened the door for Katherine before I could even get out of my door.

I watched helplessly as Dave walked Katherine up the stairs to the front entrance of the building.

"Good night, Kate," Dave said when they reached the door. "Call me about that interview."

"I will," she said, and then she turned back to the car where I stood watching. She smiled at me and in that smile, I saw appreciation as if she was glad that at least I had shown her more respect. "Thank you for the ride. Nice to meet you."

"Nice to finally meet *you*," I said and smiled back. "Take care of those knees. If you have any problems, feel free to call me."

She turned and went inside.

Dave returned to the car and sat in the front beside me.

"You know," I said, trying to choose my words carefully. "I can tell from her response to you that you make her uncomfortable."

"You think so?" he said as if genuinely unaware of how he affected Katherine. "I thought she was flirting with me."

"No," I said firmly. "She was trying to be nice. She was not flirting."

Dave turned to me and frowned. "What makes you an expert? I barely ever see you with a woman. In fact, I never see you with anyone beside that lawyer woman, Lara."

"I can tell by watching her with you that you make her feel uncomfortable. You might want to dial the attempt at seduction back just a bit."

I raised my eyebrows for emphasis, but Dave only frowned. He watched out the window as we drove to his apartment.

"Well, no loss," he said finally and shrugged. "Women are like buses. If you miss one, there'll be another along in a few minutes."

"Not like Katherine," I said to myself more than to him.

He turned to me and made a face. "You *like* her?"

I said nothing, trying hard not to smile or respond.

"Drake Morgan, the great Doctor, likes little miss Hangin' Judge's daughter?" He laughed at that and shook his head. "Well, I'll be damned. OK," he said and smiled, punching my shoulder playfully. "I'll back off if that's the case."

"It's not that," I said, not willing to admit to anything. "It's just that I'm very fond of Ethan and he's very protective of Katherine. She's not a trifle."

"A trifle?" Dave laughed at that and peered at me as if I'd lost my mind. "What are you? A throwback to the Edwardian era?"

He chuckled to himself and watched out the window as we pulled up to his apartment.

"Drake Morgan, you surprise me," he said as he left the car. He stood with the door open, leaning in so he could talk to me. "I thought you stuck with nurses or physicians. She's kinda out of your league, isn't she?"

"She's very smart," I said. "She writes very well."

"She has a hot little body," Dave said and wagged his eyebrow in the most annoying manner. "Admit it."

"You know, I *am* your boss," I said to him, trying to look stern.

He broke out laughing at that. "What? Are you going to fire me because I made a pass at her? Good God, Drake, you're *smitten*."

I frowned at him, but then I realized I was being a bit of a prude. I took in a deep breath for a moment and then I finally smiled at him. "She does have a very hot little body. Now, get the hell out of here and leave her alone or else it'll be sabers at dawn," I said, laughing at his expression.

"Later, boss," Dave said. I waved him away, knowing that we were too good of friends for this to come between us.

I left him standing on the sidewalk and drove to my apartment in Chelsea, but something he said kept echoing in my mind.

Good God, Drake, you're smitten...

I wanted her. I felt it in my gut, in my groin. Adrenaline washed through me when I thought of her being under my control. I'd have to go very carefully with her. I'd take it really slow, be really gentlemanly, respectful. She reminded me of a timid doe, and I'd have to move slowly and quietly or else I'd scare her off. To tame her to hand would take quite a lot of finesse.

I could do it. The two candidates Lara had for me as potential submissives were novices as well, but they had entered the lifestyle looking for a Dom. Neither were nearly as enticing as Katherine, despite her not being in the lifestyle. She might be a natural sexual submissive, based on her behavior and how shy she was. She might need someone more dominant to unleash her desire.

At that moment, I decided to pursue her and see how far I could get. If she was in the least bit submissive, I intended to be the one to slowly and very carefully introduce her to the lifestyle.

Good God, Drake, you're smitten...

I had only just met the lovely Ms. Bennet, but he was right.

I was.

CHAPTER 7

On Saturday night, Lara and I went to the home of a friend, who had a well-equipped dungeon in his Brooklyn basement. It was a chance to meet the two potential submissives Lara found for me. Lara sent me their screen names at FetLife and I had done some preliminary research on them based on their profiles and their preferences, but in truth, neither one interested me very much – at least, not as much as Katherine.

I knew it was wrong to think of her, wrong to want her, but I couldn't get her out of my mind. The image of her on the bed with her garters showing, her face flushed with embarrassment, her cleavage so inviting as she bent forward to cover up her gaping thighs, played in my mind.

I did everything humanly possible to shut out the image.

I spent time with my book of my previous submissives, sad now that Allie and I hadn't been able to work things out. I remembered the photo shoots, getting off to their images, but Katherine was still there at the back of my mind. Thoughts of her intruded at the oddest times – when I was sitting in the hospital cafeteria surrounded by my fellow surgeons, talking cases and conferences. In line at the grocers. Lying in bed after a grueling workout intended to drive away every sexual thought and let me sleep.

Still, I had a need for sex and didn't want to wait to see if Katherine was even interested, so I went to the dungeon with Lara in the hopes of finding one of the two submissives Lara had chosen acceptable. I wanted a temporary play partner for the interim.

I'd sent both submissives the links to my website with my letters so they'd get an idea of what I liked. They could also check out my profile at FetLife and see that I had been in the lifestyle for five years and had a number of submissives under my protection and under contract. In emails, I told them what to expect at the dungeon, and how they would be expected to dress and behave.

Fetish wear was necessary – at least one piece of clothing had to be leather, latex or rubber. Submissives were expected to be scantily dressed, wearing something that left little to the imagination if they wanted to attract attention. They would be expected to each play with me in public, do a short scene involving bondage or public sex. If they weren't able to manage public sex, it would be in one of the private rooms in the house. I had no intense desire for public sex, but it was pretty much expected that each participant would do something fetish to take part, even if there was no sex involved.

Jenna, one of the two submissives, absolutely refused to have public sex but she did want to be tied up. Chessie was up for anything I wanted, seemingly in a bid to be chosen as my new submissive, but she seemed a little eager for my liking. I enjoyed the chase, teasing response out of a reluctant sub who was afraid of the power of her own desire. It seemed so much sweeter to evoke a response from someone who was holding back.

Like a victory.

I wanted to win them over, defeat their resistance, have them surrender completely. *That* turned me on.

We arrived at the house in Bay Ridge, a renovated historic property with a fully equipped dungeon in the basement. The owner and dungeon master was a lawyer, partner in a huge firm, and could indulge in his desire for every piece of kink equipment in the catalogue. His children were grown and living elsewhere so he could indulge his lifestyle without worry. The guests were all hand-picked, friends of his and trusted completely to be discrete about who attended. I could relax and not worry about my involvement in the lifestyle becoming public.

I'd attended the dungeon parties there before many times. In fact, Lara used to take me there when I was in training to be a Dom, and so I was familiar with the owner and his milieu.

The atmosphere upstairs in the large living room was relaxed with guests arriving and getting drinks and appetizers before going down the stairs to the basement dungeon. The participants were older, in their forties and fifties with the exception of Lara and me and a few subs who had been invited to learn more about the lifestyle. Lara was there to demonstrate her skills as a Domme, and I was there to test drive the two submissives she had chosen for me. There were a few singles there to participate in any scenes that were open, but most of the people were married and into BDSM as part of their sex life.

The dungeon itself was painted black and red, with red leather benches, a large St. Andrew's Cross, several fuck machines of various design and bondage benches. Every kind of flogger and riding crop, spreader bars and restraints lined one wall, for participants to use at their leisure. There was a sex swing in one corner and someone was already inside it getting fucked very loudly when we arrived.

I watched the two subs with us to gauge their response to the scenes. I wouldn't be their first Dominant, but I would be one of their first. They were very new to the scene and excited to be at a play party.

The bolder of the two, Chessie wanted to use the sex swing, while Jenna wanted to take part in a bondage scene, with me tying her up and demonstrating various safety issues and rope techniques. She stayed close to me, always a bit behind me, her nervousness obvious by her wide eyes and reluctance to move too far from my side. I petted her as she stood beside me, my hand on her bare back to encourage her to move closer to the scene taking place in the corner of the room so she could watch.

Lara met one of her favorite male subs, a young law clerk with blond hair and a six-pack impressive enough to make every man in the dungeon envious. She immediately became involved in a scene with him, tying him up, attaching his testicles to a cock and ball stockade. Then, she took a riding crop and began to run it over his ass and thighs in a prelude to a good cropping.

The image of her topping her submissive brought me back to my own time with her and the strange and challenging weeks when I submitted to her so I could learn the ropes of being a Dom.

Lara took me under her wing when I was at my lowest, in the weeks after Maureen and I split. I had taken a leave from NYP and was doing little else but spending time at the apartment, playing my guitar and occasionally, jamming with the band.

We ran into each other on the street near the café we used to go to as students, and when she saw me, she frowned and put an arm around me.

"What is *wrong* with you?" she said, squeezing my shoulder, her voice concerned. "You look like crap, and that's saying something. You're a mess. You haven't shaved, your hair is greasy, and your clothes..." She looked me up and down, shaking her head.

I told her what happened – how Maureen had accused me of being a psycho for wanting to try bondage, and how she had finally left, obtaining a temporary restraining order so I wouldn't contact her, filing assault charges because I'd tried to stop her from leaving that fateful night.

I had no surgeries booked due to the mess I was in.

"You're a Dom, Drake," Lara said, as if diagnosing me. "You want control during sex. You also have a bondage kink. You need to get your head on straight, learn the rules and get your life together."

I said nothing, certain she was right.

"What do I do?"

She smiled. "Let me teach you how. There are rules, there are skills, and there are techniques. You become my submissive and I'll teach you."

"I'm not submissive," I said, frowning. "I don't like pain."

"You need to understand what it means to have total control over someone else. You don't just tie someone up and think everything's going to be OK. Let me show you how you introduce a new sub to BDSM. I'll explain everything and you can learn how."

At that point, I was looking for anything to move forward and so it was a no-brainer. I trusted her. She helped me find out who and what I really was. I have no doubt about it.

The first time we did a scene was at that very dungeon, in that actual room, and although we did nothing more than have sex in public, with me restrained, it was my initiation into the real world of kink. That first night, I was a reluctant sub, not really sure I wanted to be restrained or to have sex in front of complete strangers. But I turned myself over to Lara and let her lead me.

She made me wear a pair of pants made of exceptionally fine leather that molded to my body, showing every bulge and muscle. I was shirtless during our scene, barefoot. A leather-clad Lara wore a tight leather mini dress that pushed her ample breasts up into delicious mounds. She also wore thigh-high leather boots. Her long platinum blonde hair was pulled back into a smooth ponytail that reached the middle of her back.

She was beautiful in a cold, commanding way. She held a riding crop in one hand, which I eyed with suspicion, but she promised me it was just for show. She might run it over my body for sensory stimulation only. No pain would be involved unless I failed to comply, then the brief smack with it was only a reminder that I was to comply.

Our scene took place in the corner of the dungeon near some leather-covered benches, next to the sex swing. A few people watched as Lara restrained my wrists and pulled them behind my back. She eyed me up and down while I waited, my pulse racing, for what was to happen next.

"You know, when I found you again, I wished that you were a submissive, but you're not. However," she said and ran her riding crop over my shoulder and down my abs to my crotch. "You're going to have to let go of all your need for domination when you're with me. Do what I say or expect a smack with this."

"I'll try," I said.

"Try isn't good enough, Drake. Obey. It's simple."

"What if I don't like what you tell me to do?"

"You'll like it."

I took in a deep breath and tried to let go of my preference to take the lead in sex. She circled me as I stood there, waiting, and examined my body. While she did, she used her riding crop to trace my muscles, down my spine to my ass, up along the backs of my thighs to my butt, and then around my groin again, between them and up under my balls.

The leer in her eyes was starting to get to me. What would she do? What would she make *me* do?

I expected that I would service her in some way, but would I play stud and fuck her, or would I perform oral sex and make her orgasm?

My breath quickened when she ran her bare hands down my back, one finger trailing down my spine once more to the top of my leather pants. She stood behind me and as she was as tall as me with her boots on, she was able to kiss my neck from behind, her hands trailing around my waist to stroke my belly, tracing the line of hair from my navel down below the waistband of my leather pants, her fingers dipping below to my pubes without actually touching my dick.

When she bit the muscle on my shoulder gently, then licked the skin beneath my ear, I started to respond.

I didn't mind this. She was deliberately trying to arouse me.

Her hands massaged me through my leather pants as she pressed her breasts against my back.

"You're so *big*, Drake," she whispered in my ear. "I used to fantasize about sitting on you and fucking myself with your *Nice. Fat. Cock.*"

I grew thicker under her fingers, enjoying how the leather warmed and molded to my growing erection, the pleasant ache in my groin intensifying from the feel of her breath on my neck. I tilted my head back, my eyes closed, as she moved around to face me and sucked the skin on my throat.

Then, she tweaked a nipple, twisting it a bit and I grunted, frowning. "Hey," I said, stepping back. "You agreed, no pain."

"*Damn*," she said. "You really don't respond to it, do you?"

I shook my head. "No."

"Oh, well," she said and sighed. "Pleasure it is, then."

Instead of twisting my nipple once more, she bent down and sucked it briefly, and the soft feel of her lips around it, the warm wetness of her tongue tugging on it, send a jolt of desire through my groin, straight to my dick, which was getting quite hard.

I closed my eyes as she sucked the other nipple, one of her

hands trailing down my abs and cupping my balls through the leather.

"This isn't very submissive, you pleasuring me," I said.

"Ut, tut, *tut*," she said and moved the riding crop over my lips. "Don't speak unless you're spoken to or I'll have to smack your pretty tight little ass, Drake. And when you do speak to me, address me as Mistress."

I nodded.

"Let me know you understand, Drake."

I closed my eyes. "Yes, Mistress," I said. "I understand."

For the next few moments, she did whatever she could to arouse me without actually taking my erection out and sucking me. She pulled down the straps to her leather dress and rubbed her bare breasts against my chest and back, the hard nubs of her nipples exciting me. She actually bit my butt cheeks through the leather of my pants, then licked the material over my erection, looking up at me from her knees, smiling when I gasped.

I wanted her to take my aching cock out and suck it, but I knew she wouldn't. She wanted me hard and aroused, so she could gain my compliance.

Then, she unbuttoned my pants and pulled out my cock, which sprung out, heavy and thick, the tip wet with precum.

"Oh, Drake, what a pretty cock you have," she said, eyeing it. "A pretty cock on a very pretty man. I've wanted to see it for years." She gripped me and moved her hand up, her fingers sliding over the head, making me groan out loud.

"You could suck it if you want," I said, forgetting myself for a moment.

"Bad boy," she said and flicked the tip of the crop against my lips, a soft tap just to remind me. "A sub never makes suggestions to his Domme. He always waits patiently for her command."

"Sorry," I said. "The Dom in me, I guess…"

"You're *not* a Dom yet, Drake. Just a wannabe. And address me properly."

"Yes, Mistress," I said, chastened.

"Watch, listen and learn. Once you've learned and tried everything, and once you've successfully topped a sub, then you'll be a Dom. If you get really good, really trustworthy, one day, you might be a Master."

"That's my goal," I said.

She nodded. "Good boy," she said and kissed me on the lips. It was our first kiss and it felt strange to be so intimate physically with her because we had always been only friends. I was a man, however, and had often admired her breasts and her ass, which was spectacular. Of course, she was beautiful, but despite a few errant fantasies of me overpowering her with my masculine charms, I had never really considered her as a sexual partner.

She was far too much like me for that. A female Dominant.

So our first kiss was strange. I felt completely out of my element, and the adrenaline that pumped through my veins was a potent mixture of desire and excitement.

When she pulled away, she had a hard expression in her eyes, and I knew then, my free pass was used up and I had to behave.

"On your knees," she said and motioned to the floor with her riding crop, but it was difficult to get down with your arms bound behind your back. I didn't realize how much you relied on your arms for balance.

She actually put an arm under mine to help me down and it was the first time I had ever relied on a woman for assistance to do something as simple as kneel. I expect it was strategic on her part, to remove my ability to be independent and in control of my own body.

It worked. As she helped me to my knees, I finally felt helpless. Of course, I could always struggle back to my feet and demand to end the scene, but I was there to learn and had committed to give it the old college try.

Then she lifted her thigh and laid it over my shoulder so that her groin was directly in my face. I couldn't help but see her shaven folds through the thin sheer thong she wore, and smell her arousal. Despite the submissive position I was in, that scent made me even harder.

"Lick me," she said.

When I hesitated, she tilted my head up, one finger under my chin.

"Through the material."

I complied, licking her labia through the fabric, and she was already wet. She was excited about the prospect of topping me. I pressed my tongue against her slit where her clit would be, wanting to stimulate her and she pushed herself forward with a gasp.

"Use your tongue to get underneath the fabric and lick me."

I tried, running the tip of my tongue along each side of the thong, then slipping it beneath the fabric, straining to reach her slit, using my tongue to push the material aside. It wasn't easy.

Then she removed her thigh from my shoulder and stood in front of me, her skirt hiked up, her pussy a mere inch from my nose.

"Use your teeth to remove my thong."

I did, biting one side of the thong and pulling it down, then moving to the other side to do the same, baring her pussy. It took some doing but finally, I had the thong far down her thighs. She stepped out of the thong, which fell to the floor, and then she raised her thigh and laid it over my shoulder once more.

"Lick me again," she said. I moved back to her folds, licking them until they were glistening with my saliva, slipping my tongue between the lips to taste her, find her clit with the tip.

Many Doms don't pleasure their subs orally, finding it too

submissive an act, but I loved oral sex, giving and receiving. I enjoyed feeling a woman come under my mouth, her clit throbbing against my tongue during her orgasm. It made me hard as rock, and so I was becoming more excited as I pleasured Lara, despite being on my knees, my arms bound behind my back.

This wasn't so bad.

I licked her and sucked her clit until she came, grinding her pussy against my mouth, her hands on my head, fingers in my hair.

When she was finished, she stepped back and adjusted her dress, covering herself up. She picked up her thong from the floor and stuffed it in a pocket of my leather pants. Then, she went behind me and unfastened my restraints. When I tried to stand, she pressed down on my shoulders to keep me on my knees.

"Would you like to come, Drake?"

I glanced around, feeling slightly awkward with several of the other patrons watching.

I nodded.

She ran the crop over my lips. "Remember your manners…"

"Yes, Mistress."

"Yes, what?"

I smiled. "Yes, Mistress, I would like to come."

She ran the crop down my chest to my dick, which throbbed when I felt the leather against my bare skin.

"I'd love to see you stroke that nice fat cock and make yourself come. Do it for me. Keep your eyes on me the entire time."

I did, despite feeling strange, because my dick was hard and I wanted to learn what it was like to be under someone else's control.

I gripped my cock, and used the fluid leaking out of the tip to lubricate my hand. I stroked myself, my eyes closing involuntarily, trying to find a rhythm that would guarantee a quick orgasm.

"Keep your eyes open and on me."

I opened my eyes, stroking while I looked in Lara's.

It was such an intimate moment, pleasuring myself while she and the others watched. She kept glancing down at my cock, watching me jerk off, then back to my eyes, and that turned me on even more. As I grew closer to my release, she seemed to sense it.

"Come for me, Drake," she said, her voice husky. I did, ejaculating, my face hot, somewhat ashamed that I was able to do it in front of strangers, but they seemed to enjoy it and cheered as I shuddered. A look of triumph crossed Lara's face.

"Good *boy*," she said, running the crop over my cheek as I caught my breath. "Let that be a lesson to you. To assert dominance, order your sub to service you after you've aroused them. Then, order them to pleasure themselves and make sure they keep their eyes on yours. It will enforce your position of power and their subordinate status, in addition to making you closer through the intimacy of the act. A sub wants to feel your power over them. If you don't assert it, they won't feel safe and fulfilled. You make them feel safe and fulfilled by showing them you have control. Whatever it is that they need to do, they do on your orders. They're no longer responsible and can be free to enjoy their kinks, whatever they are."

CHESSIE'S VOICE brought me back from the memory of my first time in the dungeon with Lara. I blinked and watched as Chessie bounced around the room, excited to see what everyone was doing and I knew by her energy that she wasn't the sub for me. It was Jenna who was more my type, and despite her reluctance to have sex in public, I knew she'd come around eventually. She needed a lot of coaxing and to feel completely safe with me before she'd be able to let go of her inhibitions. I'd use that lesson with her, making sure to arouse her to near orgasm before ordering her to service me then demanding she bring herself to orgasm while I watched.

The fact that she wanted me to tie her up in public suggested she wanted people to look at her and know she was a sub under my control. Public sex would come eventually if I handled her properly.

It was then I saw someone I recognized from my health club – the friend of Ethan's I met earlier, a fellow justice on one of New York's courts. I couldn't remember which one. Initially, I felt the need to hide from him, but he saw me and nodded in recognition. I nodded back but his presence took me out of the dungeon and into my world outside the lifestyle. It also reminded me of Katherine and her stockings and garters.

In that moment, I wanted Katherine with me instead of Jenna or Chessie. The night lost its excitement because I was no longer satisfied with the prospect of having both Chessie *and* Jenna – something any Dom in his right mind would be very pleased about.

The rest of the night was a disappointment for me. I tied Jenna up as promised, using some soft leather straps I brought along to bind her breasts, using soft rope to restrain her. I took the opportunity to talk about various forms of Japanese rope play, talking about safety, especially with suspension bondage, and how to ensure that any restraint could be easily released to prevent unintentional pain.

As for Chessie, she wanted to try out the sex swing. I knew she wanted me to fuck her publicly, but instead, I whispered in her ear that I wasn't up to it that night but she was free to find someone else if she desired.

She looked up at me with disappointment.

"I knew you liked *her* better," she said, pouting. "What did I do wrong?"

I shrugged, ignoring her failure to address me properly. I didn't have the desire to correct her at that point. "We don't have the right chemistry, *Chessie*." I raised my eyebrows, hoping she'd get the message. "But I saw a few of the other Doms who might be interested in playing with you, if you'd like."

"Sorry, *Sir*," she said and stood with her arms folded for a moment as if in protest. I went to Lara, who had finished her scene with her sub and told her that things weren't working out with Chessie but that she wanted to keep playing with someone else. Lara arranged to have one of the other Doms play with Chessie so she didn't go home unfulfilled.

I stood with Jenna on the sidelines and we watched as Chessie's new Dom bent her over a bench, blindfolded and restrained her hands and feet before fucking her.

That *could* have been me, but all of a sudden, I felt as if this whole evening was a poor substitute for what I really wanted – to be alone with Katherine, to be spending time getting to know *her*. To have *her* there with me instead. Still, the sexual energy in the room was infectious, and I grew hard watching Chessie as she clearly enjoyed the night's developments.

Jenna looked up at me with those big brown eyes.

"Sir, could this submissive do anything to please you, Sir?"

I knew she didn't want to perform in public, and so I nodded and bent down to kiss her, to let her know I was pleased. I stroked her hair, ran a finger over her mouth, touching her lips.

"You have a lovely mouth. I want you to use it to please me."

She smiled and then glanced away, her blush visible even in the dim room.

I led her out of the dungeon and into one of the small private rooms in the back of the house that had been designated for private scenes. I closed the door behind us and pulled Jenna against my body, making sure to pull her hips against mine so she could feel my erection.

I ran my fingers over the tops of her breast, and saw her shiver in response, her skin all gooseflesh. Then I kissed her tenderly, my hand sliding down her bare back to cup her butt, which was nice and firm and round. I lingered over the kiss, then spent time nibbling on her shoulder, pulling down a strap of her very low-cut dress before baring one breast. Although smaller than I liked, her breast was perfect, with a nice rosebud nipple and I paid attention to it, sucking and nibbling on it gently. She moaned softly and pressed her breast into my mouth.

Remembering my lesson from that first time with Lara, I turned her around, kissed her neck from behind, and then used a pair of leather cuffs to restrain her arms behind her. I pulled down the other strap to her dress, baring both her breasts, and tweaked her nipples from behind, kissing her shoulder.

Then I turned her around and pushed on her shoulders so that she knelt down in front of me. I made sure to assist her as she knelt, reminding her of who was more powerful between the two of us.

"Lick me," I said, my voice husky. "Over my pants." She did, running her tongue over my erection, which strained against the leather.

"Unbutton my pants with your teeth," I ordered, and she proceeded to try, pulling at the fly, struggling to get the buttons opened. Finally, she managed the top two and I did the rest, pulling out my erection so that it sprung out directly in front of her face.

She glanced up at me, waiting for me to order her to suck me. I took my cock in hand and rubbed the wet head over her lips. She remained still, letting me, waiting like an obedient sub should.

"Lick me," I said finally, and she did, leaning forward to run her tongue over the head and then the shaft. "My balls, too," I added and she complied. She took one gently into her mouth and ran her tongue over it.

"Good girl," I said. "Now, suck me."

I leaned back against the door and closed my eyes, enjoying the feel of her velvety wet mouth on the head of my cock, letting her do the work for a while. Soon, I took over control, my hands on her head, guiding her over my cock, increasing the rhythm until my pleasure built, my orgasm near. It was then I thought of Katherine out of the blue, and then I imagined that it was Katherine on her knees to me instead of Jenna, Katherine's lips around my cock instead of Jenna's.

When I came, my hands gripping Jenna's dark hair, fucking her mouth, the warm wet lips around my cock were Katherine's and it was she who was swallowing me.

I felt only a smidgen of guilt that my focus was on Katherine instead of Jenna, but I had already decided against having Jenna as my sub.

She was too easy.

I ARRIVED HOME LATER that night after dropping Jenna and Lara off, Chessie having decided to leave with the new Dom she'd met. I felt exhausted and wanted nothing more than to have a hot bath and go to bed. I texted Lara once I was out of the bath.

How did you enjoy the night? I'm glad Chessie found herself a Dom. She was far too energetic for my tastes.

LARA TEXTED me back after a few moments.

CALL me if you want to talk. You don't seem all that taken with Jenna either. What's up?

I DIDN'T WANT to talk about it, preferring not to admit that someone outside the lifestyle had become my focus. Both Lara and I knew that way was fraught with almost certain disappointment and I didn't want a lecture from her. Despite the fact we were both Dominants, Lara felt a certain ownership of me and often tried to dominate me.

JENNA IS SWEET, but maybe a bit too easy for me. Keep searching. I'll send her a nice email wishing her luck.

LARA TEXTED RIGHT BACK.

I'LL CHECK and see if there's anyone else.

I SMILED AT THAT, and texted her back.

GOOD NIGHT, Matchmaker. We'll talk later.

CHAPTER 8

I saw Katherine again sooner than I imagined.

Dave texted me Sunday night to say that she had contacted him about the interview and was meeting him at a café close to the foundation later on Monday afternoon.

"I can do the interview if you're too busy," he said on the phone. "I know this is short notice so don't feel pressured to come by."

"I'll be there," I said, not willing to let Dave do the interview alone. "I have surgery scheduled at one but should have everything wrapped up by three."

"I'll do the interview if you're late so don't sweat it."

"*Wait* for me," I said. "She should really talk to me, since it's my foundation."

"You *are* smitten, Drake," Dave said, laughing over the phone line.

"You behave," I said and smiled in spite of myself. I hung up, a little jolt in my gut at the prospects of seeing Katherine again. I'd invite her out for lunch or a drink so I could elaborate on my foundation's work but, of course, it was really so that I could try to work my charm on her.

I was eager to get through my cases that morning and hoped everything would go well with my first surgery after lunch, but we ran into some technical problems with the equipment in the OR and were delayed about twenty minutes. I had little time so I didn't change out of my scrubs into my street clothes and even then, didn't make it over to the café for the interview until a few minutes after 3:30. Katherine was there with Dave and as I approached the table, the two were shaking hands. Perhaps they just arrived and I wasn't late at all. I laid a hand on Dave's shoulder and smiled at her.

"There you *are*," I said. "I was wondering if I'd make it down in time."

"We just finished," Katherine said and shrugged.

"I *told* Mr. Mills that I'd be right over and he was *supposed* to wait and let me do the interview." I made a face at Dave and then turned to Katherine and caught her eye. "Perhaps you could stay behind for a moment so we can speak alone."

She glanced at Dave as if surprised. Dave must have arrived early so he could do the interview himself.

Dave turned to Katherine. "I didn't want you to waste your time in case Drake wasn't able to get away from the hospital. Sometimes his surgeries take longer than planned. Nice talking to you again, Kate. Good interview."

Dave left the café, and I was finally alone with her. I sat beside her, my arm on the back of her chair, and just looked at her, drinking in every detail of her appearance.

Once more I noted her fair skin, her green eyes, soft pink lips, and her silky golden brown hair.

"Well," she said after a moment, her cheeks pink. "I'm here. What did you want to talk about?"

Her expression of bemused patience brought me back to the moment.

"How's your ankle? Your knees?" I checked her legs, which were covered by tights under a short jean skirt.

"Almost all better."

"Good."

She smiled at me but I was in no rush, enjoying how her cheeks flushed with embarrassment. I couldn't help imagining her with a sexual flush instead.

"So? You wanted to speak with me?"

"I just wanted to offer you the chance to ask me anything now that I'm here," I said.

"I think I got everything I need from Mr. Mills."

"You don't want to hear my side of things? Considering it's my father's foundation…"

She hesitated as if considering. She could walk out if she wanted. There was no reason for her to humor me. Instead, she decided to continue.

"I do have a few questions, more about motivation." She took out an iPhone and started the recording. "Can you tell me why he started this foundation?"

I moved my chair a bit closer, and leaned in, wanting to observe how she responded to my nearness. As I expected, she flushed once more, her cheeks pink.

"He was a socialist, committed to eradicating poverty," I said, remembering my father with fondness, despite his neglect. "He didn't expect to become rich and so when he did, he poured almost every extra cent into helping hospitals in third world countries, especially Africa. He said something about unequal development and capitalist exploitation – you'd know more about that than me." Dave told me she was a bit of a socialist, so I decided to check and see if he was right.

She frowned, but didn't correct me.

"The Foundation continues his work today. Everything we do in the Foundation is to try to fulfill my father's vision, even if only in a small way. He was so committed to his causes." I spoke more about the foundation and why my father started it, how it gave him a chance to give back the money he felt he didn't need or deserve.

She watched my chin while I spoke as if too shy to look me in the eye, and I enjoyed her reticence. It made me want all the more to force her to look me in the eye when she came. I was going to make her come, of that I was certain. There was nothing I loved more than the moment a sub went over the edge, her orgasm starting, pleasure washing over her, removing the last vestiges of self-control, struggling to obey my command to look me in the eye. It was a moment of such intimacy that it intensified their experience, baring them in a way that being naked and fucked alone didn't achieve.

I stopped speaking and she said nothing as if transfixed by my mouth. I couldn't stop from smiling. What was she thinking? Did she imagine kissing me, the way I was imagining kissing her?

I doubted it. She seemed far too shy to imagine me eating her while she watched me, our eyes meeting while I sucked her clit.

"I'm *sorry*." She made a face, her cheeks red. "Can you tell me what project you're most proud of?"

I said something about the pediatric neurosurgery program the foundation funded, but in truth, my dick was hard thinking about fucking her and so I barely remembered a word of it.

"Your father died while in Africa several years ago."

That jolted me back to reality, and not in a pleasant way.

"Yes," I said, feeling remorse at his death still there even now, almost a year later. "He died just after you came back from Africa."

"What happened?"

I thought about it, deciding how much to tell. I didn't really want to reminisce about my father, but she seemed interested so I told the story of how his plane crashed while on a trip to Somalia.

"He was flying into a small base camp where he was going to do some work with a local charity. Even though we were political opposites and didn't always see eye to eye, when he died, it was as if the ground was ripped out from under me." I looked in her eyes and she was listening with rapt attention. "Nothing has been able to fill the hole. *Nothing*. I took over the helm of his foundation because I thought doing his work might heal me in some way. That's how your father and I became friends. He came to the funeral and it was like he adopted me."

"I guess I just never saw my father as someone who would do that."

That shocked me. "What? Act fatherly?"

She nodded. "I mean, he's an authoritarian type – head of the family and all. But not to, you know, step in and act as a father substitute."

"He did," I said, still surprised, my voice wavering a bit at the memory. "I relied on him to get through it."

During those first months, he spent quite a lot of time with me, much to my shock. We met for dinner and drinks, and talked in the sauna at the health club.

She actually teared up a bit. "I know what it means to lose a parent."

"Your mother died of cancer a few years ago," I said, realizing that we shared a common loss. "The year before you went to Africa. Your father told me."

She nodded and stared off into the distance for a moment as if unable to leave the thought of her dead mother behind. It was in that moment that I also realized that perhaps I was wrong to pursue her after all. She was still very delicate if she teared up so easily at the talk of our dead parents, the wounds still raw.

"Well, that's all I have," she said finally, her voice sounding almost regretful that she didn't have anything more to say. "I guess I should go. Don't want to keep you from the OR."

We both stood and I extended my hand, wanting to touch her once before we parted, for I knew that it would be the last time we met.

I wouldn't ask her out. I wouldn't pursue her.

She wasn't in the lifestyle and perhaps wasn't ready to be introduced to it.

She took my hand and I lifted hers to my mouth, pressing my lips softly against her knuckles.

"People have spoken so highly of you," I said, keeping her hand in mine. "So has your father. In the past few days, I've read up a bit about you, reread your articles on Mangaize. Still so impressive. I don't know who I was expecting when I thought about meeting you. Someone older. Different. I was so surprised to actually meet you."

She pulled her hand away. "What do you mean?"

"Your writing – it's so visceral. Insightful for someone so young."

She was lovely and she was sweet and she was still fragile. I knew I would overwhelm her with the intensity of my desire for her, my need to dominate her, to control her.

I could probably completely possess her, make her do things she wouldn't otherwise imagine possible, if she let me and at that moment, I sensed that if I pressed her, she would let me.

An enormous sense of guilt filled me. She was the lovely Katherine. Champion of Africa, whose harrowing articles on Mangaize filled even me with emotion. She was the sweet sad Katherine, who lost her mother and had never fully grieved until forced to because of the trauma of Mangaize.

She was Ethan's beloved daughter, the delicious Ms. Bennet with scuffed and bloodied knees. Who wore sexy garters and retro nylons with a seam down the back.

"I'm glad we could meet and talk," I said, still fighting with myself, the darker part of me wanting to forge ahead and seduce her. The better part of me fighting to keep him in check. "I'd like to interview *you* sometime, talk about Africa."

"I don't really like to talk about Africa."

"Why?"

"It was upsetting."

"Your father told me you had problems after you came back. You were there at the height of the famine. It had to be very hard." She nodded but said nothing. Then, I made my decision and the better angels of my nature won out, a mental hand covering the mouth of the darker part of me, smothering his lust-filled protest. "I'd really like to just take you out for coffee or a drink," I said. "I feel like I've known you forever from everything your father's told me about you. But I probably shouldn't."

"Probably," she said and I was surprised that she said it. Did she somehow perceive the danger I posed to her? Did she sense the chasm so close to her?

"Can I ask why?" she added, her cheeks red.

I shook my head quickly. "You're *The Hangin' Judge's* daughter," I said, not wanting to admit it, but being truthful for a moment. "I'm not the kind of man Judge McDermott's daughter should get involved with."

She frowned at that. "He thinks very highly of you."

I smiled, but I didn't really feel amused. Instead, I felt a darkness engulf me that I couldn't explain.

"He doesn't really know me."

She frowned but said nothing in response. If she had protested even just a small bit, all my reasons for not pursuing her would have fallen like a row of dominoes.

I walked her to the door, feeling so protective of her now that my better side won out. I held the door open for her, reluctance filling me, knowing I couldn't pursue someone as sweet and fragile as her.

I would never want to see her expression of horror when she learned who and what I was, and most of all, what I wanted to do to her body and mind.

"Thank you for doing an interview," she said when we stepped outside.

I smiled, forcing it so we could part on a positive note.

"Goodbye, lovely Katherine."

Then the door closed and I walked one way, while she walked the other.

Part of me shouted to turn back and ask her out anyway, throwing caution to the wind, the promise of her deliciously soft and warmly compliant body beneath mine so tempting, but the better part of me won out once more.

I kept walking.

CHAPTER 9

THE NEXT WEEK passed slowly and I felt as if I were trapped in a fog, unable to find my way back to my real life – the one pre-Katherine when I was busy and content with things, eager to meet a new sub and start a new D/s relationship.

Instead of my usual cheerful approach to life, I went through the motions, getting up and going to work, doing my surgeries, teaching, playing in the band, but my world had become engulfed in a darkness that prevented me from enjoying life the way I usually did.

On Thursday, Lara called me to talk about Jenna, and finding a replacement.

They weren't right for me. I'd been too busy, I told myself, to spend the time needed to train either one.

Lara met with me at our usual spot and after interrogating me about Jenna and Chessie, she leaned back in her chair and studied me for a moment while I tried to avoid her eyes.

"I have a favor to ask of you. There's this *girl*..."

"Girl?" I frowned, wondering what the favor was. "How old?"

"Well, not a girl. She's twenty-four. She's special."

I hesitated, intrigued but cautious. "Tell me."

"She wants to interview a Dom for an article she's writing on the lifestyle. Would you do the interview?"

"Why don't *you* answer her questions? You know about the lifestyle as well as I do. Better."

"She wants to talk to a male Dom. I can answer questions about being a Domme but I thought of you as the best candidate for a discussion of male dominants and what they want and how they train a new sub. Besides, you're a natural born teacher."

I stirred my soup for a moment. I relied on her to find me new subs, and I felt I couldn't refuse.

"Who is she?"

"You can't know who she is, Drake. She wants to learn more about D/s but has a high profile family and doesn't want anyone to know she's interested," she said, eyeing me over her coffee. "She's a writer and is curious."

"Why is she special?"

"She's a new acquaintance with connections I want to cultivate. Can you do me a big favor and help her? Use those famed teaching skills of yours?"

I frowned, not really sure I wanted to be interviewed.

"She's not a sub?"

"I suspect she is," Lara said. "But she hasn't admitted it to herself yet. Had a boyfriend who wanted to try things out and she freaked and ended the relationship. Now she can't stop thinking about it. Don't tell her I told you that, though," Lara said and held up her hand. "I suspect this is more than just research. She's really conflicted and wants to remain totally anonymous."

"So do I," I said, considering the offer. "For obvious reasons."

"You know, one of these days you're going to have to settle down and find a permanent partner. Have a real relationship."

I frowned. Maybe down the road in my forties, I *would* settle down, but I was happy with the way things were. I worked more than sixty hours a week and barely had time for the band and fitness let alone a relationship. Since my divorce five years ago, my submissives had provided me with all the sex I needed, I enjoyed the bondage and dominance and the fact that they went away after our sessions and left me alone until the next meeting.

"So you'll meet with her?" Lara said, regarding me while I ate.

I shrugged and finished my sandwich, a bit apprehensive about the whole thing.

"Come on Drake," she said, her voice a bit impatient. "Do this favor for me."

"Sure," I said finally. "But you owe me – big time."

We ate in silence for a moment, but of course, now I was curious about this young woman who wanted to interview me.

"What's she like?" I said, trying to sound casual.

"You'll love her," Lara said, waving her hand in dismissal. "She seems really sweet."

"I'm not supposed to *love* her. I'm supposed to teach her," I said, correcting her.

"You'll *teach* her, then," Lara said and rolled her eyes. "She's pretty, and smart and despite her cover story, I think she's interested in this for real, but she's afraid, Drake. There are reasons she wants to remain anonymous, having to do with her background and family. Still, you might want to seduce her a bit. I have a feeling with a bit of your magic, she'd be signing the dotted line for real."

"I love a challenge," I said and smiled. "I love a reluctant sub who needs a lot of coaxing. You know me."

"I *do* know you, Drake and that's precisely why I asked you. Here's the contract she would sign, if this was for real." Lara reached into her briefcase and passed a document to me. I took it and reviewed the pages. It was pretty vanilla, with only a few references to bondage, hair pulling and maybe some light spanking.

I still didn't completely comprehend the need I had to be dominant, the need of these women who wanted me to be in control of them or where it came from, although I had a lot of theories. Frankly, I'd been too busy for the last few years to try to understand it. I was simply turned on by having a woman completely under my control. Helpless. Breathlessly waiting, dying for me to fuck her.

I liked the trust they placed in me, allowing me to tie them up so they were completely helpless and under my power. When they were restrained, when the last cuff was attached and they were bound and blindfolded, there was a moment of pure release as they went into subspace. Then, the submissive was open to anything, highly responsive, primed for pleasure.

I liked to train them so that they came really fast, multiple times, sometimes with just a few words, a few touches, a few licks, a few strokes, most of the buildup mental rather than physical.

Most men spent far too little time attending to their lover's mental state, so focused on the physical aspects of sex, of dicks and pussies, tits and ass, but I found that the mental preparation was the most important part of a sexual relationship. The small touches, meaningful words, the glances, the longing, the buildup, the rising desire. The actual physical act of fucking was the smallest part of it. The denouement. If you spent enough time working a woman up without even touching her, sex would be explosive.

"Let me guess – she read those books, right?"

"Who hasn't?" Lara said, laughing. "Don't complain. It's bringing in a whole new generation of material for us, although most of them don't really understand BDSM or even why the book turned them on so much."

"They like dominant men," I said. "I aim to please."

"Did you read them, too?"

"Are you kidding?" I said and grinned. "Of course I did. No self-respecting Dom would have missed seeing how our species was portrayed."

"You're the real-deal, Drake," Lara says, sipping her espresso. "Eligible bachelor, rich, good looking, smooth, smart. All the Dom without the pain."

"And without being fucked up."

She smiled at me. "If you say so."

I frowned, a bit ticked at her innuendo. "I'm *not* fucked up. I had a good upbringing."

"Whatever you say, Drake," Lara said and smiled even wider. "Have you ever thought about why you like to tie women up and torture them using pleasure? Oh, that's right... you gave up on psychoanalysis so you could study brains."

"I'm just a Dominant. I need control."

She smiled like the cat who swallowed the canary.

I gave her a look. "In the end, it doesn't really matter why something turns you on," I said. "Understanding the reasons for lust does nothing to change it."

"It does matter, Drake. You can deny it all you want, but as you know from studying psychoanalysis, the more you keep something hidden, the more you ignore it, the farther down in the darkness you shove it, the more power it has over you. Bring it out into the light and it loses that power. Why can't you let another woman into your life? Why can't you trust again?"

I shook my head, not wanting to have this discussion. There was no understanding the human psyche – at least not on a scientific level. I gave that up years ago when I switched from psychology to medicine in my senior year.

"It makes no difference why. It just is."

"Restraining women – why that in particular?"

"Lara..." I said, frowning at her. "Why do you like to beat a sub's ass black and blue?"

"Because it's so pretty like that. We're not talking about me, Drake. And I could tell you why – because I like to be in control and I enjoy the power I have over men. I like to see them cower at my feet."

"I like to have control over a woman's body so I can do what I want."

"You don't need to tie a woman up. Many women would let you do whatever you wanted, no ropes or restraints needed. There's something else going on."

"It's not me who needs it," I said. "It's them. They need to be tied up so they don't feel any guilt. I do it so I can enjoy when they surrender. When they do, they can freely enjoy everything I do to them without guilt. They can't stop it. It's not their fault they have orgasms."

"Why not have vanilla sex, with no bondage. I mean, if you don't need to tie women up for any personal reasons, you could give it up tomorrow, right?"

"I like rope bondage. I like leather."

"For purely aesthetic reasons? Or is it something deeper?"

"What are you trying to imply?"

"Abandonment issues?" she said and swirled her espresso in the tiny cup. "Mommy left you and so you restrain women to keep them from leaving?"

I pushed back from the table. "That's far too simplistic. I have no interest in fucking my mother, Lara. I like the way a woman looks when she's bound and blindfolded. That's all."

"It's a fetish, Drake. It has a history and an origin. If you don't understand it, it will have control over you instead of the other way around."

"I like a bit of mystery," I said. "I don't need to know why someone likes to dominate or be dominated. I only want to know how much they need."

"I like knowing why," Lara said. "It makes things clearer."

We sat and stared at each other in silence for a few moments, neither one of us willing to concede any ground.

Back in college when I first studied abnormal psych, I was the rebellious son who was determined not to follow in my surgeon-father's footsteps. I decided to become a psychoanalyst or psychotherapist, making my name by answering Freud's famous question *What do women want?* After an undergraduate degree in abnormal psychology, and several unsuccessful relationships of the sexual and romantic kind, I decided to give up psychology and take the easy way out.

Brain surgery.

The inner workings of the psyche were far more unfathomable than that of the brain.

We finished our lunch, silently agreeing to disagree about the whole etiology of desire debate, catching up with each other's careers, and finally, I stole a glance at my cell and saw that it was time to go back to the hospital.

"I have to run," I said. "I have a surgery in half an hour and need to prep."

Lara was done as well and finished her espresso.

"So, I can tell this girl you'll do the interview?"

"Sure." I stood, finishing the last of the coffee in my cup. "You set up a meeting." I reached into my pocket and left a couple of dollars as a tip for the waitress. "Call me and I can slip out between surgeries. I usually have an hour off at three."

"Thanks," Lara said and smiled at me. "You won't regret it. She's really smart and will likely have some good questions. I sent her a link to your website so she could read your letters. That'll probably get her so worked up, you'll have no problem getting her to sign on the dotted line. You'll probably really enjoy it."

She stood and I walked out of the café with her, my arm at the small of her back. We stopped outside on the street and she eyed me up and down as if assessing me.

"I think she'd probably be right up your alley. You might end up with a new sub after all if you put in the effort, so try to seduce her a bit. "

"Try to stop me," I said and grinned. I leaned in to kiss her cheek and we parted ways.

LARA CALLED to set up a meeting with the young woman who wanted to interview me about the lifestyle, but even the prospect of seducing someone new didn't fill me with the usual excitement. In the middle of the afternoon, after I had finished my first surgery after lunch, I pulled my lab coat over my scrubs and left NYP to make the short walk to the café where Lara and I met.

I entered the café and saw Lara immediately – she was hard to miss, with her platinum blonde hair and expensive tailored business suit. I started towards the table, curious about the young woman, whose back I saw through the window, when I realized who she was.

Katherine.

Katherine McDermott. The woman I'd been fantasizing about despite my best attempts to block her memory from my mind. I saw her face full-on when she turned to the door where I stood and I was struck once more by how pretty she was. She wore a creamy sweater that made her breasts look even more enticing – if that was even possible. Her hair was down and silky, falling around her shoulders, her features petite and pretty.

I stopped up short, frowning when I saw her with Lara, wondering if I had somehow got it wrong. I glanced around the deserted café in confusion, thinking that perhaps Lara knew Katherine and was meeting with her for coffee and that I had the date wrong.

Lara stood and waved me over to the table.

"You're *late*," Lara said, air kissing my cheeks when I arrived as if she'd been expecting me.

Then it became obvious why Katherine was there, and the truth registered as a shock of adrenaline surging through my body.

Katherine was the researcher.

She was the young woman who wanted to interview me. To interview a Dom because, as Lara said, she was curious, but was too afraid to do it for real.

The young woman Lara thought I could love…

"OH, GOD," Katherine said, glancing away for a moment, her face blanching. I stood there like a total zombie, confusion and elation battling inside of me for ascendance. I didn't know whether to laugh out loud with glee or act apologetic, still not entirely certain that I was right.

"I have to go." Katherine pulled on her coat, gathered up her bag and put on a pair of sunglasses. She walked away, her body stiff.

She was horrified that it was *me* she was supposed to meet.

"Kate!" Lara called out, but Katherine was out the door and on the street hailing a taxi before Lara could get to the door.

We stood at the open door and watched as Katherine hailed down a cab.

"You know each other, I take it?" Lara said to me, her arms crossed.

"Yes," I said, my heart pounding. I was just about to go after her, but Lara grabbed my arm and stopped me.

"Let her go," she said, her grip firm. "She's obviously freaked out. I take it there's some reason she's upset that you're the one."

"I'm very close with her father, who was my dad's best friend. We finally met about a week ago."

I watched as the taxi drove off. My instinct was to follow her, but I listened to Lara. I exhaled heavily and gave in. This would only end well if I handled it – and *her* – with utmost finesse.

Lara and I went back into the café and sat down once more at the table. The waitress brought me an espresso, and I shot it down, needing the buzz to calm me. Lara ordered another espresso and then we sat looking at each other.

"So," Lara said, hesitantly. "What do you think? Are you still interested in doing the interview?

Interested? I was fucking *ecstatic*.

"I am," I said, keeping my voice calm. "I actually *like* her."

"Oh, *oh*." Lara smiled at me over her espresso. "By her reaction, she likes you as well."

It was then I realized that she *did*, despite her response. "This could get complicated."

"Only as complicated as you let it get. You're the one in control."

I looked to the street where Kate had caught the cab. I want to follow her, talk to her. Make this right between us. Traffic was pretty heavy at this time of day, and given the recent rain, it was even slower, but she was long gone.

"Poor Kate," Lara said. "To find out you're the Dominant I was going to introduce her to. How embarrassing for you both."

"She's probably really upset that I know she's interested in BDSM. It's quite the change from famine in West Africa."

"It is. She's completely fascinated with the lifestyle but doesn't want to admit it to herself. She'll be a tough nut to crack."

"They always have the sweetest meat, once you do crack their hard shell, though." I smiled at Lara. She knew *exactly* what I meant. Submission, when a strong-willed person finally gave in, was even better than one who succumbed too easily.

Their eventual submission was total, their sexual response unrestrained.

"I should call her," I said, reaching into my scrubs pocket to retrieve my cell. I held it in my hand, indecision filling me. "Try to calm her down. Do you have her number?"

"She'll never answer your call. Let me see if I can salvage this," Lara said and took out her own phone. She entered Katherine's number but she didn't answer.

"You take it," Lara said, handing me her cell. "Try again."

I took Lara's cell and connected to Katherine's number.

"She's seriously freaked out," Lara said. "She wants it – and maybe *you* – bad."

I couldn't help but smile. "I'll try again."

I redialed and this time, Katherine answered. Before I could say anything, she spoke, her voice breathless, almost panicked.

"Before you say *anything*, I want you to remind Dr. Morgan that this was *purely* academic. This was research – nothing more. No matter what you think Lara, I'm not interested. This was nothing *personal*—"

"Kate, *Kate*, shhh," I said, keeping my voice soft. "Don't worry. I *know*. You're a serious student. This is just research. If anything, it's me who should be embarrassed."

She hung up.

I pulled the cell away from my ear and looked at Lara, who raised her eyebrows.

"Boy, does she want you," Lara said and finished her espresso. "*Real* bad. I think if you push a bit, she'll be signing a submission contract for real."

"I won't give up, then." I checked my cell for the time. "I better go. I've got a lot of paperwork to go over. I may pay a visit to Kate's apartment later this evening. Give me her number."

"Should I give it to you, Drake?" she said and eyed me from under a frown. "You sure about this? Is this manageable?"

"Never been more sure," I said, waving my hand in dismissal. "We already have a history. That will mean the walls are already crumbling. I know how to manage someone like her."

"I don't mean *her*."

I checked Lara's face to see if she was kidding.

"*Lara*..." I cracked a grin. "You know me better than anyone. Me not control myself around a sweet little girl like Katherine? I'll bend her to my will easily. I'll have her eating out of my hand in no time…"

"If you say so."

"I say so," I replied, and then I leaned down to peck her on the cheek. She rose and put on her jacket, then walked with me out of the café into the cool Manhattan afternoon.

We stood facing each other on the sidewalk and she had this strange expression on her face – part disbelief, part amusement.

She gave me a look. "I thought rule number one was to keep your life completely secret, apart from anyone in your personal life. Don't tell me you're going to go through with this…"

I smiled and walked backwards for a few steps, filled with elation.

"Try and stop me."

CHAPTER 10

Knowing someone is interested in trying out kink is one thing; actually getting them to let you bind, blindfold and dominate them sexually is quite another.

I had no idea how I was going to get Kate into my bedroom so I could gain complete control over her mind and body, but I knew I had to. As I raced up the street to New York Presbyterian to finish my afternoon office appointments, it was priority number one.

Every fiber of my being focused in on my new mission – get Kate to submit.

The panic in her voice when she thought she was talking to Lara on the phone said everything I needed to know. She found the idea of being my submissive – *my* submissive – both terrifying and absolutely undeniably desirable.

The very thought of Kate as my submissive made me hard as rock. I was a little breathless, my gut and groin filled with an ache of desire as I imagined her naked, her lovely skin pale against my dark grey bedspread, my leather cuffs around her wrists and ankles, my satin blindfold covering her beautiful green eyes...

I had to do everything in my power to focus back on my cases so that I gave each patient my undivided attention. Usually, I compartmentalized exceptionally well. It was my forte. But every so often that afternoon, while I read over patient files or dictated notes, my mind wandered to Kate. Fantasies of her lying naked on my bed, her mouth open as she panted with desire, plagued me. I had to return to the present and remind myself that soon enough, if I played my cards perfectly, Kate would be on her knees before me, naked, blindfolded, her hands restrained, her willing mouth pleasuring me.

I called her cell phone several times that afternoon, but as I expected, she wouldn't answer. Still, I left encouraging text messages in the hopes of assuaging her fears.

Kate, please answer. We have to talk.

It's okay, Kate. This is between you and me. No one but Lara will know...

Kate, seriously. You have nothing to fear from me. I won't do anything you don't want. I won't get you in any trouble...

When she hadn't answered one single call or text, I decided to take matters into my own hands and visit her apartment. Inaction was driving me crazy. My office hours could not end soon enough and I was thankful that I had a light surgical load that afternoon so I could leave my office earlier than usual.

"You seem unusually eager to leave early tonight, Dr. D," Janice said, the joint practice's administrative assistant. She winked at me as I removed my lab coat and threw on my jacket. An older nurse who had to give up the OR due to bad knees, Janice loved to tease me. "Hot date with a new lady?"

"Not yet, but," I said and winked back at her, smiling like a child, "I have hope."

"You don't need hope," Janice said and slipped a paper into a file. "Just talk to her in that deep voice you keep for anxious patients. She won't stand a chance."

"I have hope," I repeated, not wanting to sound too sure of

myself. I wasn't sure of myself. Kate was going to be difficult, but I was up for the challenge. Hell, I was a little hard once more even thinking about it.

I grabbed a turkey sandwich from the coffee shop before walking to my car in the staff parking lot, eating on the fly because I intended to stop by her apartment on my way home, see if I couldn't weasel my way inside and start my seduction of my very reluctant very new submissive.

That's the way I was going to think of Kate from that point forward – as *my* new submissive. Even though she wasn't, I had to think like a conqueror or else I wouldn't display the kind of dominance that attracted her to me. I had to wipe away our shared social life, forget whose daughter she was, and erase all the ties between us in the vanilla world – Doctors Without Borders, Columbia University, and most of all, Ethan. When we were together, we would be Master and submissive, not Drake and Kate.

Ethan could never know what I was and what Kate and I would have together. Maintaining the separation between my professional life and my personal kink was absolutely necessary to keep my practice as a neurosurgeon. Kate would be worried that Ethan would find out about her desire for kink but so was I. It would be a secret that would tie us together even more firmly than if we were two complete strangers. Secrets had a way of making everything more intense, and living this secret life, as Master and submissive, would be all the more meaningful for Kate, if only she would let me in.

I intended to make sure she did – let me in. Into her life. Between her thighs and as deep inside of her as I could get.

MY FIRST PROBLEM would be getting into her apartment.

Kate's Harlem neighborhood was pretty standard – street upon street filled with old Brownstones broken only by the occasional apartment block, school, corner store or coffee shop. I arrived as the street lights flickered on and was lucky enough to find a parking spot across from her building. I crossed the narrow road, threaded through double parked cars and climbed the steps to the entry. She'd never let me in willingly, but fortune smiled down on me. A piece of cardboard had been slipped between the door and the jamb so that I could enter without her buzzing me inside. It was a bit sneaky in a slightly stalkerish way, but we knew each other. I reasoned to myself that I was just going to surprise her.

I climbed the creaky old stairs to the third floor and stood outside her door, hesitating before I knocked, wanting to calm down a bit first.

I glanced left and right down the hallway. There were apartments on either side of the hall and a fire hose and alarm on the wall outside the stairwell. The building smelled musty and old. The flooring was faded, the once plush Oriental carpet now a muddy brown.

Kate came from a wealthy family with old money. Why did she live this way?

Finally impatient with my own indecision, I took in a deep breath and knocked on her door. I listened to see if she was in, and heard the creak of the floor behind the door. At the same time, the door to the apartment across the hall opened and I turned to see a pair of very old blue eyes with thick wiry gray eyebrows staring back at me. I turned back and leaned in to the eyehole but could make out nothing on the other side except a subtle dimming of the light as if someone – Kate – were peering out at me.

I smiled to myself. Was she debating whether to speak with me?

"I don't want to talk to you, Dr. Morgan," came Kate's voice through the door.

A surge of adrenaline went through me. She didn't try to

pretend she wasn't home. That was a good sign. Now, if only I could convince her to let me inside, I felt certain that I could get her to at least consider being my submissive.

"Kate, *please*, considering everything, call me Drake. And *trust* me. I have no interest in revealing anything about this to anyone. You, Lara and I are the only people who will ever know anything about this."

"Good," she said. "Thank you. Let's just forget this ever happened. *All* of it."

"No, *no...*" I said, unwilling to give in just yet. Not by a long shot. "No need for that." I frowned, trying to think of something to stall her. Then I remembered she was doing a paper on the lifestyle. If I could convince her to interview me, I felt confident I could convince her – eventually – to go out on a date. And then, she'd be mine. "We can still do the interviews. You want to research the lifestyle and I'm happy to help in any way I can."

"No *way*," came her voice and I could hear the hint of regret in it. "I can't. Just forget about it."

"Seriously, Kate," I said, trying to keep her talking. I remembered what Janice said and lowered my voice. "There's no need to call this off. I'm quite happy to teach you anything you want to know about," I said and lowered it even more, conscious of the pair of old eyes watching me from across the hall. "About submission. I'll even take you to a fetish night. Lara said you wanted to go. You could wear a mask, and no one would know who you are. I teach at Columbia in the department of medicine. I *love* teaching..."

"No. It's completely out of the question. It's totally embarrassing."

"*Kate...*" I said, my voice trailing off. "I understand your interest in this completely. I have a *lot* of experience. You don't have to be embarrassed with me."

"You're kidding, right? You don't think this is mortifying?"

I smiled. Every extra word she said was a victory. Every extra moment I spoke to her meant I was one more moment closer to her giving in and inviting me inside. If she did that, game over. I'd try my best to calm her, reduce her fear. She had to know that it was a risk for me that she knew I was a Dominant. I tried self-deprecating humor in the hopes of making her smile.

"For me, *yes*. For you, *no*. I'm the one who should be mortified, not you. Here I was, hoping to impress you enough that you'd go out with me for a drink some night and you discover I'm a Dom. You're just doing this for a research paper, after all…"

"I'm changing topics," she said, her voice sounding unconvincing, as if she had just made that up on the fly.

There was a pause.

I decided to play along. "What are you going to write about instead?"

"I don't know. Maybe the Administration's failure to act on climate change."

I couldn't help but smile at that. I had no doubt that Kate was interested in climate change. It was one of those liberal causes that someone like Kate would support without thinking, but it would pale next to sexual politics. "Sounds pretty boring in comparison to exploring why women are so excited by the prospect of submitting to a dominant man who knows how to release their inhibitions…"

She answered far too quickly. "I should never have even considered it."

I shook my head on the assumption she was watching out the peephole. "It's topical," I said, my voice purposely serious. "It's controversial."

"My father would *kill* me," she said, a small bit of panic still in her voice. "I don't know what I was thinking."

I *did* know what she was thinking. She was curious about

submission, about BDSM, but was afraid to explore it on her own without an excuse.

I could feel her giving in but there was still a resistance to the idea this was going to happen.

"Listen," I said, my voice conspiratorial. "We could stand here all night and talk through the door but I'm getting really hot standing here in my coat. Besides," I said, glancing back at the old woman who was unabashedly staring at me, her face pressed through the crack in the doorway. "It would be far more private if you just invited me in. Then your neighbor across the hall wouldn't keep peeking through the crack in her door and try to find out what we're talking about."

"That's Mrs. Kropotkin. I think her son's with the Russian Mafia."

I waved at the old woman. "*Zdrastvooyte.*"

She closed her door a little more tightly but not completely for I could still see one eye.

I unbuttoned my coat and loosened my tie, feeling too hot in the warmth of the hallway.

"Why do you live in a place like this?" I said, noting the fading and chipped paint. "You come from a wealthy family."

"I don't want my father's money."

"Oh, yes, that's *right*," I said, smiling. "Your father said something about you being a *socialist*…"

"I'm *not* a socialist," she said through the door, sounding insulted. "I studied political theory. There is a difference. I'm a liberal."

"Of *course*." I didn't really care if she leaned to the left – slightly or heavily. I was forbidden, politically and sexually. It would add a dimension to our relationship that would make her submission all the more exciting.

"My father would totally disown me if I joined the Socialist Party. As it is, I'm already a thorn in his side for my political positions and the fact I vote Democrat."

"*My* father was a socialist," I said, rubbing my jaw, in bad need of a shave. "A Trotskyite. I vote Republican. My father loved the Anonymous Group. He ate up WikiLeaks stuff. Probably would have stayed in Tent City if he was alive."

"I thought he – that *you* – are really rich."

"I am. He was. His company made a lot of money, but he started it for purely scientific purposes. He was what he called 'an accidental capitalist'. He saw the future in robotic surgery and wanted to help develop it. He was never in it for money. He drove one of those old Soviet cars. A really crappy, shit-brown *Lada*, but he liked the thought it was made in the Soviet Union. One of my favorite memories is of him tinkering with the engine, which was always breaking down. He spent so much trying to keep that piece of crap running."

I heard her laugh at that and saw movement under the door, as if she was leaning in to check the peephole again.

Now that he was dead, my memories of my father were mostly fond despite his foibles. I missed him.

"He was a wild man, full of life. Really gregarious." Sadness for his accidental death passed through me in a wave. His death was senseless—due to mechanical failure of his plane—but I'm sure he'd be happy that he died in his beloved Africa. "I miss him."

She said nothing for a moment and I could imagine her feeling bad for me, maybe softening towards me a bit.

"What about your mother?" she said in a soft voice as if she, too, wanted to prolong our conversation in spite of her fear.

"She left us when I was ten." I said it without emotion, for I'd turned off any feelings that I had for her long ago. I preferred not to feel sorry for myself. Self-pity was such a useless emotion that sapped you of drive.

"I'm *sorry…*"

"No, it's all right." I swallowed past the constriction in my throat. "I'm over it."

"How do you get over a mother leaving? Did your father remarry?"

"No, he never did. He travelled so much, kept the proverbial woman in every port. I had a succession of nannies and housekeepers to look after me."

Another pregnant pause ensued while neither of us said anything. I wanted to push, to use my voice on her, try to coerce her a bit but I held back. I wanted her to ask me to come in. I wanted her to pick me.

To choose me.

"You shouldn't have come here," she said finally. "It's very forward."

I smiled at that. "I didn't want any misunderstanding between us, Kate, and I don't want your father to find out about me. I admire your father and value his friendship. He's like a second father to me. I admire *you*. I…" Now it was my turn to hesitate. "I heard so much about you from your father and others. I'd like to get to know you better."

"You think I would *ever* tell my father about you? I'd have to tell him how I found out about your, you know. *Kink*. No way."

I opened my jacket farther for I was starting to overheat, a thin bead of sweat trickling down my temple. "Kate, why don't you let me in and we can talk? I'm sweltering out here and need some water."

"There's no reason to talk. I'm not writing about BDSM any longer and so we have nothing to talk about."

"I'd like to hear about Mangaize," I said, trying another tactic. I'd get her to talk about something that was important to her. "I was in Africa last year but never went to the camps. I was in several field hospitals in the Congo."

"In case you forgot, you warned me off you."

Crap. I did. What an idiot…

That was when I thought she was vanilla and would be horrified to find cuffs and rope and spreader bars in my closet.

"Oh, *damn*. I did, didn't I?" I rubbed my forehead, searching for a way to push past it. "Can I take it back?"

"Nope. My father always said that if a man tells you he's not good for you, you should believe him."

I smiled but shook my head. Trust Ethan to give Kate good advice. "Your father is a very smart man."

I sighed heavily, feeling my hopes for wearing her down dissipating. I had no idea what else to say to try to convince her.

"Why *did* you warn me off?" she said after a moment of silence.

Why did I? Because I felt guilty pursuing such a sweet innocent fragile woman like *Katherine*. Beloved daughter of the man I wished I had as a father.

"Isn't it obvious? You seemed so innocent, so young, so pure. I was sure you'd be horrified about my," I said, my voice low. "My *lifestyle*. I actually wanted to ask you out but didn't want to with Dave there, and then after the interview, I wanted to once again but I talked myself out of it. You were *Katherine*. Ethan's beloved daughter."

"I'm sorry," she said, and her voice did sound filled with regret. "I just can't."

I sighed. "Well, I should go, then. I don't want Mrs. Kropotkin to learn all my secrets." I tried to sound less disappointed than I felt but it wasn't easy. Then, I decided to leave her with something to think about. I leaned closer to the door.

"I'm sorry about all this," I said, trying to use the voice Janice told me to. "If you want to talk – about the article, about me, or the lifestyle – *anything* – you just have to call. Text me."

"I don't think I should."

She said it, but it wasn't firm. She didn't think she *should* could mean that she *wanted* to.

"Okay," I said, trying one last time. "Your call. But if you change your mind and want me, I'm willing. *Very* willing."

A silence ensued. Finally, she spoke. "Goodbye, Dr. Morgan."

"Good night, Ms. *Bennet*."

I turned away and walked down the hallway to the stairs.

I'd lost a skirmish, but I hadn't lost the war.

Not yet.

CHAPTER 11

As I drove back to my apartment, I refused to accept that we wouldn't eventually be Master and submissive. Despite her reluctance, I could almost taste the shy and reticent Ms. Katherine McDermott on my lips. I still had a huge wall to break down between us but if I had to do it brick by brick, I would – gladly.

Katherine was everything I could want in a sexual partner. Lovely, intelligent, well-bred. Submissive. Katherine was a true submissive – not just a young woman looking for a fun diversion because some book appealed to her. I'd met that kind of woman and they were fun, but often moved back to a vanilla lifestyle once they had their brief taste of submission.

No, with Kate, it was the real deal. Beneath that reluctant exterior was a woman aching to try submission but afraid of what it meant about her character. I knew her type – raised in a wealthy family by an exacting father who had high expectations for her success in whatever field she chose, high standards of behavior and performance in school and work. It had to be exhausting.

Someone like Kate just wanted to submit to someone strong and in control.

In contrast, I was raised by an absentee father who was too focused on his career and his desire for adventure and thrills to pay much attention to instilling anything in me but independence. I had to develop a sense of control – over myself and everything else – because he was never there to be my rock. I had to become dominant in order to achieve anything.

Yes, I did most of it to attract his attention, which rarely ever came, but this personal drive to be in control led to great success in my career as a neurosurgeon. I finished high school two years early, did the same with my undergraduate degree and then went through into medical school and my fellowship without break until I was fully accredited as a Board Certified neurosurgeon at thirty.

Katherine needed someone like me to feel safe. With me in control, she would be free to explore anything and everything because none of it would be her responsibility. I needed someone like her to fulfill my need for control. The fact that Ethan seemed to want to push us together made it all the easier and even more exciting. We could do anything, be together whenever we wanted, and he would be pleased. He'd be none the wiser that his little girl and best friend's son were playing dominance and submission games in the bedroom.

What we did in private was none of his business anyway.

I arrived at my building and parked my car, jangling the keys in my overcoat pocket as I made my up the elevator to my suite. I'd have to develop a plan of attack and be resolute implementing it. I knew Kate wanted this but was afraid to admit it. I'd have to push her just a little and she'd fall.

Right into my arms.

ONCE INSIDE MY APARTMENT, I threw off my coat and shucked

my boots before checking my messages. Yet another one from Allie, pleading with me to give her another chance. I'd have to speak to Lara about her. Lara had to find her another Dom because I had my mind set on Katherine and nothing was going to do in substitution.

I had a call from David in Nairobi, asking me if I'd given his offer of a position at the hospital any thought. He'd been pestering me about coming to Africa for six months to help out with the medical college's neurosurgery program. I wanted to go, but with a busy practice in Manhattan, I'd have to start slowing down in order to take a leave of absence.

The last message was from Lara.

Drake, don't push too much with Kate. I know her type – skittish like an unbroken thoroughbred filly. She'll balk at any attempt to saddle her up at first so proceed slowly... Call me back and we can talk. Better yet, meet me for lunch tomorrow and we can plot our course.

I smiled at the metaphor of Kate as a thoroughbred and the revelation that Lara was on my side. Kate was precisely a thoroughbred, with good breeding, a first-rate upbringing and a graduate education. Chestnut hair and wide green eyes, fantastic rack and tiny little waist. She was short and that always brought out the Dom in me.

God, I wanted her...

I wanted her wrists and ankles cuffed and restrained, tied to my bedframe, a blindfold covering her eyes while I played with her body, teasing her with pleasure until she begged for release. Then, I'd remove her blindfold and force her to look in my eyes as she came.

Imagining it gave rise to a semi and I rubbed myself absently, wishing I'd been more successful with her earlier. If I had been able to work my way into her apartment, I felt certain

I could have found my way between her luscious thighs. I could be very persuasive when I wanted something.

I wanted Kate badly.

After undressing and washing my face, I examined myself in the mirror. There were a few flecks of grey in my hair, and a few lines on my face. Yes, I was twelve years older than Kate, but age gave me that extra sense of dominance that would attract and tame a submissive like her. I'd been married, divorced and had been a professional for seven years. I wasn't some green under the collar frat boy who didn't know what to do with his dick or how to handle a woman like Kate.

I sat on the edge of my bed and opened the photo album containing the artistically posed photos of previous submissives and flipped through the pages. It usually provided me with a source of arousal when I was between submissive partners, but I wanted to imagine Kate in those poses instead of the woman they portrayed.

I closed the book and laid back on the bed, my eyes closed as I imagined bringing Kate to my apartment, tying her up and having my way with her delicious body and mind.

It was cold comfort to be jerking off alone instead of using her body for my pleasure but until I was successful getting between Kate's thighs, it would have to do.

I met Lara at the café across the street from NYP just after one o'clock the next day once my morning slate of surgeries was complete. As usual, she was impeccably dressed in her grey pinstripe suit and white blouse, her hair pulled back tightly in a bun, thick black framed glasses on making her look very bookish. That staid exterior hid a very kinky and domineering interior that I had come to know only too well during our time together as a new Dom in training.

I stopped at the counter and placed my order and then went to our table at the back of the small café.

"There you are," she said and bent her head to the side, expecting me to bend down and kiss her cheek. Despite the fact we were both dominants, she couldn't help but try to top me in every encounter. I smiled and bent down, placing a kiss on her cheek. Then, I slipped down to kiss her neck at the last moment, refusing to give her the upper hand completely. My small show of dominance mixed with obeisance kept us simpatico and ensured I had a steady supply of eager new recruits.

My specialty was training new submissives who were curious about the lifestyle but didn't want to try anything too heavy into S&M to start. She had a line into that supply as one of the moderators at the Manhattan branch of Fetlife.com. She taught a class on BDSM and Feminism once a semester, introducing the topic to the curious who were conflicted about their politics. I'd met almost all of my former submissives through her connections and most of them were college students or young professional women bored with the same old thing.

"So," she said, eyeing me from across the table. "Any luck with the reluctant daughter of the Hanging Judge? You sure you want to do this, given that you two run in the same social circles?"

"Not one iota of doubt," I replied and smiled at the server as she placed my BLT sandwich down on the table. I dug into my lunch, hungry after five and a half hours of surgery. "I'm even more convinced after I made a visit to her apartment last night. Our little encounter gave me hope."

Lara made a face of surprise. "You went to her apartment? She invited you in?"

That surprised me, for I was sure Kate would have called Lara to talk about the whole business.

"She didn't call you?" I said, taking a pickle chip off my plate.

"No," she said, smiling over her cup. "Tell me everything."

I shrugged. "I didn't actually go inside her apartment so there isn't much to tell. I stood outside her door in the hallway for about fifteen minutes and sweltered while she stood on the other side of the door."

"And this gives you hope because…"

"Because," I said and picked up the other half of my sandwich. "I could tell by what she said and how she said it that she really wanted to talk to me but was afraid."

"Of you?"

I shook my head and smiled. "Of herself."

"Ahh," Lara said as she fixed me with a thoughtful stare. "Of course. She strikes me as someone who is extremely frustrated with her life. She wants more but is afraid to take it. Afraid of her domineering father, I suspect."

"Precisely."

"I have the highest regard for Judge McDermott," Lara said, looking off into the distance. "But he is very dominant. I'd think she'd be happy to find another man like him. Most women want another daddy."

"She's probably happy to find another man like Ethan," I said, nodding in agreement. "She just has to realize it. If she didn't want someone like me, she wouldn't have gone looking in the first place."

"Precisely," Lara mirrored back at me, grinning. "Gotta love a confident Dom."

I grinned back. "I had the very best teacher."

On Tuesday, I saw Ethan in the locker room at the club after a game of racquetball with a fellow surgeon. Ethan was speaking with a couple of men his age, all of them wrapped in towels, preparing to take a steam.

His back was turned to me so I waited until there was a break in conversation and stepped closer. The other men glanced at me and then parted, allowing me to approach the judge.

"Pardon me, gentlemen. Judge McDermott, good to see you again," I said. "Great turnout at your fundraiser over the weekend."

He turned to me and the look on his face was priceless. Like he'd just found his future son-in-law and not the conniving Dominant out to bed his daughter…

I had to suppress a chuckle.

"Well, Drake, my boy," he said, taking my hand and shaking vigorously, his other hand on my shoulder. "So glad you could come. I've been meaning to introduce you to some of my colleagues and supporters."

"I'm one of your biggest supporters, Judge. You'd make a fantastic candidate. You have my vote."

Ethan smiled at that. After a round of introductions, he waxed poetic about my father and their time in 'Nam together and how Ethan had been 'watching over' me for the past decade. Then, Ethan narrowed his eyes and examined me as if coming to a decision.

"I'm having a little get together on Friday with a dozen or so of my closest friends and supporters to talk about my campaign. I'd be really pleased if you could join us."

A feeling of warmth for Ethan flooded through me. "I'd be honored."

"Drinks at six thirty. Dinner at seven. Then we talk strategy."

I nodded. "Sounds great. I'll be there."

"Oh, and why don't you come by a bit early? Say sixish. Katherine will be joining us for dinner. You two seemed to hit it off at the party and it was so good of you to patch her up after her fall in the alley. She can show you some of her photos of Africa."

Adrenaline surged through me at that. Ethan was inviting

me to come by and spend time with his beloved daughter, making my little seduction of Katherine all the easier.

"That would be wonderful," I said, smiling. We shook once more and I left the men alone, feeling guilty that the two of us were ambushing poor Kate this way. With Ethan and I united in the goal of pushing us together, she didn't stand a chance.

I felt only slightly guilty, of course.

Friday couldn't come fast enough.

I pushed through my day, trying to keep my mind off the dinner and my plans for the lovely Ms. Bennet. I had a class in the morning, afternoon rounds and then checked in on all my patients before rushing back to my apartment to shower and change.

I picked out a dark suit with a deep blue shirt and black tie for the event, wanting to look serious but stylish. Serious for the big wigs that Ethan would be introducing me to, and stylish to catch Katherine's eye.

There was more than a little adrenaline pumping through my veins as I drove from my apartment in Chelsea to Ethan's Park Avenue building.

I entered the parking garage, using the code Ethan provided so I could use the underground guest parking, going over my plan of attack one more time. I'd try to get Kate to talk – about her time in Africa, of which I was truly interested – and about her mother. If I could, it would raise the intimacy level between us. Revealing information to a stranger about your personal life, especially things that were painful, tended to break down the walls between you.

Once two people commiserated about deaths in the family, especially of a parent, they were no longer strangers.

They were intimates, and that was all I needed to get a little closer to Ms. Bennet's very ripe little body, and between her thighs.

I smiled to myself as I took the ornate elevator to the penthouse.

She'd be shocked that I was there. I had no doubt that Ethan wouldn't tell Kate I was coming. I had the sense that he understood that Kate was on the shy side when it came to men.

She needed a little push...

Someone buzzed me in and a servant opened the door to Ethan's luxurious apartment.

"Dr. Drake Morgan," I said to the young woman who smiled and took my overcoat.

"Please come in. I'll let Judge McDermott know you're here."

I entered the apartment and searched around, looking for Ethan, but he wasn't in sight. In the living room, I saw Katherine sitting on one of the sofas, a look of such surprise and horror on her face when she saw me that I almost laughed out loud.

Oh, Kate, Kate, *Kate*... Could you be any more transparent?

A pink flush spread over her face and she frowned only slightly before forcing a smile. I smiled back, my hands in my pockets, feeling like the cat who swallowed the canary. I stood and waited for her to get up and invite me in, wanting to make her as uncomfortable and off-center as possible.

"Doctor *Morgan*," she said, her voice quiet. She stood awkwardly and smoothed her dress, which was black velvet, the deep neckline showing off the creamy swell of her cleavage.

I drank her in like a man dying of thirst.

"Ms. *Bennet*," I said softly, my gaze lingering on her, moving from her head to her shoes and back. "You look... *breathtaking*."

She made a funny face of embarrassment – half-smiling, half-frowning, hiding her smile inexpertly behind a hand.

I offered her my hand, wanting to shake hers and kiss her knuckles. She slipped her hands behind her back as if she were afraid to touch me for fear I would ravage her right there on the plush oriental carpet – which I wanted to do, of course.

Good. I wanted her to think of me that way. Such an image would make me all the more irresistible. I kept my hand extended, unwilling to retreat and just then, Ethan walked into the living room. He was still buttoning his vest when he came over.

"Oh, Drake, *there* you are."

Immediately, Kate held out her hand and I took it and kissed her knuckles, my eyes never leaving hers. Finally, after making my point, I turned to Ethan.

"Judge McDermott," I said, extending my hand, using the formal form of address to reinforce his dominance over us all. "Thanks once again for inviting me tonight."

Ethan shook my hand, his other hand on my shoulder. There was a gleam in his eye that said he was pleased to see me treating Katherine with such courtesy.

"Drake, please, I insist you call me Ethan," he said, sounding like an old drill sergeant with his gravelly voice. "I see you've already spoken to Katherine. Come in and make yourself comfortable."

Ethan turned to Kate. "I invited Drake here a bit earlier than our other guests so you could give him the tour and show him your photographs from Africa." He turned to me. "They're really good and intimate, telling the story of her trip. You want to understand what makes my daughter tick? You see those photos. Very artistic. She has real talent. I have to take a call or I'd join you myself."

Kate looked completely flummoxed. "Of course," she said, her voice barely above a whisper.

"Good, good," Ethan said, rubbing his hands together. "The others should start arriving in a while. Get Drake a drink, dear. Be a good hostess for me, will you? The bartender had to go get more wine and Elaine is still busy getting ready. Heath isn't here yet."

He left the room, smiling like the Cheshire Cat.

Oh, Ethan... You're making this far too easy. If the prize was anyone less desirable, it would have been a bit too easy, but the prize was Katherine.

I couldn't help but smile a bit smugly at Kate, who stood there, her cheeks red.

"Would you like a drink?" she said, the dutiful daughter and hostess. She pointed to the bar in the dining room.

"Know how to make a vodka martini?" I asked, trying with all my might to keep a smile of triumph off my face.

She went to the bar and rustled around in the cupboard, retrieving a martini glass and a shaker, some vodka and vermouth. I watched as she placed some ice in the shaker, poured in a few ounces of Stolichnaya vodka and then added a splash of vermouth. She shook the mix for a moment and strained it into the martini glass like a pro.

"Lime or olive?" she asked, pointing to the small tray of lime zest and olives.

"Lime would be nice," I replied, enjoying the fact that she was serving me – like a good submissive would.

She added a twist of lime zest into the martini glass and held it out to me.

"How's that?"

"Perfect." I took a sip, all the while staring at her over the rim. It was good. It was perfect. "Where'd you learn to mix a martini?"

"I was a cocktail waitress for a few years during my undergrad. I trained as a bartender."

"That's right," I said, smiling to myself. "Dave said you're paying your own way using scholarships and working part-time." I shook my head. "Stubborn girl. You're not having anything?"

"No. I tend to get a bit argumentative when I drink. Soda and lime for me."

I chuckled softly at that. "I like argumentative."

"I thought you were a Dom."

"I am, but that doesn't mean I like dumb women," I replied. "So you get a bit loose-lipped when you drink? That tells me that you usually hold your true opinion close to the vest and only let out your honest thoughts and emotions when under the influence of some kind of mind-altering substance. Alcohol. Serotonin. *Dopamine*..." I said, my voice trailing off. "I'll keep that in mind in the future."

She frowned at that, no doubt disliking the fact that I was assuming we even *had* a future, and that I was planning on using alcohol or some other substance to loosen her up.

Which I most definitely was planning to do.

She was uptight. Wound up and in need of release. I'd be only too happy to provide that release. Nothing, and I mean *nothing* freed a woman to respond with abandon like restraints. Specifically, a pair of leather cuffs lined with lambs wool attached to a headboard. And a blindfold.

Unable to see anything, all her other senses would be enhanced and she'd respond even more fully to touch, scent and taste. Unable to move or escape, she'd be free to respond to everything I did without guilt. Her pleasure and her orgasm would be mine, not hers. My responsibility, not hers.

The very fact she would come – hard – while restrained and blindfolded would make everything even more intense because it would be our secret. Sharing a secret, especially one around sexuality, would cement our bond even more firmly.

All this passed through my mind as I watched her pour herself a glass of soda with a squeeze of lime. Finally, she turned to me, avoiding my eyes.

"How come you're here? You weren't on my father's guest list."

"I'm one of your fathers biggest supporters," I said. "We met in the health club the other day and I offered my support for his candidacy for the House. He said he wanted to repay me after I looked after your injuries at the fundraiser. When I heard you were going to be in attendance tonight, I was only too happy to accept."

She frowned at that. "If you think this changes things, you're wrong."

I made a face of mock confusion. "Changes what, Ms. Bennet?"

She finally glanced at me. "The whole business with the research agreement."

"That's entirely up to you," I said, trying my best to look serious. "I'm still all yours, if you want me." I emphasized the 'yours' to drive home the point and said nothing for a moment to let it sink in.

"Kate, I'm so glad your father invited me. I've wanted to meet you ever since I met your father and he started talking about you, but he never brought you anywhere in public. I think I was a bit infatuated with you just from his description of you." She frowned, but said nothing so I pressed on. "You took photographs while you were in Africa? I'd *love* to see them. See into that mind of yours and what makes you *tick*."

"I don't know what my father meant by that," she said, frowning. "What makes me tick. They're just photos." She started off down the hallway, her steps stiff, her back straight as if she were steeling herself. "They're in the study."

I followed her, wondering why she was so uptight about showing me her photos. Once we were inside the study, I closed the door behind us and took her arm, turning her around gently to face me.

She stared at my hand on her arm and I finally let go.

"I'm sorry if you're unhappy that I'm here," I said and stepped closer to her. I wanted a moment of intimacy between us to break down her walls, overcome her shyness. Break the ice. "Your father wanted me to come early so that you and I could get to know each other. I'm glad he did."

"Why would he want us to get to know each other?"

"I guess because I said I thought you were a lovely young woman and wanted to get to know you better."

Her cheeks flushed. "I thought you weren't the kind of man someone like me should get involved with."

"You won't let me live that down, will you?" I said and laughed softly. Me and my big mouth, warning her off like an infatuated badboy in love with the girl from the right side of the tracks.

"It's just that it would have been nice if I knew he invited you beforehand."

I stepped closer and pinned her against the huge mahogany desk. She held her glass of soda between us as if she could use it to protect herself from my advances. I could easily take the glass out of her hand and kiss her right now, and part of me wanted to for I suspected that if I did, she would be totally confused and upset, but at the same time, would most likely kiss me back. But just in case she responded differently, I held back.

I intended to kiss her tonight.

Now just wasn't the right time.

"Would you have found some excuse not to attend?"

She was quiet, turning her face away. "I would have liked the choice," she said. "But of course, my father always has to have things his way."

"He's quite a dominant man himself."

She looked up at me, finally, but avoided my eyes. Oh, *Kate*...

"I can't seem to escape them."

"Maybe that's because you don't *want* to."

That made her back stiffen. Perhaps I'd gone a bit too far, touched a raw nerve.

"I left home to get away from him. Listen," she said, pointing a finger at me, focusing on a button on my suit jacket instead of my eyes. "I can't have *anything* to do with you, do you understand? I'm writing my research paper about climate change so unless you know something about that, you and I have nothing to talk about."

I clucked my tongue. "You're trying too hard, Kate."

I took her finger in mine and turned it away. Then, I took her hand and stroked her palm, wanting her to imagine me stroking her body.

"Me thinks the lady doth protest too much and that you do, in fact, want to have something to do with me."

She pulled her hand away and blushed profusely. "I don't like being around you," she said, her voice low.

"I think you *do*. You *like* me. You don't like the fact that you like me. You don't want to like me but you can't help it."

"I don't *believe* you," she said with affront. "You're …" She clenched her fists. "You're awfully certain of yourself."

Then, she tried to escape me, but I took her arm once more and leaned in close so that my face was just inches from hers. Her perfume wafted up into my nose and I breathed in deeply. It sent a jolt of lust right to my dick.

"Yes. I know what I want."

"Well, so do I. And it's not *you*."

She pulled her arm out of my hand and turned to the door.

As if to save the day, and with impeccable timing, Ethan entered. He saw us and smiled.

"There you two are." He rubbed his hands together. "Has she shown you her photographs of Africa yet?"

I cleared my throat, still affected by her nearness. "No, she hasn't."

"Come on, Kate. Show Drake your photos. I know he's interested. He's been there many times with Doctors Without Borders. You two have a *lot* in common." He took Kate's hand and then he laid a hand on my shoulder, pulling us both towards the wall where all Kate's photos were hung.

Then Peter, Ethan's chief of staff entered the room. "Judge? There's a call for you."

Ethan raised his eyebrows. "Duty calls. I have to take that, but you two stay here. Kate, show him your photographs. I'll be back when my call is finished."

When he was gone, I turned to Kate but she refused to look at me. She stood silent, her glass of soda clutched in her hands like a some magic amulet to ward me off.

"You're not really going to make me tell you about my trip to Africa are you?"

"I most certainly am," I said, my voice soft. "I'm truly interested. I've been to Africa many times. Besides, I want to see into you, Kate. Right inside. Please, tell me." I waved at the wall and watched her, not giving an inch.

"Nothing's going to happen between us," she said, her voice low in warning. "The meeting was a mistake so you might as well forget it. There's no reason for you to see 'right inside' me. We're opposites. You vote Republican. I'm a Democrat."

I smiled inwardly but forced my voice to be serious. "None of that matters, Kate, when we fuck. All that matters is that we both need what each other has to offer."

"We're not going to... *fuck*," she said, whispering.

"Whatever you say." I couldn't stop my smile, but turned to face the photos so she wouldn't see it. "I still want you to tell me about these photos. Your father is really proud."

I heard her sigh heavily in resignation. "There are a lot of painful memories in them."

"Just the happy ones, then."

She pointed to a large picture of her with Nigel. I leaned closer, wondering about her friendship with Nigel, who I already knew was into BDSM, having seen him several times over the past few years at private dungeon parties.

"That's us, the day we arrived in Niger. Our driver took it. Nigel had been there before but I had no idea what to expect and so I was excited."

I peered at the pictures and listened as she told me about her trip. She talked about working for the UN program to provide food and medical care to new mothers. The photos captured the camps, filled with refugees who were desperate to escape the horrors of war.

She studiously avoided talking about one picture in particular, so that was the one I focused on.

"What's this one?" I pointed to one depicting two figures alone in the vast emptiness of the African desert.

She covered her mouth and shook her head.

"I can't."

I tried to turn her face gently towards me but she fought and turned away. I decided not to force her, and instead, merely touched her arm to show that I recognized she was upset.

Then Nigel himself walked into the study.

Damn… Just when things were starting to open up between us…

"Kate, my *dear*." Nigel pushed into the study and bent down to Kate, speaking in a conspiratorial tone. "Your father let slip that Dr. Morgan was coming a bit early, and so I thought I'd be chivalrous and offer my services…"

I bristled at that. Did he imagine he was somehow protecting Kate from me?

Nigel hugged and kissed Kate on both cheeks and on her part, Kate looked relieved, as if she'd been rescued.

"Can I get you a drink?" she asked.

"Please." Nigel smiled at me but I could tell he wasn't pleased to see me. "My usual."

Kate left us standing in front of the wall of photographs.

"Look here," he said, wasting no time in speaking to me as soon as the door to the study had closed. "Kate is a very delicate young woman, who has suffered quite a bit of trauma in the past couple of years."

My back stiffened at his tone. "And you're telling me this because…?"

"I'm telling you this *because* she's not for you," Nigel said, moving a bit closer to me, staring down at me the way a headmaster does his students. "Kate is not your usual kind of woman."

"And my usual kind of woman would be…?"

"You know very well what I mean. I've known Kate for years and she is not your type, *Dr.* Morgan," he said, emphasizing the Dr. "Kate is *not* the kind of girl to be trifled with."

I smiled. Almost my exact words to Dave the night I drove Kate home from the fundraiser.

"I assure you that I don't intend to 'trifle' with Kate. Quite the contrary. And perhaps you don't know Kate as well as you think." I stepped away, not willing to have him intimidate me with his larger physical presence any longer.

"If you hurt her, there will be repercussions," he said, stepping closer to me once more.

The door opened to admit Kate carrying a glass of red wine for Nigel. Nigel raised his eyebrows at me before turning to Kate and smiling once more, the happy lovable big brother.

Kate turned to me without meeting my eyes. "How is your drink, Dr. Morgan?"

"Please, call me Drake." I bent down and tried to catch her eye. "Considering. And it's still fine, thank you."

When I stood back up, Nigel gave me a look that said 'back off' but there was no way in hell I was backing anywhere from Kate.

Full steam ahead was more like it.

As much as I tried to stay by Kate's side over the next half hour, Peter pulled me around the room to introduce me to the other high rollers who were in attendance. Ethan himself was still busy on a conference call and couldn't join us right away, so he'd asked Peter to take over and introduce me to his group of financial supporters.

Every time I got within three feet of Kate, Nigel stepped in between us and tried to keep me away from her. It was almost comedic at first as the two of us jostled for position, but after a while, it became tedious.

Finally, about half an hour later, Ethan entered the room and pulled Nigel and Kate together, urging me and a few of the other guests to follow. I followed in their wake, only slightly peeved that it was Nigel, and not me, in Ethan's grasp.

"Kate has some wonderful photographs from her trip to Africa. Come dear," he said to Kate, "and talk about your trip."

Kate seemed quite unhappy that she was being forced to perform and frowned as her father pulled her down the hallway.

"Go ahead, dear," Ethan said to Kate once we were all in the study. "Tell us about your trip. Start here, with this one."

Kate spoke about her trip to Africa, going through each photograph, talking about the relief camp. When she came to the one photo that she avoided with me, Ethan wouldn't let her off the hook.

"Tell them about Alika and Chinua," Ethan said, turning to the rest of us who were gazing at the photos. "A couple and their baby that Kate and Nigel rescued from the desert."

Kate looked as if she wished a hole would open up in the floor and she could disappear, but I saw her steel herself, taking in a deep breath. The story was quite emotional – of she and Nigel finding a young couple with a newborn who were lost on the road to the relief camp, wandering in the middle of nowhere. Kate was overwhelmed at one point and had to stop. Nigel took over and told the rest of the story.

Then Kate picked back up again, her voice shaky, but she was trying.

"He crawled like a crab because his knees were bloody," she said, her voice barely audible. "Alika was carrying her baby. They hadn't named him yet because they weren't even sure if he would live. I thought he was a newborn because he was so small, but he was three months old and starving. Her breasts," she said, shaking her head, her voice almost inaudible. "She had no milk left. They were like deflated balloons."

Kate had to stop speaking, and covered her mouth with a hand, tears in her eyes. Nigel stepped up to the plate and finished the story of how they had saved the trio, but the husband died once they got back to the camp and he knew his wife and baby were safe.

I remembered Kate's articles in the Columbia Journalism Review and how impressed I was with them, how well-written and objective they were. From speaking with Ethan, I knew that a few months after returning to Manhattan, Kate had a breakdown. She hadn't properly mourned her mother's death and then, the trauma of the camps proved too much. Sympathy for her filled me. She was brave to take on such a harrowing ordeal so soon after a personal loss.

I was impressed.

Ethan stood watching Kate, his eyes filled with emotion, tears visible in them as he listened to his daughter speak.

"Excuse me," Kate said left the rest of us behind, closing the study door quietly behind her.

Nigel turned to follow her, but Ethan took his arm and stopped him.

"Let her go. She gets very emotional when she talks about the camps. It was very hard on her. She was very brave."

Nigel nodded and turned back to the wall of photos, talking

to someone who asked him to describe one of the photos that showed Kate and Nigel together. I took that as my cue to leave and follow Kate, wanting to be with her when she was especially vulnerable.

I quietly opened the door to the study, hoping Nigel didn't see me. He was occupied, but Ethan saw me and smiled as if he approved.

God, he was making this so easy...

I closed the door and went down the hallway, peering in each room to see if Kate was there. I found her in a small bedroom at the back of the apartment, which looked as if it had been hers for the furniture was feminine and a bit girly, French Provincial, white with gilded detailing and ornate. There was a cork-board on the wall over a small student desk with a half-dozen ribbons of blue and red – the kind you won in school for sports or for academic achievement. I wanted to check everything out, curious about this woman I was planning to seduce and dominate, but I held back. She needed my attention by the looks of her, sitting on the side of the bed, a tissue clutched in her hand, daubing her eyes.

When I entered the room completely, she glared at me and then turned away.

"I'd like to be *alone*."

I sat beside her and nudged her with my knee, bumping my shoulder against hers. "Being alone is the last thing you need right now." I purposely sat a bit too close to her, wanting our bodies to touch, make a connection. I rested my elbows on my knees and craned my head so I could look her in the eye. "I'm sorry. Your father doesn't seem to understand how upset Africa still makes you."

She frowned. "He always sees everything, every event, every word, for its strategic purpose. How it can aggrandize him and our family – or hurt us. He doesn't really pay attention to people," she said, her voice petulant, still emotional. "What he said about those photographs being key to what makes me tick? He thinks it means I'm some great humanitarian – some angel of mercy – but really, I was just a student looking for a topic for my honors thesis. I had *no* idea what I got myself into."

I was a bit taken aback at her confession. "You didn't like Africa?"

She said nothing for a moment, her arms wrapped around herself. She was very emotional, almost childlike in her response to her father. Part of me was surprised, for she was twenty-four but part of me completely and totally understood. How many times had I cried as a boy over my own father's neglect? How often did I see fathers and sons together, deep in conversation as two adults, and ache to have my father still alive and treating me as a real son?

He never did. I never had that kind of relationship with him. Even now, it hurt.

Here Kate was, well-educated, well-bred, obviously self-sufficient to a fault with her scholarships and part-time jobs, trying so hard to impress her father and she never really felt he was impressed.

How could she be so wrong? Ethan clearly loved her very much and was completely impressed with her.

"I hated it – the corruption," she said. "It was so hard. Painful. As soon as I could, I changed my topic. I couldn't *do* it. I'm not strong enough, but he can't see that because it would mean *his* daughter isn't up to snuff."

"You saw the worst of the worst." I turned to her, trying to catch her eye. "Where the people have resources, they're full of hope. I see it in the hospitals. The young doctors and nurses – they've been trained in America and they want to raise their countries out of poverty."

I leaned against her again, trying to nudge her into feeling better, thinking that she needed some affection at that moment. Of course, she didn't respond, but I thought I felt something between us. Something cracked just a bit in her reserved and tightly controlled demeanor.

"I admire you for going. You didn't have to so that does say something about you, what makes you 'tick'."

"You'd be wrong to think that." Her voice was bitter. "My father has *no idea* what makes me 'tick'. He practically chose my thesis topic and arranged everything. I *wanted* to do something on the fine arts, but *no*. It had to be political."

I frowned. "Your father *chose* your honors thesis topic?" I was shocked that Ethan had intervened so deeply in her life that he would choose her thesis topic. That went a bit too far. My father barely heard me talk about my schooling, my courses, my career path. Her father was practically engineering it for her.

"You're surprised?" She turned away. "You obviously don't know my father."

I thought I knew Ethan pretty well as a man and by the way he talked about his children, as a father. He seemed totally smitten with his daughter, speaking of her to me whenever we met. He was clearly proud of her accomplishments.

Was he too controlling? If so, she seemed to resent it . I'd have to watch myself with her if that was the case. Many submissives loved to have their Dominant make all the decisions – in all aspects of their lives together. It gave them some relief. Kate must not be that submissive if it bothered her so much. I'd have to give her a lot of freedom if we were going to be a couple.

I corrected myself. If we were going to be play partners. And we *were* going to be play partners. I was more determined than ever.

"What did *you* want to do?"

She didn't say anything for a moment. Finally, she sighed. "What did *I* want to do? *I* wanted to do a series on young artists in Manhattan, and how they're using social media and new technology in their art, but that was too 'airy-fairy' for him, as he put it. He only sees art for its value as an investment, not for its social or cultural value. I tried to explain but he just dismissed me. I was too much of a chicken to fight him and do what I really wanted."

That was the kicker. She saw herself as weak and afraid, not making her own decisions.

"I'm sorry. University should be a time when you explore who you are and what excites you. It shouldn't be a time to please your parents."

Of course, I had tried to please my father almost all my life, even finishing high school early through the accelerated program for gifted students. I had planned on going into Medical School, but when he went away for six months, leaving me with a housekeeper when I was only fourteen, I gave up on that and decided to do an undergrad degree in Psychology. Of course, I changed my mind when I realized that I was as interested in medicine as my father had been. That was one thing he instilled in me – a love of science and of medicine.

So we both had father issues. It was one more thing we had in common. A point of identification.

Then, our eyes met and she looked at me for perhaps the first time since we met. Really looked in my eyes. We connected in a way that we never had until then and I felt it right in my gut and in my dick.

I smiled at her, a little surprised that I felt such empathy for her all of a sudden. It felt a bit like standing at the edge of a precipice.

The door opened and Ethan popped his head just inside.

"Oh, *here* you are," he said and smiled. "I *thought* you two might have a lot in common. Sorry to interrupt, but my dear wife has announced that dinner is served."

CHAPTER 12

Dinner was amusing.

Ethan sat me to his right and Kate beside me. I felt a stab of warmth for the man at giving me such a privileged position at his table. The rest of his group of supporters were seated around the large table in the formal dining room, with Elaine sitting at the other end, entertaining them all and Heath and his wife across from us.

I could almost feel Kate bristle beside me, angry that she had been assigned a seat beside me. I smiled at her barely concealed anger as I pulled out her chair. While she was upset, I was extremely happy with the arrangements. I enjoyed myself immensely, drinking the wonderful wine Ethan served, the food delicious, and Ethan's conversation about politics engaging.

Kate ate in silence, and despite how Ethan tried to force her to make conversation, she politely refused, answering his questions in a monotone, with single word replies.

But at one point, she glanced sideways at me and when our eyes met, there was this expression in hers that I found hard to place. If I hadn't been so aware of how unhappy she was with my presence and how it unnerved her that her father was so openly and delightedly trying to match us, I would have thought it was some kind of dark lust I saw in her eyes. I felt it again – this connection with her that made my heart jump.

I held her gaze, unable to look away, hoping I wasn't mistaking that look which felt like pure desire.

Whatever that look meant, I felt it in my groin. For a moment, I had this insane desire to drag her to the washroom just off her bedroom and fuck her while facing the mirror, thrusting hard and fast until we both came, watching each other's faces.

When she finally glanced away, her cheeks red, I did as well, a bit unnerved once more by this woman beside me. Something in my brain kept saying *Choose me...* Which was completely the opposite of how I found new submissives. It was usually the other way around with them wanting me to pick them.

I took a long drink of wine, needing it to quell the feeling in my gut that bordered on desperation.

I didn't do desperation.

When the serving personnel came to remove our dessert plates and coffee cups, Ethan stood and cleared his throat, drawing the guests' attention.

"Now, if everyone here to discuss politics could join me in my study, we'll get down to the real business."

At that, Kate almost sprang up as if she couldn't wait to escape.

I caught up with her at the door to the hall and took her arm. "Can we talk later?"

She glanced at my hand on her arm as if it offended her, but I wasn't going to give in that easily.

"We have nothing to talk about."

"Please?" I said, my voice soft. "Just hear me out."

She hesitated. "I was going to leave after we 'ladies' have our tea."

"Okay. I'll come by your place," I said, hoping she'd decide to wait and talk to me to avoid such an encounter. "Can we talk *inside* your apartment instead of through the door this time?"

She responded as I expected, her jaw tightening. No. She wanted to avoid me showing up at her place.

"I'd rather you didn't come to my apartment."

"Fine," I said, smiling to myself. "Why don't you wait for me and I'll give you a ride home when we're done here."

Ethan stood at the door and looked at Kate expectantly. "Hey, sweetie, you're detaining Drake. We have important business to attend to."

Kate looked between Ethan and me and so I nodded, not wanting to delay Ethan.

"We'll just speak in the car." I held up three fingers. "I won't come in. I promise. Scout's Honor."

She looked exasperated but she finally gave in, probably thinking it was better than having me show up unannounced. "Very *well*."

I let go of her arm and joined Ethan as he walked with a group of his guests back to the study. He slipped an arm around my shoulder and I felt warm at his show of affection.

If he only knew how much I was fantasizing about his beautiful beloved daughter, and what plans I had for her sexual pleasure, I wasn't so sure he'd be as friendly.

The talk around the table was about Ethan's candidacy for the open seat and what party powerhouses we could get on board. I admitted to being a lightweight in the group, but was glad to be invited to take part. It would provide me with an education about how real politics worked, and besides, I loved Ethan like a father.

Once we were done with the discussion and pulled out our

checkbooks to make a personal donation to the campaign, I shook hands with everyone once more, accepted a few invitations to play racquetball at the club or join them for drinks. Then, I made my way out of Ethan's study, hoping that Kate decided to stay behind and wait for me. Ethan grabbed me before I left, and held me back while the others left.

"Thanks for your support," Ethan said, one hand on my shoulder. "I'm sure your father would hate to see you working behind the scenes at a Republican strategy session, but I'm really honored to have you as one of my supporters."

I shook my head and smiled at him. "There could never be any doubt that I'd support you, with my vote and checkbook. I know you'll make a great Congressman."

He led me out of the study and down the hall to the living room where Elaine, Christie and Kate were seated. I was relieved that Kate stayed behind. It reinforced that she was interested after all, despite her reticence. I buttoned my jacket and entered the living room.

Ethan seemed interested in delaying my departure and leaned in close.

"Can you give my irritatingly independent daughter a lift home? She insists on taking the bus or subway, but I don't like to see her out late at night all alone."

"Of course," I said, taking my coat from the closet. "I'd be pleased to give her a ride home."

Kate stood and after kissing Elaine on the cheek, she came over to us.

"What are you two conspiring about?" she kissed Ethan's cheek and gave me a look I couldn't quite decipher.

"Us? Conspire?" Ethan laughed. "Just how to take over the world." He smiled and glanced at me. After one last goodbye, I opened the door and led her to the elevator.

"I didn't think you'd actually wait for me." I pressed the

button. "I thought you'd be long gone, so I'm pleasantly surprised."

"I said I'd wait." I could see her brow furrow as she stood beside me, buttoning her coat.

The door to the elevator opened and Kate entered first. I stood behind her and leaned past her to push the button for the basement. I couldn't help but remember a passage in those books about elevators and smiled to myself.

"Why are you smiling?" she said, bristling just a bit as if she knew precisely why.

"Oh, let's just say that I have a hard time riding alone in elevators with pretty women and keeping a straight face these days."

"Don't get any ideas."

I chuckled out loud. "Kate, I've already had so *many* ideas. And that's what I wanted to talk to you about."

She said nothing in reply, as if trying to avoid the conversation entirely.

I helped her into my car once we arrived at the garage level and got in the driver's side, still smiling, waiting her out.

"Well, talk away," she said finally, reluctance in her voice.

I drove out of the garage and onto the streets bordering Ethan's building. I'd already been formulating my appeal in my mind as we drove.

"I know it really upset you that I'm the one Lara was trying to match you with for your 'research'. You wanted anonymity and are embarrassed that I know who you are. I think we should still go through with the agreement you wanted – for one reason. Who could be safer than me?"

"How are *you* safe?"

I glanced at her, to check her expression. She was frowning. She was still afraid her father would find out she was interested in kink. She had to know I was as well.

"I know and admire your father, so there's no way I'd want

to screw things up with him. I admire you and don't want you to think less of me than you probably already do. I understand your need for anonymity, at least, for no one to find out what you're doing. You understand my need for secrecy, too. We're not going to expose each other."

She said nothing as we drove down the street, unable to counter my logic, her face turned away from me as she watched out the window.

"Look," I said, trying once more to let her know that I was safe. "I know you're worried about your father finding out about your interest in BDSM but I'm well-respected in my field and I don't want to screw that up. If people found out I frequent fetish nights and have submissives, it would hurt my reputation. *You* want to learn about the lifestyle and understand female submissives and male Dominants? I can help you," I said as we stopped at a light. "We can *pretend* to be dating, and that way there'd be no reason that we couldn't be seen together. We wouldn't have to make up excuses in case anyone found us together. I won't do anything you don't want me to do. We can write it all out, formally in an agreement, and I'll stick to it. The only way anything will happen is if *you* want it to and specifically negotiate for the agreement to change. I am an honorable man in that respect. You can talk to Lara if you want verification."

We drove along, but still nothing on her part. I was going to try another tack, but then she finally spoke, her voice hesitant.

"Drake, it's just…"

I watched her, noting her flushed cheeks.

She shook her head and then continued. "I'm so embarrassed."

"I know." I took her hand in mine and squeezed, wanting physical contact with her to show I was human and not some kind of scary monster. I also wanted to break down the physical wall between us as much as I could get away with. "How do you think I feel? Your father actually *likes* me. You don't know how much that means to me."

Strangely enough, she didn't jerk her hand away as I thought she might. She let me hold her hand and while I was tempted to stroke her palm, I decided against it and let her hand go much earlier than I wanted to. I wanted her to know I could control myself.

"I know you and he don't really get along well," I said, remembering how upset she was at her father for what she felt was his interference in her life. "But he's like the father I *wish* I'd had. My own father was so self-absorbed and away from home so much that I always felt as if I was just not important enough. He was always, *'Hey, I love you man,'* but I never felt it. If he had loved me, why was he always away?"

We sat in silence at another stoplight. "Your father is maybe *too* involved in your life but as someone who felt neglected, I envy you that. When I met your father at my dad's funeral, he took me under his wing immediately because he and my dad were such good friends. So, if he found out about *me*..." I shook my head. "I've read some of his judgments. I know what he's like."

"And yet you *like* him."

I glanced at her, shocked that *she* was surprised that I liked her father. Did she really think he was an old bastard?

"He's like a second father to me. He's smart and competent and powerful and has so much history with my dad. And he *likes* me, Kate."

We arrived at her apartment and when the car stopped Kate jumped out of the car and started walking up the steps as if she couldn't wait to escape me. I followed her quickly to the door, unwilling to let her get away.

"*Kate*." I took her arm and tried to turn her to face me. "Don't run away. I want to talk. Straighten this out between us."

"There's nothing to straighten out," she said and tried to pull away. "We're square, OK? Let's just go our separate ways."

I let go, discretion the better part of valor, and she opened the door and kicked the piece of cardboard aside that was holding it open. She slipped inside the door, and tried to close it before I could enter completely, but I was able to get in before she could.

Yes, it was a bit forward on my part, but I knew if I could calm her down, we could make some progress. I didn't want her to run away before I felt we were on the same page.

"You said you wouldn't come in." She glared at my chin as if she couldn't stand to look me in the eye and I realized that eye contact was difficult for Kate. It was intimate to her. I'd use that little tidbit and make her look me in the eye – eventually. When she came.

"You said you'd talk to me," I countered.

"I did."

"*Kate...*" I put my arm out and stopped her before she could leave and make it to the stairs.

"Are you really going to try to stop me from going upstairs?" she said, still not looking me in the eye.

"I want to keep talking."

She exhaled in frustration. "Is this what Dominants do? Always try to control things?"

"*Yes.*" I took in a breath. "I like control Kate. I'm a Dom. It's what I do."

She stood with her eyes fixed on the wall, her jaw clenched. I'd have to loosen her up if I was going to make it up to her apartment. And of course, that was the end goal. Her apartment. The rest would be a foregone conclusion if I made it there.

"I'm listening."

Good. She wasn't going to force matters and leave without talking to me.

"Write up an agreement," I said, keeping my voice soft – the way you'd speak to a frightened animal. "Include anything you want in it, any terms, and I'll sign."

She said noting for a moment, either to confirm or reject my proposal.

"What *is* that?" she said and pointed to my wristband. "Is it some kind of kinky *bondage* thing?"

I fingered it, remembering Kwesi, my first pediatric patient from Africa. The Foundation brought him to NYP for treatment.

"This?" I twisted the band so that the tooling was visible. "No, it's not some kinky *bondage* thing, although I do have a real leather fetish. I love leather, how it feels and smells, and how really fine hide warms when it's against naked skin." I smiled, thinking how delicious Kate would look with my leather restraints on her naked body. "I make my subs wear leather corset dresses, naked underneath, but I'm thinking of adding in a garter belt and black stockings with a seam in the back." I glanced at her and saw her expression, which was a mixture of shock and a bit of titillation. "And thigh high leather stiletto boots when we go to fetish parties, but maybe in your case, I'd settle for shorter heels..."

She smiled at that, against her will for she turned her head away to hide her amusement. "Not fair."

"*What?*"

"You trying to make me like you."

I laughed out loud at that. Of course, I was trying to make her like me. I wanted her to lust after me, more than anything, but like was fine as well.

"See? You *do* like me." I cleared my throat, trying not to gloat too much, at least, not yet. I'd gloat once I was between her thighs. Until then, nothing was certain. "Really soft leather is also nice for restraints, but you have to know how to tie them carefully." I glanced at her, and saw her wide eyes. She couldn't help but listen and imagine what I described. "But this?" I lifted my hand and showed her the band once more. "This was a gift from a patient."

"What does it say?" she said, her voice less defensive.

"It's French. Here," I said and held my wrist so she could see it. "Do you read French?"

"Just a bit." She took my wrist and examined the carving, peering down at it carefully.

"It's from *Fern Hill*."

"I know that poem," she said. "Dylan Thomas."

"You know it?" I said, a bit surprised, but she did study journalism. Maybe she took a few literature courses. "It's my favorite poem. The end especially."

I recited the last line, which I remembered from my college days.

She smiled shyly. "My favorite line was something about being easy under the apple boughs."

Now it was my turn to be impressed. "That's the first line." I recited it as well.

"Do you know the whole poem by heart?"

I shook my head. "I can only remember the first and last stanzas. I memorized the whole thing once, back in college. I loved it because it made me think of my childhood. How happy I was and how unaware that soon, it would all come crashing down."

"How did it come crashing down?" she asked, her pretty brow furrowed, genuinely interested.

"Oh, you know. Life in general." I didn't really want to talk about my youth. "I had a patient, a young boy of thirteen from South Africa. He suffered from inherited dystonia. A muscle contraction that makes the body contort. He had it all his life. It's hell, but he had such a great attitude. The Foundation brought him here a few years ago to do the operation and we became friends. He made this after he recovered from surgery and went back home. You know – touristy 'native' jewelry sold in the gift shops. I wear it because it reminds me why I became a doctor and a surgeon."

"Oh, that's…" she said, hesitating as if searching for words. "That's so… *nice*."

I smiled to myself. It was special to me – the young boy seeing me as a favorite uncle or father substitute. I never had children of my own and given what a neglectful father I had growing up, I wasn't sure if I'd make a good father. Without any siblings, I had no nieces or nephews and expected I'd never marry so would die alone, some old bachelor living in a barren apartment…

"But the quote?" she said, frowning. "How did he know to include that?"

"He was here for six months and we arranged for him to have tutors," I said. "He liked poetry the most of all his classes. He asked me what my favorite line of poetry was and I told him."

This was getting far too sentimental. I cleared my mind of thoughts of Kwesi and returned to more comfortable topics. Like sex – specifically bondage and dominance.

"So about our *agreement*,' I said, raising my eyebrows, trying to inject a note of humor into the discussion. "You can include sex if you want, but remember I'm only *so* kinky. I have limits…"

She didn't smile or reply. Instead she frowned. Not what I intended…

I decided to move things forward. "Give me your phone," I said, motioning to her bag. If she wouldn't volunteer, I'd take matters into my own hands and put my phone number into her contacts. Then, I could text her. Texting might be less intrusive.

"Why?"

"Just give it to me."

She reached into her bag, handing me her iPhone. I opened her contacts, entering my information. There. Simple. As long as she didn't erase it before she got home, I'd be able to text her while she was lying in bed, thinking of the evening. I wanted her to think of me while she was in bed. I wanted her to connect me with her bed in her mind.

"There," I said, handing her phone back. "At least consider what I've suggested. Draw up an agreement with whatever you want included and send it to me in an email."

She took the phone and turned away without a word, starting up the stairs. Before she reached the top, I called out.

"Remember, send me an email. I'll sign anything you want."

"Goodbye, Dr. Morgan," she said without looking back.

"Good *night*, Ms. Bennet."

I smiled as I watched her climb the stairs. I'd gotten under her skin – I was sure of it. It was now only a matter of time before we were carrying on intimate conversations via text message.

I went to my car and texted her right away, hoping to ensure she didn't erase my contact info.

You seem surprised that I like poetry. What you must think of me... I'm not a Neanderthal, Kate. Write up an agreement between us. Whatever you want. Include as much detail as you feel is necessary. I'll honor it to the letter. Your father would be only too pleased if we were to date and that can be our cover.

At least <u>he</u> thinks I'm a decent sort...

She responded, but not the way I planned...

Imagine how surprised he'd be to find out how wrong he is...

I made a face. Talk about not sparing my feelings...

Ouch...

She didn't text back and part of me was upset that she'd threatened, in a passive kind of way, to reveal me to her father. But that would mean she'd have to reveal how the whole matter came up in the first place, and I was sure she wouldn't do that.

I was sure of one thing, and one thing only: she would never reveal to her father her interest in BDSM. She would never reveal my involvement in the lifestyle. She might not ever let me tie her up and fuck her, but she'd keep my secret safe for there was no way she would even know about it unless she was interested as well.

I was safe with Kate. I just wish she understood that she was safe with me. I wasn't the kind of Dom she feared – a sadist who would hurt and humiliate her. My only kink was leather and bondage. Other than that, I was pretty vanilla when it came to sex.

I needed control. That was my true kink.

She was perfectly safe with me. All she had to lose were her inhibitions. If she took a chance on me, I'd make sure she lost them and fast.

She'd probably thank me for it in the long run.

I drove back to my apartment in Chelsea and threw off my coat and boots, going to the kitchen for a glass of water before bed. I was still a bit up from my encounter with Kate – a bit restless and in need of some kind of release. I didn't want to resort to masturbation yet again, feeling a bit like a failure for doing so since I was just outside her apartment building. Instead, I went for a late-night run to blow off some steam and drain off some of the pent-up sexual energy I'd been hoarding for Kate. When I returned, I checked my email and saw one from her.

I sat at the island in my kitchen and read it over, surprised that she sent it to me so quickly, and that she apparently couldn't sleep either.

> From: McDermott, Katherine M.
> Sent: November 07, 11:31 PM
> To: Morgan, D. L.
> Subject: The Agreement
> Attachments: The Agreement.doc (50 KB)
>
> Drake: I've attached the agreement for you to review and agree to.
>
> Please don't push any of my limits. I know it's in your nature to do just that.
>
> If you do, I'm gone.
>
> Seriously.
>
> Kate

I read her document over, noting how determined she seemed to be about keeping our distance, making our relationship one purely of research with me as an 'informant' and her as the 'researcher'. I went to bed and lay awake for quite a while, considering how I was going to approach this. I wasn't going to quibble with her about her document. Instead, I'd revise and send her my own version in the form of a submission agreement, based on one of the most popular documents currently in use in the lifestyle.

I didn't get to sleep very quickly despite the run, for now that I had her document, I couldn't stop thinking about how I'd get her to accept and sign mine, which was far more explicit.

In the morning, after a fitful sleep in which I tossed and turned, thinking of having Kate under my complete control, I got up and showered before drinking a cup of coffee at my desk, laptop open to my boilerplate submission contract.

I dithered, unable to get my wording correct, not wanting to include anything too frightening to Kate that she'd reject it out of hand, but not wanting to appear too easy to sway either. I considered including a few clauses that I knew she'd reject just so she could cross them off the list and feel some degree of control over the contents, but they couldn't be too extreme. When I checked my watch, I had only a short time to get to work and scrub in for my first surgery so I sent her an email.

From: Morgan, D. L.
Sent: November 08, 5:31
To: McDermott, Katherine M.
Subject: The Agreement
Attachments: The Agreement.doc (50 KB)

Katherine, I received your agreement and will read it over. We can discuss when we meet.

Drake

All week, I kept busy with work, waiting for Kate to contact me so we could do her interviews. On Friday while I was dictating notes after a surgery, I received a text from her:

Why don't you send me your schedule so we can set up some dates to meet next week and discuss the lifestyle. We can discuss the agreement at that time. I'm pretty free for the next couple of weeks with the exception of Monday and so I'd like to get started with the interviews.

I texted her back right away, wondering what she was doing on Monday. I had Wednesday off and Friday and had a practice session with the band on Monday, but I was curious. What could she be doing on a Monday night?

I'm pretty busy all week with my surgical slate and personal commitments... What are you doing on Monday night? What time are you done? I could make a late meal at a restaurant, if you're free after 10 PM.

She texted me right back.

I'm going to Carnegie Hall with my father and his wife.

I quickly Googled Carnegie Hall's schedule and saw it was a special Veteran's Day performance. I had to take her. I'd rearrange my schedule, tell the guys we had to change our practice session to Tuesday instead.

I want to take you.

There was a very pregnant pause and I tapped my foot, waiting for her response. I was that close…

We could meet after. I don't know if I'm ready to start the whole 'dating' ruse yet…

What difference would it make to meet after the concert? A date for coffee was still a date but I wanted to go with her. I wanted to see how she responded to music, and share something that was important to both our fathers. She didn't want it to be an official date, but there were ways around that.

We could meet there by accident during intermission. I could invite you out for a late meal. I'm sure your father would be pleased. We could start the whole interview process.

When she didn't respond right away, I sent another text in the hopes of assuaging any concerns she had and prevent her from outright declining.

I'll have you home by midnight as I have surgery early in the morning. No funny business. Scout's Honor…

Finally, after a few minutes of delay, she texted me back.

I'll go for coffee and dessert with you but this is a special family event. We always have a family dinner before the concert.

Then I had a brilliant idea – I'd take her out for dinner to my favorite restaurant after the performance. Coffee and dessert was nice but I wanted to pull out all the stops with her. If we went to the Russian Tea Room, she'd be on my turf, in my comfort zone while she'd be in unfamiliar territory. I would be in complete control, thus beginning my seduction of her as my submissive.

Can you hold off eating and join me at The Russian Tea Room? I feel like some Pelmeni and blini. Have you been and tried their blini? To die for. I would love company.

Quite a few moments passed and I waited to see if she would agree. If she did, it was game over for the delightfully reticent Ms. Bennet. She'd be mine if I could get her to go out for a late meal with me. I'd ply her with vodka and hand-feed her rich food. I'd sit close to her and look deeply into her eyes, treating her like a princess. She'd be eating out of my hand, literally and figuratively. Getting her to invite me back to her apartment would be all the easier if I could feed her. I'd know at the first forkful of food I scooped into her mouth.

Finally, she texted back.

My father is very rigid about these things but I told him you invited me to go for a meal after the concert and he said I could miss our usual family dinner. Boy, does he like you… If he only knew…

I texted right back, wanting to keep the momentum of her acceptance going before she gathered enough courage to stop me.

He doesn't know and I want things to stay that way. I don't want him finding out about my… pastimes. Just keep that in mind when you worry that I'll push your boundaries. I won't.

She was fast to respond:

I'll hold you to that. Good afternoon.

Success.
Adrenaline surged through me at that and I couldn't resist.

I'll meet you in the lobby during intermission. Until then, Ms. Bennet…

She was falling, and it was only a matter of time before she was tied up to the headboard of my bed, crying out my name.

CHAPTER 13

On Thursday, I was at the club working out when I ran into Ethan once more. The fact we both were members had been a godsend with Kate.

"There you are, my boy," he said in his gravelly voice. "I hope Katherine invited you to sit with us in our box seats."

I smiled at Ethan and to myself, for imagine my surprise to learn Ethan asked her to invite me to sit with them for the entire performance. The better angels of my nature told me to be good and 'find' her at intermission. The lesser angels won out easily. I was only too happy to accept Ethan's gracious invitation and would especially enjoy Kate's face when she saw me walk up and sit right beside her.

"I was planning on joining you at intermission, but I was able to rearrange my practice session with Mersey until another day so I'm free."

It was a lie, but that could be easily made true. I'd call Ken later and ask if we could practice on Tuesday instead. It would be no problem as we occasionally changed dates depending on people's schedules.

Ethan clapped his hand on my back and we said our goodbyes. Monday evening couldn't come fast enough.

My weekend went slowly, especially now that Kate was going out with me on Monday. Despite being busy with the band, and having a monthly general meeting of the local chapter of Doctors Without Borders to attend on Sunday afternoon, time seemed to drag. I was eager to see Kate and so my usual weekend pursuits seemed tedious. They were events to get through, not to enjoy.

I was sitting with my fellow band members after Sunday dinner with the O'Riley's when the subject of my love life – or lack thereof – came up as it usually did.

The pub closed early on Sunday and each week, we were all invited for dinner. Everyone, from the cooks to the waitresses and waiters, as well as our band members, had a standing invitation and for a few hours, the pub was taken over for a sit-down meal. I didn't always attend, but I needed a distraction. After we finished eating, I sat with the other band members enjoying a drink in the deserted bar, when Mrs. O'Riley leaned on the back of her son's chair and peered at me pointedly.

"So when are you going to settle down, Drake?" she said, patting her son on the shoulder. "My other boys are always bringing their wives and children here for Sunday dinner, but you're always alone. If *anyone* should be married, it should be you. Don't tell me you're afraid to walk down the aisle again?"

I smiled. With Mrs. O, the talk usually turned to my bachelorhood. She couldn't stand the thought that one of her 'boys' was single – especially not a doctor. She saw it as an affront to the female species.

"Once bitten, twice shy?" I said, finishing my beer so I could escape any further grilling.

"You? Shy?" she said, scoffing. "You're the great brain

surgeon. Handsome. Rich. Accomplished. I'm surprised some society gal hasn't snapped you up. What's wrong with you?"

She said it only half in jest. I knew she worried about me, but frankly, I wasn't used to having women concerned with my well-being. My mother abandoned me. My wife left me.

Only my submissives seemed to actually want me.

"I don't know what's wrong with me, Mrs. O," I said and shrugged. "No one has captured my heart yet." I placed my hand over my heart and made a face of sorrow.

The guys all laughed at that.

"He has too many women to choose from. Why only have one?" Ken said, punching me lightly on the shoulder. "He dates college girls who only want to party. But Drake's getting old. Soon, he won't be able to keep up."

"Someone will catch you," Mrs. O said, nodding as if she'd made a decision. "Take it from me, Drake. Life's awfully lonely when you're single and old. You can only fill your day up so full with work and the band." She had only recently lost her husband of thirty years to a heart attack, so she must have been feeling her widowhood particularly hard that night.

"I have a busy practice. I have the company," I said, forcing a smile. "I have the Foundation. The band. I keep really busy. I'm not lonely, so don't worry about me."

Mrs. O pointed at me and squinted. "You find someone. Don't die alone."

She walked off, and the other guys all glanced at me for my response. I stayed steadfast in my silence.

"No new girlfriend?" Johnny asked. "You and your last girl broke up. Nothing new on the horizon?"

"As a matter of fact, I'm seeing someone new." I didn't say anything more, but I couldn't keep a huge smile off my face.

"Uh, oh," Ken said, grinning like a mad man, cuffing the back of my head. "That smile betrays you, my single but soon-to-be attached friend. Tell us all about her."

"It's not really a date," I said, trying to downplay it, but my gut told me I was more excited about seeing Kate than I let on. "I'm meeting her and her parents at Carnegie Hall for a concert tomorrow."

"Holy crap – her *parents?* Why haven't we heard about her?" Ken said, making a face of mock anger. "That's huge!"

I shook my head. "It's nothing serious. Just the daughter of a family friend." I took a drink and avoided Ken's eyes, not wanting to see the huge grin on his mug.

"What's her name?" Cliff asked, leaning forward expectantly.

"Kate," I said, putting my empty beer glass down. "And that's all I'm telling you bastards."

"Come *on*," he added. "How old is she?"

"Is she pretty?" Johnny chimed in. "What color is her hair?"

"What does she do for a living?" Ken added.

I laughed at their exuberance. "Twenty-four, beautiful, chestnut brown, journalism grad student, nice rack." I stood up, trying to escape the inevitable twenty-questions. "And that's *really* all I'm saying.

They all laughed and protested when I started to walk away.

"Have you nailed her yet?" Cliff asked, his face poker straight.

I frowned. "Have I *nailed* her yet? *Jesus.* Are you in high school?"

They all laughed uproariously at me and for a moment I was pissed, but then I saw the shit-eating grin on Ken's face. "He really *likes* this Kate woman. Could she possibly be *'the one'*?"

The others nodded, not even trying to hide their amusement.

"The one to haul in the big fish."

"Seriously, I have to go," I said when Ken grabbed my arm to stop me. "I have early surgery in the morning."

"One of these days, Drake will realize the emptiness of all that free sex, medicine and rock'n'roll. He'll succumb like the rest of us," Ken said, releasing my arm and holding up a glass to everyone. "Let's toast the impeding end to Drake's bachelor days."

The guys all laughed at that and toasted me, raised their glasses as well, but I was pretty much convinced that I'd die a bachelor. Marriage and family were not in my cards.

On my way out of the pub, I walked by Mrs. O's office, where she sat sorting through the night's receipts.

"Drake," she said as I passed. I stopped and leaned into the office. She glanced at me over her reading glasses. "I hope you didn't take what I said the wrong way."

I bent down and kissed her on the cheek. "Not at all. I know you're only being motherly. I was married. I didn't do a very good job at it. Don't worry about me."

"What happened?" she said, although we'd spoken of my divorce before. She couldn't seem to get her head around the idea that my ex-wife, or any woman, would reject me.

I shrugged, not willing to get into it again at that late hour. "It didn't suit my temperament."

She nodded. "You were younger. Just a boy. You're a man now. You'll find someone."

I smiled and pecked her cheek once more before leaving.

Monday passed quickly, and I was glad to have a full slate of surgeries for the day. It kept my mind off Kate and the concert. I had some time to kill at lunch, and it was only then that I thought about the night and how I'd approach her.

Kate was the proverbial good girl who tried to please her father, obey the rules, and make people happy. It was obviously not making her happy and she felt oppressed by her own obedience and yet unable to break out of the mold. She wanted freedom, but was afraid of it as well. She was also uptight sexually, but had an undeniable attraction to BDSM and the idea of sexual submission. If it didn't appeal to her on some primal level, she would have never even considered it for a research topic. That was an excuse to indulge her fantasies.

As much as she balked at being under her father's thumb, she craved submission to someone strong. She wanted personal freedom but at the same time, someone strong who knew what he was doing sexually. That's why she wanted to interview a Dominant. She wanted to see what it would be like to be with a man who was in complete control – who wasn't her father. Someone who made her feel secure and protected but who controlled her sexually.

Lara was right.

I was perfect for her.

After my day was done at New York Presbyterian, I went to my apartment and showered, changed into a suit of slate grey with a white shirt and black tie. One last buff of my shoes to remove the dust and I was off to Carnegie Hall to listen to the concert. I arrived just before the start of the concert so Kate would have little time to respond to my presence. I'd show up and sit down beside her and that would be that. No protests. No escape.

I wouldn't put it past her to run, given her history with me. She couldn't run tonight. I knew I had Ethan on my side.

I found my way to Ethan's box and slipped through the door, catching Kate's eye immediately. In contrast to Kate's glare, Ethan smiled, and reached out to shake my hand.

"There you are, my boy. So glad you could make it. Come and join us!"

Kate frowned. "Drake…"

Kate looked ... *beautiful*. I tried not to leer at the delicious amount of cleavage showing from under the low neckline of her dress as I stood over her but I couldn't help myself. I pulled my eyes away only when I had to, focusing instead on her hair, which was up in a loose up-do with tendrils falling around her neck, and then her lips, which were red and slightly pouty.

I had the crazy urge to kiss her, pulling her into my arms and damn discretion.

Ethan was gracious, as usual, and took a seat farther away so I could take the empty one beside Kate. The look on her face... It was priceless. Shock. Confusion. I smiled and took her hand, leaning down to kiss her cheek.

"I ran into your father at the health club and when he asked me if I was joining you, I told him I was able to rearrange my jam session with my band to another night and was pleased to keep you company."

"Oh," she murmured. "That's ... good to know."

I said hello to Elaine, commented on her dress and then sat beside Kate, enjoying that I'd completely thrown her off balance. That was key – she had to be kept off balance so I could retain control over her and the situation. If she felt too in control, she might just shut things down between us. I would not accept that.

I leaned in close to her, breathing in her perfume, the scent intoxicating.

"Don't sound so pleased to see me. Nice move, by the way, forgetting to invite me to sit in your box as your father asked," I said, my lips hovering over her cheek. I fought my urge to kiss her there and then and almost gave in, but Ethan turned to me and began asking me questions about Mersey. I answered, keeping half my attention on Kate as she sat in silence beside me. Petulant silence, a frown over her beautiful eyes.

Ethan showed me his opera glasses and I pulled out mine, which I found in my father's belongings after he died. I remembered them at the last minute and brought them with me so I could watch the performance.

Kate was completely shut off. She sat rigid, her hands folded in her lap, twisting the program in her hands nervously.

Finally, she leaned over to me, avoiding my eyes. "I consider this pushing my limits."

I smiled and leaned down to her. "I'm a good Dom, Kate," I whispered, my arm slipping over the back of her chair. "We push our sub's limits. It's the only way they experience anything new or as intensely as they could because they're too afraid on their own."

"You said you'd honor the agreement to the letter."

"It hasn't taken effect yet. Not until November 15th, if I recall correctly. This is just me being who I am."

She sat back and frowned even more deeply. If she thought she'd convince me to leave, she was sadly mistaken. I was here for the duration.

"This is a special event for me," she said, her voice low. "I don't want you here."

"What do you mean?"

"Why don't you ask my *father*?"

It was my turn to frown. I leaned over to Ethan. "Kate said this is a special night for her."

"Oh, yes, that's right. Katherine used to go with her mother each year to hear this performed. *Symphony No. 3* by Gorecki. About the Holocaust. Lost some family on her mother's side in the camps. Isn't that right, dear?" he said and smiled at Kate. "Katherine and her mother used to cry like babies when they listened to it."

Kate turned away from her father as if she couldn't stand to look at him. She was not pleased. At all.

I thought she'd be surprised, but I didn't expect her to seem so adverse to my presence. I hoped I'd be able to warm her up, lean down and whisper in her ear, but she wasn't buying it. She pulled out her phone and texted. Who was she texting? A friend? Was she complaining about the man who was bothering her?

Then my cell dinged with an incoming text. I took out my phone and checked. It was from Kate.

I frowned and read it.

Drake, <u>please</u>, can you find some excuse to leave during the first part of the performance? It has special meaning to me and I get very emotional. It has to do with my mother. I'd rather you not be with us. Can't you pretend to get a page about a patient and leave for half an hour? I'm asking you this as one human to another…<u>please</u>…

Damn…

I didn't want to leave, especially during a very emotional moment. I wanted to be there to share it with her.

Still, I wanted the evening to go well, and for me to end up between her luscious thighs. If I didn't leave, she would resent me.

So I took the high road.

I typed a message on my phone and sent it to Lorraine, the unit clerk on the surgical ward where I had patients.

Do me a huge favor and buzz my pager in a minute – I need an excuse to leave and you're all I have. I can say someone on the ward needs my attention. Are you game?

Of course Lorraine was game. She was an apple-cheeked women with Albinism who joked with me constantly when I was at the nursing station to read charts.

Sure thing, boss man. Woman problems?

I chuckled to myself and answered.

You have no idea…

She sent me one last text.

You have to tell me all about it when you're in tomorrow… Promise?

I replied, knowing damn well that she'd grill me if I admitted that I needed her to help me with a date.

You drive a hard bargain but OK. Tomorrow. Thanks for this.

I slipped my phone back in my pocket just in time for Ethan to ask me more questions about my band. Kate was still silently fuming beside me so I answered, happy to pass the time until the program started.

As the lights dimmed to mark the start of the concert, my pager went off, so I pulled it out and checked it.

"Ah, *damn*," I said and showed it to Ethan. "Gotta run out for a bit. Have a patient post-op who's experiencing complications. I'll run back to the hospital and check on him, but I'll come back as soon as I can."

"That's too bad, Drake," Ethan said. "You'll miss the first part of the performance. That's Katherine's favorite part, isn't it, dear?"

"That's too bad," Kate said and turned to me, our eyes meeting. It was the first time that night she actually looked in my eyes. I sensed relief and appreciation in them so it was a good thing I decided to be a gentleman and honor her request.

"I'll be back as soon as I can," I said, holding her gaze. "I'm sad I'll miss your favorite part."

I made my way to the door, glancing one last time at Kate before I left the box, but I had no intentions of missing the performance or Kate's response to it. I had my own seat a few boxes away and the angle would afford me a profile view of Kate.

I stood in the back of my box for a few moments, until the concert was underway and the soloist had begun, before moving forward and training my opera glasses onto Kate. I only half-listened to the performance, my focus on her, but soon even I was diverted from my observation of Kate to listen to the music. It was very emotional, and I glanced at the program, which included the lyrics in both Polish and

English. The words were by a young Polish prisoner to her mother, asking her mother not to weep for her. Extremely emotional, I couldn't help but calculate how Kate would respond to it. Based on what I knew of her already, she'd be emotionally overwrought by it and – to be honest – more open to me.

While I watched her, I saw her break down completely, a tissue to her mouth, tears in her eyes. When the audience rose for an ovation, she sat back, gathering her composure.

Then she glanced around and saw me watching her.

She leaned back, trying to hide but I didn't stop watching her or hide what I was doing. I wanted her to know I saw her. It would be one more moment we shared. One more intimacy. One more brick I'd removed from the wall between us.

I left the box at intermission and made my way to the mezzanine where people were congregating. Ethan had already left his own box with Elaine and was standing with a small group of people I didn't recognize. I went up to him and of course, we shook hands and he introduced me to everyone. I glanced around, but Kate was nowhere to be seen.

"She's in the washroom. Always gets a bit emotional during the concert. She'll be out in a minute." Ethan nodded at me knowingly.

Ethan's friends all spoke of the music and how wonderful Upshaw was, but all I could think of was Kate and how much the music affected her. She was a delicate young woman, her emotions close to the surface. I hated being so calculating but the thought excited me. I knew I could get a lot out of her and that's what I wanted more than anything.

Finally, Kate emerged from the washroom and when she saw me standing with Ethan, I smiled at her. She wasn't ready to face anyone and left the mezzanine, almost racing back to the box.

"Excuse me," I said to Ethan, who raised his eyebrows at me as if he understood.

I followed her back and when I was inside, I sat down and put my arm around her on the back of her chair.

"How are you?" I asked, keeping my voice soft.

She tried to avoid looking in my eyes, glancing everywhere except at me directly.

"Fine," she said, pausing. "Thank you for understanding and leaving."

"You're welcome." I moved a bit closer. "I've never heard that piece before. It was…" I searched for the right word, wanting to convey how much it moved me. "*Devastating*."

I took out a handkerchief from my jacket pocket and wiped a spot of mascara from her cheek. I wanted her to know I knew she had been crying from the music. It was a moment of emotional nakedness that would lead – eventually – to one that was physical.

"Here, let me get this," I said. "Your mascara ran a bit from your tears."

When she resisted, I took her chin in my hand and turned her face so that she could no longer avoid me. Finally she met my eyes and a jolt of adrenaline went through me, surprising me at how much I responded to her.

I kissed her, my hands on either side of her face. A kiss meant to knock yet another brick out of the wall between us. Soon, there'd be nothing there and she'd be mine completely.

Of course, Ethan and Elaine returned so my brief moment of intimacy with Kate came to an end. I turned to Ethan and smiled at his expression. He wanted us together so badly. I felt more than a touch of guilt at taking advantage of his fatherly desire to match me with his daughter. But only a touch.

I wouldn't be bad for Kate. On the contrary, I'd help her find out more about herself.

I turned to Ethan and Elaine, welcoming them back. Kate

was clearly trying to hide that she had been so emotional, her face turned away from us. I let her have her moment to recover her self-control and then sat back beside her as the program started.

Getting her into my bed would take a bit of finesse, even though I could feel her cold reluctant exterior starting to crack under my constant pressure. My mind was occupied with thoughts of her seduction and so I barely took note of the performance, the music a distraction from my mental images of Kate lying beneath me, blindfolded and restrained. When she stood up and excused herself, I thought at first she had to use the washroom, but then I realized that she was far too emotionally overwrought and was probably trying to escape.

I followed her out of the box, patting Ethan on the shoulder when he made a face of concern.

"Is she all right?" he whispered.

"I'll take care of her," I said, my voice quiet. Ethan nodded as if he approved and was glad to know I was taking care of his daughter.

God, he was making this so damn easy…

I couldn't find her down the hallway and so I checked the mezzanine but it was empty. Finally, I saw a side door and realized she might have taken it so she could get some air. I opened the exit door and saw her leaning against the wall, staring up at the night sky.

"Kate, what on Earth are you doing out here? It's freezing out, for God's sake," I said, and grabbed her arm, wanting to pull her into an embrace, but she resisted me, pulling free, wrapping her arms around herself protectively.

"Just leave me. I need some air."

She was close to tears again, and so I removed my jacket and draped it around her shoulders, tightening it to keep her warm. I had to take control, show her that I could understand her and take care of her needs.

"There," I said and then tipped her face up so I could look in her eyes. I wanted her to connect with me, to look at me and not retreat into herself. When she finally met my eyes, a surge of desire for her raced through my body right to my cock.

"Oh, fuck, *Kate*," I groaned, surprised at how she affected me. I pulled her into my arms and against my body, unashamed that she'd know how hard I was. I wanted her to know I was aroused by her emotions and her delicious body. I pinned her against the wall and kissed her and this time, I didn't hold back, devouring her mouth, needing to feel her lips part and for our tongues to touch. I slipped my hand behind her head and ran my fingers through her hair, then kissed her chin and her neck, pulling her hair out of the clip so that it fell softly around her shoulders.

She let me kiss her, not resisting, turning herself over to me and I took over, jamming my thigh between hers, my fingers caressing the tops of her breasts, the other hand trailing down her back, over her buttocks, and then beneath the hem of her dress.

I wanted to see if she wore garters and stockings again.

"Drake, *no*..."

I stopped, breathing heavily, not wanting the moment to end.

"Tell me you don't want me," I said, my voice low.

She turned her face away, not able to deny her desire for me.

"I thought so."

I kissed her again, this time even more aggressively, my mouth claiming hers, sucking her tongue inside, my fingers searching for her mound, her clit...

"Oh, you're already wet." I almost groaned out loud when I felt her dampness. "*Fuck*, I want you right here, right now." I stroked her over her hose and panties, wanting to stimulate her even more. Then I pressed my hips against her so she could feel me, imagine me inside of her.

Then, she kissed me back.

I lost all control and struggled to find a way beneath her pantyhose, my fingers slipping under the waistband and beneath her panties until I reached her pussy. I slid one finger between her lips and felt the hard nub of her clit, my cock throbbing in response.

Then she pulled away and pushed against me. "*Stop!*"

I did stop, pulling my fingers away, removing my hand from beneath her dress, but I leaned against the wall, my elbows on either side of her head so she couldn't escape.

"What?"

"I'm not *ready*," she said, her breath coming in small gasps.

"Yes, you are," I said and licked my fingers methodically, one at a time, my eyes not leaving hers. "You're more than ready." The salty taste of her juices made me even harder, if possible.

"No," she said, her voice barely above a whisper. "I'm not ready for this. For *you*. Not yet."

Of course she was ready. Physically, she wanted me as much as I wanted her. Emotionally, she was still afraid. I pulled my horns back in and tried to calm myself. She adjusted her dress, and smoothed her hair.

"Well, I'm ready for you." I stood up straight and adjusted myself, running a hand briefly over my groin to hide my still-erect cock. I felt her eyes on me and smiled to myself, knowing she'd be curious about how big I was. Let her wonder. I hoped that she'd find out by the night's end.

"Any time, Kate. You just have to sign the revised agreement I'm sending to you when I get home tonight." I turned away and took in a few deep breaths, trying to will my erection away so we could return to the box. When I felt a bit less erect, I went to the door and opened it, pointing inside. "We better go back. Your father will be starting to worry about us."

She appeared to have regained some composure and walked past me and back into the building.

I glanced back at the wall where we had stood and saw that her bag was on the ground. Chuckling to myself, I picked it up and handed it to her.

Not so in control after all.

"Here," I said, and couldn't stop from smiling. "I really must have affected you if you forgot your bag."

She grabbed it from me, and quickly turned away as if to hide her smile but I caught it.

Yes, Kate. I saw your smile. You can't resist me.

We returned to the box and stood at the back in the darkness, not wanting to interrupt the final performance of the evening. I leaned against the wall beside Kate, an arm beside her head, watching her without looking away.

When she finally looked at me, after avoiding my eyes for as long as she could, I held my fingers under my nose and breathed in her scent, which lingered on them, tantalizing and arousing. That was a bit too much for her, and she glanced away again, her cheeks flushing. I wanted her to know I found everything about her desirable, right down to how wet she was.

When the second standing ovation was over, Ethan turned to us, smiling like he was pleased to see us in such an intimate pose.

"There you two are!" he said and made his way to the back of the box. "I'm so glad Drake went to find you, Katherine. Did he help you calm down a bit? I know that song always gets to you."

"I'm fine," she said quietly.

I almost laughed out loud at that. *No, I didn't calm her down. I made her wet and swollen and breathless.*

"Good good." Ethan rubbed his hands together. "Now, weren't you two going out for dinner? The Russian Tea Room, wasn't it, Drake?"

He glanced from me to Kate and back.

"That's right," I said and turned to Kate, catching her eye despite her attempt to avoid me. "We have reservations for two in about ten minutes. I could really *eat* something right now."

I smiled, enjoying the small expression of shock that my words elicited. It would focus her mind on me eating her rather than food and that was the desired effect.

She removed my jacket from around her shoulders and handed it to me. I slipped it on, enjoying the way her perfume clung to the collar. Then, I took her coat from the hanger and helped her with it, standing close, breathing in the scent of her hair, now loosened from its clip.

I had no real interest in eating anything besides her but I had to go through with the seduction. Feeding her my favorite food, getting a bit of vodka into her, and forcing her to talk about her desires would be necessary if I was going to feel that swollen nub beneath my tongue.

I was determined I would feel it before the night was out. I licked my fingers once more, imagining it as we left the hall.

CHAPTER 14

WE DROVE in silence to the Russian Tea Room.

My silence was deliberate. I didn't say anything in an attempt to keep Kate off center and make her uncomfortable. She would feel slightly out of control, and I would then take control so that she felt my dominance. It would show her what it felt like to be with a real Dom.

At least, that was my plan.

"You're not going to talk to me?"

"I'm too busy recovering from our little kiss."

"Little?"

I smiled at her and she turned away.

"For me it was little," I said. "Maybe for you it wasn't. I don't usually kiss a woman unless I'm in scene and I'm fucking her, so for me, that was nothing."

"If it was nothing, why are you still recovering?"

I grinned at that. "Touché. But as I said, I don't usually kiss a woman unless we're fucking, so I'm still a bit uncomfortable. How about you?"

She crossed her arms and looked out the window, avoiding my gaze. "Never better."

"Good. I *knew* you needed some attention," I said, enjoying this little dance between us.

"Do you ever take things seriously?"

I laughed at that. "Oh, I assure you, Ms. Bennet, that I take some things *very* seriously. Sex, for instance."

There. Let that sink in. Sex wasn't just something I did, like eat or sleep. It was a passion. Something I did with the same deliberateness that I applied to my music or surgery.

Since I became a Dom, I thought a great deal about sex – what women want and what they need, especially women like Kate – the kind of woman I wanted. Smart. Well-bred. Professional. With a mind of her own but at the same time, eager to be taken by someone who knew what he was doing. Who knew how to please her and how to get right into her mind and give her what she needed.

I wanted her to have no doubt that I could and would please her, make her come again and again until she was spent and in a blissed-out state.

She said nothing more as we drove through the Manhattan streets towards the restaurant. I didn't try to make conversation, preferring instead for her to spend the time thinking of what I had said.

Imagining it.

I FOUND a parking spot a block away and walked with Kate, my arm around her protectively. She was still silent, as if waiting to see what I would do, letting me control things.

The hostess greeted us and took us to my table, which I had reserved earlier in the week. I asked to be seated at a curved banquette so I could sit close beside Kate. I wanted her to feel the warmth of my body. I wanted to put my arm around her on the back of the seat. I wanted to be close enough to smell her hair and perfume. I wanted to be able to feed her, because nothing says I have control more than feeding a person.

"I love these tables," I said as she slid into the booth. "If you were already my submissive, I'd have made you wear garters and black fishnet nylons instead of pantyhose. With no underwear on, I'd be able to sit real close and have my way with your pussy while we ate. Your mind would be occupied with what else I was going to eat when we were finally alone."

She glanced at me, her cheeks flushing. When the waitress arrived to take our drink order, I ordered some blini with caviar to start and a shot of Anisovaya for us both.

The waitress was new. I didn't recognize her so she didn't know my preferences.

"I'm sorry, but we don't have Anisovaya on the menu."

"Tell the bartender that Dr. Morgan is here. He keeps some especially for me."

The waitress nodded. "Certainly."

Kate turned to me, her mouth open. "You drink Anisovaya?"

"Yes," I said and folded my hands on the crisp white linen of the tablecloth. "I love Russian vodka, especially infused with anise."

She said nothing for a moment, and merely stared at her hands, which were folded primly on her lap. "*You* wrote those letters."

I frowned, realizing what had happened. Lara must have sent Kate the link and password to my letters to my subs. I posted them online on a password protected site as a resource for new subs, so they could get a glimpse into the mind of a Dom.

"I take it that Lara gave you the link and password."

She nodded but didn't speak, as if she wasn't sure of her voice.

"You weren't supposed to read those," I said, feeling a bit exposed. "They're for my subs to read after we sign contracts so they know what to expect. I feel somewhat at a disadvantage because usually I know what my subs like before they know what I like."

"You read my profile on FetLife," Kate said, her voice soft.

"Yes, but I want the narrative, not just a list. I want your fantasies so I can fulfill them. Most couples are too afraid to be honest about fantasies, sexual kinks, Kate. The great thing about a relationship like we'll have," I said, leaning closer, "is that you can be totally honest with me. I won't be offended or shocked or jealous or worried about them the way a normal boyfriend would. I'm only here for the sex so I want to make it incredibly good and rewarding. There'll be none of those messy emotions to get in the way of pure pleasure."

Just then, the cocktail waitress arrived with the caviar and vodka, placing them in front of me. Good. I needed to get a few shots of vodka into Kate so she'd relax a bit. I was going to be brutally honest and I wanted her lips a bit looser, so she'd open up as well.

"How can you keep emotions out of a relationship? They're bound to leak in."

"Not if you don't let them," I said, trying to sound certain. "I won't let them. Now, down it fast," I said, pointing to the shot of vodka. "The Anisovaya goes down smoothly."

"I shouldn't drink." She bit her lip as if afraid that she'd become too pliant and say something she would regret. That's exactly what I wanted.

"Oh, you most *definitely* should. I want you to loosen up a bit, Kate. Enjoy yourself. Relax. We need to talk and I want you to be completely honest with me. For a change. Here." I pointed to the shot. "Pick it up and we'll do it at the same time."

She did, but I could tell she was still reluctant. Her hand shook a bit when she picked up the shot glass.

"*Za vas,*" I said in Russian. "To you."

"*Za vas,*" she replied and together, we shot back the vodka. She made a face but licked her lips.

"*Vashee zda-ró-vye!*" I said. "To your health."

She smiled just a bit, which gave me hope. I smeared some sour cream on a blini and added caviar, then added a few bits of red onion.

"Here." I held it up for her, waiting for her to open her mouth. "You never drink vodka without eating."

"I don't *know*…"

I made a face of disbelief. "A rich kid like you never had caviar?"

"I had a huge aquarium when I was a kid and bred guppies. I could never get used to the idea of eating fish eggs."

I laughed at that but pushed the blini closer. "Trust me, Kate. This is so *good*. You'll love it."

Finally, she gave in and opened her mouth. After chewing for a moment, she smiled. "It's good. I didn't think I'd like it."

"Like I said, you have to trust me. I know what's good. The more I know you, the more intimate we are, the more you can just let go and I'll lead the way."

"You're so sure of yourself," she said and opened the menu. "What's good to eat?"

"I'll order my favorites," I said, wanting to maintain control over everything. "Can you trust me?"

She nodded. "Russians don't eat eyeballs do they?"

I smiled to myself. She was such a reticent woman. I wondered how she managed to go to Africa and stay in the camps. Her desire to please her father must have been incredibly strong to overcome it.

"No, at least, none that I know."

I ate the rest of the blini and then fixed us another, which we shared as well. She allowed me to feed her without any fuss and it pleased me, for it was another show of her willingness for me to take the lead, take control. She seemed to enjoy it, and

I could sense her relaxing beside me, her body no longer tight and tense.

When the waiter arrived, I ordered for us in Russian, requesting my favorite dishes, including the stuffed dumplings, crepes with white truffle, and to start, the famous Tea Room borscht.

When we were alone again, I moved closer to her, my arm on the back of the seat behind her.

"So, Kate. You read my letters. How did they make you feel?"

She shrank a bit at that, as if her own response embarrassed her. "I don't know what to think..."

"Don't tell me what you *think*," I said, wanting to know how the letters affected her emotions. "Tell me how you *felt*."

She held back. If she was interested at all in Dominance and submission, she should have responded to the letters in a visceral way.

"You're a good writer."

I laughed to myself. "You are so *stubborn*. Look, Kate, this couldn't be easier," I said, moving a little closer. "Your father wants us to be together. We can meet, talk and I can take you out to functions as much as we want, we can do as much as *you* want, explore as much as you want, without having to hide our relationship. No one has to know *why* we're together. They'll all assume they know why, thinking it's because we've *fallen in love*. It's great cover."

Her back stiffened. "I haven't agreed to become your sub."

"No, you haven't," I said and traced a pattern on the back of her hand, wanting any excuse to touch her. "I hope to convince you to sign a modified agreement. I'm going to be honest with you, Kate." I caught her eye, refusing to let her avoid me any longer. "I want you. There's nothing I love more than initiating and training a new submissive. I think I can satisfy your needs. In fact, I think this is perfect for us both."

She actually blushed and blinked rapidly. It was so sweet and such a telling response to my very frank words.

"And if I said I just want to write a research paper and interview you? Nothing more?" she said, her voice a little fearful.

"You didn't *feel* like you only wanted to write a research paper earlier. You were nice and wet and for a moment, you kissed me back."

"I was overly emotional," she said and I could see her muster her strength again. "You caught me at a vulnerable moment."

Exactly. That's when someone was less able to hide his or her true emotions. Which was why I wanted to put her off her game, let her guard down.

"When you're vulnerable, your true feelings come out. It's when you're feeling strong that you're able to hide them. Look, Kate," I said and took her chin in my hand. "There's something between us. I felt it. You felt it. Pure sexual attraction. You want to try submission – I *know* you do. You want to try it with *me*. Why fight it?"

I let go of her chin and she glanced away unable to hold my gaze. "You're so blunt."

"I *have* to be blunt," I said as gently as I could. I didn't want her to think I was an asshole. Just strong and determined. "I have to tell you the truth about how I feel and what I want and what I can give. You have to be completely open with me about what you desire. You have to feel complete trust in me in order to really let go."

She fiddled with the cutlery. "I feel like you're pushing me. I don't like being pressured."

I turned her face towards me once more. "Kate, this is all about *you*. People think that it's the Dominant who has all the control – and he does, once they're in scene, but to get to that point, it's all about the sub. Her limits. You have all the control. You dictate the terms. I fulfill them. You don't have to be afraid.

I'm not going to hurt you, if that's holding you back. I'm not going to reveal anything about this to anyone. It's just between you and me – and Lara of course. She's not going to let anything slip. She's totally professional. All I really *want*," I said and leaned closer, staring at her mouth, before deliberately moving up to her eyes. "All I really want is to do whatever it is you need so I can make you come, over and over again. Is that so bad?"

I deliberately licked my lips, wanting her to imagine them on her, my tongue on her. I wanted her to think of me as in control and sexual, focused on her pleasure.

"If it's all about me, then let me decide on the pace," she said, still a little resistant, but I could tell she was afraid of herself, not me. She was afraid of falling.

"I will," I said, wanting to reassure her. "This is just me trying to assure you that I *want* you. You don't have to worry about that part of things. This is now all up to you. Like I said, I'm sending you a revised agreement with my preferences later tonight when I get back to my apartment, but if you've read my letters, you already know most of it. I want you to strike off what you don't want to try and include everything you do want. Then we can negotiate."

"How soon would you," she said and hesitated in a totally endearing and submissive way. "Usually start things?"

"We can have sex right away, if you want." I deliberately stared into her eyes, enjoying how vulnerable she was, her pretty green eyes wide, her cheeks pink. "Tonight. But it will take time before you're ready for the bondage. I won't move too fast for you. You'll decide when we start."

She swallowed nervously. "So, we just go somewhere and have sex?"

"My place or yours?" I couldn't hold back a smile. She really was so sweet and almost innocent. "Kate, have you never just had casual sex with anyone? A one-night stand?"

"No," she said softly, shaking her head. "I've always known them first. Dated. Never sex on a first date or a one night stand."

"You've never *wanted* to fuck a man you just met?" I said, trying to coax it out of her. I wanted her to admit her desires freely. Doms and subs had to be open and honest about their needs and desires.

She avoided my eyes. "I've been attracted to men I've met, but I can't just have sex with someone right away."

"Why not?"

"*Because*," she said, frowning. "This is embarrassing."

"Kate, you have to be honest. You have to get over your shyness with me. *Tell* me. Why can't you just fuck me tonight?"

She took in a deep breath. "It's so ...*intimate*. Being naked with someone? Letting them touch your skin? Opening your legs to them? Letting them inside your body? It's so ... *you're* so ...*vulnerable*."

She finally looked in my eyes, as if hoping I could understand. I did. I knew that submissives often felt incredibly restrained by society's conventions. Submission allowed them to give in to their own desires and enjoy themselves for the first time.

"Thank you for being honest."

I leaned in and kissed her and she let me. There. She didn't pull back and reject me. She let me feed her. She let me kiss her. She'd let me fuck her before the night was out.

When the waitress came with our soup, I broke the kiss and sat back, a bit surprised at the surge of adrenaline in me at the prospect we'd fuck. As I was pulling back, I stared at her lovely mouth and saw once more the tiny scar on her bottom lip.

"What happened here?" I touched it, running my finger over the small scar.

"I fell when I was a kid."

"Don't tell me – wearing your mother's high heels during a dress-up game?"

She shook her head and fought with a smile, adjusting the napkin in her lap. "Stilts."

"*Stilts?* You?" I grinned widely at the image of Kate as a small girl trying to walk with stilts. It jibed with what Ethan said about Kate trying to keep up with the older kids.

She wanted so much to please… I wanted so much for her to please me. Of course, pleasing me meant she let me tie her to my bed and make her come multiple times.

Win-win.

"So," I said, spooning some sour cream into her soup, "tell me about flyboy."

"How do you know about *him*?" she said and frowned.

"Lara told me."

"I'd rather not. Can't we talk about something else?"

"This is important," I said, for I had to get her to open up about her past sexual experiences and the pilot who tried to introduce her to BDSM – very inexpertly – was the most important piece of her background I wanted. "I need to understand what happened, what he did, how you responded. It will help me know what to do to make you relax and trust me."

She sighed in resignation. "I don't like talking about him. He's a bad memory."

"I need to know why your memory of him was bad. Look, he obviously made mistakes with you. He was a total amateur. I won't make those mistakes. Besides, think of this as research. You tell me what he did, and I'll tell you where he went wrong and how I'd do it properly. If we never do anything more, at least you'll understand."

She said nothing for a moment, stalling for time. "I met him through Doctors Without Borders. He used to fly people into remote camps as a volunteer. He was doing his MBA when we started to date."

"How soon did you have sex with him?"

"A couple of weeks. We went out for coffee a lot at first, and then had dinner. Then we went to a movie and he came over and we had sex."

"What was it like for you the first time? Did you come?"

She exhaled heavily and glanced at me, frustration with my persistence clear on her face. "Are you going to ask for a moment by moment accounting of our relationship?"

"Yes." I turned back to my soup and took a spoonful. "I need details to understand what your experience was and why it went wrong. So," I said again. "Did you come the first time?"

That was pushing the envelope, but I knew that if she answered, I was on my way to having her reveal even more. I wanted to know what worked and what didn't.

"No, I didn't. It took a while. But I did eventually."

"What did it? What was it that allowed you to have an orgasm?"

She glanced at me. "You sound like a sex therapist."

That made me smile. "That's one way of thinking about me. But seriously, what did you do that allowed you to orgasm?"

"I don't *know*." Now she was sounding frustrated. She glanced around as if afraid that people would overhear us. "We were a bit drunk, and I just, I don't know… I was more relaxed. He *did* things for a long time and I was more ready."

"How exactly did he work you up?" I said, knowing I might be going over the line even more firmly. I had to keep pushing. She'd never reveal anything on her own.

"Drake! We're having supper."

I smiled. "I'm not asking because I want to become aroused. I'm asking so I understand what you need. What you like. A Dom must trust his sub to tell the truth at all times. She must trust him enough to tell the truth. Otherwise, it won't work."

"I thought that was what the agreement is for."

"It is but we have to talk openly. I want you to get used to being totally honest with me about sex. You can say anything. *Anything*. I've heard it all."

"Not from *my* lips."

"No, not from *your* lips," I said, smiling. "And I can't *wait* to hear it from your lips in particular. I happen to love your lips, especially your scar. All I can think of when I'm with you is kissing you, licking your scar, sucking your lips, biting them. And I mean both sets." I licked my lips again for emphasis and bit my bottom lip, knowing it would make her think of me licking her, but also think of those books.

They titillated her. They made her want it for herself. I wanted to be the one to give it to her.

Oh, I was no sadist, which was her fear. I wasn't into humiliation, which was another fear of hers. I wasn't into anything but sexual domination. Using her body for my own pleasure, which of course, meant giving pleasure to her.

Having total control over a woman's body – of her sexual response? It was what drove me.

"So, enough about your delicious lips that I want to suck and lick and bite. Tell me about flyboy. When did he start to introduce the idea of BDSM into your relationship?"

"After the books came out and it was on the news."

"What did you think at first?"

"I read the books but I didn't want it," she said and I knew she was lying. She *did* want it, but it scared her. "I thought BDSM was about men who hated women and just wanted an excuse to hit them and get away with it. I thought it meant I wasn't good enough the way I was. He wanted me to shave. He wanted to do anal. He wanted to spank me. He wanted me to let him mock-rape me."

"And how did that make you feel?"

She frowned as if the answer as obvious. "Upset, of course. I had just started to enjoy sex and then he starts with all this kinky stuff that scared me and made me feel inadequate. Why wasn't I good enough as I was?"

I finished my soup and sat back, wiping my mouth with a napkin. "For someone with a kink, plain old orgasms aren't enough. It's like eating vanilla ice cream after you've had chocolate truffle. You can eat it but it's not the same pleasure."

"You and Lara," she said and smiled. "With the ice cream metaphor. Except vanilla ice cream is still sweet. Anal and mock rape aren't."

"They *can* be," I said, and it was then I realized how sheltered she had been. Flyboy hadn't known how to initiate her into the pleasures of anal. I wouldn't make that mistake. A lot of women were shocked to realize they can orgasm during anal sex. "It's all in your preparation and build-up. Flyboy should have studied BDSM before he ever tried anything. He should have gone to someone and been trained like I was. I *know* how to do this, Kate. You can relax."

"So, is this dinner and this talk part of how to *do* this?"

She said it while avoiding my eyes so I had to bend down a bit, catch her eye.

"Not my usual MO," I said, for it was the truth. I usually didn't give a running narrative with explanations of why I was asking and doing certain things. But she was a student. She wanted to learn. I loved to teach. "But the general approach is the same. I have to find out what a sub needs and if we're compatible. Sometimes, I have to seduce them a bit."

"So, in your mind, you're seducing me right now."

I smiled. "I hope so."

Her cheeks reddened once again and I could have leaned over and kissed her right then, chuckling at how open she was despite her unwillingness to say the words. Her body betrayed her. I relied on it.

"What do you *hope* will happen?"

I moved closer to her and brushed a strand of hair from her cheek.

"I *hope*," I said, speaking softly. "I hope that we'll continue to talk like this, with you telling me in intimate detail what you did that made you feel pleasure and what he did that scared you. Then I hope you'll agree to take me to your apartment. I hope that you'll agree to let me fuck you tonight so that the first time is out of the way. I promise to make you come at least twice if you do. Nothing will happen tonight in terms of bondage and dominance. It's too soon. But it's not too soon for us to fuck, given our obvious mutual attraction."

"This is all too, I don't know – *clinical*."

She was still resisting me.

"I thought you wanted to understand. I thought if I explained everything, you'd feel more comfortable. I can just *do* it, if you'd prefer. Just train you without explaining."

She said nothing for a moment as if considering. "You seem to have this all plotted out."

"I do. It's my specialty. I like to study a problem. I like to break it down into its parts. I like to create a strategy for solving it, lay out all the steps. I like to follow through."

"So I'm a problem?"

"I want you as my submissive. The problem is how I can get you to submit. I have to understand you, what you need and want in order to have you, satisfy your needs. Will you at least consider my request?" I looked deeply into her eyes.

She glanced away, unable to hold my gaze as if embarrassed by her desires. "I'm thinking."

"Good,' I said, deciding then to move to another topic. She was obviously unnerved and while I wanted her to feel out of her element and in mine, I didn't want her to get mad. "Now, tell me about your love of the fine arts. Do you paint or draw?"

We talked about her studies and how she felt her father disapproved of her interest in the arts. I thought it was strange that Ethan would be anything but supportive of Kate and whatever she decided. It didn't seem in character.

She surprised me once more when talk turned to her mother and whether she encouraged Kate's love of art.

"You want to talk about submissives? I think that sometimes, mother was afraid of him."

That surprised me once more. I couldn't imagine Ethan, who I knew as a jovial mentor, making his own family afraid. Perhaps in my haste to welcome Ethan's attention, I misjudged him. "He wasn't violent was he?"

She shook her head. "No. He just has this *way*... You *know* when he disapproves. He doesn't even have to say anything."

"Sounds like an old bastard," I said, wanting to be sympathetic even as I had a hard time accepting it. "So, now, instead of writing about politics, you're writing about culture and the arts. That's a good compromise. You're a very good writer."

"Thank you," she said, and I could tell she was beginning to calm down, warm up a bit. "It makes me happy to be able to write about what I really love."

The rest of our food came and I cut up the Pelmeni and held the fork for her to eat.

"Here," I said, "taste this. It's so *good*."

She took the food willingly off my fork and I couldn't help but smile in triumph as she ate it.

She closed her eyes. "That's so *good!*"

I smiled. "I love that face."

I imagined her closing her eyes when I touched her naked body. Hopefully I would know in an hour or so, if I took extreme care. "I bet it's like your orgasm face. At least, I *hope* so."

I could see her trying not to respond to that in her body language. She hesitated and blinked several times. "Do you talk like this to all your submissives?"

"Like what?" I bit back a laugh at her forwardness, which I

enjoyed. I didn't want to insult her, but I wanted to play a bit. Loosen her up.

I ordered another round of Anisovaya from the cocktail waitress. It would help loosen her up a bit as well.

"So," I said, lowering my voice. "Will you take me to your place tonight and let me fuck you and make you come at least twice?"

She had regained enough composure from my last comment and was unfazed. She stabbed a Pelmeni with her fork. "I don't know if I can – *tonight*."

"But maybe *some* night? That's a step forward," I said, not wanting to admit defeat – yet. I still had a few weapons in my seduction arsenal. "Look, if you're unsure about sex, just let me come over and see your apartment at least. I'd love to see what your apartment looks like from the inside instead of just what your peephole looks like. Besides," I said and leaned a bit closer, smiling. "If you make me stay outside, Mrs. Kropotkin might call the cops if she thinks I'm harassing you. You're an artist. I'd love to see your art. "

She was unable to hide her smile. "You want to come in and see my etchings?"

"I really do want to see your art. I want to *know* you, Kate. Your art is part of you."

"You don't need to see my art to be my Dom."

She was right of course. I didn't have to see her apartment or her art to be her Dom. I wanted to see her apartment and her art so I could understand her better. I was damn curious.

"Look, Kate, I *promise* I'll keep my hands to myself. If you change your mind and want to fuck me, you'll have to make the move."

She looked in my eyes as if trying to determine if she could trust me. She could – I would never force a woman. I had no interest in real resistance. Only the kind that the sub wanted as part of role playing. I got off seeing a woman willingly turn over her power to me, making herself vulnerable, trusting me completely. Force was the very opposite of that.

When we finished our main course, the waiter brought us the blini with whipped cream. I fed it to her, enjoying watching her eat and savor the delicious dessert.

She opened her mouth and let me feed her the crepe, closing her eyes and murmuring in delight.

"I love it when you close your eyes like that," I said. "But when I make you come, you'll keep your eyes open and focused on mine."

That threw her, but not as much as before. We'd been making small talk – mostly about the restaurant and its history in the city so my comment came out of the blue. I hoped she was imagining me making her come in some manner. What did she prefer? Oral? Intercourse? I'd do both of course. I'd make her come once through oral and then I'd fuck her and make her come again.

She was quiet and I wondered if she wasn't thinking the same thing.

"What's going on in that too-intelligent mind of yours?" I said, seeing that she was overthinking.

She frowned. "Why am I too intelligent? You said you didn't like stupid women..."

I laughed. "I should have said *too active* mind. Sometimes very intelligent women over-think certain things – like sex and pleasure. You have a very responsive body, Kate. You should just free yourself to feel."

"Women are *always* wet, you know," she said, her voice irritated. "You're a doctor. You should know that from your Gynecology rotation."

"Not *that* wet." I smiled, remembering how wet she was. It sent a rush of blood to my dick. "Don't be embarrassed. I was hard as a rock so we're even."

"You seem so certain of yourself."

"You like that I'm so certain of myself." She did. She was attracted to me. She might feel safer with a milquetoast of a man who deferred to her and was sweet and gentlemanly, but she wouldn't get wet for him. "If I wasn't, what kind of Dom would I be?" I held a fork up to her mouth. "You have to believe that I'm dominant for this to work. If you doubt my ability to take control over you, you'll never be able to yield power. That's key." If she could admit it to herself, she'd finally let go and be happy but she was fighting with herself every step of the way.

"So this is an act to convince me you're able to take control?"

I shook my head and caught her eye. "This is no act," I said, for it wasn't. I was being true to who I was and what I was with her, so she saw me as I really was – not what might be seen as polite and safe. "I'm being as open and honest as I can with you. I *understand* you, Kate. You can relax with me. You can just *be*. Believe me, I won't judge you except when you disobey my orders or don't try hard enough to comply."

Submissives needed to feel the Dom's control or they would fight. They wanted to feel his control. It was what they craved. Kate craved it, but her mind fought with her body.

"I'm so conflicted about this."

"I know you are." I reached out and took her hand, stroking my thumb over her palm. "You're afraid. Your modern feminist sensibility thinks this is wrong, that submission is wrong, but that primal part of your brain knows it's right."

I watched her while I ate, searching her face for a sign of what was going on in her mind. She felt such guilt for wanting to be dominated sexually.

"You have to get over your self-judgment and accept this for what it is. Submission for you is just the way you prefer to experience sex. Nothing more, nothing less. There's no deep meaning to it. It just turns you on."

"It shouldn't."

"There you go – that judgmental Superego," I said, recognizing it for what it was. "Kate, D/s the way we will practice it is safe, sane, and most of all, consensual. That's not just a slogan. I believe it." I let that sink in for a moment. I had to reinforce the safe part. The consensual. This would be her choice. She would choose it. Choose everything that would happen between us. I would fulfill it.

"D/s is not illegal, it's not damaging. It doesn't diminish you in any way. If you sign the contract, we'll have lots of mind-blowing sex in the way that really appeals to us both and you'll sleep really well at night when we part." I popped a strawberry in my mouth. "Simple."

I could tell that appealed to her. She wanted to experience mind-blowing sex. She wanted someone who knew what he was doing and how to do it. That's why a Dominant appealed to her.

We talked a bit about my schedule, my surgical slate, my band's practice sessions and gigs. I told her I'd come to see her at her apartment on my nights off, or if she preferred, she could come to my place.

Usually, I met my subs at their place or sometimes, a hotel room. With Kate, I wanted her to come to my place. I wanted to see her tied up on my bed, ready and waiting.

"But tonight, I want to come to your place so I can see who you are when you're not with your family."

"I don't *know*..." she said, making a face of indecision.

"If you want, no sex tonight. Just talk. We can go over my personal limits and discuss yours. No touching and no sex unless you initiate it."

"And if I sign an agreement? How much say do I get in what happens between us?"

This was a tricky subject. While it was true that the sub gave over her power to her Dom during a scene, she listed her hard limits and she knew his kinks and preferences. They agreed to do everything on their lists, at his discretion. He chose how and when.

"When we're together? Sexually? *None*. The purpose of the agreement is for you to give that power over to me to decide what happens. The only out you have is your safe word, but once you use it, that's it. We stop. *Full* stop. So don't use it unless you really mean it. Don't use it unless what's happening is too much for you to bear. At first, you can use 'yellow' as a sign you need to slow down or pause. Red will be only for full stop, and once we're over the initial training. A submissive enjoys some uncertainty, because it's arousing. But real fear and bad pain? That's when you use your safe word. Other than that, other than your hard limits, you leave everything up to me. What, how, when, where, how often."

"I shouldn't need a safe word, Drake, if all we're going to do is fuck. Remember – no pain."

She was so afraid of pain. "I told you I'm not a sadist. But sex can get intense. Bondage scenes can get intense." I moved closer and stroked the back of her hand to show her I was warm and affectionate, not cold and sadistic. "I'm not into pain, but a binding can accidentally get too tight, or you can be emotionally overwhelmed. I will punish you if you misbehave. Sometimes, punishment can be too intense."

"What kind of punishment?" she said, pouting a bit. I could tell the thought of being punished upset her. For some subs, being punished was enjoyable for it reinforced the relationship. For others, they avoided it like the plague.

"We'll have to negotiate that."

"Lara said you'd likely spank me."

I smiled. "Does that upset you?" Spanking wasn't a kink of mine, but I could do it. I could even enjoy a sensual spanking intended to enhance pleasure. Not a spanking in punishment.

"I'm not a child."

"Spanking is merely to reinforce dominance. It's not supposed to be about hurting you."

"How can it not hurt?"

"It won't hurt too much, then."

"How do you know what too much is?"

"I'll show you. You'll tell me. I'll stop at that point."

She moved away from me, subtly distancing herself from the issue. I knew the next few moments would be key to whether I would end up in her apartment and possibly in her bed or whether I'd be left standing outside her apartment in the cold, staring up at the stars.

"Look, Kate," I said, keeping my voice as soft and unthreatening as I could. "Hopefully, if I do this right, you'll never *need* to use a safe word but it's there just in case."

"I don't know about the spanking part," she murmured. "We're going to have to talk about that."

"We will." I stroked her cheek, noting the wide-eyed expression of wonder mixed with fear. "I won't go too far for you. I want this. I don't want to make a mistake with you."

She sighed, and I could hear the last bits of resistance draining out of her voice. "You won't push me tonight?"

"I won't push. *Much,*" I said, biting my lip to hide my grin. "But you have to know that I want you." I leaned closer, so that my face was only a few inches from hers and stared at her mouth. "I want to fuck you tonight. I'd love to tie you up and have my way with you, but I know it's too soon. You need to trust me before you can give over your power willingly. But a kiss goodnight would be nice."

She bit her bottom lip to stop a smile. "I'll consider it."

I paid the check, and made sure to run my hands down her arms as I helped her on with her coat. Unlike her, I had no hesitation to let her know exactly how I felt. I wanted her. I wanted her to be my submissive.

I don't think I'd ever wanted a woman to be my new sub as much as I did Kate.

That should have set off alarm bells in my mind but it didn't. I was too excited, too busy imagining seducing her, gaining control over her mind and body to notice.

CHAPTER 15

We arrived at Kate's apartment and I wondered how this would go. Would she invite me in? We stopped at the top step and I moved nearer to her, wanting to at least be close enough in case this was good night. I wanted to be in a position to at least kiss her if I had to leave.

I waited.

And waited. She glanced around, stalling for time. She wasn't going to invite me up but she wasn't saying goodbye either. That was a good sign.

I decided to press my case.

"Kate, invite me in. *Trust* me. I won't risk anything with you, given who you are and who your father is."

"You won't touch me?"

I tilted her chin up so she had no choice but to meet my eyes. "I may touch you, but I won't force you to do anything. I don't rape women, Kate," I said, trying to be patient. "I don't like *real* resistance. Only the fun kind. The play kind."

"We won't have sex, Drake," she said, chopping her hand down. "I'm not like that. I don't have sex on a first date."

"I know." I was being honest. I knew Kate wasn't promiscuous. Far from it.

"I'm serious. No sex. I'll think about the goodnight kiss."

I checked my cell phone for the time. Then it hit me – she could call Lara... A safe call was always advised when a Dom and sub were meeting for the first time. We weren't strangers, but it would make Kate feel safer if Lara spoke with her and reassured her that I wasn't a psycho-killer.

"Why don't you call Lara and let her know I'm coming into your apartment? Tell her you'll call her in an hour and if you don't call, she should take action. That way, you'll feel safe."

Kate plucked her phone from her bag and dialed Lara.

"I'm standing on the front step of my building with Drake. He wants to come in and just talk, and suggested that I call you so you know I'm alone with him. That I'll call you in an hour to let you know things are okay."

Kate listened for a moment and nodded. Then she turned to me. "Lara said if I don't call in an hour, she'll bring Bruno over."

I laughed at that. I leaned down to the phone in Kate's hand "Oh, you're threatening to use the heavy artillery. You've never had to use Bruno with me yet and won't have to tonight."

Kate listened to Lara for another moment.

"Thanks, Lara." Then she put her phone away and sighed. "Who's Bruno?"

"Her Rottweiler," I said, smiling widely.

Kate laughed and I saw the last shred of resistance leave her. "Come on up."

We climbed the stairs to her apartment, stopping at the door while Kate searched her bag for her keys. She said something under her breath but her voice shook with nervousness. Finally, she found the keys and just as she was unlocking the door, Mrs. Kropotkin from across the hall opened her door. I saw her grey hair and kerchief through the narrow crack in the doorway. I smiled.

"*Zdrastvooyte.*"

She closed her door.

"Did you study Russian in college?" Kate asked.

"My father had a cassette tape with Russian lessons on it and I used to listen as a kid." My own voice wavered a bit and I was surprised at my nerves. I wasn't usually this excited about going to a new sub's apartment. "I don't really speak Russian well. Just enough to order in a restaurant or make a few toasts."

Kate opened the door but blocked me from entering. "You'll keep your promise to just talk? No sex?"

I held up my hands. "Kate, it's up to you. You'll be the one to decide what happens. Whatever *you* want."

"We're *not* having sex. Tell me you understand."

"I understand."

She was still hesitant, eyeing me as if having second thoughts. "Come in," she said finally.

I entered, so curious about her and what her apartment looked like, but on first impression, was surprised at how small and dark it was. I turned around in a circle, glancing down the hallway to what looked like the main living room.

"Kate why do you live like this?" It struck me once more how much she had deprived herself of her father's wealth. "This apartment looks like it belongs to a poor kid, not the daughter of a wealthy judge running for election."

"I don't want his money and I don't earn enough even with the scholarship to live anywhere else."

I walked down the hallway, checking out her place, breathing in deeply the scent to see if it smelled like her. Like Kate – a mixture of floral shampoo and citrus. Kate removed her coat and hung it up and then came to me.

"Let me take your coat."

I removed it, slipping out of my boots and then I loosened

my tie. I hoped I would be removing all my clothes before the night was over, despite Kate's protestation to the contrary.

"Do you mind if I take a look around?"

Kate shook her head, but said nothing, her face blanched. She was really nervous. I went to her and tipped up her chin with a finger.

"Its okay. I know you're nervous. A bit excited. You know what? So am I."

I was nervous and took in a deep breath to show her, smiling. She glanced away.

Still not able to look me directly in the eye. That would have to change if we were to work out as a couple. I'd force her to look in my eyes as she came, as she sucked my cock, as I fucked her, as I ate her. It would break down all the walls between us until there was nothing left but raw lust.

I checked out the rest of her apartment, interested in the art hanging on the walls. There was one piece in particular I examined closely -- a drawing of a knight in armor with a naked woman lying beneath him.

"You did this?"

She came to my side and examined it, tilting her head to the side. She pointed to some initials at the bottom right hand corner. *KMcD.*

"I did it in my Freshman year. I took a fine arts elective."

It was good. Even I could see that. The realism with which she drew was impressive. "It's good. Actually technically skilled." I turned to her. "Tell me about this."

"What's to tell?" she said, shrugging. She didn't seem like she wanted to discuss it any further. "It's a pencil drawing of a knight and his lady love."

"And why is she naked while he's in full armor?"

She hesitated. "Our assignment was to show contrasts in textures. I thought that metal and flesh were opposites – almost mortal enemies – and contrasting, kind of like male and female, masculine and feminine. My professor said I took the assignment way too literally."

"Metal and flesh aren't always enemies. I use steel to cut out tumors, open the skull to let pressure off a swelling brain."

She frowned. "I never thought of that. I was thinking more of war."

"It's all in your point of view. Even in war, metal can save lives. Trauma surgeons like my father worked in hospitals on the front lines in Vietnam using steel and cutting flesh to save lives." I leaned forward and examined the picture more closely. The detail was amazing. I was even more impressed with her than before. Underneath the shy and sometimes petulant exterior was a woman of real potential. She had convictions and talent. "Did you at least get a good grade? This is very good."

"I got an A."

"Good. But why a couple?" I asked, frowning. "If you wanted to show contrast between flesh and metal, if you wanted the war theme, why not a hand holding a sword?" Then it came to me and I turned to her, smiling a bit. "Or were you thinking of a different kind of war – the war between the sexes?"

Kate said nothing, her hands behind her back.

"It was after a boyfriend and I broke up and I was all upset about it. You know what it's like when you're nineteen. You'd think it would be the other way around, right? The woman would be covered in armor while the man would be naked, so willing to have sex."

Ahh... She thought men were the ones to wear armor.

"Oh, very deep," I said, really getting it. "He can't really touch her even when they have sex because he wears armor to protect himself. It's symbolic of men's psychological armor. There she is, naked, open, and he can't really touch her even when he's fucking her." I examined her face, amazed that she was thinking that deeply about sex and gender for her age. "Did you study psychology?"

She avoided my eyes. "Yes," she said in a soft voice. "I took a course in my Freshman year."

"So you're implying that despite the fact that men want to have sex, they're not really touching the women they fuck. There's always that male armor keeping them from intimacy. Am I right?"

She forced a smile. "You're one of the few to get it."

"I have a degree in psychology. I was trained to look for underlying explanations for behavior."

I moved to the next painting, which was an abstract with different colors and lines. It wasn't at all in the same vein as her drawing, and when I examined the signature, I saw it was someone else's work.

Still, I couldn't get my mind off her picture of the knight and lady. There was another dimension to her that wasn't apparent on the surface. She thought deeply about things like relations between the sexes, even if she wasn't very experienced and even if she was repressed. Did she really think that men kept emotional armor around themselves for protection? That sex was different for men than for women?

"Research suggests that men fall in love more easily than women," I said, keeping my voice light for I didn't want to sound too critical. I wanted to keep the dialogue open so I could learn more about her, open her up a bit more. Well, make that all the way. "Do you really believe that men never let down their armor even during sex?"

"You tell me," she said, her voice sounding slightly mocking. "You're the expert at keeping things compartmentalized."

"What could you possibly mean by that, Ms. Bennet?" I said in mock surprise, keeping with her tone. "Are you suggesting that I use D/s as a way to keep my distance from the women I fuck? I assure you, it's quite the opposite. I get right into their minds."

"But you don't love them. You're not really intimate with them, despite controlling them sexually."

"I'm exceedingly intimate with them." I smiled, but her assessment of me was irritating. "It all depends on how you define intimacy. Back to you and your difficulty sleeping with men on the first date." I stepped closer to her, forcing her back against the wall. She was getting a bit combative – for her – and I wanted to shut that down right away. Physical proximity usually helped. "You can't open your thighs without being intimate with a man and it bothers you that men can fuck women without being intimate, without actually caring about her the way you *think* they should. Am I right?"

She nodded without meeting my eyes. "My body is private," she said and I could tell that she was upset that I couldn't understand. But I did understand. "How can I get naked with someone I don't care about?"

"My *heart* is private," I countered. "How can I care about someone who won't get naked with me?"

I stepped even closer. I could smell her perfume and her hair from where I stood. It was intoxicating. I lifted a strand of it and ran it under my nose, breathing it in. I wanted to rub my face in her hair, between her thighs and it was getting increasingly difficult to focus on the issue we were discussing with my raging hard on starting to raise its head.

"What if I was to tell you that your inability to have casual sex was because of your father's and society's influence on you, not because of anything inherent in male-female sex differences? We're both animals with drives, Kate. Society has just controlled women's drives more, redirected them, couched the control in moral platitudes."

"I forgot you wanted to be a psychoanalyst. I never did like Freud and his focus on fathers."

"He was right, but in the wrong way. Your father – the generalized father of patriarchal authority – made you believe that if you were purely sexual, if you *needed* to be fucked, you were bad. Isn't that right?" I said and watched her face closely for her response. She blinked rapidly at that, so I knew I'd hit home. I pressed on. "He and the Church made you believe you were a bad girl to just want a hard cock inside of you. So you always held back, using this idea of intimacy as a shield – as *armor* against just feeling pleasure for its own sake. You use the demand for intimacy as an excuse so you can maintain the façade of being a good girl when really you're just an animal like me."

She stood in front of me, her face turned away as if what I said was too hard to face – I was too hard to face. I knew she had probably reached her limit so I turned and went to the small living room filled with shabby furniture and worn parquet floors. I removed my jacket and tie and sat on the couch.

Right in the middle.

She'd have to decide where to sit – beside me, or across from me. Where she sat would tell me if I was going to get her naked tonight or if we would continue to talk with me going home with blue balls. I leaned back, and stretched my arms out on the back of the couch, my stocking feet up on the rickety old coffee table.

I caught her eye. "Am I right?"

"Maybe," she said, staring at the couch beside me, then glancing at the chair across from me. Oh, she was torn. Where to sit? What would it say about her? "But whose approach is more satisfying in the end?"

"I've tried your approach," I said and shrugged, thinking back to my disastrous marriage. I thought when I met my future-wife that I needed a woman as strong as me so we were 'equal'. I'd quashed my tendencies towards dominance sexually in order to be a sensitive lover. What it did was ensure I never really enjoyed sex as much as I could, with women who were never really satisfied with me. Performance wise, I was fine but there as a lack of spark. When I tried to push things with my wife, she couldn't handle it and thought I was too controlling.

It didn't end well.

"I was married for five years," I said, not wanting to dwell too much longer on it. "You haven't tried mine. *Yet*. Why don't you give it a chance? Then you'll know."

She looked doubtful. "I can't imagine that meaningless sex can be rewarding in the long run."

I sighed. Meaningless sex was a relief from sex that was wrapped up in anger and frustration and misunderstanding. "It's not. But it's good enough for now."

She stood and stared at me, and I could tell from the expression on her face that I was forcing her to confront issues that were difficult. "I only want to fuck someone who loves me. Is that so wrong?"

"Someone *will* love you, Kate," I said, for someone would. Kate was not the kind of woman to remain single for very long. I was surprised she'd been single for as long as she had, but there were several traumas in her life to recover from. "Do you really want to wait until he does? Is masturbating all alone in your room at night, for what – a year? Is that really good enough for you?"

As soon as I said it, I knew it was a mistake. I could almost see her wince.

She left the living room and I heard her opening and closing drawers and cupboards with quite a lot of force. She was hurt. I followed her into the kitchen after a moment and stood behind her as she fiddled with a teapot.

"I'm sorry." I reached out and touched her, wanting to reconnect and mend things.

"You're a *bastard*."

"No, I'm not. I'm just being honest." I turned her around and tried to catch her eye but she avoided me. "Kate, you *deserve* to have pleasure when you need it. You're not a bad girl for wanting to feel it. I can give it to you. I *want* to give you the pleasure you need in the way that most appeals to you, deep down inside if you're brave enough to admit it to yourself."

She actually closed her eyes and turned her head away.

"Here," I said and pulled her into an embrace, needing to break the icy silence between us. She didn't respond, her body stiff.

"I'm sorry I hurt your feelings by speaking the truth so plainly," I said softly. "If this is going to work between us, you have to let me break down those protective walls you've built up around yourself. Otherwise, you won't really experience submission the way you need to."

"So you're telling me you have to be mean to me in order for me to be able to submit?" she said, her green eyes wide.

"*No*, you have to be honest with me about what you need and want. You have to honest with *yourself*."

I watched her chest heaving. She was close to tears. I had to save the moment or the night would be over, and fast.

"Kate, *are* you sexually attracted to me?"

"You already know you're very handsome."

"I didn't ask that. I asked you if you were sexually attracted to me." She didn't answer so I spoke even more softly "Do you want to fuck me? Is there a part of you that just wishes you could right now and to hell with convention?"

Finally, she replied, but I could hear the emotion in her voice. "Yes. But I'm afraid."

"*What* are you afraid of? That you'll have a great orgasm or three?"

"I'm afraid that you'll hurt me."

"I *told* you and Lara told you that I'm not into pain. I don't want to *hurt* you, Kate. I want to make you feel *pleasure*."

"Not that kind of hurt."

I shook my head and stared at her for a moment. I knew what she meant. I had to get it through to her that we would keep things from becoming too tangled emotionally.

"That won't happen. We'll only have sex. None of that relationship stuff. We won't have breakfast together or go to movies or on dates. We'll fuck. I'll tie you up and make you come until you scream. I'll come. Then I'll go home. You'll sleep like a baby. End of story."

She looked doubtful, her brow furrowed. "What if I fall in love with you?"

I smiled. "I won't let you."

"That's like saying you can control the weather. You can't."

I smiled even more widely. "I can control the weather, too."

She turned away slightly so I couldn't see her, but I caught her grin nonetheless.

"I know this is all new to you. I know you're afraid." I embraced her once more, pressing my hips against her so she knew how hard I was. How much I wanted her. Then I let her go and went back into the living room and sat back in the center of the sofa. She'd have to follow me eventually, and I'd know by how she responded and where she sat whether I was going to make any progress with her or whether I had gone too far. My sense was that she was fighting with all her might not to want me, not to want this, but that she was failing. And more importantly, that she wanted to fail.

She wanted me to convince her.

She returned and stood in front of the coffee table, her cheeks pink.

"Just theoretical, but if I was really your sub-in-training, what would you normally do at this point?"

I looked her over, deciding how much to admit. In truth,

most of the subs I trained already accepted they were submissive sexually and were eager to learn. They *wanted* me to take control and show them. Tell them what to do. It was a relief for them. It was exciting.

Most could hardly wait for me to tie them up the first time.

With Kate, I had to be careful for she wasn't eager. She looked as if she was being led to her own slaughter.

"I'd suggest that you come and sit with me and we can talk some more."

She sat on the edge of the sofa, her back stiff, her hands folded in her lap.

"Did you go to a Catholic school as a child?"

"Yes," she said. "Why do you ask?"

"You have very good posture," I said, examining her. Your hands are folded."

She immediately unclasped her hands, smiling guiltily.

"Yes, they expected us to sit properly. The nuns gave us the cane if we were *slovenly* in our dress or behavior."

"A good Catholic school upbringing," I said with a grin. "Making uptight women out of excited little girls full of life and promise. Only the really rebellious ones escaped with their libidos fully intact."

"Yeah, the nuns really did a number on us."

She visibly relaxed, and I decided to push things. I patted my knee. "If you were really my sub-in-training, I'd tell you to come closer. Sit on my lap. So why don't you?"

She frowned and for a moment, I thought I'd lost the battle. "Am I a child?"

"No, but I like to sit close together at first. Just touching for a while with all our clothes on." I let that sit for a few seconds. "If you decide to stop at any time, you just have to get up. I won't prevent you."

She stood before me but seemed at a loss as to how she should sit on my lap. "How do I…"

I grabbed her arms and pulled her down, positioning her body so that she sat with her legs over to one side. It meant she had to put her arms around my shoulders. There was an awkward moment when she seemed as if she was going to try to sit with her arms around herself, but she relented, her arms threading around my neck, resting on my shoulders. Our faces were inches away from each other. I could smell the anise from dinner on her breath.

She finally met my eyes and *God…* blood rushed to my dick, which was already hard as rock against her soft thigh.

I adjusted her on my lap, for she was pressing hard against my now aching erection. "Sorry, you're pressing just a bit too hard on my…" I adjusted myself. "That's better."

Her cheeks actually flushed deep red at the suggestion I was erect. I breathed in her scent and it was a delicious mixture of her hair, her perfume and her female scent, which almost made me dizzy.

God, she was delicious.

"You smell so good," I said and slid my hand along her thigh to her hip. I wanted to slip it between her thighs to feel how wet she was, but I held back. She'd make the first move or nothing would happen.

"It's my perfume," she said. "It's called *Mystique*."

"I wasn't referring to your perfume."

"Oh." She tensed, her back straightening. "Maybe I…"

She was uncomfortable with the fact I could smell her arousal but I had to get her used to how I responded to her. I loved how she smelled, how warm she was, how soft. I imagined sliding my cock inside of her velvety wetness.

She tried to get up but I stopped her.

"I *love* how you smell. Your female scent and the thought of how wet you are makes me so *hard*."

I took her hand and pressed it against my erection, sliding her fingers along its length

She closed her eyes and I felt her tremble just a bit.

Yes. That unnerved you, didn't it, sweet Kate?

You want to know how it will feel inside of you, stretching you, filling you completely.

A moment passed while she breathed in deeply as if trying to calm herself.

"So we just sit here like this?"

"Yes." I stretched my arms over the back of the couch so that she felt in control. She had to be the one to push now so there'd be no doubt about her willingness for this to happen. If she was sitting on me, if she was touching me, if she kissed me, she was the one who signaled it was okay to proceed.

Of course, I was doing everything I could to arouse her and seduce her into giving over control to me.

"We can just talk. With my new subs, I always let them choose the time of our first fuck. If they want anything to happen, they have to make the move. If they want me, all they have to do is kiss me. But I warn them," I said and caught her eye, frowning just a bit so she knew I was serious. "If they do, I take that as a sign they want to fuck me and I take over. I take control and I fuck them. If they change their mind, they have to use a safe word. If they do, it all stops right then, and I go home. So be warned. Don't kiss me unless you mean it."

I held her gaze for as long as she let me and when she tried to glance away because it was becoming too intense for her, I took her chin in my hand and stopped her.

"I can sit here like this for as long as you want and talk if that's all you want tonight. Sure, I'm hard as rock," I said, wanting to reinforce how aroused I was, "but it will fade eventually if nothing more happens. But if you *kiss* me, I'll take it to mean you want me to fuck you. I'll take your clothes off and I'll eat you and then I'll fuck you. I'm not a frat boy, Kate. I don't like to play games."

She blushed at that and her back straightened. I hoped I hadn't gone to far.

"I thought you *liked* playing games. Isn't that what people in the lifestyle call it? Playing?"

"*Fuck* games, Kate," I said, my voice firm. "Not emotional games."

She tilted her head to one side, still frowning a bit, but she didn't stand up so I knew the battle could still be won.

"Why do your subs need a safe word if the first time is just vanilla sex?"

"It's always good to have a safe word. Things get passionate. Heavy. Hard. Fast. If I overwhelm the sub and she can't handle it, I need to know. But Kate," I said and turned her face to me. "Using red as a safe word isn't a request just to slow things down a bit or to adjust things. It's a signal for a full-stop. Once they use it, it's over. So I warn my subs not to use red unless they really are unable to go on."

"What exactly do you mean by heavy? Hard?"

"*Kate...*" I smiled at her. Was she really that inexperienced? Had every man she'd been with fucked her gently? Afraid to be a bit rough with her? Passionate?

Our bodies were made to fuck. Hard.

I tried not to laugh but it took every ounce of my self-control. "Have you never had really passionate sex with a man before? A little desperate? He's pounding into you from behind, grabbing your hips, thrusting hard and fast?"

I watched her cheeks flush. They were a barometer of her emotions. Her skin was so fair she flushed very easily.

"Red is a stoplight," I said, trying my best to sound like an instructor to calm her down a bit. "You say red, everything stops."

"How do I know you won't run a red light?"

I closed my eyes and smiled. She was so afraid... "Unlike flyboy, I'm not into rape, Kate. Not even mock rape. If I do it, it's because my sub needs it and asked for it." When I opened my eyes, she was examining my face as if trying to detect if I was being truthful. "I can only get off with a woman who wants it. Who wants *me*."

"*I* want you."

There. She admitted that she wanted me. I waited for her to lean closer and kiss me. She was *sooo* close…

Nothing.

She couldn't do it. She couldn't make the first move. My whole body was vibrating with lust, my cock hard as rock as I imagined how close I was to spreading her thighs and tasting her, filling her up.

I actually held my breath, waiting for the kiss. It didn't come.

"Then *kiss* me."

She froze. "I can't."

"Oh, *Kate*…"

I pulled her down on top of me as I lay back in the couch.

"Oh, *God*." She gasped as I pulled her hips against mine.

"*Jesus*, Kate, are you that repressed that you can't even *kiss* me?"

"You said it yourself. If I kiss you, you're going to fuck me."

"You said you want me, so just *do* it."

"Why are you making *me*?" She sounded as if she could cry. "You already kissed me *three times* tonight. Why do I have to be the one now?"

"You *have* to be the one."

"Why?"

"You have to say yes. I have to know that you want me to fuck you. That this is what you *really* want. What you really *need*. I don't want any doubt."

"Then, *yes*, for Christ's sake, *yes*," she said, her eyes wet. "I *want* you to fuck me. I *need* you to fu—"

Then I kissed her. It went against my own rules, for I had to know, without a doubt, that my sub wanted me to take control. Kate wanted me, she wanted this to happen, but she couldn't make the move. She couldn't bend down to me, make her lips kiss me.

I shouldn't have kissed her, but dammit, if I didn't, she never would.

But I didn't take over just yet. I needed to feel her respond to me. I needed her to kiss me back.

Passionately.

She ended the kiss, her brow furrowed. "I thought," she said, her voice wavering with emotion. "I thought you were going to take control after I kissed you."

I smiled at her naiveté. "Who's to say I haven't?"

"I don't understand. You said—"

Then I had enough of her stalling. "Stop talking."

I switched positions so that now, she was under me and pressed my erection into her belly. I watched her response as I trailed my fingers over her skin, the soft curve of her cheek, and over her plump bottom lip that I wanted to kiss, suck and rub my cock against. Her breasts were squeezed by her position, and almost bursting out of her dress. I traced each mound with my finger, enjoying how her skin went all gooseflesh. I squeezed one breast and found the hard peak of her nipple, squeezing it a bit harder than I should have, but I waned her to feel it.

I smiled when she gasped out loud.

Oh, yes…

She would be so delightful if she was as responsive as this all the time.

I spread her thighs with my knee a bit roughly and she didn't object. I pulled up her dress, my hand finding her pussy, my fingers slipping down between her lips to find her clit.

She was damp and hard and she groaned when I pressed

my cock against her. She closed her eyes but I wouldn't let her escape that way. I wanted her right there with me.

"Keep your eyes open."

She did, her eyes so open and vulnerable and filled with desire. I grasped the top of her hose and started to remove them.

"From now on," I said, making my voice as authoritative as I could, "you're only wearing garters and nylons when you're with me. No underwear."

I pulled down her panties and spread her thighs quickly, before she could close them. Moisture glistened on her flesh.

She was ready. "Oh, you're so nice and *wet*."

Then she tried to cover herself, her hands slipping down to her groin but I kept my hands on her thighs, spreading them despite her attempts to close them.

"I should take a bath…"

"What?" I said, frowning. "*No*. Kate, you're supposed to be wet. Your scent makes me rock hard. I can't wait to taste you."

I stopped and lifted her up off the sofa, wanting to get her naked as fast as possible before she ran. I moved her hair out of the way and kissed her neck from behind, running my lips over her shoulder, biting just a bit to let her know I was aroused. I slipped her dress off and now, she was naked except for her bra, which I was going to leave on for a bit longer, for I knew her breasts were going to be spectacular. I wanted to linger over them as I exposed them for the first time.

I ran my hands over her soft round hips and belly, then cupped each breast and they more then overflowed each hand.

When she leaned back against me, she sighed audibly, finally relaxing. I pulled the fabric down to expose her breasts, and was delighted when her nipples hardened in the cool air. Small, rosy nipples, I couldn't wait to suck each one and hear her moan out loud.

I slipped a hand down to her pussy, grazing over her mound, covered by closely trimmed pubic hair.

"Spread your legs."

It was not a request. It was a command, and she complied, exposing her lips to my searching fingers. While I stroked her clit, I licked her neck and sucked the skin beneath her ear.

I wanted her to think of me licking her pussy.

Finally, I wanted to see her breasts full on and turned her around. She was still a bit shy despite everything and tried to cover her beautiful breasts, which were perfect, heavy, full, with small rosy nipples.

"Don't cover yourself," I said firmly. "You look so delicious, I want to lick you. I want to run my tongue over every inch of you."

I did. I wanted to eat her, suck her, lick her, make her cry out.

I admired her as she stood naked in front of me, my eyes moving over her body.

She was luscious.

Now, I wanted her to take off my clothes. "Undress me."

She reached for my shirt as if relieved to have something to do besides stand and be admired. Still, she was hesitant in the most delightful way, her hands shaking just a bit, her cheeks flushed. She took care with my cuffs and buttons, unfastening them slowly. She avoided my eyes, biting her lip when she opened my shirt to expose my bare chest. Her fingers trailed over my pecs and down my abs to my hip, sending a shiver of delight through me.

I shed my shirt, throwing it behind me, and waited for what she'd remove next, eager to see her tackle my belt and zipper. My erection strained at the fabric of my slacks when she reached for the belt buckle. I watched with some amusement and a lot of lust as she unzipped gingerly and then pulled them down. I stepped out of them so that all that was left were my boxer briefs. When she pulled them down and my cock sprung out, already wet and leaking, her eyes widened as she realized how thick I was. She knelt down and removed my socks, one at a time, glancing up at me waiting for my next command. I imagined her sucking my cock in that position, her mouth stretched wide, her lips swollen.

"See how ready I am for you?"

She looked in my eyes, and I could see desire in them. She liked this – me taking control, telling her what to do. It aroused her. She was submissive sexually, at least, but afraid of what it meant about her.

It meant nothing except she was perfect for me.

"Touch me," I said, wanting to feel her fingers around me. "Feel how hard I am because of you."

She did, stroking my length with her fingers, spreading the fluid over the head, eliciting a gasp from me as her thumb rubbed over the tip.

Desire built in me, my cock thickening further. "Kneel down and lick me. Taste me."

She did without hesitation, her tongue lapping at the head, then down the shaft, her eyes closed.

"Suck me."

She pulled the head into her mouth, her lips soft and wet, her tongue warm against my skin. She moved her mouth over the head, pulling off softly, then pushing back over it in a way that drove me wild. I moaned and she glanced up, our eyes meeting, her mouth full of my cock.

"That's so *good*, Kate."

I was hard and ready, but I wanted to tease her, work her up more, hear her moan while I stroked her with my cock, eat her and bring her off once before we fucked. I pulled my cock out of her mouth with reluctance, and helped her up, pulling her down the hallway to her bedroom.

"Do you have any condoms?"

She shook her head and her cheeks flushed a bright pink. "No, I haven't had sex for a long time. I wasn't planning… "

"That's all right." I went to my coat and reached in the pocket for the condoms I brought along, just in case I succeeded in my plan to seduce her. "I honestly didn't really think we'd end up here, but I brought a couple just in case lady luck smiled down on me." I held them up. "I prefer bareback and we will once we're both tested and clear. Are you on the birth control pill?"

"Yes, I'm on the pill and I was tested a few months ago. There's been no one for a year."

I hesitated. With my established subs, I usually fucked bareback once we had both been tested and had been exclusive for a while. I knew Kate was probably clean, for she wasn't very experienced sexually but I wanted to be safe.

"Look, Kate, I get tested regularly and I make sure all my partners are tested. I'm clean. But until we both get the all clear? We have to use these."

She nodded. "You're the doctor."

"Doctors still get HIV."

"I trust you."

I pulled her over to the bed and sat on the edge, positioning her between my thighs. Now, her heavy breasts were there for me to enjoy and I pushed my face between them, wrapping my arms around her so I could pull her close.

I squeezed each breast, enjoying the heavy fullness, and licked each nipple, laving the puckered areola with my tongue. She breathed rapidly, groaning softly as I sucked hard on the first nipple and then the other.

Then I leaned back and held out the condom.

"Put it on."

She took the condom but seemed unsure. "I've never…"

"You've never put a condom on a man?"

"They always did it."

Another first. I enjoyed when my new sub would sheathe my cock the first time and could anticipate how it would feel inside. "Hold the top between your finger and thumb and then place it over the head. Unroll it down as far as it will go."

She did, her hands shaking as she unrolled it over my shaft. Once she was done, I stood and pushed her down on the bed, spreading her thighs wide so I could see everything.

"You're so nice and wet, Kate," I said, sliding the head of my cock over her labia and clit, stroking slowly over and over again until she groaned out loud, her body arching "Oh, you like that do you?"

I had planned on eating her first, but she seemed to enjoy what I was doing so I continued, slipping the head of my cock into her a tiny bit more with each stroke.

"It's been a while, hasn't it, since you had a cock inside of you."

She said nothing, her eyes closed, lips parted. When I pushed inside her a bit deeper, she gasped.

"You're so nice and *big*."

I withdrew and stroked her clit once more with the head of my cock, slick with her juices.

"You're so nice and *tight*."

Now I closed my eyes, enjoying the sensation of her tight wetness around me, my thumb stroking her clit while I slid deeper inside of her, trying to hit her sweet spot with the head. When she thrust her hips up, meeting my thrust, I opened my eyes and watched her writhing in pleasure beneath me, her mouth open, lost to the sensations. I hadn't expected her to be so responsive to this and was very pleasantly surprised, my own lust building.

"Feels good, doesn't it? So *sweet*…"

"I feel," she said, her eyes closing, " that feels *so*…"

She watched me, her eyes almost closed as I thrust a bit

deeper, repeatedly and purposely hitting her g-spot while I circled her clit with my thumb.

"*Ohhh*," she gasped, her eyes closing, her back arching. "Oh, God…" I could see her grit her teeth.

"Don't come yet," I said, stopping my thrusts. I hadn't even tasted her yet. "This is too fast. *Breathe*, Kate. Wait and it will be even better."

But she didn't stop, thrusting her hips up, trying to find me and I could feel her body clenching around my cock.

"Oh, *baby*, you're already gone." I entered her fully and thrust as hard and fast as I could, and she shuddered, her flesh spasming around me, her nipples hard nubs beneath my fingers.

Oh, fuck, Kate….

CHAPTER 16

SHE CAME *HARD*.

I stopped thrusting when she finally relaxed, her back no longer arched. I enjoyed the lingering spasms of her body around my length and I touched her clit softly, eliciting little groans of pleasure when I did.

"What are you doing?" she asked as if startled.

"I like feeling you clench around me." I couldn't help but smile in triumph as she lay before me, my cock filling her up, her body like a fine instrument that I was playing – better than I expected.

"Why are you laughing at me?" She covered her face with her hands and I realized she mistook my pleasure for humor. I wasn't amused. I was ecstatic. It wasn't easy to make a woman come with just the head of your cock and your fingers. Usually, it took a while to find the right rhythm and the specific way a woman liked to be stimulated.

Kate responded perfectly to my seduction and my touch. More perfectly than I expected or was prepared for. I was so caught up in how she responded to me, I hadn't kept on top of things, and her orgasm got away on me. I always wanted to control when and how my partners came.

It was my thing.

"Oh, *Kate*." I tried to pull her hands away from her face. "I'm not laughing at you."

I was laughing because I was in a state of fucking bliss but I wasn't going to tell her that.

"*Don't*," she said and turned her face away.

I wouldn't have it. She couldn't retreat now for my cock was deep inside of her. She was going to look me straight in the eye and know I made her come *hard* with very little stimulation.

"No modesty allowed with me." I thrust once more inside of her, my thumb pressing on her still-hard clit and was rewarded with another clench of her body around my cock. "That was just so *fast*. You really needed a hard cock in you."

Then, she struggled with me, twisting and turning on the bed, turning her face away from me, her cheeks red.

Why was she so damn embarrassed? Most women would be happy to come as easily as Kate had.

My cell phone alarm beeped, and I remembered. "Oh, *fuck*. Lara…"

I had to withdraw from Kate's delicious body, my cock still hard as rock, and get my phone.

It was Lara, right on time. I'd taken longer than I planned and forgot about the call. It was another slip in my usual firm control over things.

"Hi, it's me," I said.

"Drake… What's going on? You know the rules. You should have called me five minutes ago."

"We're in the middle of things…"

"Yeah? I don't care what you were doing. This isn't like you. You're usually fastidious about safety routines. Put Kate on so that I know she's okay."

I frowned. Why wouldn't she be okay? I knew Lara was just

following proper procedure, unlike me, but it still irked me that she could even imagine I would hurt Kate.

"Just a minute." I went to the bed and tried to hand the phone to Kate. "It's Lara. She wants to talk to you, make sure you're all right."

Kate turned on her side and pushed the phone away, not looking at me, her voice barely a whisper. "I'm fine."

I held the phone back up to my ear. "She says she's fine."

"Not good enough, Drake. You know the rules. Put her on. I have to speak to her directly."

I exhaled in frustration. Damn. This wasn't like me. What did Kate do to me that I lost control over the situation, lost track of time?

I tried to hand the phone to her once more but she fought me, covering her face with her arms. I gave up and left the bedroom so I could speak with Lara more openly. I went down the hallway to the living room and stood looking out the window at the street below.

"Lara, she's a bit *emotional* right now," I said quietly, not wanting Kate to hear.

"Why is she emotional? What happened? Drake, this isn't like you. You're the pro at this."

I shook my head, surprised at it myself. "I barely even had it *in* her. Seriously, I hardly did anything. Like, two minutes…"

"You should have taken it slow. She's obviously upset."

"I'm not an idiot *frat boy*," I said, a bit too forcefully, pissed that Lara saw me as inept. "I *did* take it slow. Christ, She was just so ready…"

"Look, I know you really like her. Maybe too much, but you have to get things under control, Drake. Calm her down. Have her call me so I know she's okay. I'm only letting you off because I know you really like her and want this to work out. Do it now."

"I will. *She* will," I said. "Thanks for understanding."

When I returned to Kate's bedroom, she was gone. I saw that the en suite bathroom door was closed, the light on. I knocked.

"Kate, let me in."

She replied, her voice sounding mortified. "Just *go*."

"Don't be like that," I said, using my calm voice. The voice I used during surgery when I had a patient on the table who was upset. "Let me in. We have to talk."

She didn't respond so I went inside, knowing I had to get control over the situation and fast or else things would go south. When I entered, she was standing at the sink with a washcloth covering her eyes. I put my arms around her from behind, pulling her against me, my cock still semi-hard and pressed against her lower back.

"Kate, *why* are you crying?"

"I'm not."

I turned her around and removed the washcloth, and she was lying of course. Her eyes were red, her nose red. I embraced her, pushing her head against my shoulder, holding her for a moment.

After a moment, she seemed a bit calmer, so I led her out of the bathroom and to the living room. I pulled her down on the sofa, positioning her so that she straddled my hips, my hard cock trapped between us.

She relaxed finally and laid her head on my shoulder.

"I should have been more aware of how you were doing, Kate," I said, my voice soft. "I was just so aroused myself, too busy enjoying myself to notice, a little shocked. That was sloppy of me and won't happen again. I really didn't think anything would happen…"

"You were laughing at me."

"No, *no*," I said, shaking my head. "I wasn't laughing *at* you. I was delighted *with* you. I was ecstatic. You're so *responsive*."

I tried to catch her eyes but she was still embarrassed.

"Look at me," I said and took her chin in my hand, turning her face toward me.

Finally, she made eye contact and when our eyes met, my cock jumped, for she was so deliciously disheveled, her hair a bit wild, her eyes wide. She looked as if she'd been well-fucked and satisfied. God, what an effect she had on me.

I inhaled shakily. "I didn't think you'd come so fast and so easily. I didn't even get to *taste* you."

"I'm so *embarrassed*," she whispered, her eyes closing. "You barely did *anything* to me. I've never been that fast before."

"Don't be," I said, smiling softly. "It means you can come many times in a session. You don't know how pleased that makes me." I brushed hair off her cheek. "Sweet submissive Kate. You really are a sub, little one. I just proved it without even trying."

"What do you mean?"

"I didn't really even have my Dom hat on with you – not fully," I said, smiling at the expression on her face, "…and you were totally responsive to me and what I was doing and saying and how I was touching you. You have no idea how that kind of response is so addictive."

It was addicting. I wanted more of it – right away.

"You didn't," she said, glancing down at my still-semi hard erection. "You *know*…"

"No, I didn't *come*," I said, stifling a laugh at her shyness. "Way too fast for me. Next time you can do me twice in payback."

She tucked her face into the crook of my neck. "Won't you get blue balls or something?"

"I'll be fine, Kate. But I did want to ask you something," I said, trying to frame my question just right so I didn't scare her off answering. "Do you always come during intercourse?"

"No," she said, shaking her head solemnly. "Never with a partner."

I frowned. "What does *that* mean, with a partner?"

"Well," she said, her cheeks reddening.

"What?"

"I do with…" She paused, shrugging one shoulder, and when she spoke, her voice was barely audible. "You *know*."

"With what?" I said, still confused, trying to interpret her words. "Tell me, Kate. You can't shock me. Your fingers?"

She shook her head. "I got this gift at a bachelorette party and…"

Then I got it. She used a sex toy. "A dildo or a vibrator?"

"The first one."

A jolt of blood shot to my dick, which was now even more interested in this conversation. "You use a *dildo*?"

I pushed her down onto the couch, unable to hide my grin, filled with lust and mirth that threatened to spill out in laughter. And made my dick hard as rock again.

"Sweet little Ms. *Bennet* using a dildo to get off? Oh, *God*…" I dipped my mouth next to her ear and whispered. "I won't be able to sleep tonight imagining it."

When I pulled back, she had covered her eyes. "I can't believe I admitted to that!"

"Oh, you *have* to admit to things like that with *me*, Kate," I said, absolutely totally delighted that she admitted it and that she had actually made herself come with a dildo. "I have to know these things. You *are* a little kinky after all. A dildo? How big? What color?"

She bit her lip and turned away.

"Come on," I said, leaning down closer. "*Tell me*!"

"I looked it up on Google," she said, covering her mouth to stifle a laugh. "It's flesh colored and called…" Then she giggled, her eyes lighting up. "Mr. *Big*."

I laughed out loud at that. "Well, then, I'm perfect for you!"

Kate was almost crying with laughter at that and I pulled her closer, my arms around her, my face nestled in her neck.

Visions of her playing with a dildo, making herself come with it, made me even harder. But I was enjoying how free she had been, admitting to something so personal and intimate.

"So, tell me details," I said, pulling her up and positioning her so that she once more was straddling my hips. I had a thousand questions, the answers I knew would be fuel for my masturbatory fantasies. "When did you start using it? Was it before or after flyboy? How often do you use it?"

"*Drake*! I can't talk about this!" She squeezed her eyes shut and tried to turn her head away.

"Oh, yes you can," I said and held her chin so she had to look in my eyes. "You *must*. This is like Pandora's Box. Once you mention it, you have to tell me everything. Did you use it before or after flyboy?"

"After," she said. I was pleased that she was willing to continue revealing little tidbits about her sexual history. Not only would it give me insight into what she was like sexually, it would create a degree of trust and intimacy between us so I could really take control during sex. "My friend's bachelorette party about eight months ago. We all got one. It was a Carrie *Sex in the City* party."

"And? Details. Come on."

She shrugged her shoulder. "I tried it, but it was too big. So I just kind of played with it a bit. You *know*..."

"No, I don't know," I said, urging her on. "You have to describe it."

"I *can't*..."

"I'll make you show me right now if you don't tell me." I gave her a mock glare.

"No way!" She shook her head. "I do just what you did. You know, just playing around a bit outside, going in a bit but not too deep at first... Eventually, I got the hang of it and I think I found my G-Spot."

"You sure *did* get the hang of it."

I pulled her against my body and took in a deep breath, kissing her neck. I wanted to assure her that what she told me was not at all shameful. It was wonderful.

"Oh, sweet Kate, don't be embarrassed about that. You don't have any idea how much men want to learn something like that about their lover."

"It's embarrassing."

"Oh, no, *baby*. There isn't a heterosexual man alive who'd think less of you if he knew. In fact, he'd be pleased that you can come from his dick alone. That's not all that common."

"I wanted to be able to. It frustrated me that I couldn't. I only used to be able to through oral and it felt like there was something wrong with me. So when I got *Big*, I decided to try…"

I smiled and stroked her cheek, trying to keep her talking. I wanted to mine as much of her secrets as I could so she'd feel completely at ease with me sexually. I wanted her to let me do what I wanted, when I wanted, where I wanted and how I wanted. To accomplish that, she had to trust me.

"You call it *Big*?"

"After *Big* on Sex and the City. Carrie's boyfriend. We used to joke with each other about it. *Has Big visited you lately?*" She raised her eyebrows suggestively. " *How's Big doing? Still such an upright kinda guy? Still as reliable as ever? Never lets a girl down.* That kind of thing."

I laughed and then pulled her against me, burying my face in her neck. My arousal, my desire for her fought with this growing sense of affection for her, sympathy for her.

I wanted to fuck her so badly.

Instead, I decided that she'd had enough for one night. It was late and I had to get home and get to bed. I had surgery early and was fastidious about being in top shape for the grueling six hour procedure.

"Come," I said and pulled her back into the bedroom. I lay

on the bed and pulled her on top of me, my arms stroking down her back. Nothing sexual, just affection and physical contact to calm her and take care of her after such an emotionally charged experience.

Sex with a new lover as always difficult and fraught with emotions. I had to provide Kate with aftercare so she'd feel positive about what happened.

She lifted her head and looked in my eyes. "You don't want to…"

"To what?" I said, playing deliberately dumb.

"You *know*…"

"Fuck you?" I had to bite back a laugh. "It's getting too late and I don't like to rush." I glanced at my watch. "It's almost past the witching hour." I took hold of her face and stroked her cheek. "I have to go in five. Have an early morning in the OR but I wanted to just lie here for a while with you. Make sure you're OK."

"I'm fine," she said, and she did sound good. She sounded happy – as if she had overcome some kind of hurdle or obstacle. Or fear.

I thought she was pleased that I was pleased. I kissed her softly, my dick still a bit hard, but quickly flagging.

"Are *you* OK? You're still a *bit*…"

"I'll be fine," I said, smiling at the way she avoided saying it directly. "It's not the first time I've left a woman half-erect and won't be the last time."

"You don't want to *just*…" she said, raising her eyebrows again.

I squeezed her, delighted in her shyness. "Just have a quickie? A quick ram from behind?"

She nodded, her cheeks heating.

"I'm tempted but no," I said and rolled over on top of her, watching her as I stroked her cheek. I suspected she feared that I was going home unfulfilled sexually, but she couldn't have been more wrong. Despite the miscalculation on my part about how close she was to her orgasm, the fact she came so easily made me ecstatic. I didn't expect it to be so quick or easy. I actually felt a little dizzy remembering how I had to fuck her hard and fast once I recognized she was over the edge.

I couldn't wait to eat her and feel her coming beneath my mouth and tongue.

"I don't want to use your body like that right now but next time?" I said, trying to look serious, Dom-ish, although I felt anything but at that moment. "Next time I *will* use your body for my pleasure entirely. I intend to fuck you without you coming, just a straight desperate fuck so that we're even."

She responded physically to my tone and words.

Oh, Kate... You are a sub – a reluctant one, but you truly are...

"Why not now?" she asked, her eyes wide.

"Not now – not the first time. The first time is all about you. We don't have time to get you back in the mood after that laughing fit. As fast as you were, I know you won't be that fast again and I don't have time. I can wait until next time."

We remained like that for a few more minutes, a pleasant silence between us that was not at all awkward.

I sighed, not wanting to go, wishing I could call in and cancel my first surgery so I could work her up again and fuck her properly, but I had patients waiting, desperate for my expertise.

"I have to go."

I rose from the bed and went to the bathroom, removing the condom from my still-semi hard cock. I felt Kate's eyes on me from where she stood at the bathroom door. She probably hadn't been with a man often. I enjoyed knowing she was curious about me, my body. I took a piss, and smiled to myself when she averted her eyes.

"I have no shame, Kate, about anything to do with the body. You shouldn't either. Not with me."

After washing my hands, I went to the bedroom and dressed with her as my audience. After I draped my tie around my neck, leaving it loose, I went to her and tipped her chin up with a finger, kissing her, a kiss that surprised me with how much affection I felt for her. I felt as if we'd been through an ordeal together that ended well.

How I wished I could call in sick, arrange to have someone else take my OR time, cancel, but I couldn't do that.

"Until next time," I said, catching her eye. "There will be a next time, I hope? You'll give me another chance?"

"Yes, please," she said, the eagerness plain in her voice.

"I look forward to it," I said. "I'm going to edit your agreement and send you a revised copy in email tonight. I want you to read it and consider it. Sign it. I want this for real, Kate. I think we're a good match." I kissed her again. "Promise me you'll consider it."

"I will."

She gave me my coat and I pulled it on and then kissed her once more, stroking her cheek with a thumb, feeling as if I couldn't get enough of her. I hadn't had enough of her.

Not nearly enough.

"Call Lara now, so I know you have," I said as I stood at the door. "She'll be waiting."

Kate retrieved her phone from her bag, dialed and then waited, her eyes meeting mine without shyness.

"Hi, Lara?" she said and smiled at me, and her smile did something to my insides. "It's Kate. I'm fine."

I nodded, pleased that she was so relaxed now, so calm. Then, as much as I hated doing it, I left her apartment.

As I walked down the stairs to the street, a feeling of euphoria built in me so that when I got out onto the sidewalk, I could have jogged all the way to the parking garage down the street.

Then I realized I would look like a fool. I had the biggest

grin on my face, which no matter what I did, would not go away because *I had her*. She had given herself to me, let me take control – although I'd done a piss-poor job at maintaining it.

She wanted me.

I'd rip up that silly agreement she sent me and write up a real submission contract.

Then she'd be mine completely.

I exhaled and walked calmly back to my car.

CHAPTER 17

THE NEXT MORNING I woke early and worked on the boilerplate submission agreement I had started on my computer the week earlier while I drank my coffee. I wanted to put a few finishing touches on it after my night with Kate.

I was running late, so I'd have to send it later, once I finished my first surgery.

The morning went by very fast and I was in an exceptionally good mood, with great tunes over the sound system and my favorite OR team in place. Surgery went well and I was finished earlier than I anticipated, so as soon as I spoke with the patient's family, I went to my office and looked over the agreement once more while I had my second cup of coffee.

SUBMISSION AGREEMENT

SUBMISSION AGREEMENT BETWEEN
Drake Liam Morgan (hereinafter referred to as "Master")
AND
Katherine Marie McDermott (hereinafter referred to as "slave")

Said Submission Agreement, hereafter referred to as "the Agreement", refers to total dominance and control of Master in his sexual relationship with said slave.

1.0.0 Slave's Role

The slave agrees to submit sexually to the Master in all ways. This applies to all situations in which the Master and slave interact sexually, both in private and if applicable, in public. Failure to obey will result in punishment as the Master sees fit with the exception of the slave's veto right (section 1.0.1). Once entered into the Slavery Agreement, the slave's body belongs to the Master, to be used as He desires, within the guidelines defined herein. When they are together, the slave exists solely to please the Master and will do so to the best of her ability.

1.0.1 Slave's Veto

The slave may refuse to comply with any command or act that is illegal or would result in permanent bodily or psychological harm to said slave, that would shed blood or involve breaking of any law.

2.0.0 Master's Role

Once He signs the Agreement, the Master takes on full responsibility for the slave's body and is given license to do with her sexually as He sees fit, under the provisions determined in the Agreement. The Master will care for the slave, arrange for her safety and well-being, as long as He owns her. The Master commits to treat the slave properly, to train her, punish her, and use her as He sees fit.

3.0.0 Punishment

The slave agrees to accept punishment the Master chooses to inflict. Failure to comply with Master's demands immediately and properly will result in discipline, until it is performed satisfactorily. Refusal to comply with Master's demands will result in punishment, to include any of the following: bare handed spanking, denial of orgasm, denial of attention.

4.0.0 Others

The slave may not seek any other Master or lover or relate to others in any sexual or submissive way without the Master's permission. If the slave does, it will be considered a breach of the Agreement, and will result in termination of the Agreement. The Master will not give the slave to other Masters.

5.0.0 Limits

The slave agrees to the following activities, which the Master shall engage in at His discretion:

- All forms of sexual intercourse, oral sex and play, anal sex and play, masturbation, mutual masturbation, vaginal fisting;

- All forms of bondage with the following: Rope, leather, and other suitable restraint materials, and other restraints as the Master sees fit;

- The use of appropriately designed sex toys, including but not limited to vibrators, dildos, anal training toys, vagina beads, etc.

I sent it off, certain that it didn't go too far for Kate, eager to see how she responded. I dictated some notes on the surgery and then studied the file on my next case, wondering one last time before I focused back on my work when I'd hear back from Kate and what she'd say.

When I finished my second surgery, and returned to my office, I saw that she'd sent me an email a few moments earlier. It was late afternoon. I probably would be able to slip by her apartment after my practice session with Mersey if she was interested in talking about the submission agreement.

To my dismay, the letter wasn't at all what I expected. In fact, I felt sick about it, wondering what I'd done to receive her email. Was it the vaginal fisting? I didn't really need that, but put it in so Kate could strike it off is she wanted.

I opened the email and studied it.

From: McDermott, Katherine M.
   Sent: November 12, 5:31 PM
   To: Morgan, D. L.
   Subject: Re: Your Submission

DRAKE, I read your agreement, but I'm afraid I just can't go through with this. I made a mistake and I'm going to just put this behind me. I'm sorry but this isn't going to work between us after all.

Please don't come over or contact me again.

Goodbye.

Kate

WHAT? My heart sank at that. I sent a reply immediately.
From: Morgan, D. L.
Sent: November 12, 6:46 PM
To: McDermott, Katherine M.
Subject: RE: Your Submission

I'll be right over.

BEFORE I COULD LEAVE my office, as I was cleaning up my desk, I received another email.

To: Morgan, D. L.

Sent: November 12, 6:48 PM
From: McDermott, Katherine M.
Subject: Re: Your Submission

No, please don't. I don't want to see you ever again.

I called her cell phone, but she wouldn't answer so I texted her as I left the hospital.

KATE, what happened between last night and lunch? Tell me.

Let me talk to you. Please…
I want you.

She responded and I frowned as I read the text, trying to understand what she meant.

This is just the way it has to be for your own good. Please stop calling and texting me. It won't do any good.

What? What the fuck did she mean, my own good. I texted back:

For my own good? What does that mean?

Kate, don't do this…

KATE, please call me.

Kate, what happened? You were fine when I left you…

Will you at least answer my texts so I know you're OK?

Kate, I'm coming over to talk to you. Please give me the chance to make it right…

NOTHING.

I drove by her apartment building but she didn't answer when I tried her buzzer. I sat on the steps and texted her once more.

AT LEAST TELL *me why you don't want to be with me. What was it? Did the contract scare you? Don't be afraid, Kate. You can strike off anything that you don't want to do. I just included those things that I know probably upset you so you'd have something to cross off. I don't need to do them. I don't need to do anything that you don't want to do. I want to be with you.*

Please, give this time.

She texted me back almost immediately.

DRAKE, *I'm doing this for you. To protect you. I can't say anything more but you have to stop trying to see me. You have to just stop for your own good. I can't say more…. I'm sorry.*

I WENT to my own place and sat on my sofa, my phone in my hand. I sat back and covered my head with my hands trying to figure out where I'd gone wrong.

I had to fix this. I had to find a way to calm whatever fears she'd developed in the hours between being at her apartment and when I received her email.

I was not going to let her get away.

CHAPTER 18

I DIDN'T ALLOW myself any time to sulk, despite the void I felt in my gut. Self-pity wasn't going to get Kate back. I had to figure out what had happened and fix it before too much time passed. Nothing killed intimacy quicker than absence. I had to get back to Kate as soon as possible.

My first step was to contact Lara, but she had nothing.

"I don't know, Drake. Everything sounded fine when I spoke to her last night. She confessed how quickly she came and was shocked and embarrassed because she's so inexperienced."

"She *is* inexperienced," I said. "But you know me. That's a plus, not a minus."

"She may be inexperienced but she did tell me something I found surprising."

I waited, but she didn't elaborate. "Such as?"

"She told me that she used a dildo."

I laughed out loud at that, despite the sensation of dread I felt about Kate. "She calls it 'Big' – as in Sex and the City."

"She told you that?" Lara laughed with me. "You did pretty well getting her to open up if she actually told you."

"I plied her with liquor and rich food. I hand fed her. And I used my serious doctor voice."

"Does it every time," she said and I could hear the grin in her voice.

"Whatever happened, she's not biting now," I replied, a sick feeling in my gut. "I honestly don't know what happened. I sent her the contract this morning and then I got an email breaking it off."

"You sent her your usual contract?"

"Yes," I said and rubbed my forehead. "She must have been shocked at a few things I listed. I put them in the contract because I thought she'd want to strike them off."

"Such as?"

I shrugged, mentally knocking myself in the head for including anything I knew would be objectionable. I should have included only what I knew she'd accept, but I wanted her to feel some kind of power over the contract. "Mock rape. Anal. Vaginal fisting."

I heard her sharp intake of breath. "The mock rape is probably a no-go with someone like Kate. That was why she broke off with her last boyfriend."

"Yeah," I said. "Bad choice on my part. He was the one who tried to introduce BDSM into their relationship. He wanted mock rape and it frightened her. I suspect she's now curious about it and would only need someone who knew what they were doing to make it work."

"You may be right." Then I heard her sigh. "She's *young*, Drake. She might be a bit more flighty than you like. Are you set on this? Why not just let her go? I have several other submissive-hopefuls you could take on..."

I shook my head and even the thought that I wouldn't have Kate as my own caused my throat to constrict. "I want her, Lara."

"Oh, dear..." she said, her voice trailing off into a sigh of resignation. "This isn't like you. You're usually much more cool and in control with a new submissive."

"She's not my usual submissive."

There was a pause. "If she calls me, I'll see what I can find out, but I'm not convinced you two are good together."

"Why not?" I said, my back stiffening.

"You need someone who knows that being a submissive is what they want, Drake. Kate was never completely honest about her desires, even to herself. My advice?" she said and paused for a brief time. "Just let her go… Seriously."

"Not going to happen," I said, more convinced than ever that Kate was who and what I wanted. "If she calls you, I'd appreciate it if you could find out why she changed her mind."

"I will, if that's truly what you want. Take care, Drake. Underneath that cool controlled exterior, you're a human like everyone else. You know and I know that you can be hurt just as much as the next person. I remember you after your divorce. You were a mess."

"Don't worry about me," I said, remembering with a real sense of remorse my post-divorce blue period. "I'll be fine. But thanks for agreeing to put in a good word if you talk to her. I appreciate it."

I hung up, frowning as I thought about what Lara said. It was true that I hadn't been my usual self with Kate. I hadn't treated her the way I usually would a new submissive. I would never take my new sub – or even an established sub – out to the Russian Tea Room or a concert. I didn't want them to expect anything other than a B&D session three times a week. I told them that at the outset. I wouldn't be a boyfriend. I was a Dom who tied them up and made them come and that was all I could ever be.

With Kate, I definitely wanted to be a Dom, but part of me knew what the other part of me tried to deny.

I wanted more.

I SPENT the rest of the evening sitting at my desk at home preparing for my convention in the Bahamas, going over the paper my co-author and I would present on pediatric movement disorders. I wasn't looking forward to going – I had a heavy sensation in my chest at the thought. I called and texted Kate several times, with no response. She really was determined not to respond. I felt the dreariness of New York in November and not even the prospect of sun and sand could bring me out of my funk. My only hope was that Ethan and Elaine would bring Kate with them when they came to the Bahamas – if they came to the Bahamas.

As luck would have it, I had made a stop at my fitness club earlier that afternoon and ran into Ethan, who was coming out of the steam room with a few of his fellow judges who frequented the club. He was busy toweling off his face, which was red and sweating from the steam.

"Oh, Drake, just the man I wanted to see."

I smiled and extended my hand for our usual shake. "How are you, Sir?"

"I'm fine."

We moved to an alcove where there were a few benches next to some old lockers, speaking a bit more quietly.

"How are you doing?"

"Good," I said. "I'm leaving for the Bahamas on Tuesday."

"The Bahamas, hmm?" Ethan said, frowning for a moment. "You said you were going there for a conference, if I recall correctly."

"I am." Then a thought popped into my head. "You and Elaine should come. The beach is beautiful and the weather is fine. Consistently in the 80s every day."

Ethan considered for a moment as he dried off. "That sounds like a capital idea. I imagine it would be great to get

Kate there as well," he said and quirked his eyebrow. "A break from all her studies would do her good. You two could spend some time together, get to know each other."

I smiled. On his part, Ethan examined me for a moment and I wondered what he was thinking. He obviously saw me as a good prospect for Kate and was eager to put us together on a tropical vacation. It gave me a warm feeling that he was so open about his interest in seeing us as a couple, but it also brought out a bit of guilt. He had to know I wanted Kate sexually. No heterosexual man in his right mind wouldn't want her. I wouldn't be harming her, or doing anything degrading... Still, I felt as if I were deceiving Ethan. He couldn't know about my involvement in the lifestyle. I couldn't bear the expression of disgust I'd see on his face if he found out.

But I wanted Kate...

"I'll call my assistant and get her to book us a flight and hotel," Ethan said finally, as if he'd made a decision. "Where are you staying?"

"The conference is at the Hilton in Nassau."

He nodded. "We might just be able to make this work out." He winked at me. "Leave it to me. I'll call you and let you know if we're going."

I smiled and shook his hand, feeling a bit sheepish, as if I'd just traded a half-dozen head of cattle for his daughter's hand in marriage in some bronze-age tribal rite. Kate had no say in any of this, and I hoped that she would agree to go. *And* that she wouldn't hate me or Ethan when she found out we'd been conspiring behind her back.

If she did go to the Bahamas, and we had a chance to be alone, I was pretty certain that I could get her to sign a revised and far less threatening submission agreement. I felt confident I could exert control over her fairly well. If I could just get her alone... I'd be insistent. I'd be as persuasive as I knew how to be.

She'd be unable to resist.

I hoped.

If Ethan brought Kate with him, I'd have a chance to repair whatever damage had been done by the clauses in my submission agreement that caused her to balk. If that is what caused her to call it off – and I was pretty sure it was – I knew I could fix things. I kicked myself mentally once more, wishing I'd kept it even more vanilla than I had made it.

DESPITE SEVERAL MORE CALLS AND texts, it appeared that Kate was determined to shut me out of her life. A few days before my trip, I met Lara for a drink after work at the bar close to her office. She was still wearing her business suit, but had unbuttoned her blouse and let her hair down. She looked as beautiful as I remembered her from our college days. That beauty hid a strong sadistic streak and I was glad I was a Dom and not into S&M. She was beautiful and wickedly sexual. Any man inclined to submission would be unable to resist her.

I kissed her cheek as I arrived and sat beside her on a stool at the bar.

"Drake," she said and smiled, her ice blue eyes coolly appraising.

"Lara," I said and turned to her.

We made small talk for a while, passing the time while I waited for the bartender. She was busy with some big case and had been working like a dog. I told her about my upcoming conference and the paper I was presenting with a colleague.

"Okay, so now that we've impressed each other with our successful careers, any luck on the more human side? Have you won Kate back? Is she at your beck and call?" Lara winked at me, a sly look in her eye. "She never called me."

I shook my head and ordered a beer from the bartender when he finally came over. "No," I said, and loosened my tie.

"She hasn't answered a call or text. Do you think she'll call you?"

She shook her head. "I doubt she will. She's skittish."

"She's afraid. It's understandable, given who her father is."

My beer arrived and I took a big sip, needing the alcohol to relax me for the penetrating interrogation I knew was coming. Lara was always on my case about finding a permanent partner who could share my life as well as my kink.

"It seems as if Ms. McDermott has given up on being your new submissive, Drake. Speaking of which," she said and nodded in the direction of a young woman sitting down the bar from us. I glanced over and saw the look that passed between Lara and the pretty young blonde. She slipped off her stool and came over, an expectant smile on her face.

"Drake, this is Kira," Lara said, gesturing towards her. She wore a sexy black number with ample cleavage. Her wide blue eyes in combination with being on the petite side, gave her the kind of look Lara knew I was into. I had to hand it to Lara – she knew what I liked.

"Kira, this is Drake," Lara said pointing to me. "I told you about him and thought you two might hit it off."

I gave Lara a glare, for she didn't warn me this was a matchmaking session, but then I tried my best to be chivalrous, considering the young woman was obviously looking for a Dom. No doubt Lara was hoping to divert my focus from Kate to someone she felt was more suitable – and available.

Problem was that I was simply not interested in anyone else. I'd kissed Kate. I'd had her naked beneath me. I'd touched her skin and had my cock inside of her – barely. There was so much I wanted to do with her, so much I wanted to try, so much I wanted her to experience. She was already mine. My task was to convince her of the fact.

I wanted Kate.

"Nice to meet you, Kira," I said and shook her hand.

"There's been a misunderstanding. I'm not in the market right now." I shrugged and smiled, hoping to nip this little matchmaking game in the bud before Kira became too interested.

"Drake..." Lara glared at me, her expression frustrated. "Not like you to hold a torch," she said under her breath. Then, as if resigned, she turned to Kira, who looked embarrassed. "Let's go, sweetie. I know a place where you might be able to meet someone who *is* available." Lara turned to me. "Sorry, Drake. We have to go. You understand."

I did understand. Lara would try to salvage the night by taking the girl to *Diamant*, a bar in the Upper East Side frequented by people who were active in the lifestyle. Lara would parade her around, introduce her to the Doms she knew and try to fix the young woman up with one of them.

I sighed in relief, and turned my back to the bar so I could at least watch the Nicks while I finished my beer.

I SPENT the next day at my office seeing patients for their pre-op appointments, post-op follow-ups and consultations.

At around three in the afternoon, I receive a call from Ethan to let me know that he, Elaine and Kate would be coming to the Bahamas for Thanksgiving Weekend.

"What did Kate say when you asked her?"

Ethan paused before he spoke. "I didn't say anything about you being there," he said. "I figured she'd find some excuse to back out. She needs a break and some sun. Would do her a world of good."

"It will be great to have her there," I said, wanting to be as up-front about my interest in Kate as possible. I needed all the help I could get.

"I'll call you when we get in."

"If I don't answer, it's because I'm in the conference. Just leave a message with the front desk. We should meet for dinner.

The hotel puts on a Thanksgiving spread for all the American tourists so we could do the whole turkey dinner thing."

"Sounds great."

We said our goodbyes and I hung up, a huge grin on my face. Then I kicked myself mentally. Don't get ahead of yourself, Drake. She's not yours yet.

But I was determined to make her mine. When I was determined about something, I did everything in my power to make it happen, whether it was having a career as a surgeon, playing in a retro Brit Rock band, or seducing and winning the reluctant heart of a submissive and very shy Kate.

KEN CALLED around five in the afternoon. I checked my calendar and saw we had a practice session at O'Riley's that night, but it would mean a late night before my flight the next morning. I wanted to cancel but I'd be gone all weekend and we'd already cancelled several practices and a paying gig.

"Drink a can of Red Bull and meet us at ten," Ken said when I groaned about how tired I was. "You can sleep on the beach."

"I'm attending a conference."

"I know what you doctors do at conferences," Ken said and laughed. "You play golf, go to clubs to watch exotic dancers and get lap dances and drink expensive wine."

I smiled. "I'm delivering a conference paper."

"Yeah, cry me a river, Drake. See you at ten."

DESPITE BEING GENERALLY EXHAUSTED after two days of surgery and a day in my office, I made it to O'Riley's at ten that night after rushing home for a shower and bite to eat at eight. I'd just done evening rounds with my residents and would really rather have spent the night on the couch, but Ken would not be denied.

Once the evening dinner crowd had finished, we brought our instruments out of the basement and set up, using the bar dance floor as our stage for a practice session. People knew we practiced and were getting their seats at the small tables surrounding the stage. Others sat at the bar, their backs turned so they could watch.

Once we were set up, we fooled around on our instruments, tuning and getting everything set up properly, discussing amongst ourselves what we'd play first.

"How about Tell Her No by the Zombies?" Cliff said. "We haven't played them for a while and they're doing a North American tour."

I nodded. My voice wasn't as high as Colin Blundstone's so we adjusted the key so I could avoid having to use falsetto too much. I liked *Tell Her No*. It was one of my father's favorites. The song was about a woman's betrayal and warned the listener that if a woman tells you she loves you and tempts you, you shouldn't believe her.

TELL HER NO, *no, no…*

HE'D PLAY it when I was younger, singing along, winking at me. "Take the Zombie's advice, Drake. Women are fickle. Quick to love and quick to hate. Don't ever think you can trust them."

Like everything else my father said to me, I tended to reject it out of hand. Maureen taught me just how right my father was after all.

We were a bit rusty, but after a couple of minutes of playing around, we found our rhythm and started over, playing Tell Her No completely through without stopping. A round of applause followed and we all smiled. For a group of over-the-hill wanna-be musicians, it was music to our ears.

Just as the song was ending, I looked out over the small crowd and saw Allie at a table against the far wall. It threw me, knocking me off my place and I fucked up the words to *Time of the Season*. Luckily there was a long coda so I was able to collect my wits before we moved into *She's Not There*.

When we were finished, Ken leaned over to me. "What happened to you?"

I gestured to Allie with my head. "She happened."

Ken glanced over to where Allie sat, a drink in her hand, her face expectant. "Ahh," he said. "Ex girlfriend not willing to be an ex after all?"

"Something like that," I muttered.

"Don't let her throw you."

I nodded to Ken and strummed my bass.

"How about we play some American music for a change," Ken said to the others. "The Turtles."

I didn't really care what we played, distracted by Allie's presence. I wondered why she'd come to one of our practice sessions. Did Lara send her?

We played *You Showed Me*, *Eleanor* and then *Happy Together*. It was in the middle of *Happy Together* that I thought the song choices weren't the best, given my ex-submissive was sitting in the audience and was obviously not over the relationship.

The crowd applauded when we were finished, and after we took a bow, I put my bass down and left the stage, determined to confront Allie and settle things once and for all.

"Allie," I said when I sat across from her. "I'm surprised to see you here."

"Are you really?" she said and I could already see she was upset by the way her mouth turned down. Her eyes sparkled in the dim light of the bar. "Are you already over me? Was coming here once really such a crime?"

I sighed. "Allie, I told you right from the start that I don't do girlfriends. I don't do sleepovers. I don't do breakfast in bed. I fuck. Period. You knew my terms. You were the one to break them."

"Can't we try again? Lara said you haven't found a new sub yet. I haven't found a Dom. I promise I won't push. Just sex."

"You came here tonight, I said and shook my head. "You should have let Lara contact me. Besides, Lara's wrong about that. I have found someone new."

Allie frowned. "Lara said she broke it off."

"No, she didn't. Things are just…" I hesitated. Was I fooling myself? Kate *had* broken it off. She wasn't answering my texts or answering my calls. "Things are just complicated. I'm not in the market, Allie. I'm sorry."

"Give me back my fucking key, then," she said, frowning, real tears in her eyes.

"I don't have your key."

"I left it here that night. I thought you'd at least drop it off, but you're so selfish and self-centered you didn't even think to do that."

Then I remembered that Allie had left her key on the table when we broke up.

"Hold on a minute," I said and went over to the bar where Chris was bartending. "Did you find a key on a keychain a couple of weeks ago?"

"Let me check," Chris said and bent down, rustling through a box. He pulled out the key to Allie's apartment and plopped it down on the bar. "This it?"

I nodded and took the key chain. "Thanks."

I went back to where Allie was and placed it on the table in front of her.

"I'm sorry you're so upset, but things didn't work out with us, Allie. Both of us have to move on."

She looked up at me, tears in her eyes, a determined set to her mouth. "Eight months for nothing." She grabbed the keychain and left, bumping into me hard as she rushed by.

I went back to the stage where Ken and the other guys were dismantling things.

"That looked rather unpleasant," Ken said, his voice low.

"Tell me about it," I said and helped carry the large amp out the back to the basement.

Very unpleasant. I sure hoped to see Kate tomorrow so we could hash things out. Seeing Allie reminded me that something was missing in my life. There was a hole, gaping, where bondage and dominance, sex and pleasure was supposed to be.

I wanted Kate to fill that gap.

Badly.

CHAPTER 19

My flight to the Bahamas was quiet and as I sat in first class, alone by the window, I read over my paper one last time, checking the tables in the PowerPoint presentation. I had a day to rest before the conference was scheduled to start and I planned to get some sun, catch up on sleep and take it as easy as I could, considering I'd been working straight for almost a year without a vacation.

I took a limo to the hotel in Nassau, located on the northern coast. A beautiful old colonial building built during the British colonial era as the name suggested, the hotel was grand and luxurious. After checking in and unpacking my bags, I changed into some casual slacks and a white linen shirt, open at the collar, rolled up at the cuffs and went for a walk along the beach. The sand was sugar-white, the surf gentle, and the water azure blue. I rolled up my slacks to the knee and waded in when I grew too heated from the intense sun, and then splashed along the shore, enjoying having absolutely nothing to do but wait until seven for dinner.

I made my way back to the hotel after about an hour, and into the lounge, sitting at the huge mahogany bar surrounded by dark wood, glass and crystal, and had a vodka tonic with a lime wedge. It was refreshing after my time on the beach. While I was sitting nursing my drink, a very attractive and very well-dressed woman in her twenties leaned against the bar two stools down from me. Dark hair and dark eyes, tanned skin, she was exotic and beautiful in a white dress with a frilly low-cut neckline and short skirt. She ordered a drink and glanced my way, smiling when she caught my eye.

A working girl.

She sipped her drink and then took the stool next to me at the bar.

"Hello," she said in a husky voice. "You look like you're new here."

"Why is that?"

She pointed to my face. "Sunburn. Gives it away every time."

I laughed and took a sip of my drink, wanting to see how this played out.

"So," she said and leaned closer, displaying her décolletage. "You in for the neurosurgery convention?"

"I am," I said, and took another sip.

"Neurosurgeon, huh?"

"That would be why I'm attending the neurosurgery convention." I smiled at her. "I don't pay for it, sweetheart. Sorry."

She shrugged. "For you, I'd be tempted to give it away."

I shook my head and swirled my drink with the swizzle stick. "I'm meeting my new lady here, so I'm not looking for a hookup either."

"Shame," she said and licked her lips. "Like I say, I'd give it away for a piece of that." She glanced down my body, a feral smile on her face.

Then she sighed and looked around. "Any of your single physician friends here I could meet, maybe party with?"

I glanced around the bar but didn't see anyone I knew. "I'm here a bit early. The rest will be coming later tonight or tomorrow morning for the first sessions."

"Keep me in mind if any of your colleagues need an escort."

"I will," I said, although finding hookers for fellow doctors was not on my list of skills.

She wandered off, eyeing the other patrons for a likely target.

I MOVED to the patio for dinner, and sat under a crisp blue and white umbrella at a small table overlooking the beach and enjoyed a feast of fresh seafood and a bottle of very good chardonnay. The breeze was warm, the sunset beautiful, and I was ready for a good night's sleep by the time nine o'clock rolled around. After a quick shower, I stood at the window in my room and watched the harbor lights while I listened to the news on cable. The world seemed so far away. All the pressures of my practice, the work of the foundation and my father's company, and my band were forgotten. I felt lighter, refreshed by the bright sun and warm salty air.

My cell dinged and I checked. An email from Ethan. They would be arriving late that night but would see me tomorrow for lunch before the afternoon session.

Kate was coming and when I read the news, a surge of adrenaline flowed through me. She knew nothing of my presence at the hotel and I wondered how she'd respond. Probably not well at first, but I was lucky to have Ethan on my side.

I felt only a tiny bit guilty that Ethan and I were ambushing her this way, but I was sure after a while, she'd accept it and she and I would have a little chat about her needing to protect me.

Was it something to do with public knowledge of me being

in the lifestyle? That was the only thing I could think of that she would have to protect me from.

Unable to keep my eyes open any longer, I shut off the lights and lay in bed, the windows open to admit the breeze. I could have turned on the air conditioning, but I wanted to smell the salt air while I slept. Luckily, the weather wasn't too hot and I fell asleep to the sounds of a ship's horn in the distance, the lovely Katherine on my mind.

I WOKE EARLY the next morning and after a walk on the beach, I had a shower and met some of my colleagues for breakfast. Laurisse Marchand and I sat on the patio and spoke of previous conventions, catching up on each other's news and current interests. My co-author for the paper I was presenting, Laurisse was there with her husband. We agreed to meet for an hour just after lunch to go over the paper once more although both of us had the final PowerPoint presentation for a week and knew our parts.

The first session started at nine and was on deep brain stimulation in pediatric movement disorders. I was considering a specialty in pediatric neurosurgery as there were few in practice with my expertise in deep brain stimulation. Working with children in Africa had given me a fondness for pediatrics and although it would mean a few more years of training, I was interested in going down that pathway. Laurisse and I worked on transitioning the procedures for pediatric patients and I was eager to enter into the new field.

Keeping busy with the conference kept my mind off Kate, but when I stopped and thought about seeing her, I felt a twinge of adrenaline, and had to stop myself from smiling too widely. Around eleven, we took a break and a group of us headed up from the convention level to our rooms, to check our email.

As we were mounting the staircase to the main floor, I glanced up and saw her.

Katherine.

Wearing a skimpy cotton sundress that displayed her delicious cleavage, and highlighted her pale skin, which was now showing signs of a light sunburn, she looked ravishing with her hair twisted up in a knot.

Our eyes met and her eyes widened, her mouth open.

"Excuse me," I said to Laurisse as I watched a rapidly retreating Ms. Bennet. "Kate!" I called after her but she didn't stop. I turned back to Laurisse. "I'll see you after lunch." Laurisse had the grace not to ask me about Kate, so I followed Kate to the elevator, where she stood poking the button.

I reached out and touched her arm. "*Kate*," I said, stopping her when the elevator doors opened. "You arrived."

She turned to me and her face was flushed. "I *arrived?*"

"Yes," I said and let go of her arm. "I was expecting you."

Kate entered the elevator but if she was hoping to escape me, she was mistaken. I pressed the close button before anyone else could get on so we could be alone, then I cornered her, my arm on the elevator wall beside her head. I could barely suppress a smile.

She avoided my eyes, in her usual way. I'd have to break her of that habit when we fucked.

And we were going to fuck. At that moment, I wanted it more than anything.

"Was this all a set-up?" she whispered, frustration in her voice.

I said nothing, biting back a huge grin. She glanced up at my face cautiously. "You could call it that."

"You and my father?"

"Me and your father. He thought it might be a good idea for us to get away from it all, work through this 'difficulty' we're facing, I think he said. Of course I agreed."

Kate frowned. "What did you tell him?"

"Oh, I made something up about how you were concerned about my schedule, and how busy I was, thinking I wouldn't have time for you. That kind of thing. He bought it completely." I moved a bit closer, running my fingers over her cheeks. "You're a bit burnt. Your skin is so fair..."

"I told you we can't be together."

I leaned down and caught her eye. "You said you were doing this for my own good. I have to know what you mean by that or else I can't accept it. I'm the one who should decide what's for my own good."

"Drake this can't happen."

"*Shh*. When I told your father about a conference I had to attend and that I was *not* looking forward to it because I was worried about you, he offered to bring you here for a bit of a getaway. Of course, I thought it was a *spectacular* idea…"

When the elevator door opened, I stepped away and Kate rushed off the elevator, using her keycard to open the door to her room. She went inside and I followed. This was not going to end with me on her doorstep, her on the other side of the door. I heard her exhale as if in frustration and went to stand beside her at the large picture window.

"*Kate*…" I said, and took her shoulders in my hands, turning her to face me. "Come *here*."

She stiffened. "Who was that woman you were with?"

What? She was jealous of Laurisse? There was hope for me yet. "Her?" I said and grinned. "That's Doctor Laurisse Marchand, from Quebec. She does the same work I do and we've collaborated on a paper we're presenting. She's very happily married with kids and is a few years older than me. She also has a very dominant personality, like me. In other words, not my type, so don't even let your mind go there."

She blushed profusely and it made me want to ravish her.

"Nothing can happen between us, Drake."

I took her hand and pulled her over to the couch. I sat in the middle, and pulled her down onto my lap so that her face was just inches from mine. I wanted to remind her of that first night and how intimate we were. I wanted her to think of us fucking.

"You look absolutely ravishing. I want to ravish you."

"I'm serious," she said, but I could hear the fight was gone from her voice. " We have to end this. For your own good."

"Tell me how ending this would be for my own good."

"You have to trust me. Someone knows about you. Your kink. They threatened to expose you if we kept seeing each other."

"What?" I said, frowning at the thought someone wanted to expose me. "*Who?*"

She shook her head. "I can't say."

"You can't or won't say?" As much as I though Kate might be overblowing this threat, I had to play it safe with my reputation.

"Both."

I exhaled heavily. Despite this so-called threat, I wasn't going to go gently. I wanted Kate and I was going to have her. I'd deal with whatever threat arose myself.

"Kate, I can't just end 'this' like you seem to think we have to. You're an unanswered question. You're unexplored country and I very much want to explore you. Every single *inch* of you, inside and out."

I nuzzled her neck, kissing the skin beneath her ear. My lips brushed her earlobe.

"Unless you can tell me who is threatening you so I can understand it, and agree or not, find a way around it, I am *not* giving you up," I said. "You said you'd sign my agreement last week. I don't think anyone's threatening you. I think you read my limits and you're afraid." I pulled back and examined her face, trying to meet her eyes. "What was it that shocked you? Was it vaginal fisting? Anal sex? I *told* you I put those in specifically so you could strike them off and feel some degree of control."

She glanced away and I knew that she had been shocked by those items. Once more, I wished I'd shown better judgment.

"It wasn't that. I'm telling you the truth."

"Then, who is it?" I demanded. "Tell me or I won't believe you."

"Drake, I *can't*" She pulled out of my arms and stood but I followed, determined not to let her back out without a full explanation. Hell, nothing could get me to accept that she didn't want me. She did. I could feel it in her body. I could see it in her eyes. She was afraid.

Finally, I had her pressed against the table. "Tell me, or I'll keep after you. I won't give up on you, Kate."

"Why not? Barely anything has happened between us. It would be a lot easier to end it now rather than later when we're forced to after you've been disgraced because of my carelessness."

"What about your carelessness?"

She shook her head, "I," she said, fumbling for words. "I left the agreement on my desk and someone found it."

I closed my eyes and exhaled heavily, dismayed that someone had seen it. "*Who* found it?"

"Just someone who doesn't want me to be with you, Okay?"

"Nigel," I said, thinking he was a likely suspect. "It was Nigel, right?"

"No!" she shook her head.

"Don't protect him, Kate. I know he doesn't really approve of me."

"What do you mean? Why wouldn't he approve of you?"

"Did he force you to stop seeing me? He knows that I'm in the lifestyle." I shook my head and then I realized I could deal with Nigel. He wouldn't want to be exposed either. I was sure Nigel was just bluffing.

I stroked her cheek, then brushed my fingers against the tops of her breasts. "I can talk to him, assure him that I mean you no harm."

"It wasn't Nigel. Does Nigel know about you?"

"Yes."

"How does he know?"

"I can't tell you how he knows. That's private. He just knows. I thought he was okay with it, but if you're protecting him, you have to let me know. I'll have to speak with him if he's pressuring you."

"Nigel's *kinky?*" she said and frowned.

I rubbed my forehead, kicking myself for suggesting it. Kate obviously didn't know.

"I can neither confirm nor deny that statement," I said, angry with myself and my lapse. "It's not my place to out people. I take this seriously. Kate, I've known people who've lost their jobs and their lives because of adverse publicity around BDSM. All I can say is that he knows about me. Please, just tell me who's threatening you so we can figure this out."

"I can't and we can't just figure this out," she said, her voice firm. "This person will not back down, no matter what. This person is very morally judgmental. And irrational. If they think we're together, they will tell my father about you. Now, you'd better go." She had this look in her eyes and sound in her voice – resignation and a hint of regret. "This can't happen."

"Who is it?" I said once more, determined to find out so I could fix things.

"It's someone who doesn't understand BDSM. They never will. Listen, this is just too much trouble, Drake. Why are you so *insistent?* "

It wasn't too much trouble. It wasn't any trouble at all. Or if it was, my mind wasn't letting me see it. "Because I *want* you."

"That doesn't *matter*."

I sighed in frustration and stood staring at her, wishing

there was something I could say that would make her realize that we couldn't let this drop. I couldn't let this thing between us – whatever it was – end before it ever really started.

"Look, I won't touch you, if you really don't want me to," I said and tried to catch her eye. "I promise we'll just talk."

She wasn't having it and shook her head. "It's not that I don't want you to touch me. I *do*, God do I want you to," she said, her voice emotional, "but you're in danger." She looked up into my eyes, her expression earnest. "Can't you understand?"

"So you *do* want me to touch you," I said, a jolt of adrenaline surging through me. I wrapped my arms around her and pulled her against my body. She had no choice but to put her arms around me or else fall into my arms.

"*Drake…*"

"Sorry, you said the operative words," I said, pulling her even closer, leaning down so I could kiss her. "I need to finish what I started that night before we were so rudely interrupted by my cell phone alarm."

I kissed her, my lips on hers, my mouth hungry for her, my hands roving over her body as if I were a horny teenager with his first girl. I couldn't help it – the thought that she wanted me after all, and that this wasn't some excuse to break it off out of fear but was done out of some sense of chivalry, made me feel as if my chest would explode. My tongue found hers and I sucked it into my mouth, one hand finding her ample breast and squeezing, the other on her ass.

"*Fuck*, I need you." I pressed her down onto the table, sweeping the gift basket and chocolates onto the floor. I couldn't get enough of her, my mouth trailing down her throat to her neck and cleavage. I pulled her sundress over her head and stood over her as she lay on the table in her tiny white bikini. Her breasts spilled out of the top and the bottom barely covered her. "God, you're *luscious*. I want to eat every inch of you."

Her cheeks were pink, her breathing fast, and I knew she was as aroused as me. No longer worried about consent, I untied her bikini top and pulled it down to expose her breasts entirely. What beautiful breasts... heavy and full, the nipples pink and hard in the cool air of the air conditioned bedroom. She must have been too long in the sun, for the start of a sunburn was evident on the tops of her breasts along the bikini line.

"You're sunburnt, you bad thing. As your doctor, I must chastise you severely for that."

Her eyes widened for a moment but then she smiled. "If you're my doctor, isn't there some kind of ethical issue with becoming involved with a patient?"

"Fuck ethics," I murmured against her skin, too aroused to be engaging in playful banter anymore. I couldn't get enough of her breasts, squeezing and sucking her nipples one after the other, my tongue circling the areola, my lips tugging at them, teeth grazing over them softly until she groaned in pleasure, pressing her hips up against me.

I barely heard the knock at the door, my mind so focused on her luscious body, my mouth trailing down her belly and hovering over her pussy to lick her through the fabric.

Ethan. Damn him!

"Katherine? Are you there?" came his gravelly voice. "We have reservations for lunch."

Kate immediately tensed. "Drake!" she whispered.

Finally back in the current moment, I exhaled and rested my forehead on her belly, my mouth still above her pussy.

"Fuck, *Ethan*," I whispered. "You have *horrible* timing." Then I rose up and laid on top of her, grinning. "So close and yet so far."

She smiled back and it was that smile in that moment that

told me she could be my partner in crime. My *willing* partner in crime.

"Katie? Are you OK sweetie?" Ethan said through the door. "We were worried about you." He jiggled the door.

"*Katie?*" I whispered, grinning. "You better answer him. Tell him we'll be right down."

"I'll be right down, Daddy. Give me five minutes, OK?"

"All right, dear," Ethan said. "We're waiting."

Did he know I was in the room with her? Neither Kate nor I said anything for a moment, waiting for them to leave. Once I was sure they had, I buried my face between her naked breasts, wanting to drown myself in her body. I kissed each nipple and then stared in her eyes. "Jesus *Christ*. Am I ever going to get to actually *come* inside of you?"

"You want to?" Kate said and grinned.

"Right now, there is absolutely *nothing* I want more in this world," I said, grinning back widely. "An end to poverty? World peace? Human rights for all? No. I want to fuck you until I come inside of you. Bareback."

"We haven't been tested yet…"

"I have been. I'm clean. I'm know you are as well. You told me and I trust you. I want to see my come dripping out of you."

"*Drake!*"

"Seriously," I said. "You've brought out the animal in me, Kate. We're talking caveman. Warlord claiming territory, plundering." I couldn't stop myself from laughing like an idiot.

"*Plundering…*" she said, smiling.

I rose up over her and brushed a strand of hair from her flushed cheek. She was so delicious, lying there almost naked. I had never wanted a woman as much as I wanted Kate at that moment. Never in the heat of passion or in a moment of total and complete control had I felt this way.

"Once we're alone, once we're *finally* alone, I'm going to fuck you and come inside your body and I'm not even going to worry about making you come, because you owe me one, remember? After that, I'll bathe you and shave your sweet little pussy, and I'll tie you up and make you come three times. Once with my tongue and mouth. Once with my fingers, and once with my cock."

"Oh, *God*." She closed her eyes as if it was too much.

"You like that idea, do you Kate?"

She opened her eyes once more. "Yes," she whispered like she was afraid to admit it. What was she afraid of? For the life of me, I couldn't understand. She wanted it – me – but was still afraid.

"You want me to tie you up and make you come?"

"Yes."

"Yes, what?" I said, wanting her to say the words out loud. I had to have complete certainty that she wanted to submit, that she wanted me to take control, that she wanted me to do what I wanted how I wanted.

She shook her head. "Yes... *Sir?*" she said hesitantly.

I closed my eyes and leaned down, pressing my forehead against hers, smiling. "No, *no*. I want you to say the words." Yes, I *wanted* her to call me 'Master' some day, but I wanted her to feel it. For it to be real for her, and not just something she said to please me or because she thought she had to. That would take time. I had to be patient.

I kissed her, smiling in spite of myself for she was just so damn sweet. "Just say what I said. That you want me to tie you up."

"Oh, yes, please tie me up and make me come, Drake," she said softly, finally understanding my intention.

"You're not ready for *Sir* yet," I said, my gaze moving over her face. "You don't feel it yet. But one day you will be ready and you will feel it. And I will *enjoy* hearing that word come from your sweet lips while you beg me to let you come."

She exhaled, closing her eyes and I could see that those

words affected her deeply. She wanted to submit, to lose control and for me to take it.

I stood up, running my hands down her inner thighs to her pussy. "*Damn*. You're so nice and wet. But we better go or Ethan will be back with firefighters to break down the door."

I pulled her up so that she stood in front of me, her head tilted back to look in my eyes. I leaned down and kissed her.

"I like that you're short," I said. "Petite. It brings out the Dom in me."

"I like when the Dom in you comes out."

"Oh, Kate, you ain't seen *nothing* yet. All you've tasted is vanilla ice cream."

She frowned a bit as if unsure.

"Don't frown," I said, stepping closer. "If you like it now, all I mean is that you'll like it even more when we actually play."

She nodded. "I better change," she said and pointed to her room.

"I'll wait, although I feel like I need to go and jerk off in the bathroom to get rid of this," I said, grasping my still-hard cock, taking her hand and placing it over my length. "But I want to save it for you."

She took in a deep breath, but eagerly squeezed me to test my size.

"I wish I could help you with this," she said, her voice a bit quivery.

"You will. *Later*."

"You know, I still haven't signed anything."

"You will. *Later*," I said, grinning.

"You're so sure of yourself."

"No, I'm not," I said, pulling her into my arms. "I'm just sure of what I want." I was sure. Never more sure. I was sure I wanted her completely to myself. I kissed her, my emotions welling up inside. "I want you."

She sighed audibly and pulled slowly out of my arms. "I better freshen up…"

While she went to the washroom, I took out my cell and called Laurisse to confirm our meeting prior to the conference session. When Kate was done, I waved her over and pulled her against my body.

"Yes, I'll meet you at 1:30," I said to Laurisse. "We can review the slides once before 2:00."

Then I ended the call and put my cell away.

"Business?" she asked.

"Just preparing for our presentation this afternoon at the conference. My colleagues and I are presenting the results of a three-year study on pediatric neuro-electrophysiology. Dr. Marchand and I are doing the presentation at 2:00."

She nodded.

"Let's go down to the restaurant," I said, kissing her on the cheek. "Ethan will be expecting you and I don't want to keep the judge waiting."

She smiled and took my hand when I opened the door to her suite.

We went to the dining room where Ethan and Elaine were seated.

"Look who I ran into on the way over here," Kate said, pointing to me. I felt rather sheepish, considering I'd just been in her room, ravishing her when Ethan had knocked.

Ethan feigned surprise but he wasn't a very good actor. He stood and extended his hand and we shook vigorously. He winked at me.

"Drake, how nice to see you again."

"You can cut the act, Daddy," Kate said, smiling. "Drake already told me you two conspired to bring me here so I could 'get away from it all'."

Ethan looked between us but couldn't keep up the ruse. "Guilty as charged. I confess."

AFTER A NICE MEAL, during which we discussed the conference and made plans to go on a scuba diving excursion, I left and met with Laurisse to go over the conference PowerPoint presentation.

"You're looking very happy," she said when I sat down across from her in her suite.

"I am," I said. "This conference is turning out to be more than entertaining."

"Your girlfriend seemed surprised to see you."

"We had a little misunderstanding back in Manhattan. She wasn't expecting me."

She smiled. "You two made up?"

I nodded. "Everything is straightened out."

It was and I was filled with a sensation of elation and was barely able to focus on the slides as I thought about Kate possibly signing my agreement before the weekend was out.

CHAPTER 20

THE AFTERNOON SESSION went very well, and once Laurisse and I finished answering questions, it was almost four. I left the conference room early, without staying for the second session and met up with Ethan, Elaine and Kate in the lobby.

We took a limo to White Beach Diving Adventures several miles down the coast from our hotel. I greeted the owner, who I had already met on a previous trip to the Bahamas, and we had an hour's worth of instruction on scuba diving. Once the lecture was over, we all suited up but Kate was a bit more difficult to fit. She had mistakenly worn her underwear instead of her bathing suit, and so had to be fitted while in her underwear. Kate was petite with thin bones and an ample bosom, so the only woman's size left was too big in the body and too small in the bust.

The instructor held up yet another wetsuit for her to try.

"This is all we have left. It's old."

Kate made a face as she examined it. "Maybe I should just stay behind."

"Nonsense," Ethan said. "Suit up and let's go."

Kate disappeared behind the curtain but after several long moments, she popped her head out of the stall. "Um, I need a bit of help with this zipper…"

Elaine was getting dressed herself so I went in the change room where she was struggling with the zipper.

"It's a bit rusted," she said, trying to hold the two sides of the zipper close together. I tried to keep a smile off my face but she looked so desirable, her hair up, her cheeks pink, her breasts squished together. Finally, I took hold of the zip loop and pulled, but it didn't budge. I jiggled the zipper up and down, but it was completely stuck.

"That's what you get for having such luscious breasts," I whispered as I gave one strong jerk on the zipper latch. "Squeeze them a bit more, pull the two sides closer."

She did, her cheeks reddening.

"Christ, you're going to give me a boner, Kate."

"You better not get one," she said. Then, she glanced down at me and her eyes widened. "You look like you already do."

I glanced down. "No, I'm soft. I'm just a *shower*, not a *grower*."

"A *what?*"

"A shower. I *show* my length all the time, and only thicken up and harden when I get an erection. Most men are growers. They're smaller when soft and grow in length when they have an erection."

"*Oh*," she said, smiling up at me shyly. "So what I see is what I get?"

"More or less," I said. "In terms of length, at least." Then I caught her eye. "As you learned from Big, length isn't as important as girth when it comes to a woman's pleasure…"

"Drake!"

I grinned widely at her expression and gave one huge tug and the zipper finally complied.

"There," I said, straightening her shoulders. "Confined." I glanced at her body, which looked luscious all wrapped in rubber. "I might be convinced to put you in some latex at some point. A nice black latex cat suit would be really delicious…"

Kate wiggled around in the suit, trying to make it fit better.

"We have to get going," the instructor said through the door. "Those suits are thin but if you wear them for any length of time in this warmth, you'll overheat. Most accidents in triathlons are due to people overheating while waiting for their wave of swimmers to leave the shore."

We all went to the boats, where an assistant instructor loaded our gear. I had already been scuba diving several times, so I buddied up with Kate instead of one of the staff. I was pleased to be her partner, for it would allow me to 'take control' over her and show her how I could be the one to lead.

Our dive was short but enjoyable, and although I was ready to keep on exploring the reef, we had only a short dive planned. We returned to the marina and Kate had as much difficulty getting out of the suit as she had getting in.

Ethan stood outside her stall. "Sweetie? Do you need some help?"

"Yes," Kate said, her voice sounding frustrated. "Its just as hard to unzip."

I went inside her stall and took hold of the zipper and gave it a few good yanks, but had no luck. I tried everything I could think of but the zipper would not budge. The instructor came in with some oil and drizzled it over the zipper, but that did nothing to help matters. All it accomplished was to make our hands all oily.

I had changed into my board shorts and sandals, my chest bare. Ethan and Elaine were also back in their street clothes, leaving Kate in her rubber suit. I could tell by the color in her cheeks that she was starting to overheat.

"Phew," she said and waved her face with a hand. "I'm getting hot."

"We need to get you out of this," I said, feeling a touch of alarm.

"Is everything all right in there?" Ethan called out.

I went out to speak with them. "There's a problem with the zipper. It'll take a bit but we may have to cut her out of the suit. Why don't you two go back to the hotel and we'll meet you back there for a drink before dinner?"

Ethan nodded. "I'll send the limo back. Are you sure everything's all right?"

"No problem," I said, not wanting to alarm him.

The instructor came in with me and both of us took turns yanking on the zipper, but it was firmly stuck. Then just when the instructor was going to get a pair of scissors to start cutting Kate out of the suit, I was able to get the zipper down about six inches, right below her bust.

"Maybe you should take the top off so you can cool off," I said. She tried to pull the arms off but the suit was too tight around her bust, the zipper not down far enough.

"*Goddammit*," I said, frustration building. Kate held the top of the suit and I pulled and jerked the zipper but had no luck.

"I'm feeling a bit faint," Kate said, the sweat now running down her neck and face.

"*Christ*," I said, examining her. "We have to cut you out of this – *now*."

We found a small pair of scissors in one of the desk drawers, but they were more suited to cutting fingernails than a rubber wetsuit. Luckily, the instructor found a box cutter in his tool box, which I used to cut around the zipper and down to Kate's crotch, peeling the suit off her, her body slick with sweat. She was faint and her knees gave out so we had to lay her down on a bench and cool her off with bottled water from a cooler. The instructor pointed a fan at her and soon, Kate started to cool down, her heart rate slowing from its rapid pace. She lay practically naked, dressed only in flesh-colored sheer panties and bra, both of which were soaked and left nothing to the imagination. Her pubic hair and nipples were visible through the sheer wet lace.

I fanned her with a magazine and pressed a wet cloth against her forehead and soon she came around. When she sat up, concerned about her state of undress, I knew she was better. A really sick patient is oblivious to how they appear.

When I was certain the danger had passed, I helped Kate sit up and rest for a moment, wanting to ensure she didn't faint when she stood up. The instructor brought her a bottle of fruit juice and some ice-cold water and soon, she was feeling better. I helped her with her sundress, lifting it over her head to cover her wet bra and panties and then we left just in time for the next crew of divers.

The limo was waiting for us and so we returned to the hotel. I held onto Kate as we drove up the coast and back to the hotel on the bay.

"You scared me," I said, running my fingers through her hair. "You were overheating and could have developed hyperthermia if we hadn't gotten you out of the suit. Plus, you have quite a sunburn."

"I'm just glad it's over," she said and sighed. "I thought I was going to faint."

"You almost did."

I lifted her chin with a finger and kissed her softly, glad that I was there to care for her and glad that nothing came of the mishap with the old rubber wetsuit.

Once we were back in the hotel, she yawned and wrapped her arms around herself as if chilled. "I feel really tired," she said. I took her back to her room, knocking on the door to Ethan's room to let them know we had returned. They came right in, just as I was getting Kate onto the bed, comfortably propped up with pillows and a blanket. Ethan went right over to her, after unlocking the adjoining door which connected both rooms.

"What took you so long?" he said.

"We had trouble with the suit and had to cut Kate out of it. She overheated a bit."

"Is she OK?" he said, his bull-dog face concerned, his brow knit.

I nodded. "She just needs to rest. Get some more fluids into her."

Ethan sat on the bed beside Kate. "Maybe you should stay in your room for dinner. Drake can order something in for you. They could send up some turkey and fixings."

Kate smiled faintly and nodded. "I'll just stay here and watch TV."

I put my hand on Ethan's arm. "I'll make sure she's all right. She needs to just rest. We can order something from room service when she gets hungry. You two go ahead."

Ethan and Elaine kissed Kate on the cheek and then left us alone.

"I'm hungry," I said, checking out the menu. "What would you like to eat? Do you really want turkey? Or something local, fresh?"

Kate shook her head. "Whatever you want. I'm just going to close my eyes for a bit."

I called room service, speaking quietly because Kate was starting to drift off, her eyes closing. When I was finished ordering our meal, I sat beside her on the bed and took her wrist to check her pulse. It was fine, slow and steady. I leaned down and kissed her forehead.

"Just rest a bit. I'll watch some headlines."

I stretched out on the bed beside her and turned on the television, switching channels until I found the international news. Beside me, Kate closed her eyes. The afternoon hadn't turned out quite the way I hoped, but I was glad to be there with her.

After a while, I grew sleepy myself and so I turned down the volume to the television and snuggled down behind Kate, who lay on her side with her folded hands tucked under her cheek. She looked so sweet and vulnerable, lying there in her pretty sundress, her skin slightly burnt, her hair fanned out on the pillow like satin. I carefully pressed up against her, spooning my body next to hers, one hand gingerly slipping around her waist and sliding up beneath her breast where I could check her apical pulse if I wanted. It also provided me with a nice handful of her breast. We lay like this for some time, but after about half an hour, she rolled over onto her back and I adjusted my position, all warm and comfortable. I kept my hand on her breast.

"You like keeping your hand there?" she said and smiled.

"I was just taking your pulse, making sure you were okay."

"Yeah, *right*..." she said, grinning up at me.

"Seriously," I said, trying to keep a smile off my face but failing. "You overheated. I wanted to make sure you were all right. I was feeling your apical pulse, just under your left breast." I tried to sound official, but I was bluffing. Of course, I felt her pulse once but it was fine and there was little chance that she'd decompensate at this point. I was enjoying the chance to feel her delicious breast.

"Oh," she said, her cheek pink. "I didn't realize doctors did that."

I couldn't resist her – she was so earnest. I leaned in and nuzzled her neck, pressing my nose against the skin beneath her ear so I could inhale her scent. "No, you sweet thing, I was just kidding. I just like squeezing your lovely breast. But I did also feel your pulse and it was perfect. I *could* have felt it here," I said, slipping my hand down her body from her pubic mound to her inner thigh. "It's called the femoral pulse, but I thought that might be a bit dangerous…"

Of course, it was then that room service showed up with three quick knocks on the door. "That's room service with our meal."

I jumped up and opened the door to admit a waiter wheeling in a cart covered in white linen, with several dishes covered with metal domes to keep the food warm. I signed for the bill and gave the waiter a tip. When we were alone, I lifted the domes and examined the food.

"What did you order?" Kate asked from the bed.

"Fresh fish and vegetables, some salad," I said, inspecting the food. "Not much of a turkey man. Hope you're hungry, because I sure am."

Kate sat upright, watching as I arranged the table, setting out the dishes and pulling the chairs into proper position.

"Come," I said, motioning to the food. "You need some food in you, get your blood sugar up. I'm going to keep you busy tonight and you need your strength."

Kate smiled at that. "You have it all planned out?"

"You know it."

I pulled a chair out and motioned to Kate to join me. She smoothed her hair and dress and then did, taking the seat to my left. Then, I began to feed Kate her meal, wanting to continue looking after her needs while she recovered from her ordeal at the diving club.

"Do you always feed your subs?" she asked, tilting her head to the side while she watched me cut up the fish.

"I don't usually eat meals with my subs," I said, holding out the fork. "But I enjoy looking after them."

"Why?" she asked as I spooned some rice pilaf into her mouth. She chewed for a moment. "Why don't you eat with them?"

"The relationship is just about sex."

"Eating is too personal?"

I nodded. "But I like taking care of a sub's needs. *All* of them. It also reinforces my dominance, which is necessary for submission to work. A sub needs to feel totally cared for, totally safe and cherished if she's going to submit completely. That," I said and examined her as I fed her some more fish. "Your complete submission is what I want."

She let me feed her and seemed to enjoy it as much as I was.

"Have you figured out why you want a woman's complete submission?" she asked while I served myself a plate and sampled the fish. "I imagine, given your training, you'd have some theories..."

I shrugged and cut up some fish, then held the fork up to her mouth. "I need control. I *love* having a woman completely under my control."

"What does that control give you?"

I considered for a moment. Having thought about my interest in D/s a great deal over the years, I thought I had myself figured out.

"When she's tied up completely, willingly, waiting for me to do what I want to her, I am," I said and paused, taking in a deep breath. "Completely *satisfied*. It also makes me incredibly hard. Hearing her moans of pleasure, seeing her response to my touch, my words? Nothing else can get me off as well. But it's that she *wants* it, that she *chooses* it, that she trusts me completely to have her under my control that gets me off."

She nodded. "Lara said she taught you to top someone. You can't get off if the woman takes control?"

I chewed my food for a moment. How to phrase my response? I didn't want Kate to see me as anything but dominant, and telling the story of Lara teaching me to be a Dom might make her question the strength of my need for it.

"I can, and did when Lara topped me. I actually tried out pain, but it did nothing for me personally, either giving or receiving. Lara even got me subs who were painsluts to see if I enjoyed it, but it did nothing for me." I shook my head, remembering. Administering pain never worked for me because while I could work my mind around D/s and the need for power exchange as part of desire, pain was like a black hole to me. I couldn't see into it enough to understand. I always avoided pain with my patients. I treated them for intractable pain. It wasn't something that signaled success to me as a surgeon. Quite the opposite.

"I always felt bad for damaging such lovely flesh. A surgeon is used to cutting into the body, but it's always to heal, fix, improve. We create wounds, yes, but the patient never feels pain while we do it and we pride ourselves on a patient who experiences the least pain possible post-op. I'm curious about sadists and masochists, but in an entirely clinical way, not sexual."

I looked at Kate pointedly. "You don't have to worry. There isn't a sadist hiding inside of me, waiting to get out. I had ample opportunity to see if there was, and no."

"I'm not worried."

"Good. Don't *ever* be."

Kate sighed heavily, and I knew then that something was bothering her still. "What was that sigh about?"

She shook her head. "I just wish this person could understand, Drake. I can't see that they ever will. They had a very traumatic experience and that's made them unable to understand. You and I? We can want each other and be good for each other, satisfy each other's kinks, but this will always be dangerous for you. You have to really think seriously about this. We'll have to really be extremely careful if we carry on when we get back to Manhattan."

"*If* we carry on?" I said, the thought we wouldn't making me upset. "You mean, *when* we carry on back in Manhattan." I leaned down to her, fixing my gaze on her. "I'm not giving up on you that easily. I have yet to plumb your depths, Kate. I want to plumb them. See how deep you go."

She smiled softly at that, and then glanced away.

After we finished our meal, I felt a need to get outside. "Let's go for a walk along the beach now that the sun is down."

WE WENT out of the hotel to the beach and walked along, hand in hand. It was really nice, comfortable and I felt as if Kate's previous reluctance to become involved with me was fading. It felt as if she was starting to trust me. To feel relaxed with me.

"Tell me about your band," she said, glancing up at me when we reached a break wall and had to stop.

"Just a bunch of guys from college," I said, my arm around her shoulder. "We started to play during our Junior year and never stopped. We found our niche and even though we're older than most bands, we enjoy playing."

"I'd like to hear you some day," she said quietly, "or is that also off-limits for your subs?"

I said nothing for a moment, watching the ocean as we stood in an embrace. I didn't like my subs to come to my performances. I didn't like them to be part of my life at all, except sexually. Although I felt more for Kate than I had for my other subs, and had let her more deeply into my life than I usually would, I held back.

"You may not like our music."

"Retro-psychedelic rock?" Kate said, and I could tell from the sound of her voice that my answer hurt her feelings. She forced a smile that didn't reach her eyes. "British Invasion? I heard you talking to my dad at the concert. I like some of it. I've heard my father play it before on those Oldie Goldie satellite radio stations. I don't have to hear you play, if it makes you uncomfortable."

Her response told me everything I needed to know. If I let her in more deeply, she'd want more. Despite the fact I wanted her badly, I wasn't sure that I could give it. I was horrible with relationships.

"I tend to keep things separated. The different parts of my life don't intermingle, Kate."

"I know. I'm sorry. I won't expect anything."

We walked along in silence and I knew I'd blown the evening with my response, but I didn't want to encourage Kate to expect anything more than I could give. I was great at sex. I was terrible at love.

I stopped her and pulled her into my arms, not wanting to bruise her delicate heart. "Lovely *Katherine*," I said and stroked her cheek. "I've already gone off my usual routine with you, broken my own rules. Let's play things by ear, okay?"

She looked up at me with those wide green eyes, so open and so guileless and I felt a stab of something in my chest.

"Okay," she said but her voice was resigned rather than hopeful. "You're the one in charge."

I stroked her cheek, wishing more than anything that she could be happy with what I could give her.

"Thank you for understanding."

Back in the hotel room, Kate knocked on the door to her father's suite to say goodnight, but they were out. I sat and checked my email while Kate brushed her teeth. At first, I wondered whether she would actually invite me into her hotel room, fearing that she'd be afraid to have me stay the night due to her father's proximity.

I popped my head into the bathroom. "I'm just going to zip to my own room for a moment," I said. "I have to get a few things, but I'll be right back."

She nodded and so I left the room and went to my own to get my briefcase and overnight bag. I wanted to show Kate the agreement I sent her and get her to open up about it, tell me how she felt and what upset her so much that she reconsidered. Kate was not the type to be so candid, but I had to force the issue with her. If she was going to be my sub, and I was determined to make her mine, she had to be absolutely truthful with me about how she felt, what she liked and didn't like, and what she needed. If she hid things, if she lied to please me, the relationship soon would fall apart and I knew that it would probably end up hurting me more than her.

With Kate, I felt as if the stakes were higher for me than for her. I was a gamble for Kate. I was something different that she might find exciting and out of character for her given her very vanilla past. I was older than her by quite a bit. I had a very busy life and she might need more than I could give her. On the other hand, she was perfect for me in every way. If I failed with her, I would fail big time.

I returned to the room with a slight pall of dread hanging over me for some reason. She was standing by her bed, dressed in a tiny black lacy nightgown which barely covered her delicious breasts.

"You look lovely," I said and ran my fingers over the tops of her breasts. "Come with me. I want us to talk about the agreement."

I led her into the living room where I left my briefcase. I removed my print copy of the agreement and sat down on the sofa. "Come here and sit on my lap," I said, patting my lap.

She complied, sitting across my lap, her hands resting on my shoulders. As usual, she avoided looking me in the eye. I held out the agreement.

"I want to talk about what upset you when you read it the first time."

She took it from me and glanced at it, her eyes moving down over the page. "Do you have a pen?"

"Yes, but before you sign, you have to tell me what you want removed," I said, wanting to ensure she knew how important it was to be truthful. "How you feel about the limits I've listed."

"Where's your pen?" she said again. She checked my shirt pocket and found the fountain pen I'd brought along in the hopes that at some point during the weekend, she'd sign. My father's pen, it had a polished burled-wood barrel and a gold nib. I carried it around even though I didn't use it much.

"This is beautiful."

"That was my father's pen," I said and examined it. "He was so old fashioned about some things. Felt that disposable pens were bad environmentally."

"You're so sentimental, Drake."

I smiled. "I guess. So," I said and pulled her closer, wanting to get to the meat of the discussion. "Tell me about what parts of my limits bothered you when you first read it. We can negotiate. I want you to feel completely secure when you sign."

She nodded and pulled out of my arms, then went to the desk and opened the document to the page with signature lines.

"Is this where I sign?"

I frowned and followed her to the table. Her hand was poised with the pen, ready to sign. I stopped her, my hand on hers.

"Kate, you haven't answered my questions. You can't sign until we've gone through each item."

"I've already read this," she said softly. "I've thought about it ever since I received it." She signed her name.

"Kate," I said, my eyes meeting hers. "I know you were concerned about something. Tell me. I won't sign until you do."

"I trust you, Drake," she said, handing me the pen. "You won't hurt me. I'm OK with the agreement the way it is."

"What about this?" I said, and pointed to the clause mentioning anal sex. "And this?" I pointed to vaginal fisting.

"I trust you, Drake," she repeated. "I know you'll keep me safe and only go as far as I can handle."

I stared at her for a moment, needing to see how serious she was. She surprised me completely, signing so quickly, insisting on it. I expected to have to calm her fears, spend time – maybe all evening, talking about everything. Finally, I took the pen and signed below hers. Then I turned to her and pulled her into my arms.

"Oh, sweet *Katherine*," I said, emotion welling up in me. "You surprise me. But you've made me very happy."

"I want to make you happy."

I leaned down and kissed her, and it was a very tender emotional moment for me. For Kate, it was probably just an adventure, but for me, someone experienced in the lifestyle, signing a contract was far more meaningful. More solemn. I didn't think she was truly ready for it yet, but I think she wanted to be ready. I hoped I hadn't made a big mistake in signing so quickly.

Then, I pushed all doubts aside and pulled her into the bathroom and took off her nightgown, staring at her beautiful nakedness before me. As much as I wanted her right then and there, the physician in me couldn't help but notice her sunburn. Only momentarily though. I had imagined this night – when she signed my contract and was mine completely. My first order of business was to shave her smooth. Then, I was finally going to eat her the way I wanted to from the moment I first thought of having her as my sub.

"Your burn is getting worse." I went to my overnight bag

and removed my shaving kit where I had a can of shaving cream and a razor. "Here," I said and brought them to the bathroom. "I'm going to shave you and then I'm going to eat you and fuck you. Are you ready?"

"Yes," she said, her voice wavering with excitement.

"Yes, what?" I said, looking at her squarely, trying to appear dominant even if I felt a bit out of control and ecstatic at the prospect she was all mine.

"Yes, whatever it is you want me to say."

"You signed the contract," I said, my eyes hooded. "What does it say?"

"Yes, Sir," she said, smiling coyly.

"Don't you smile when you call me *Sir*, or you'll ruin the whole effect," I said, having to keep myself from smiling and ruining the mood. "When we're together, I want you to consider us in scene. I'll call you either *Katherine* or slave, depending on how I feel. When you call me Sir, make sure it has a capital 'S'. Do you understand?"

"Yes, Sir," she said, and I could tell she was fighting to keep a straight face, her lips pressed tightly together. "Why Katherine, if I may ask?"

"It's what I first knew you as – *Katherine*," I said. "It's more formal and will keep me in proper Dom headspace. I'll give you a bit of leeway at first with proper forms of address," I said, fighting a grin as well, "but if you continue to be saucy, I'll have to spank your delicious little ass. Do you understand?"

"Yes, *Sir*," she said and she managed just barely to keep a straight face. "What if I said I wanted you to spank me, just so I could know what it felt like?"

I shook my head, my brow furrowed. "I'll be spanking you soon enough, Katherine. There's no way with that mischievous look in your eyes that you won't need one. But first, I'm going to fuck you the way I want." Then, I ran a bath while she stood and examined the bottle of aloe gel on the counter.

"Come and sit in the bath," I said, pointing to the tub. "We need to soften up your pubic hair before I shave you."

She obeyed, sitting in the warm water while I arranged the shaving kit on the counter. I had a razor, shaving cream, and an electric wet/dry shaver. I ran hot water in the sink and threw in a couple of washcloths.

"Stand up," I said, and sat on the toilet beside the bathtub. She complied without a word. "Spread your legs wide," I said, my voice firm. Shaving a sub was both very sexy and at times humorous. I'd try to keep it sexy. She rested her hands on my shoulders while I shaved her pudenda and inner thighs.

"Put one leg on the side of the tub," I said, pointing to her. She obeyed once more without question, although this exposed her labia to me. I glanced up and saw her flushed cheeks and knew she was both embarrassed and probably quite aroused. I added more shaving cream and used the razor to get the rest of the hair between her thighs and labia. Soon, she was completely bare, her skin smooth.

"Perfect," I said, running a washcloth over the area, then my fingers to check for stray hairs. I glanced up in her eyes. "Nice and smooth. I can see everything now." I stood and took her hand. "It makes me hard as rock. Now, I'm going to eat you the way I wanted since I first met you, when you were on the bed with your garters and nylons showing. Before I do, I have to apply some of this," I said and picked up the bottle of aloe vera.

"What's that?" she asked, her brow furrowed.

I noted that she forgot to say 'Sir' and caught her eye, my brows raised.

"I'm sorry," she said immediately. "What's that, Sir?"

"It's aloe vera. It's for your burn. Can't be fucking you roughly if your burns are hurting."

I poured some of the aloe gel into my hand and then applied it to her burned skin, on her cheeks, the tops of her shoulders and breasts, the front and back of her arms, her belly, and the tops of her thighs.

"Are you being Doctor or Dom now, Sir?" she said, her voice breathless.

"Doctor Dom," I replied, grinning in spite of my best attempts to sound all Dom. "Now, stop being so cheeky, Katherine, or I'll have to put you over my knee and teach you about punishment."

She covered her mouth to hide her grin. When I saw it, it made me smile even more widely. "Oh, *you*," I said and pulled her into my arms, squeezing her tightly. I kissed the top of her head. "I can see I'm going to get nowhere with you tonight, Ms. Bennet. If you were any other sub…"

"If I were any other sub what?" she said and then caught herself. "Sir, I mean."

"If you were any other sub, I wouldn't be smiling."

"Smiling is good, Sir. I read that it releases good brain chemicals."

"That it does. Now, *Katherine*," I said and pulled away, forcing a stern expression on my face. "No more talking. Time to submit and become my slave as you agreed in the contract."

I took her hand and led her back into the bedroom. We stood beside the bed, and I stood behind her and kissed her neck and shoulder. I had to get her into the proper mood and had to replace the playful mood we'd been in with one more serious.

"Close your eyes," I said as I touched her softly, pulling her hair away and over to one side, my lips at her ear. "Just give yourself over to me."

She leaned back against me and I felt her body relax as she tried to do what I commanded. I touched her firmly but not aggressively, my hand roving down her body, over her shoulders, down her arms, one hand squeezing one breast while the other slipped down over the soft curve of her hip to her pussy.

I kissed her neck, licking her skin while I pressed my fingers against her mound, making slow movements so I could build sensation. I wanted her to imagine me licking her labia, her clit under my tongue. She made little whimpering sounds that pleased me, a short gasp when I slipped a finger between her lips and stroked her clit.

Then I sat on the edge of the bed and pulled her between my thighs, my arms wrapped around her for a moment while I continued to stroke her skin. With one hand I kneaded her buttock, the other cupping her breasts, tweaking her nipple, pulling it into a hard point. My cock was rock hard in response, straining at my shorts, my heart beating more rapidly. I felt almost dizzy with lust as I touched her, listened to her breathing, felt her warm skin under my lips.

"I told you I was going to use your body for my own pleasure, Katherine," I said, using a firm tone with her to keep her in the proper submissive mood. "And I'm going to. You're not allowed to come, do you understand?"

Of course, she would come, but giving her the command not to do so would make it all the more exciting as she tried to obey.

"What if I can't help it?" she said, gasping when I sucked one nipple, my teeth grazing the puckered areola. "Sir," she quickly added. I smiled against her neck.

"A simple yes or no is all that's required."

"Yes," she said, her voice husky. "*Sir*."

"You have to learn that you're only allowed to come when I want you to," I said firmly. "I know when you're ready and when you deserve an orgasm. If you feel like you're going to come, you must tell me immediately."

I slipped my fingers between her lips and stroked her clit firmly and she gasped and pressed herself against me hungrily.

"I don't want you to come this time, Katherine," I said. "I

want you to just feel well-used. I want you to get used to being an object for my pleasure."

"Then why are you arousing me, Sir?"

"Shh," I said, a finger on her lips. "No talking. I want you to feel how I felt the other night when you came so quickly and we were rudely interrupted. You have to yield up every bit of power to me, Katherine, when we're together. I decide everything. What we do, how we do it, if and when you come, and how you come." I continued to stroke her clit, then slipped my fingers a bit deeper, teasing the entrance to her body. "You've probably spent most of your life trying to keep quiet when you have an orgasm, Katherine. I want you to be loud. I want your eyes open and staring into mine."

She groaned when I stroked her g-spot, her hips thrusting against my fingers.

"You're so nice and *wet*, Katherine. You're almost ready for me."

Then I removed my fingers and pushed her back onto the bed.

"Crawl up farther," I said as I removed my shirt and shorts. She moved up farther on the bed as I commanded, her eyes expectant.

"Are you going to tie me up?"

I frowned, for not only was I *not* going to tie her up, she hadn't used 'Sir' when addressing me.

"*Sir*, I mean," she said when she remembered.

"Katherine, a slave doesn't ask her Master what he plans. She merely submits happily."

"But you said…"

"Shh," I said and took her hands and placed them above her head. That was as far as we were going to get in terms of bondage. She was nowhere near ready to be really restrained. "Keep your hands together like that. Imagine that they're restrained and tied to the bed frame. Don't let go no matter what."

"Why aren't you going to restrain me for real?"

"*Kate*," I said, a bit frustrated with her continued questions. "You have to let *me* decide these things."

She finally complied and said nothing, her hands stretched above her hand.

"Now, close your eyes and keep them closed until I tell you to open them," I instructed. "I don't want you distracted by anything besides how your body feels."

She nodded.

I spread her thighs and lay between them, kissing her neck and then her breasts, sucking each nipple, squeezing them before running my teeth softly over each nub. I wanted to tease her with the knowledge that I'd soon eat her, but I'd make her suffer a long wait first. I wanted her almost ready to come when I did finally lick her. I wanted to feel her body shake beneath me.

Her pussy was smooth and now hairless and I licked it all over, the external labia, and around her inner thighs. I avoided her clit and inner labia for as long as I could, until I saw her holding her breath. Then, when I finally licked her inner lips and clit with one long sweep of my tongue, she groaned out loud. When I sucked her into my mouth completely, she gasped, her body trembling.

"Remember," I said, pulling off her. "You can't come this time. You have to tell me if you feel like you will."

She said nothing, her eyes closed, and I knew she was close. I slipped my fingers inside her warm silky wetness and began sucking and licking once more.

"I…" she gasped, her hands in my hair. "I'm going to…"

I pulled off and removed my fingers, letting her come down a bit. She lay still, almost panting,

"Good *girl*," I said. "Keep your eyes closed."

I stood up and pulled her back to the edge of the bed, her legs spread wide, and positioned her feet on the edge. "Put your hands above your head again. Now, I'm going to fuck you until I come inside of you. You're not allowed to come this time."

She nodded, licking her lips, her eyes closed.

Now, I stimulated her with my cock, which was heavy and thick in my hand, the tip wet with fluid. I ran the head all over her external labia and then over her slit, nudging it in at the entrance to her body before stroking her clit with it once more. I repeated this, slipping a bit deeper each time. As I had done with her at her apartment – I knew this would get her ready.

"I'm going…" she said, gasping as I pulled out, her thighs quaking. I waited another couple of moments for her to cool down again before I started stimulating her once more. When I was fully inside of her, I kept still and leaned over her so I could look at her face.

"Open your eyes," I said, my voice firm. She complied, her eyes languid, half-lidded with desire. "I'm teaching you patience, Katherine. You have to get used to obeying me. You have to turn your body and mind over to me completely. Just *feel*."

She nodded without speaking.

"Now close your eyes again."

She did and so I began again, slowly entering her a bit more with each thrust. I didn't touch her clit, just fucked her until my entire length was inside her warm wetness. I closed my eyes and just enjoyed the sensation, I knew I'd have to watch myself, keep my focus on Kate. I reached down and stroked her clit, wanting her to come now, despite telling her she couldn't.

I wanted her to lose control. For me to make her come and for her to be unable to stop herself.

"I'm going to…" she said through gritted teeth, and I could

see she was trying so hard not to come but was ready, oh so ready, to go over the edge. I leaned back over her.

"Open your eyes," I said quickly. "Look in mine."

She did, and instead of stopping once more to let her cool down, I kept thrusting, close to my own edge, having to focus on her to stop myself from coming.

"Oh, *God*..." she gasped, her body tensing, eyes rolling up a bit.

"Say my name," I ordered, wanting to hear it from her lips. "Say my name when you come."

I fucked her hard and fast, wanting to push her as far as I could.

"*Say my name.*"

She tried but could barely speak above a whisper. "*Drake...*"

Then her body arced and her face slackened and I knew she was coming. I thrust harder, faster, watching her as I did. Then I came, the pleasure surging up from my balls and through my groin.

I collapsed onto her, my face in the crook of her neck, gasping for breath in her ear.

Finally...

Finally I'd fucked her, after weeks of imagining it, planning for it. Needing it and her.

"I don't understand," she said, a look of confusion on her flushed face. "I thought you didn't want me to come, but you made me come on purpose."

I pulled back, my face over hers, my eyes locked on hers. Finally, I smiled, enjoying how innocent she was.

"Kate, my whole reason for existence when we're together is to make you come."

"But then, why did you tell me..."

I kissed her neck once more and then rose up. I spread her legs and watched as I pulled my now-softening cock out of her.

"Perfect," I said as I watched my come dripping out of her pussy.

She smiled and covered her face with her hands.

"Why did you tell me I wasn't supposed to come?" she asked again.

I leaned back down between her thighs, my face above hers, and stroked her cheek.

"I have to learn your body like it was my own because I want to own it. You have to get used to taking orders from me. You have to get used to me controlling your response. I watched you get closer and closer with what I did to you so I could learn to judge when you're no longer able to hold back. I watched your body and your face. I listened to your breathing for how erratic it became when you started to come, watched your skin for how it flushed when you were ready, saw your nipples as they puckered when your orgasm started, how your belly tightened as your muscles tensed. They're all clues that let me know how you're feeling, how you're responding to each thing I do to you. Eventually, I'll be able to tell you're close without you having to tell me. But you'll still have to ask permission. I want to control your orgasms, Kate. It's my kink."

She nodded, as if finally understanding.

"I want your every orgasm to be mine."

"Why?" she said, opening her eyes.

I shook my head, having wondered the same thing many times before. Psychoanalysis requires you to understand your own motivations. I was as curious about my need for control as my own analyst had been. It was a combination of things, primarily due to a feeling of loss of control as a child.

"Why does it matter?" I said, not wanting to get into it. "I just do. There's no big mystery. It gets me off. When I really feel your complete submission, that moment when I know you are completely mine, it will be," I said, pausing for the right words. "Bliss."

"Bliss," she said, mirroring my own words.

"Hopefully, when you do submit completely, you'll feel it, too."

"I thought I did."

I smiled. "No, not even close. We're just starting, Kate," I said, stroking her cheek with the backs of my fingers. "I have to learn every inch of you. I have to learn all your little kinks. All the things that send you over. I have to feel you give more and more control to me. Unquestioning. You have to do things without a thought and you're still thinking. It will take a while. But it will be so worth it for us both."

I kissed her neck, her throat and the tops of her breasts, feeling for the first time since I met her that she was actually going to be mine.

We went to bed after washing up and brushing our teeth side by side in her bathroom. Usually, that kind of mundane relationship thing would kill my mood, but with Kate, it felt good. We slipped beneath the covers and I pulled her against my body, one hand beneath her breast.

"Why are you sleeping here with me?" she asked. "I thought you'd go back to your own room."

I said nothing for a moment. "I thought I'd stay with you tonight, make sure you're all right after the day you had. You've got a bad sunburn, and you had a touch of heat stroke."

"So you're in charitable doctor mode?"

I kissed her shoulder. "Something like that." I sighed after a while, thinking to myself that I was really breaking my rules. "To tell you the truth, I've gone a bit off the reservation, so to speak."

She rolled over onto her back and looked at me, her eyes shining in a sliver of light from the window.

"Off the reservation?"

"I've broken my own rules with you."

"How?"

I stroked my hand over her shoulder and down her arm. "I told you. I keep things in their own place. I don't like them to mix."

"Why? Were you one of those kids who kept their food on separate parts of the plate, not letting them touch?"

I laughed at that but it was a good metaphor for my life. I tried hard not to get too enmeshed in the lives of my subs. I didn't want to need them. I didn't want them to need me.

"It gets messy."

"*What* gets messy?" she said.

"*Katherine…*" I kissed her forehead. "Is this twenty questions?"

She didn't speak for a moment and I knew then I'd hurt her. "You want to understand *me*, Drake. Why can't I want to understand you?"

"That's *not* how it's supposed to work," I replied. "You're supposed to just let me do the thinking. Let me do the knowing. You just let go of control when you're with me and relax. I should remain this dark and powerful enigma."

"Dr. *Enigma*," she said, smiling just a bit. "I think I get it. You want to stay a bit mysterious so I feel more submissive when I'm with you. Am I right?"

"Something like that. Now, shush," I said softly. "Go to sleep. I'm going to fuck you first thing before the conference starts and I want you all bright eyed and bushy tailed. Fair warning."

"*Bright eyed and bushy tailed…*" she said chidingly. "How will I be able to sleep after you tell me that? Too bad I didn't bring *Big* along…"

"You've got the real Big right *here*," I said and thrust my hips against her. "Don't you try to get me all hard again, Katherine." I nuzzled her neck. "I have to present my paper tomorrow morning in another session. I have to *sleep*."

Beside me, Kate sighed. "Good *night*, Drake."

"Good night, Ms. *Bennet*," I said, smiling at her. "I'm beginning to think that name suits you to a tee and I should start calling you *Elizabeth*."

"Did you read *Pride and Prejudice*?" She sounded surprised.

I pulled her closer, my arms around her. "Dave isn't the only person in the world to take a Victorian Lit course in college. I read *Pride and Prejudice*, but I'm more a Brontë *Wuthering Heights* fan."

She didn't say anything for a moment as if digesting that fact.

"Why did you like *Wuthering Heights* so much?"

"*Kate*..." I yawned, not really wanting to get into the whole identification I felt with Heathcliff. "Tomorrow. I promise that, after I fuck you, I'll tell you all about my love of Emily Brontë over breakfast..."

"*Wuthering Heights* is so ... depressing," she said. "Tragic. *Pride and Prejudice* is happily ever after."

"Shh," I said, squeezing her once more. "I don't believe in *happily ever after*, Kate. I've studied psychology. I've been divorced. Now *please*. Women's brains have this tendency to become more active after a good fucking. Men need *sleep*. Very strong *hint*..."

She said nothing more after that and for a moment, I felt a bit bad for shutting her down when she obviously felt like talking. It wasn't only that I was exhausted. It was that I felt strange talking to her like that. I didn't do the whole sleepover schtick. I didn't get into deep conversations with my subs. I didn't wax poetic or philosophic with them. I tied them up, tortured them with pleasure, made them come several times, and then fucked them until I did. End of story.

This whole trip was probably a huge mistake, but for whatever reason, I went along with it and even encouraged it. I felt conflicting emotions as we lay together in bed, her snuggled into my arms. Part of me was ecstatic. I'd finally fucked Kate – something I'd been fantasizing about way too much for someone like me, who didn't do that sort of thing.

The other part was on guard, as if some dark and ominous threat loomed just out of sight. I knew it was there.

I had no idea when it would rear its ugly head and break my heart.

I closed my eyes and exhaled heavily, determined to shut my mind off and not let my worries about this – relationship – whatever it turned out to be – ruin my peace of mind.

CHAPTER 21

When I next woke, I was alone in bed. Kate was in the bathroom for I saw a sliver of light under the door.

I rose and went to the door, opening it to see if she was okay. Kate was sitting with her head in her hands.

"What's the matter?" I started inside, conscious that she was on the toilet but she looked as if she were in distress "Are you feeling OK?"

"Drake, I'm taking a pee..." she said, putting something in her bag. "Can you give me a moment?"

"Sorry." I stepped out of the bathroom doorway. "I was worried you were feeling sick from your burn."

She finally flushed the toilet and came out, frowning.

"Are you OK?"

"My burn hurts," she said, her voice a bit quivery. "I thought I'd put some aloe on it."

I nodded and ran my fingers over the burn on her breasts. "Let me do that."

"I can do it," she said, pushing my hands away.

"I *like* to do it." I took the bottle out of her hands and turned her around, lifting her so that she sat on the vanity, her back to the mirror. I leaned closer between her thighs and pulled down one of the straps to her nightgown. Seeing her delicious breast like that sent blood rushing to my dick. I was determined to take care of her before I fucked her, so I squeezed some aloe out and smoothed it over the burns on her shoulders and breasts.

"This is going to make me hard."

"It's still really *early*…" she said, a hint of protest in her voice.

"Six hours of sleep is my usual." I smiled at her, trying to get her mood lighter but she wasn't responding to me. "You're so delicious in that black lace. But even more delicious out of it." I hiked up the hem so that her thighs and newly shaved pussy were exposed. Then I poured a bit of aloe gel on her thighs where the burn was worst and spread it over them. "Oh, I am definitely getting hard because of this."

"I need to take a shower first," she said and I got the sense that she wanted to avoid me for some reason.

I put the bottle of aloe down and leaned against her, kissing her throat and neck, hoping to ignite her desire as mine had been seeing her half-naked and touching her skin.

"This is waterproof," I said, sliding my fingers up her inner thigh to her groin. "Oh, you're so nice and *smooth*…"

I pulled away, my erection jutting out, hard as rock. "I'll turn the shower on. You get naked."

I turned away and started the shower, entering it, motioning to Kate to come in with me. There was enough room for four people and I decided I was going to fuck her in the shower.

Once she was inside, I took a bar of soap and lathered up, then washed her, starting with her shoulders and moving down over her breasts. I was going to work her up slowly, my soapy hands sliding over her skin, squeezing her breasts, pulling her nipples until they were hard nubs.

I moved lower over her belly and between her thighs. She

gasped softly when I slipped my fingers between her labia, one hand sliding around to her ass.

"There," I said, turning her back, letting the spray rinse off all the soap. I was going to eat her first and so when she was all clean, I shut off the water. "All clean."

I knelt down on the floor, taking her leg, placing it over my shoulder. I glanced up at her, wanting to hold her eye while I licked her to increase the intimacy. "I'm going to eat you, Kate. Put your leg over my other shoulder. Hold on to those bars for support. Remember to tell me if you feel like you're going to come."

She did, her thighs shaking when I spread her lips and began to lick her all over, my tongue circling her clit, then sliding lower to the entrance to her body. I slipped two fingers into her warmth and was rewarded with another small gasp and her body clenching around my fingers. I couldn't wait to slide my aching cock inside of her.

"Drake, I..." Kate whispered, but I didn't stop. I kept licking, sucking her clit into my mouth, my fingers stroking inside of her. "Drake, I'm going to *come...*"

I glanced up and saw her gritted teeth and knew she was going to come, and was fighting it as best she could. Finally, she moaned out loud. "Oh, *God...*"

Then I felt her orgasm start when her muscles clenched rhythmically, rapidly, her whole body tensing. I pulled my mouth away and stared into her eyes as she gasped above me, her arms shaking.

Then I let her stand upright again, my rock-hard dick pressing against her belly.

"Turn around," I commanded and she complied like a good submissive, spreading her thighs without me having to ask, gripping the safety bars for support. I entered her from behind, sliding deep inside of her, easily because she was nice and wet from her orgasm. I slid my hand around her body and stroked her clit, determined to make her come again while I fucked her. I angled my cock so that I bumped her g-spot with each slow shallow thrust, while I stimulated her clit with my fingers.

Soon, she was helping me, pressing back against me with each thrust.

"Drake," she said, breathless once more, "I'm going to come again."

I didn't stop, just kept sliding inside of her a few inches, my fingers never stopping their slow, agonizing tease. She was breathing rapidly, and I knew she was close once more.

"*Drake*…"

"*Come* for me," I said, and started thrusting faster, entering her all the way. "Say my name when you come," I whispered, biting her shoulder. "Say my *name*."

She gasped but didn't respond.

"*Say my name*," I demanded, so close myself I thought I wouldn't be able to control myself.

"*Drake*…" She groaned, and shuddered, her whole body quaking.

Feeling her clench around my cock sent me over, the pleasure blinding. I gripped her hips, thrusting through my ejaculation until I had to stop. I leaned against her, my hands spread on the wall, my cock still deep inside her.

"*Fuck*…" I gasped in her ear and then slipped one hand down to stroke her body, from her neck and over her breasts, then to her pussy once more. "That was so good."

She gasped when I touched her clit softly and I smiled. Finally, I slipped out of her and turned her around, bending down to kiss her, pulling her into my arms.

"There," I said and stroked her cheek. "That's two for one, I think."

She smiled and closed her eyes, but I had this sense that she was holding back. "Are you keeping track?"

I leaned down and pressed my face in her neck, hiding my smile while I kissed her skin.

"I'm greedy that way."

I left Kate in her room and went back to mine for a while, to change my clothes and sort through my notes before the conference started. I felt ecstatic for despite the little problem with Kate's suit and her hyperthermia, we had a very good night together and the sex, while vanilla, was really good for us both. It wasn't mind altering life changing sex, but it gave me hope that we were simpatico and that I would eventually be able to read her when we were in scene and know what she needed and how far she wanted to go. Then, we'd reach mind-altering. Life changing. Frankly, I would have been satisfied to have a plain vanilla relationship with her, but was glad that she was at least intrigued by kink and wanted to try it. I had no idea how deep we would get, but I wanted to explore everything with her.

I wanted to go as far and as deep as she wanted and needed. Whatever that ended up being, I'd be content.

I knew Kate was more than just a sub. I could feel myself sinking into something that felt like infatuation, but bigger. I'd done so many things with Kate that I had written down on my "never do this with a sub" list. We'd gone out for a meal and to my favorite restaurant on top of it. A place with so many memories of my father and my youth. It had great sentimental value for me. I'd gone to the concert with her. We were together in a paradise, and had spent the night together. I'd slept over.

I was including her firmly in my life outside of kink.

I should have been keeping her at arm's-length, I shouldn't have pursued her or encouraged Ethan to bring her to the Bahamas, but there was a part of me that was running headlong towards her and the other parts just didn't care enough to stop me. In fact, I had this sense that they were cheering me on.

I pushed the whole business out of my mind and tried to concentrate on the day and my responsibilities. I met my fellow presenters in the coffee shop for a quick bite before the conference started, eschewing the conference fare of Danishes and bagels for some eggs and toast. We talked about the conference schedule and what we expected in terms of questions from the audience. We went over the agenda for the session.

I was doing really well and almost forgot about Kate and the whole issue of our relationship. Almost. Then, I glanced out at the water and the white beach, and thought about my walk with Kate the previous evening. She wanted to hear my band play but it was on the list of no-no's. Subs did not become enmeshed in my life, especially not my music or band.

It had meant the end to my relationship with Allie.

I felt reluctant to invite Kate into that part of my life, seeing it as a bulwark of sorts against full encroachment. Not that my music life was so very private – after all, I performed in front of an audience, however small. It was just one more way someone could get into my head, into my life.

I had the sense that if I denied Kate, she'd be the one to leave me but of all people, Kate should understand how personal music could be. After all, she didn't want me to be there when she listened to the first part of the Veteran's Day concert. Still, I had the sense that Kate would want me to be part of it if we were a couple. I knew she'd want to be part of my music, too.

I sighed and tried to focus on the conference, and on my presentation.

THE CONFERENCE SESSION went without a hitch. Our slides worked, my presentation was smooth, and there were interesting questions and really little in the way of criticism.

My colleague from Mass General invited me along with his

small group of physicians for lunch, and I agreed. It would be good for Kate and I to spend time apart. I sent her a text to let her know that I'd come by later. I'd be glad to miss the afternoon sessions and thought we could spend time together.

I escaped the others when the afternoon session started and went to Kate's room. I had a key card and so I entered and went inside.

Kate lay on the bed, her back to the room. I took off my shoes and slid onto the bed beside her, pulling her into my arms. I was ready for a nice kiss from her, but she seemed startled and pushed against me.

"Drake, I was *sleeping*."

"Sorry," I said, stroking her hair, thinking I must have scared her. "I missed you all day. I've been thinking of you, planning what I was going to do to that luscious body of yours when I was finally finished with the conference, which is, *now*."

I nibbled her neck, wanting to feel her relax into my arms, but instead, her body stiffened.

"Not now," she said, pushing me away again.

I pulled back and leaned on my elbow, trying to read her face. "What's the matter?"

She sat up on the bed and wrapped her arms around her legs. She yawned. "I didn't sleep well I guess."

"I know how to wake you up," I said, grinning suggestively. I ran the backs of my fingers over the tops of her breasts and while she shivered in response, she frowned.

"Ow, my burn." She pulled away.

"Sorry." I lay back on the bed, my hands behind my head and watched her for a moment. "What have you been doing?"

"We went for a boat ride and then had lunch. I've been sleeping."

"What would you like to do?"

She shrugged her shoulder again, and I knew something was wrong. "I don't know…"

I sat up and moved closer to her, kissing her shoulder. "Kate, I know something's wrong. I can tell. What is it?"

She yawned again. "I don't know. I'm a bit bored, I guess."

"You're probably not used to leisure time, having nothing to do. Your father said you've been working like a dog for years, working on your degrees and for *Geist*."

"It's just that most of the people here are older than me," she said, her voice a bit choky as if she were upset. "There's no one here my age. I feel like I'm in an old-folks home or something."

I watched her face, surprised for that didn't seem at all like something that would concern Kate. Then I remembered what Lara said – Kate was very young. Was I making a huge mistake with her? Was she really too young?

"Would you like to go out to a bar? The locals have some nightlife. Dancing."

She made a face. "Whatever." Then she sighed. "Not really. I don't know if I want to be out among *the locals*."

"Come here," I said, holding my arms out. She needed some affection and lots of it. She needed to be touched. She needed to be reminded that she wanted me.

"Why?"

"I need to hold you."

She shrugged and climbed onto my lap but I could feel the distance in her, as if her mind was somewhere else. I tilted her head up and looked in her eyes, completely alarmed now that she was unhappy. That she'd changed her mind. "Kate, what's wrong?"

"I don't know," she said. "Just bored, like I said."

I kissed her, desperate to elicit something other than disdain from her, for only hours earlier, she was completely mine and now, she wasn't.

I ran my hands over her body, pulling her tightly into my arms. I pushed her back on the bed and lay on top of her, cradling her head while I kissed her, one of my knees between hers, pushing her legs apart. Maybe she needed to feel my dominance to respond. Maybe she felt I was too vanilla.

Had I misread her so badly that I'd already lost her?

I thought she needed to be handled with kid gloves, introduced to kink slowly so she would open up like a new flower to the sun. Maybe I was wrong about what she needed, but if so, I'd really have to rethink everything with her.

I kissed her intently, completely focused, and pressed my hips against her, wanting her to know I desired her but I felt nothing in response from her.

Finally I pulled back. I stroked her cheek, and waited. Then, my cell rang and I pulled it out of my pocket and checked the ID.

"Crap," I said, and answered. It was a colleague from the afternoon session asking me where I'd been and wanting me to join them for supper. "Not tonight. No. I have something planned." He told me to call if I changed my mind and suggested we get together for a meal the next day. "Sure," I said. "Tomorrow before the plenary. See you then." I ended the call and turned back to Kate.

"You really are tired," I said, grasping at any straw to explain how cold she'd suddenly turned toward me. "I'm not feeling the usual response in you."

She yawned and stretched. "Maybe," she said. "It's just so dead here. Nothing to do."

"I can think of lots I want to do." I forced a smile, hoping that something would break that icy reserve that had taken over the usually-warm Kate I'd grown used to.

"Yeah?" she said, her face blank. "Like what?"

"Do I even have to say?"

"Oh," she said and crawled away from me, standing up. "*That*. I'm thirsty. I'm going to get a drink." She took her bag and left the room without a word. I rose from the bed, frowning, and followed her to the hall, watching as she walked across the hall to the vending machine where she bought a drink.

She opened the drink, taking a sip, saying nothing and not acknowledging me in the least as if she wanted me to leave.

"Kate?" I leaned against the doorjamb. "You want to go somewhere?"

She shrugged and returned to the hotel room, walking past me, actually taking care to skirt me so she wouldn't touch me. I followed her into the living room. She took the channel changer and switched on the television.

"Wonder what channels they get here?"

I sat on the couch, right in the middle, my arms outstretched on the back. On her part, Kate ignored me and flipped through the lineup of shows.

"Come here," I said, trying to use my Dom voice. My serious Doctor voice. She turned and looked at me but only shrugged and put the channel changer down. She sat beside me on the sofa. I knew then that she was either topping me from the bottom or didn't want me anymore. I patted my lap, determined to play this out no matter where it led. "I mean here."

She sighed dramatically and climbed onto my lap, her hands resting on my shoulder.

"What?" she said, her voice petulant.

"What's wrong?"

She shook her head. "I don't know, Drake. I'm just not *feeling* this."

"What do you mean?" I felt as if my stomach fell out of my chest.

"This," she said pointing between us. "Submission. It's just not there. This feels too much like a traditional relationship. You know. Boyfriend / girlfriend."

"You seemed to enjoy yourself this morning," I said, unable to stop myself from sounding bitter.

"Yeah, but it was just ordinary sex. You rub my clit the right way and I'll come. I could do that with any man. There was nothing kinky about it." She raised her eyebrows. "Maybe we're just not working out. Now that we're alone, it's just not really," she said as if searching for the word. "Exciting. Lara told me that sometimes, a Dom and sub just aren't compatible. You must really *feel* it. I just don't feel like we're the right match. I want to *feel*, I don't know… really possessed. I *don't*. It's like, I can't even call you *Sir* and feel it. I mean, Nigel's a Sir. He's an actual Knight and I don't even call *him* 'Sir'."

So that was it. I had totally and completely misread her. She didn't feel anything for me besides curiosity and I'd failed her test, whatever it was.

"I'm sorry," she said quickly. "I just don't feel it with you. You're really sweet, Drake. Maybe Lara has someone else who I won't have any history with. Someone really anonymous. I might be able to feel it more with a stranger. You know how this works. What do you think?"

I felt disappointment welling up inside of me, sadness biting at my throat and chest. I watched her face in wonder that I had been so wrong about her. She wasn't deep and serious, needing someone like me to mine her depths. She was just like all the other young women of her age. Into excitement and the thrill of the conquest.

I'd been so wrong. I'd gotten my hopes up for her so much.

I'd let her in far too deeply and now, I felt a mixture of sadness and like something caught in my throat. Anger at myself and at Lara, for thinking there was a chance with Kate.

"I think you might be onto something," I said, fighting to keep my voice calm.

Kate nodded. "I *knew* you'd understand. You've been doing this for a long time and have lots of experience. I already talked to my parents. I think I'll go back tomorrow morning, try to salvage a couple of days of my vacation."

She was going back to Manhattan already? Then, I had a

brainstorm. "And this has nothing to do with the person trying to keep you from being with me?"

"*No*," she said and frowned. "Of course not. Like you said, we could just keep this agreement under wraps."

"Why did you sign the contract?"

She shrugged one shoulder. "I have to admit I was a bit shocked by your contract, but I thought, you know, maybe I needed to just sign the damned thing and take a risk, give it a shot. But once I did, it was like all the thrill was gone. So maybe I expected more than I should have. You know, it was just straight sex after all."

She climbed off my lap and went to her drink on the table, taking a long sip as if she had now completely forgotten about me. I sat there watching her, trying to digest what she'd just revealed.

"Well, then," I said and stood, feeling my chest constrict. "I guess I'll go to the bar after all and meet my colleagues. Have a good trip home."

I left the room, taking my bag and shaving kit with me, closing the door behind me without another word.

As I walked down the hallway to the elevator, I felt as if I could punch something.

THAT NIGHT I didn't go to the restaurant to meet with colleagues. I was in no mood to celebrate anything, and if I'd been anywhere near to a bottle of vodka, I would have downed the entire thing. Instead, I went for a long walk along the beach while the sun set, the orange rays warm on my face. The sound of the surf was usually calming and peaceful, but it did nothing to comfort me.

"What the fuck, Drake?" I said to myself as I stood staring at the ocean. "She's just a girl."

A fucking *girl*.

There were a million others like her in Manhattan alone.

But I knew I was just rationalizing. I'd found someone I thought was perfect for me. She loved music. She'd volunteered at the Mangaize camp in West Africa during the famine and wrote heartbreaking investigative journalism pieces on the politics of the camps. She came from a good family and was well-educated and well-raised. She was beautiful, she was intelligent and was curious about kink but needed someone like me to safely show her the way.

How could I have been so damn wrong?

I WENT HOME EARLY from the conference, not able to face endless sessions about my specialty, despite usually finding them inspiring and invigorating. I spent Saturday alone in my apartment, wandering around in my robe and boxer briefs, not even bothering to stop in at the foundation or go to the fitness club to work out.

Finally on Monday morning, after moping around all weekend watching reruns on television, I called Lara during a break in my cases.

"I was expecting your call a lot sooner Drake," she said, her voice sounding tired. "What took you so long?"

"Kate already called you to find another Dom?" I said, a stab of pain in my chest surprising me with its intensity.

She laughed. Actually laughed.

"Drake Morgan," she said, her voice filled with amusement.

"Tell me," I said, steeling myself for the truth.

"My God, you *are* smitten."

"Just tell me the truth."

"No," Lara said, her voice firm. "You tell me what happened from your point of view first."

I sighed, not wanting to replay the disaster of a week over again. "You obviously know Kate left the Bahamas after ending it with me. She said she was bored and that she wasn't feeling it with me. I thought we were good together. I was wrong about her, Lara. You were wrong about her, too."

"*I* was wrong about her?" Lara said, her voice sounding affronted. "I'm never wrong about people, Drake. That's why I'm such a hotshot lawyer."

"You said Kate was perfect for me. You said she needed someone like me to bring her out of herself. To help her discover her inner sub."

"And I was right."

I shook my head, frustrated by her seeming incoherence. "She broke it *off*, Lara. Weren't you listening?"

"I'm always listening, Drake. Listening to you tell me why you can't have a life partner and have to keep your submissives limited to just sex three times a week. I'm always listening to your excuses why you aren't able to have a real relationship."

"So you should know how hard this is for me. I actually really *like* Kate," I said, angry that Lara was acting as if this was nothing. "A lot. Too much."

"It hurt when she ended it?"

"Yes, dammit. It hurt. I still don't understand how I could be so wrong about her."

She laughed lightly. "You weren't wrong Drake. Neither was I. We were both right about her."

"Tell me what you know," I said, almost seeing red with Lara. "Quit with all the BS."

"Oh, Drake. It's so amusing to hear you all upset over this girl. The great Drake Morgan, the Dom who won't let anyone get close to him, who keeps his women at arm's length. Who keeps his heart protected with clauses and rules. Fallen."

I was ready to hang up. "I'm glad my pain amuses you."

"So you admit you're hurt that Kate broke it off."

"I already said it, damn you. Why are you doing this? Tell me what you know or I'm hanging up."

"You are so sweet, Drake," she said and sighed. "Kate wasn't bored with you. If anything, she likes you far too much, considering your usual demands for keeping your distance. She's being blackmailed by her best friend over your relationship. This friend threatened to tell Kate's father about you if she didn't break it off."

"What?" Hope surged through me, followed by anger. "Her friend?"

"Yes, her best friend. She found your contract and freaked out. Kate told her she broke it off with you and was despondent. She went to the Bahamas with her father to get away and was totally shocked to see you there. Her friend called her house and was told by Kate's brother that she'd gone to the Bahamas with her father. She was suspicious and found out that you were at the conference in the Bahamas as well and put two and two together. She called Kate at the hotel and threatened to contact the hospital about you so Kate promised to break it off."

I sat with my head in my hands, enraged that Kate's friend would do that to her, and absolutely ecstatic that in fact, Kate hadn't wanted to end things.

"What did you tell her?"

There was silence on the line for a moment too long.

"What did you *tell* her, Lara?"

"I told her that she should seriously think about what it would mean if your involvement in kink was made public – how it would affect your career."

"So you told her to what – end it with me?"

"You have to protect yourself, Drake. Is Kate worth the risk? You could have any sub you want. There are dozens I know of right now who would be only too happy to be your sub in training. Think about this, Drake. I mean it. Is she worth it?"

My face was hot with anger. Anger at Kate's busybody

blackmailing friend. Angry with Lara for making Kate rethink our relationship.

"I can't believe you did that. You of all people? I thought we were friends."

"We *are* friends, Drake," she said, sounding impatient with me. "Old friends who know each other better than anyone. You're a great doctor, Drake. Do you *really* want to put that on the line over a woman? A girl? Snap out of it!"

"Snap out of it?" I said, almost shouting. "Jesus, Lara, I've never met anyone as good for me as Kate. She's everything I could want in a partner. She's smart and beautiful and loves music and wants to explore kink. I—"

"Then go and get her."

I sat there, my mouth open. "Go get her?"

"Yes," she said and laughed out loud. "Go the fuck and get her, you big dumb lout. Honestly, Drake, sometimes I wonder about you. So smart about everything else except your own heart. You're in love with her. Go and *get her*. She's yours for the taking, if that's what you really want."

"Why did you try to talk both of us out of the relationship?"

She sighed audibly. "Drake. If I succeeded in talking you out of each other, then I'd know you both weren't right for each other. Go and win her back. If you really are right for her, she'll be only too happy."

"Jesus, Lara…"

"Yes, I know," she said, matter of fact. "Cruel but effective. Now quit your moping and go and get her."

I DID, but before I left for Kate's apartment, I called Ethan.

"Drake, just the man I wanted to speak with."

"How's Kate?" I said, cautious. "When she left, I was concerned for her. She seemed a bit upset."

"She was upset but wouldn't say much of anything to either

Elaine or me. She's been moping around the apartment all weekend in her pajamas, barely eating. I'm worried about her."

"I'm worried about her as well. I think I'll call her, try to make things right. We parted on a bad note over a misunderstanding."

"I thought as much, but she was pretty tight-lipped about things. I hope things work out for you both. You know I'm very fond of you, Drake, but I have to think about my little girl."

"Of course. I hope you know that I'm very fond of Kate and will respect her decision about us."

"Good man," he said. "If things don't work out between you two, no hard feelings on my part, Drake. I've known you for too long to let this come between us. Your father asked me to watch out for you as if you were my own son. I hope I have."

"You have, Sir. I appreciate it. Seriously."

We hung up and I knew that no matter what, Ethan and I would remain friends.

I LEFT my office and got in the car, driving over to her place, determined to get her back. The door to her building wasn't propped open and there was no answer at her apartment so I sat on the stairs outside her building and sent her a text.

Kate, I know everything. I talked to Lara and she confessed that she guilted you into saying goodbye to me. I was confused the other day when you claimed not to feel anything for me. I tried not to respond – to respect your wishes. In truth, I was hurt.

Talk to me. Please. I'm not letting you run away just to protect me from something that might never happen. It's up to me what risks I take in my life, not you.

Your father is worried about you. He says you've been sick all weekend. You know what I think? I think you're upset about this. Maybe as upset as I am.

Kate, please... Don't give up on this – on us – without a fight.

There was no reply for a few moments and I was almost ready to get up and go back to the hospital when my cell chimed.

I'm in the deli across the street from you.

I glanced up and saw her sitting in the window of the deli across the street. If she hadn't wanted me back, she could have just sat there and watched me leave. That gave me confidence that in fact, she did want me.

At that moment, I knew that nothing – no meddling best friend or threat of exposure – would keep me from her.

CHAPTER 22

My heart was in my throat as I crossed the street and entered the deli. Kate was sitting in the window seat so I wasted no time pulling up a chair and sitting right beside her, my knee between hers to stop her from trying to leave before I'd had my say.

I leaned in close, taking her hand in mine and kissed her knuckles. Her eyes were wide, as if she was afraid of what I'd do or say.

"Drake, you can't *do* this," she said, her voice barely above a whisper. She tried to pull her hand away but I held on tight. She wiped her eyes with the other hand, so I knew she was really upset. "We have to just end this. Better to do it now before any damage is done."

"It's already been done. I *want* you," I said, surprised at how emotional I felt. "Don't you want me?"

She said nothing, glancing away.

"*Tell* me that you don't want me." I was determined to make her admit she still wanted me. She kept trying to avoid my eyes, sighing heavily as if exasperated.

"*Tell* me, Kate," I said in my best Dom voice. "If you don't want me, I'll leave right now."

"It's not that I don't want you," she said. "I *do* want you but we can't be together. It's for your own good."

I couldn't accept that. If she wanted me, there was no way I was going to let someone come between us. Although I was vulnerable if word got out about my involvement in the BDSM lifestyle, my life wouldn't be over. I'd still have my inheritance and the corporation. I could always quietly move to another city in another state and practice neurosurgery. I'd thought about the possibility many times in the past five years, being as careful as I could be but prepared in case the worst came to pass.

"If you still want me, we'll find a way to work around this, whatever it is. Tell me who knows. What did they say?"

"I can't *tell* you." She leaned away from me but I kept hold of her hand, knowing that I needed to maintain physical contact with her or she'd get up and leave.

"Look," she said, her voice soft, "barely anything has happened between us. We had sex a couple of times. We should just let this drop. I'm sure there are other subs with far fewer ... impediments than I have."

"*Impediments*..." I said, smiling just a bit. "Something happened between us, Kate. I know it's only been a short time, but I don't want this to end, especially not in this way because of someone else forcing us. If we stop seeing each other, it should be because of how *we* feel, not someone else's judgment."

She said nothing, but she did meet my gaze. "This person told me there was a restraining order against you. Your ex-wife..."

I closed my eyes and bowed my head, a sick feeling in the pit of my stomach. The restraining order was always hanging over my head like some personal sword of Damocles. How could I make Kate understand what it really was? "That was a long time ago in a different life."

"You can understand why they, and why I, might be concerned," she said softly. "You *are* into BDSM."

"Not the SM part," I insisted. "Kate, I didn't injure her. I tried to prevent her from leaving our home. That's all. I prevented her from leaving for a while. I wanted to talk to her. I wanted to try to work things out. She wasn't listening."

"Why?" she asked, frowning. "What happened between you? Why did your marriage fail?"

I searched her face, looking for some kind of sign that she would really listen. How could I explain what happened between us?

"Why does any marriage fail?" I shook my head, the futility of explaining it frustrating me. "Because the couple is no longer in sync. *We* were no longer in sync. I wanted more control. She didn't want me to have it. I was so ambitious about my career, traveling around the country doing conferences, presenting papers. We grew apart, and when I did finally try to assert more control, she was already gone emotionally."

"You were just starting to recognize your Dom tendencies?"

"Yes," I said, "but not very clearly. Look, I may have been a self-centered asshole, but I never hurt her. *Never*."

"Why were you a self-centered asshole?"

"I spent too much time away. You know…"

"No, I don't."

"I was like my father, Kate," I said, hating to admit it for I always swore I would never be like him. "I was too busy and neglected her."

"Why? Didn't you love her?"

I shrugged, filled with exasperation. "I don't know. Part of me thinks I did still love her. Part of me thinks I had no idea what love was." I glanced away, remembering so many nights where I stayed longer at work than I had to. How I'd kept my distance emotionally and all we had together was great sex, and even that was starting to be affected by my need for dominance. "I neglected her and she fell out of love with me. She said I was a self-centered prick who cared only about myself."

"Do you agree?"

I nodded, because I had been a self-centered prick. But part of me knew that I was also afraid. Afraid of being hurt. How foolish I'd been. My behavior led directly to my broken heart. "I didn't know what it took to make a relationship work. I'd never seen a marriage. Never knew what a woman wanted, what she expected. I can do sex, Kate. I do it really well. Everything else in a relationship? Not so much."

She nodded as if she understood. "What happened in court? Lara said you got off really lightly."

"Lara helped me," I said and inhaled deeply. "She's very rational and saw what was happening and set me on the right path. I started training with Lara at that point."

"You already knew her?"

I nodded. "Yes. We were old acquaintances and took classes together during our undergrad years. When I needed a lawyer, I called her. When I needed to be taught how to do this properly, she trained me. Kate, I've never hurt anyone purposely except during training and that was consensual. If anything's happened otherwise, it was an accident. Incidental to what was happening."

"What happened?"

I thought back to all the times when something happened by accident during a scene with one of my submissives. None of the pain my subs experienced, with the exception of the first subs Lara paired me with to test my interest in S&M, had ever been intentional. "A binding a bit too tight. A bruise or abrasion on a wrist or ankle. Nothing permanent. Nothing inflicted on purpose. I've always chosen my subs very carefully. I don't *want* anyone into pain. If a sub needs pain, I refuse to sign. Just D/s.

Just pleasure. You can ask Lara for more details if you need them. I'll tell you anything you want to know." I glanced at my cell. "Look, I hate to rush this. I know you need to process this but I have a surgery in a very short time. I want you to come with me. I don't want to leave you alone right now."

"Come with you where?"

"To the hospital," I said, not willing to let her go at that point for fear she never answered my cell or texts again and was out of my life permanently. "You can sit in my office while I take care of this procedure. It's pretty short—only about forty-five minutes. Then I have an hour off before my final surgeries of the day. I want to figure this out."

"I can go back to my apartment and wait there."

"*Come* with me. I don't want you out of my," I said and hesitated, trying to find the right word. "Out of my *reach* right now."

"I'm not going to disappear…"

"Kate, for all I know, you might," I said, unwilling to take the risk. "Come with me. Wait for me. Then we'll figure this all out."

She looked hesitant. "I shouldn't go anywhere with you. If anyone saw us..."

"No one is going to see us."

Finally, she gave in and exhaled. " Okay."

I still held her hand in mine and so I squeezed it, and then leaned in and kissed her. She let me and I knew then that she *did* want me, but was afraid that I'd get hurt if we were found to be together. I wanted to push her down on the floor and ravish her right then and there. My mind went immediately to my office at the hospital and how I'd lock my door and have her right there on the sofa after my procedure was completed.

"Come," I said, standing and pulling her up with me. She followed me without question. We left the deli and took my car to NY Presbyterian, to the wing where my office was located. While we walked hand in hand back to my office, I explained to her what I would do in the procedure. I ushered her into the small room with a sofa, flat screen television for watching procedures, and my desk. A small exam room was off through the side door.

"Here," I said and pointed to the couch. "Have a seat and make yourself comfortable. I have a collection of out of date magazines to read." I switched on the huge screen so she could watch me operate. "There's a coffee and vending machine down the hall if you get thirsty or hungry. You can watch the surgery on the screen if you want. We're recording all procedures and you can watch live feed here."

"I can watch you operate?"

"Yes," I said and held up the remote. "I do really specialized robotically-assisted procedures and record every case for my clinical course in neurosurgery. You can use this to turn the volume up or down. If you get bored, you can switch to cable and watch television." I brought up a screen that had three views, one with a slightly elevated view of a high-tech looking OR theatre, another directly above a gurney, and a third staring at what resembled an open CT scanner. Inside, the scrub nurses and technicians were busy preparing for surgery.

"That's your OR?"

"For the procedure this afternoon, yes. It's a really advanced OR suite equipped for neurological procedures like I'm doing this afternoon." I pointed to a CT scanner. "That does real-time images of the brain for really delicate surgery."

"What are you doing?"

"Implanting electrodes in a man's brain to stop Parkinson's tremor. That's for imaging the brain during the procedure. The patient will be sitting with his head inside the machine so we can watch as the electrodes are inserted to make sure we get them in the right location. Speaking of which, I have to get ready or I'm going to be late. Gotta go scrub in."

I handed her the remote control, then I bent down to kiss

her. She raised her head and let me. I touched her bottom lip, the tiny scar, and then stared into her eyes, searching for some sign that she was really here to stay. "Wait for me?"

She nodded, but didn't reply.

"I'll be forty-five minutes, maybe an hour, depending on how things go. Okay?"

"I'll be here."

I went to the door and looked back at her. "I won't be long."

She smiled and waved so I closed the door and left her alone.

I SCRUBBED outside the OR in the anteroom while the rest of the OR staff finished preparations for surgery. One of my neurosurgery residents would start the procedure, opening the cranium and preparing the patient for my part of the surgery.

When I was gowned up and ready, I went up to my patient to say hello, and then I turned to the camera to describe the procedure. I returned to Mr. Graham and spoke with him to reassure him.

"How are you doing, Bob?" I said, keeping my voice firm but warm. "Ready?"

"Cut away, Doc. Great tunes, by the way," Mr. Graham said. "When you asked me, I didn't really believe you'd play Led Zeppelin in the OR."

"I find music relaxes patients," I said and smiled beneath my mask. "Luckily, we have the same taste in bands."

"You're too young to like this music."

"It's my father's music. I love it, too."

I consulted the CT images, checking to make sure everything was in proper alignment. I described what I was doing for the benefit of my students, who would watch the video in preparation for their own OR time. Then, I went ahead with the procedure and threaded an electrode into a precise position in the brain, guided by a CT-generated image on a screen beside the operating table.

"When I stimulate the section of the brain where the electrode has been placed, Mr. Graham's hand should stop shaking. Slowly at first, maybe not completely, but there will be noticeable improvement."

Graham's head was imprisoned in a metal cage. He lifted his hand at my instruction and it shook wildly, the tremor reaching all down his arm.

"We are now going to send a charge down the electrode to the *subthalamic nucleus* and the *globus pallidus interna*, the structures responsible for motor movement."

In a few seconds, Mr. Graham's hand stopped shaking. Slowly at first but in about ten or fifteen seconds, it was almost perfectly still.

"Oh, God, *oh God*," Mr. Graham said, his voice breaking. "Oh, *God* I can't believe it." Graham was obviously overcome with emotion, and for good reason.

"*Thank* you, Doctor," Mr. Graham said, his voice breaking. "Thank you, *God*."

I bent over Mr. Graham, but kept my hands away from the man, to keep sterile. "I *love* my job," I said, smiling to myself. "I can't believe they pay me to do it."

About twenty minutes later, after we finished closing and the nurses wheeled my patient out of the OR, I spoke briefly with the family to let them know how the procedure went and went back to my office in my scrubs, my cap still on my head. I glanced at the screen and saw the technicians cleaning the OR. Then I turned to Kate.

"How are you?"

She came over to me and to my surprise, she slipped her arms around my waist, squeezing me.

"What's this?" I said, smiling, my arms closing around her.

"That was amazing." Her eyes were warm, brimming just a bit as if she was emotional.

Despite wanting to kiss her then and there, I pulled out of her arms and closed the door. Then I removed my cap and pressed Kate against the door.

"Mmm, Ms. *Bennet*," I said, and pushed one of my knees between hers, my hips pressed against her, my arms on the door beside her head. "I hope this show of affection means you've reconsidered and you're planning on giving this a chance."

"I still want you," she said, and ran her hands up my chest. "I never stopped. If anything, I want you even more. But if this person finds out that we're seeing each other, they'll tell my father about your involvement in the BDSM community and send the restraining order to your boss."

I watched her, my gaze moving over her face. "You won't tell me who?"

"I can't."

"If I talk to them, maybe I can assure them I won't hurt you and—"

"I *can't*. You *don't* understand. They're serious and completely irrational about this."

I pulled her over to the couch and we sat down. I slipped my arm around her. "So, it's back to the secret affair? We can't see each other in public?"

She nodded.

"Well, at least you *want* to try."

"I do."

Relief flooded through me. I knew what I wanted and needed. I wanted her that night. "I have a jam session tonight but I'm done at 9:00."

"I can't be seen with you, Drake," she said, her hands splayed on my chest "I can't go to your apartment. You can't come to mine. I don't know where we'll meet. A hotel?"

"No, that's too…" I brushed hair off her cheek. "Too cliché. I have a small apartment on 8th Avenue from when I was in school. It was my dad's when he was a student. He bought the whole building when he started to make serious money and I decided to go to Columbia. We could use that. I spent a lot of years there and it has some of my old junk from when I first lived away from my father. I store a lot of his stuff there as well."

"This person works three nights a week," Kate said. "Every Tuesday and Thursday for sure. One night on the weekend. On those nights, I could probably go there. I might be able to make excuses for a night now and then, but this person is determined to watch me. I have to make them think we've truly broken up so they stop."

"You seem so much more positive about this," I said, surprised and glad at the same time. "What happened?"

She shook her head and just stared at me as if trying to find the right words. "This made me face up to what it was that I wanted. Having to say goodbye to you made me realized that I *want* this," she said and ran her hands up my chest to my shoulders. "I want *you*."

I leaned closer and kissed her softly, affection for her flooding through me, mixed with arousal. When I pulled back, I stroked her cheek. "Look, I only have an hour. Will you come with me? Surely this person isn't tailing you? We could go to my place on 8th Avenue but we'll have to hurry because of traffic."

"Why don't we just stay if you only have a little while. We can talk here," she said and brushed hair off my forehead.

"Ms. *Bennet*," I said, grinning. "I don't want to *talk*." Then I leaned down and kissed her throat and then the tops of her very luscious breasts.

"Do you think it's advisable?" she said, when I pulled her onto my lap so that she lay across me, her arms around my neck. "I mean, do you think someone might come in? One of your nurses? Or maybe…"

"Enough talking."

I pressed her down on the tiny couch and kissed her and it took no time for me to be rock hard with her soft curves beneath me. While I kissed her tenderly at the start, my arousal built quickly and soon I was practically devouring her, one hand searching her body while my tongue searched her mouth, my fingers slipping under her sweater to cup a breast through her bra, stroking the flesh that spilled out above the fabric. Then I slid my hand down over her belly to her thigh, pulling up her jean skirt until I found her pussy.

"I'm going to lock the door and fuck you right now," I whispered, pressing my fingers against her, searching for the hard nub of her clit through her tights. She gasped and pressed against my hand, signaling that she was aroused as well. I rose reluctantly and went to the door, turning the lock then I came back and lay beside Kate again, kissing her neck, pulling open her sweater, running my tongue over the tops of her breasts. When I pulled the fabric down to expose one nipple and sucked on it, she gasped.

I stopped sucking and pulled on the nipple gently with my teeth. Then, I took her hand and ran it over top of my scrubs so she could feel my erection.

"See what you do to me?"

She smiled coyly. "That was your own doing."

Someone spoke outside the office door, and Kate stiffened in alarm. "Drake, is this a good idea? Will you get in trouble if someone comes? Maybe we should stop…"

"Shh," I said. "You signed the contract. No resistance." I kissed her again, leaning over her, stroking her cheek, my fingers running over her bottom lip. "I want you *now*."

"Do you," she whispered as I nuzzled her neck. "Do you

think it's a good idea before surgery? Won't it, like, sap your vital essence or something?"

I smiled against her neck, then I moved back down to her breasts. "*Quiet*. You talk far too much. I'm going to eat you," I said, taking her hand again and moving it down over my balls. "*Right now*."

Then I pulled away and bent down, taking her feet and removing her shoes, before unzipping her jean skirt and pulling down her tights and underwear. I finished undressing her as fast as I could so that she was completely naked and then I pushed her back onto the couch. Still fully dressed, I knelt down and examined her. "I'm going to have to shave you again tonight," I said, noting the hair was growing back, short and sharp. "I look forward to it."

I buried my face between her spread thighs, my fingers opening her up, my mouth and lips and tongue finding her clit. She leaned back and closed her eyes, finally surrendering to me.

I licked and sucked her clit, my tongue stroking all over her lips, while I slid two fingers inside of her. When I heard her breathing fast and shallow, I knew she was close. Then, I pulled her up and turned her around so that she leaned over the couch, her knees on the seat and her body over the back. After untying my scrubs, I pulled out my cock and stroked her pussy with the head to rekindle her arousal. When I finally entered her, moving slowly inside of her just a few inches, she gasped. I bent over her, one arm around her waist so that I could stroke her clit.

"Tell me when you're close," I said. I kept my fingers on her as I began to thrust and soon, she was breathing fast again, pushing back against me.

"Drake, *I*…"

While I would usually build her up several times before letting her come, I increased my tempo, and soon, I felt her spasms and thrust even harder. I wanted to come with her and was so close, a few more thrusts would push me over. I came with my mouth at her ear, grunting through my ejaculation, blinded with the pleasure.

I leaned against her, breathing hard, my hands covering hers on the back of the couch.

"*God*, I needed that…" I kissed her shoulder and bit it gently. "I needed *you*." Finally, I slid out of her but when she tried to turn around, I stopped her.

"No, stay like that so I can admire you. My come is running down your leg."

I stepped back and examined her from a few feet away, her nice round ass in the air, her pussy peeking out at the base of her cheeks, a slither of my semen dripping out.

"Um, my legs are a bit shaky," she said, craning her neck to see me.

"I know. I like seeing you shake because of what I did to you."

Finally, I turned her around and cleaned her using some tissues from my desk. After she was clean, I pushed her down on the couch and lay on top of her.

"This won't affect your surgical performance, will it?" she said, her voice playful, a cheeky grin on her lips.

I laughed out loud. "Probably. Might improve it."

"I thought men got all sleepy after an orgasm."

"Sometimes, but it depends on the time of day. Right now, I feel great. I was feeling very *deprived*, Ms. Bennet. Very unhappy so a few extra pleasure endorphins will only help." I closed my eyes and sighed, pressing my forehead against hers. "You have no idea how relieved I am. When I went up to your apartment, I made poor Mrs. Kropotkin so frantic I thought she was going to call the police. It took every neuron I ever made studying Russian to convince her I didn't have ill-intent. I was really worried about you."

"I'm sorry," she said, her voice soft. "Lara asked me to think about what was more important—my happiness or your career. I left the apartment because she told me you were coming over."

"You were planning on not seeing me ever again?" I asked, shaking my head at her sense of honor.

"I was afraid I'd hate myself if I did meet with you. I knew I wouldn't be able to resist you if I got within a foot of you. I was right."

I smiled. "I can't resist *you*. I don't want to. Kate, I can't leave this thing between us hanging. I have to *know*. I have to know how far I can go with you. If anything happens, it will be because someone else made the wrong choice, not either of us. It will be because you're important enough to me to take that risk." I kissed her and stroked her cheek. "Your father was glad to see me and even he encouraged me to go to your apartment and not give up."

She smiled. "He said he thought we were really intense with each other and well-matched."

I nodded in agreement. "We are." I kissed her once more, unable to get enough of her soft lips.

"Maybe I should leave you alone for a while before your next surgery."

I sighed. "Probably. I don't want you out of my sight though."

"I'll go back to my father's for the rest of the afternoon. I'll make an excuse to go back to my apartment for the night. Then, we can meet at the apartment on 8th Avenue after your practice."

"Maybe I'll cancel tonight."

"*Don't* because of me," she said, her tone insistent. "Your music is important to you."

I stroked her cheek with the backs of my fingers. "I don't want you out of arm's reach, Kate."

"I can't stay here all day," she said, smiling. "We can spend the evening together at your secret hideaway. *After* your practice."

"Tonight." I kissed her again, softly.

"I should go now," she said and stood up. "Let you focus before your next surgery."

"I wish I could cancel that, but I can't. Poor man's been waiting for a while to get the procedure."

She started dressing and I helped, handing over her jean skirt, zipping it up for her, buttoning the button. I helped her with her bra and fastened the front clasp. Then I pulled the sweater on and around her shoulders and buttoned it up.

"You like dressing me?" she said, eyeing me with a smile.

"Dressing and undressing a woman is a total turn on and pleasure." Finally, I smoothed her hair before leaning down to kiss her once more. "Where should I pick you up tonight?"

"I can meet you. It's probably better that I don't get a ride with you anywhere. I'll take a taxi."

"I don't like leaving you alone. I don't like loose ends, Kate."

"Just give me the address and I'll meet you there."

"Give me your iPhone."

She handed me her cell and I called up my address on GPS, getting directions from Ethan's apartment.

"There," I said. "You can find your way there easily with that."

After she took the phone back, I walked her to the door of my office. "Are you sure I can't drive you back to your apartment?"

She shook her head. "No. I can take a taxi. I don't want to be seen in your car just in case we run into anyone. We already risked a lot coming here."

I exhaled in frustration. " Okay, but I don't like leaving you alone now. You can always call me and I can pick you up if you change your mind. Text me and let me know you're on your way, okay? Otherwise, I'll worry."

"I will."

I kissed her once more before she left. Then I watched her from my office door as she walked down the long hallway to the exit.

I turned back to my desk, and the stack of patient files on the surface, with a smile.

CHAPTER 23

MY NEXT CASE was complex and I needed every ounce of focus to perform. My afternoon delight with Kate hadn't stunted my skill so the operation went off without a hitch and I was able to tell the husband that his wife's tremor was vastly reduced and might even disappear completely in time.

After I finished dictating notes on the surgery, I went to my apartment, had a quick shower and changed clothes. I listened to my messages and checked my email but there was nothing of much interest, except for an invitation to play a game of racquetball the following week with another surgeon.

Then, I drove over meet the guys for practice at O'Riley's. I should have cancelled the practice because all I could think of was seeing Kate at 8th Avenue, but I forced myself to play and sing. Even Ken noticed my distraction.

"What's up with you tonight?" he said, frowning at me when we were putting our instruments away for the night.

"Have a date," I said and smiled. "Sorry."

Ken grinned. "Hey, say no more. Is it that new girl?"

"The very one."

Ken raised his eyebrows knowingly. "Bring her to Mom's

for dinner on Sunday. Seriously. Mom would love to meet her."

I shook my head. "Maybe."

Ken laughed. "You really do like her if you almost agree to bring her."

"I do," I said and pulled on my coat, eager to leave. "Now, stop with the questions and let me get to her, okay?"

Ken slapped me on the back and nodded. "Understood. Have a good one."

"More than one, I hope." I ducked away from his playful punch and left the pub for my car.

I drove to the apartment on 8th Avenue and parked my car in a parking garage and walked down the street to the old building, seeing it for the first time in a couple of weeks. I tried to see it as Kate would -- a corner brownstone walk-up with ornate windows and wrought iron window boxes with faded ivy, the building very old. Browning ivy crept up the building's façade. My father bought it for me when I was at Columbia and I never sold it. It had too many good memories of my life in medical school and the times my father would come up to Manhattan to visit. He would sleep on the couch rather than in a hotel, despite how uncomfortable it was because he wanted to wake up and make coffee, fry some bacon and eat brunch with me over the newspaper. Those are some of my very best memories of my father and there were far too few and far too late.

I needed those kind of memories when I was a child, not when I was already a grown man.

I climbed the stairs to the third floor and entered the cramped living room, filled with boxes from my father's apartment that I had shipped here after he died. His old furniture competed with my college-edition sofa and coffee table. It bore no resemblance to the wealth my father, or I, had accumulated. It wasn't that I couldn't afford to buy new furniture and have the apartment professionally renovated and decorated. It was the only thing I had left of my father.

The apartment was a one bedroom that was open-plan except for the bedroom off to the rear of the building. Bookshelves covered most of the walls, filled with thousands of books I had collected during my years in school. There were windows on three walls, providing ample light during the day. The floors were hardwood planks with faded Persian carpets covering the most worn parts of the surface. I was thinking of getting the floors refinished but had let it slide, not wanting to make any decisions about the place. The living room led to a combined kitchen and dining room.

I went to the windows and opened one to let in some fresh air. The windows were huge and looked out over the streets on either side. In the living room stood my collection of six old guitars on their stands. I'd covered the walls without bookshelves in posters of old bands – the Beatles, Led Zeppelin, Deep Purple, The Who. So much of my life was shaped by my father and it showed in the contents of my apartment.

8th Avenue was my refuge from everything, and I went there to practice and when I needed an evening alone with my music and memories. Bringing Kate there was probably a mistake, but I was already so in over my head, one more transgression of my rules would make no real difference.

Before she arrived, I spent some time tidying up. Since I hadn't used it for anything other than a practice space for some time, it was dusty and a bit messy. While I was cleaning up, I came across the sheet music Ethan had given to my father years earlier, with a photograph of them attached. Wearing fatigues and dog tags around their necks from their time in 'Nam, they stood side by side smiling at the camera, their arms around each other's shoulders.

Kate would probably really enjoy seeing it, so I left it on top of the desk. I wouldn't show it to her unless she seemed interested, but it was there to be found if she was curious.

I'd only been there for less than half an hour when my cell chimed and I checked my messages.

I'm on my way. Be there in 2.

I texted back immediately.

I am so ready for you, Ms. Bennet...

I went to the window overlooking the street and watched for her, excitement in my gut, a surge of adrenaline going through me when I saw her taxi drive up and she got out and looked up at the building. I'd left the door open so I went to the landing to wait for her, listening as she walked up the steps. The old wooden staircase creaked as she climbed up to me.

When our eyes met, I couldn't help but smile. "There you *are*," I said and went to her, pulling her into my arms. She laid her head on my shoulder and hugged me back warmly. I tilted her face up and kissed her, a rush of blood to my dick when our tongues touched, my body ready for more.

"You may have to carry me up the rest of the way," she said, her voice shaking a bit from nerves. "I feel a bit weak-kneed."

"Ms. Bennet, are you nervous to be alone with me?" I smiled, pleased that she was excited even though she was still a bit shy.

"Yes," she said. "But the good kind of nervous."

"Good. I want you a little nervous." Then I bent down and picked her up, one arm under hers, the other under her legs.

"Oh, no, *don't*," she said when I started up the stairs. "I was just kidding! Put me down, please! Let me walk."

"I don't *think* so, *Katherine*. I think I *want* to carry you up and into my *lair*." I grinned at her, enjoying the look of helplessness on her face.

She buried her face in my shoulder as I carried her up the rest of the way to my floor and through the doorway.

"Are you going to put me down?"

I smiled. "I don't know *what* I'm going to do with you, Ms. Bennet. I haven't decided yet. One thing I *might* have to do, if memory serves me, is kiss you to keep you from talking."

I kissed her, a soft kiss, just lips on lips, my mind already imagining the rest of the night to come.

"I *must* be getting heavy..." she said, a slight hint of protest in her voice.

"You're light as a feather."

She relaxed in my arms and glanced around the apartment. "You have so many books. And all these guitars...I want to explore your apartment."

"I want to explore *you*."

Her eyes widened. "You do, do you? I think you already did after lunch..."

"Ms. Bennet, there's so much more of you to explore. So much more of your body. So much more of your mind."

I put her down finally and removed her coat. She took off her boots, leaving them on the mat by the front door.

"Take a look around. I'll get us a drink."

She put her bag down on the table and walked around while I went to my sideboard in the living room to get us a drink. I kept glasses inside and old bottles of liqueurs and scotch. Vodka I kept in the refrigerator. I watched Kate wander around, examining my things, sorting through the piles and piles of magazines including *Guitar, Rolling Stone, Bass Player*, and then scientific journals – *Annals of Internal Medicine, Lancet, JAMA* and others.

She peeked into the bedroom, probably wondering when she'd end up there. Soon, if I had my way, a delicious stab of desire running through me when I thought about her lying naked on my bed. When she returned to the living room, I had two shot glasses of Anisovaya ready for us.

"Here," I said, handing her one of the crystal shot glasses I inherited from my father. "These are my father's glasses that he got from an old woman named Yelena Kuznetzova, who was rumored to be Stalin's housekeeper at his dacha in Soviet Georgia. This is Anisovaya. Drink up."

"I should have *known*," she said, smiling. "Stalin's housekeeper?"

"It was one of my father's favorite stories," I said and laughed. "Probably just his bullshit wishful thinking."

"He was a Stalinist? I thought he was a Trotskyite."

"He was a Sovietophile. Anything Russian, especially Soviet. He was sad to see the Soviet Union fall. Said it was their folly in Afghanistan."

Kate nodded. "It was probably Afghanistan."

"Anyway, *Za vas*," I said, giving a Russian toast, not wanting to get into any political discussions. "To you."

"*Za vas*," she replied. We shot the vodka back and she grimaced when she downed it. On my part, I loved the bite of Anisovaya and smacked my lips in appreciation.

"Oh *korosho*, that's so good." I smiled at her and was rewarded with a smile in return. She was still a bit hesitant but definitely more relaxed than during our previous times alone.

"This is a nice old apartment."

I took her glass and watched as she started to explore the apartment a bit more.

"My father bought it for me when I started college," I said, remembering the first time he brought me here to show me my new place. I loved it from the start. "Until then, I lived in Baltimore with him. He worked at the University of Maryland Shock Trauma Center until he died."

"So you came to Manhattan and lived here all by yourself?"

I nodded. "He hated that I was moving away, but I wanted to come to New York to Columbia, get away from Baltimore – and him."

"Why him?"

I shrugged, not sure I could explain. How can you describe feeling betrayed by someone and at the same time, craving their attention and affirmation nonetheless? I always wanted more from my father than he could give and was always disappointed. Even when he spent his money on me, I felt nothing but sad.

"He wanted me to become a doctor like him," I said finally. "And I was in rebellious youth mode at the time. I wanted to study psychoanalysis. So I came here. When he couldn't talk me out of it, he made sure to come here and buy me a place to live. He wanted me to live here because he'd been so happy here, and so he made the owner an offer way over its market value. It was his only real splurge despite his wealth. He approved because it was a rent-controlled building and he let the other tenants stay, not raising the rent once. Such an idealistic socialist…"

"It's yours now," she said. "Have you raised the rent?"

I shook my head and smiled guiltily. "Nah. I'll let the current tenants keep the units until they decide to move out. Rent controlled units are so rare, it's a shame to lose them. I keep this place just for the memories."

"Sounds like a bit of his socialism rubbed off on you." She raised her eyebrows skeptically.

I grinned and refused to be drawn into her game. "It's just lazy rich boy, actually. I can't be bothered to change things." I glanced around at the place with affection. It was all I had left of my father except memories. "I don't want to."

I put our glasses down and watched as Kate stood in the center of the living room and examined the space. The apartment was dim at that time of night, and the furniture looked drab and well-used. The living room was crammed full with his furniture and mine – leather and dark wood and overstuffed cushions. A huge old wooden desk sat below the window, a wooden office chair on rollers parked in its space. All the boxes from my father's apartment were stacked high in one corner, marked with *Dad*.

"Is this your father's furniture?"

I smiled briefly. "Yeah, I know. Sentimental, right? When he died, I couldn't bring myself to sell it or give it away so I closed up his apartment in Baltimore and had it shipped here."

She turned around in a complete circle. "How often do you come here?"

"I practice here," I said, standing a few feet away, watching her, planning my moves. "Luckily, old Mr. Neumann downstairs is practically deaf, so it doesn't bother him."

"You practice here with your band?"

"No, just me," I said, giving her time to completely relax. "I come here when I have time off and just play."

"Do you ever have time off? You sound so busy… Your surgery. Your band. The foundation. Your subs…"

"I'm rich. I only work as much as I want to. Interesting cases only. I keep busy."

"Do you play this?" She went to my acoustic guitar standing next to the desk and wall of books. "I thought you played the bass guitar."

"I play lead and acoustic as well."

Then, she picked up the sheet music I'd left on the desk. I went to her side and glanced over her shoulder. Simon and Garfunkel. "Old Friends/Bookends". On the top of the sheet music was a hand-written note.

'To Liam. From your 'old friend'. E'

Her father's handwriting, given to my father years earlier. She held the piece of sheet music up and beneath it was the faded Polaroid of our fathers as much younger men.

"Oh my *God*," she said, staring at the Polaroid, a hand covering her mouth. "This is *them*." She turned to me and I nodded.

"Your father gave that photo and sheet music to my dad a long time ago. I remembered them when I came here tonight and found them so you could see."

She examined them closely. "They really *were* friends." She glanced up at me as if she was surprised. "Somehow, I didn't really believe it. Like it was just a story my father told me about this crazy doctor friend of his from 'Nam."

I took the photo out of her hand and looked at it more closely myself. The two seemed so happy then, despite the wars. Seeing it sent a stab of regret and sadness through me. "They thought they'd be friends forever."

"Will you play this for me?" She held the sheet music out.

I shook my head and took the sheet music away. "I don't think so."

She frowned, and I knew then it was the wrong answer but I just didn't want to go too deep into each other's personal lives.

"Why not?"

I forced a smile and put the sheet of music down on the desk, saying nothing. How could I tell her that I wanted to get as deep into her life as I possibly could so I could know her inside and out so I could better understand her, but I didn't want her doing the same?

"I understand," she said, and made a face like she'd done something wrong. "That's getting too personal, right?"

"No, it's just that I had other plans when inviting you here…" I said, trying to change the subject and the mood. I raised my eyebrows, hoping she got the hint. I watched, actually saw resignation fill her, her eyes becoming distant, closed off.

"I get it, Drake." She sighed and went to the window, looking down at the street below. "You don't want us to cross that line. I'm sorry. This is just new to me. This *fucking* without emotion thing."

I knew I had to do something and fast to overcome the sense of gloom she obviously was feeling at the thought we'd never be more than Dom/sub. I went behind her and wrapped my arms around her, taking her hands in mine, our fingers threading together.

"Oh, there's lots of emotion, Kate," I said, wanting her to

know that I would care about her – about her pleasure and happiness. "Just very contained and appropriate."

She nodded, but I had the sense it was her being a good girl and not that she really felt it was okay.

"I know. You want to keep things compartmentalized. Your food in all the right spots on the plate. No messy mingling of flavors. I'm used to piling everything on the fork all at once. I don't know if I can do this."

"Shh," I said, knowing I had to push through this. I kissed her neck, her shoulder. "Stop over-thinking. Just *feel*. Feel this," I said and pressed my erection against her to remind her of why she was there. "I've been imagining fucking you all afternoon. You don't know how difficult it was to blank you out of my thoughts because I kept thinking of your tight wet little pussy and getting hard. Not quite a good thing when you're supposed to be focused on delicate brain surgery…"

She leaned back against me, her eyes closed. "You're exaggerating."

I chuckled and nuzzled her neck, one hand slipping around her waist. "Maybe not *during* surgery but in between."

She nestled into my arms. "I apologize if I intruded in your thoughts." Her voice had taken on a slightly playful tone, so I hoped I had salvaged the moment.

"No apology necessary."

We stood at the window, the faint light from the street filtering through the wrought iron trellis covering the window, my arms around her, her body warm against mine.

"And *now*," I said, wanting to move beyond the moment. "Now that I have you all to myself, alone in my *lair*, it's time for you to put that signature on the agreement into effect. You understand what that means?"

"Submission?" she said, her voice a bit husky.

"Yes," I said, my lips at her neck. "No hesitation. No questions. Just comply."

"What if—"

I stopped her, my finger on her mouth, my lips at her ear. "Shh," I said. "No *what-ifs*. You know the safe words. Yellow if you need me to slow down. Red if you absolutely have to stop what's happening. You also know what red means."

"Full stop and I go home?"

I could hear the excitement in her voice. "Yes. But remember – I don't want to go too fast or scare you. I want you to trust me. I want this to work so I plan on keeping a very close watch over you and how you respond to me and what I'm doing. You don't have to be afraid. *Much*. Do you understand?"

"Much?"

"Kate," I said, needing to calm her. "A little fear is arousing to a sub. A little uncertainty about what I'll do to you. What I'll make you do to me. Admit it. It makes you wet."

She closed her eyes but said nothing.

"*Admit* it," I said in her ear, my mouth on her neck, my arms tightening around her so she felt completely possessed. "You have to learn to be completely honest with me. It arouses you. I can tell, Kate. Your heart rate just increased. Your breathing is fast and shallow at the thought. If I was to slip my fingers between your lips, I'd feel how wet you are. Tell me I'm right."

"Yes," she said softly.

"Yes, what?"

She hesitated. I wasn't sure she was ready to call me Sir or Master, but I wanted to test her out.

"What do you want me to call you? Sir? Or Master?"

"What do I *want* you to call me? I want you to call me Master when we're in scene. I know you don't feel it yet. If you say it enough, if I make you *feel* it, eventually it will be second nature. I'll enjoy that. But more than that, I'll enjoy you calling me Master even if you don't feel it."

"Why? Don't you want me to feel it?"

"Of course. That's what I long for. But I also just want your submission. Your obedience. I know you don't feel that I'm your Master now, but your willingness to just do what I command will please me in itself."

"Yes," she said, her voice soft. "*Master*."

I knew she didn't feel it, and that it felt silly, but she had to get used to it.

"Good *girl*," I said and stroked my hands over her body, over her shoulders and down her arms, then over her breasts, of which I couldn't get enough. "When we meet from now on, after you cross that threshold and I kiss you the first time, it's a signal that we're in scene and I expect obedience. I'll call you Katherine or slave, you call me Master. Now, no more talking. No hesitation."

Still standing behind her, I caressed her breasts through the fabric and then moved lower over her belly and to her thighs. I was hard as rock already, just touching her and thinking of the control I had over her body and mind. She pressed back against me, her buttocks against my erection and I was pleased that she was showing interest although I wanted to take control. I reached up beneath her sweater to cup her bra and with the other hand, I reached under the hem of her skirt and felt her garter belt.

"Mmm, I *like* this, Ms. Bennet…" I murmured against her skin.

I reached up between her thighs and felt her naked flesh beneath the garter belt.

"Oh, I *really* like this," I said. "I like that you remembered and thought about this and how to please me." My fingers slipped between her labia and down lower to the entrance to her body. "I really *really* like that you're already so *wet*."

I kissed her neck while stroking her clit and she gasped, inhaling when my fingers penetrated her. Then, I released her and turned her around to face me.

"Take your clothes off except for your bra, the garters and

nylons," I ordered. I backed away and sat on the wing chair against the wall, my arms on the arm rests, my legs spread wide. "Undress, Katherine. *Slowly*." I licked my lips. "Touch yourself while you do."

She looked a bit hesitant at first but proceeded despite it.

"It's a shame that you don't have some nice high heels," I said, smiling, "but I know you're not good on them."

She unbuttoned her sweater slowly, pulling it down over her shoulders, letting it hang for a moment before removing it from her arms. She dropped it on the coffee table. Then she ran her hands down her body and over her breasts, cupping them briefly before moving down to the zipper in back of her skirt. She unzipped it slowly.

"Turn around and do that."

She frowned, but complied, turning around so that her back was to me. She pulled the skirt down and over her hips, bending down as she did. Bending over like that gave me a very good view of her ass and pussy.

"Oh, Ms. *Bennet*..." I said and exhaled loudly. "I like this view very *much*..."

"You said you'd only call me Katherine or slave," she said, and I could hear a touch of impertinence in her voice.

"Shh," I said quickly, hiding my smile behind my hand. "A slave never corrects her Master."

She stepped out of the skirt and turned back, dropping it on the coffee table as well. Finally, she stood before me in nothing but her black lace garters and bra, sheer black nylons. She stood quietly, waiting. At that point, I believed she enjoyed the performance, her shyness gone completely.

I twirled my fingers. "Turn around, slowly. Let me see you from all angles."

She turned around slowly and I admired her curves and smooth skin.

"Lift your hair up. Hold it up as you turn."

She complied, pulling her hair up above her shoulders. She could be a model for an artist with skin and flesh like that.

"Come here and straddle me on the chair."

She stopped her turn. "Don't you want to shave me first?"

"*Slave*," I said and shook my head, my voice impatient although I enjoyed the chance to correct her. "No questioning my decisions. Besides, I'm going to send you to get waxed. It lasts longer."

She came over to the chair and straddled me, one knee on either side of my hips, her arms resting on my shoulders. I glanced down her body to her bare pussy and then up to her face.

"Your cheeks are nicely flushed, Katherine," I said. "You're nice and wet as well. I suspect you're also nicely swollen inside. Almost ready for me."

I continued to simply examine her, taking her in, knowing that it would arouse her to be the object of my gaze. Finally, I pulled down the fabric of her bra to expose her nipples and tweaked each one to points. Then I leaned up and sucked one after the other, pulling on the areola gently with my teeth, knowing that the tiny bit of pain would arouse her, especially when I sucked immediately after. She gasped and closed her eyes.

"Stand up."

She did, standing with a foot on either side of me on the cushion so that her groin was level with my face. Then, I reached up behind her and squeezed her ass, pulling her closer.

"Put one foot on the arm rest," I said, wanting to open her up so that I could lick her all over, slowly, biting her softly before slipping my tongue between her lips to find her very swollen clit. She trembled beneath my mouth and had to prop herself on the wall behind the wing chair while I bit and licked and sucked her. Finally, I slipped two fingers inside of her while I sucked and licked and soon, her thighs began to tremble.

"Tell me if you feel close. Remember, you can't come until I say you can."

I continued to eat her, focused on the sounds she was making, wanting to learn her signs.

"Drake, I *think*..." she said and I was almost going to stop and correct her but I didn't need to. "I mean, *Master*..." she said quickly so I didn't stop. Instead, I increased the tempo, adding another finger, sucking her into my mouth. She groaned.

"I'm *going to*..."

Finally, her orgasm started, her body clenching around my fingers, her legs trembling. I continued to suck and lick her while her body shook.

"Oh, God, please *stop*..." she gasped.

I stopped and enjoyed the sensation of her spasms around my fingers, her flesh so warm and wet and silky. I wanted to push myself into her and fuck her until she came once more and then I would, wanting to make sure she had at least two orgasms.

Above me, Kate leaned against the wall, breathing deeply, her forehead resting on the plaster.

"Should I get down?" she asked after a moment. She tried to pull away but I stopped her with one hand, keeping the other where it was, my fingers still inside her.

"No, wait. I like to feel this."

I covered her once more with my mouth, my tongue flat against her still-hard clit. After a moment, I pulled her back down when her thighs shook too much, and guided her so she straddled my lap again. I kissed her, and the touch of her tongue on mine sent a jolt of lust through my body, my dick throbbing.

I pulled back and looked at her, at her pink cheeks, her eyes languid with fulfilled desire.

"My turn."

CHAPTER 24

"I THOUGHT I got two for every one of yours," she said, a hint of a smile on her lips. I wanted to kiss her again, but I had to pretend to be angry so I frowned.

"That's a *very* saucy mouth you have." I touched the scar on her bottom lip. "I might have to just silence it with something."

"Not a ball gag," she said, pulling back, a look of apprehension on her face.

"That's not *quite* what I had in mind…" I grinned, wanting to lighten the mood. "And remember your manners…"

"Oh, sorry," she said and made a face. "*Master*…"

"Good girl," I said, trying my best to sound stern. "Now, on your knees."

She slid off my lap and on her knees between my spread legs, her hands on my thighs, her eyes locked on mine as she waited for my command.

"Take me out and lick me," I said and even ordering her to do that made my cock thicken.

She reached for my belt and unbuckled it and then unzipped my pants. I was commando, so my cock sprang out when she pulled the material aside. She held my shaft in both hands and began licking me, working her tongue up to the head, circling it before lapping the fluid that leaked off it.

"That's very nice, Katherine," I said, my voice husky with desire. "Now, take me in your mouth and suck."

She did as I commanded, taking me into her mouth, sucking as she moved her lips over the head, up and down, while she stroked my shaft with her hands.

Her hair fell over her face so I pulled it back, holding it up and twisting it in my hand, wanting to see her mouth on my cock and control her movements.

"More," I said, guiding her head just a bit. "Deeper."

She let me guide her, trying hard to please me but she gagged when I pulled her down too forcefully. I let up, loosening my grip on her hair.

"That's good, Kate," I said, wanting her to know how well she was doing. "Stroke with your hands."

She did, taking me more deeply, stroking with both hands. I watched her, aroused by the view of her mouth on me, the thought that she was eagerly sucking me, the sensations washing over me almost overwhelming. My cock hardened under her lips and the warm wet motion of her tongue. Soon, I was so close I had to distract myself, breathing in deeply to stop from coming too quickly.

"Pull off, *now*," I said, needing her to stop or I'd go over. She licked the head once before glancing up at my face, waiting for my next command. "Good *girl*," I said. "You have a sweet mouth, but I want your other lips on me now."

I pulled her up and then stood before her. "Undress me."

She did, pulling the shirt off my shoulders and down my arms, dropping it onto the pile of her clothes. Finally, I was naked in front of her, my cock hard as rock and wet from her saliva.

I took her hand and led her back to the bedroom, picking her up and throwing her onto the bed so that she lay across it sideways on her back. I climbed over her, spreading her knees with my own and leaned down, kissing her, rubbing my cock over her pussy. When I pulled away, I admired her beneath me, my gaze moving down over her face and lower to her naked body, thighs splayed wide, completely open and ready.

"Are you going to tie me up?" she said, breathless, waiting. I was amused by her eagerness and knew then—finally—that she was turned on completely by the idea of bondage. Still, I had to teach her not to question me. She had to learn to let go, to accept whatever I chose for her and for us, to not anticipate.

I frowned purposely. "Kate, a proper submissive doesn't ask questions about her Dom's plans on how to top her. And she makes sure to use the proper form of *address*…"

She covered her eyes with a hand. "I'm sorry, *Master*. It's just that I'm *curious*—"

I silenced her with my mouth, kissing her in mid-sentence. Then, I pulled back, examining her, trying to determine how far to take her and how quickly.

"I don't want to move too fast with bondage so I didn't bring any gear," I said, keeping my voice soft. "It can be very arousing but also scary at first. Maybe just a bit for now. Your hands perhaps…"

I rose up and went to an armoire, sorting through my belts, testing them one after the other, but I was unhappy with them all. The leather was too thick and unyielding. She'd get abrasions from them if she tugged on them too much in the heat of the moment. Then I examined a hanger with several ties on it, selecting a black leather tie. It was supple enough that it wouldn't chafe. I returned to the bed and held it out in front of her so she could see it. Thin and flexible, it was from my time in college. She grinned as I examined it. I caught her grin and turned to her.

"Ms. Bennet, that grin is entirely *inappropriate* to the mood I'm trying to create…"

She covered her mouth, trying to hide a huge smile. "Master, I'm sorry," she said, her voice betraying amusement. "But I was imagining you wearing it when you were a college student... So hip with your thin leather tie. I bet the co-eds were all over *you*."

"Oh, I was very *groovy*, Ms. Bennet, in my day," I said, grinning back at her, enjoying her impertinence despite my best attempts to get her to take this seriously. To bring her back into scene, I took her hands very roughly in mine and held them over her head, my grip firm, my expression as stern as I could muster given my own amusement. "You are too cute, *Katherine*," I said as I loomed over her, "and able to distract me too well, but I want you to focus on what I'm doing here and *now*."

Her eyes widened, the smile fading on her face. I didn't want to scare her, but I wanted her in the right headspace. She had to take this seriously if it was going to work. It couldn't become a joke. It was serious.

"I'm sorry, *Master*," she whispered.

I stared into her eyes, trying to impart as much dominance as I could. "If your mind wanders, I'll have to bring you back with me," I said. "I want you here, with me, mentally and emotionally, Kate. With *me* in the moment. Focused."

She nodded but said nothing and I hoped I hadn't gone too far too soon. She was being disciplined through my show of displeasure at her attitude. I kept my eyes on hers, waiting to see her compliance. She breathed in deeply beneath me and I watched her physically relax, her body going limp.

"Good *girl*," I said. I held her hands above her head with one hand and reached down to touch her bottom lip with a finger, stroking the tiny scar there. How I'd imagined kissing her lips, licking that scar... Then I leaned down and kissed her deeply, passionately, my lust and need for her almost overwhelming.

She let out a little groan when I ground myself against her pussy.

I pulled away and bound her hands together with the leather tie, the knot tight but with some space so that there was no pressure on her skin.

"Test them. Feel them. They won't get any tighter than that, no matter what you do. I've used a special knot so don't worry. They should be fine no matter how you pull on them. But if they do get tighter, tell me right away if it becomes painful in a way you can't tolerate."

She nodded and tried to pull her wrists apart. Then, I moved her on the bed so I could fasten the other end of the leather tie to one of the spindles in the headboard. There wasn't much give. She pulled at the tie to feel how secure it was. She wouldn't be able to get free if she wanted to. Truly confined now, she was here until I released her. She couldn't run away.

I saw the transformation in her. I always looked for it the first time I tied up my new subs—that moment when they realized they were at my complete mercy. It was subtle, just a change in breathing, a look in their eyes when their helplessness finally hit home. I could tell Kate panicked a bit when the reality of her bindings hit home. Her eyes widened in surprise, and she starting breathing fast. I placed my hand around her neck to check her pulse, which was elevated, and watched her intently.

"Now you understand," I said, my own arousal growing. That moment was always such a turn-on for me. It was why I was attracted to bondage and dominance. I loved having total control over my sub. I loved her surrender to me and the trust she had to place in me. "You're completely mine now, Katherine. All you can do is kick me and scream, but I can easily gag you if I want, and besides, Mr. Neumann won't hear you."

"Are you *trying* to scare me?" she said, her eyes bright.

"*No*," I said softly, "but this is serious now. You have to trust me completely to let me do this." I let that sink in for a moment. "*Do* you? If you don't, we'll stop right now."

She searched my face. I waited for her to decide, my breath held. She could shut this down right then and there if she wanted.

"Yes," she said, her body relaxing fully, her body limp beneath me. "*Master…*"

Then I kissed her, watching her as I did, one hand cupping her cheek. The kiss started off soft and tender, but soon became more intense, more needy, my tongue finding hers, insistent, searching. I closed my eyes and sucked her tongue into my mouth, then licked her bottom lip as I had fantasized about for weeks, biting it before moving down over her chin and neck, stopping over her carotid to feel her pulse again to monitor her level of excitement.

She was excited.

I squeezed her ample breasts, kneading them, pulling the lacy fabric down once more so that they jutted out. I began sucking her nipples, biting them gently, before sucking them once again, increasing the pressure of my teeth each time, always licking and sucking afterwards until her nipples were rosy and erect, her breasts swelling. I bit just hard enough for her to notice I was biting but not enough for any real pain and always laved the nipple with my tongue to soothe it.

"I don't like *pain*," she said, sounding almost drunk. "*Master*," she added quickly, her voice shaky.

"I'm just seeing how far I can go with you," I said softly. "You don't really know yet what you like and what you don't like if you haven't really tried. I can tell you *like* what I'm doing now by how your body responds," I said, thrusting two fingers between her labia to see how wet she was. "I won't go too far. Now keep completely still or I'll have to tie up your feet as well."

She closed her eyes as I moved lower, tracing my tongue

down over her belly to her pussy. I began to lick her all over again, slowly, pressing my tongue flat against her, not making direct contact on her clit just yet. Finally, I spread her thighs and ran my tongue up and over her clit. In response, she moaned out loud.

When I slipped several fingers inside of her, she clenched around me. I knew she wouldn't last long if I moved my fingers.

"Master, I'm so close…"

"Good girl," I said, pleased that she remembered. I pulled away and lifted her, turning her over so that she was on her knees, her weight borne by her elbows, her face to the side pressed against the bed. I ran my hands over her, stroking up and down her back and down her thighs. Then I slipped fingers between her labia and began stroking slowly up and inside her wetness. When my thumb made contact with her anus, she tensed completely.

"Please, *no*…" she whispered, her voice alarmed.

"Shh," I said, leaning over her, my fingers still inside of her, thumb pressed against her. "You signed the contract, Kate. This is part of it. I won't penetrate you now. I'm getting you used to the sensation. *Relax*."

She remained tense, so I wrapped my other arm around her and played with her clit, hoping that the pleasure from the contact combined with that of my fingers inside of her overcame her reluctance and she'd relax. When I finally felt her body go limp once more, I kissed her shoulder, then bit it gently.

"That's my good *girl*," I said. "No moralistic judgment of what you enjoy allowed, Katherine. Just let yourself *feel*."

I kept stimulating her in that position, fingers on her clit, fingers stroking her just a few inches inside, my thumb moving in a circle over her anus, and I brought her once more right to the brink of orgasm, her breathing fast, her thighs trembling.

She gasped, barely able to speak. "I'm *going to*..."

I immediately withdrew my fingers and remained still, my cock pressed against her pussy but unmoving.

"Just breathe, Kate," I said, kissing her neck and shoulder. She breathed in deeply, her breath shaky, and soon, I felt her relax.

Finally, I turned her over, kneeling on the bed and pulling her hips into position on my lap, spreading her thighs wide. I stroked the head of my cock over her labia slowly, circling her clit each time. I pushed just inside of her, then pulled out, stroking her clit, repeating it over and over again, building her back up so that she was breathing hard and fast.

"What do you *want*, Katherine?" I said, watching her face. "Tell me what you want. *Beg* me."

She panted for a moment as if considering. "Please, Master," she said and licked her lips. "*Fuck* me."

It was a first—a first of many times she'd beg me to fuck her, so close to the edge that it would take no more than a few thrusts to send her over. I slid into her, filling her entirely, my fingers on her clit. She groaned, her eyes closing.

"Yes, you like that, don't you?" I pulled out completely and stroked my cock over her clit again. Then I thrust inside all the way again and kept thrusting, my fingers light on her clit and soon, I saw her grit her teeth and knew she was going over.

I leaned over her, sliding into missionary position quickly, my hands on either side of her head, my face over hers. "Look in my eyes," I commanded. "Say my name when you come."

She tried, but all that came out was a hoarse whisper. I thrust faster, harder, until finally, I came as well, my eyes locked on hers, the pleasure almost blinding me. Then I collapsed against her, my face in the crook of her neck.

For the next few moments, we both recovered, not saying anything. I kissed her neck, shoulder, her face, and finally, her mouth. Then I withdrew slowly so I could watch my come ooze out of her. I saw her smile and then turn her face away to hide it.

"What's that smile about, Ms. Bennet?" I said, smiling myself. "Does my kink amuse you?"

She said nothing, but I could see she was holding back.

"*Well*?"

She didn't—or couldn't—speak, but I saw mirth in her eyes.

"I can't wait to see it over other parts of your very delicious body," I said. "Maybe your luscious breasts. Or that smirking mouth, which I'm going to kiss right now, just to wipe that smile off your saucy face."

I lay on top of her, kissing her again, barely able to keep the smile off my face. Then I pulled back and looked in her eyes. "A Dom isn't supposed to lose control of the scene so easily. I may have to spank your delicious ass to remind you to show proper respect for your Dom's kinks…"

Her eyes widened at that. "Now?"

I shook my head. "Oh no. Not *now*. Your first spanking will only come before a good fucking. I wouldn't want to waste getting you all wet. I'd only spank you when I was going to fuck you immediately afterward. And my spanking would make you very wet."

Her eyes widened at that, and I hoped I'd planted a seed that would bear delicious fruit for us both.

"We're still two to one," I said, smiling. "I won't be really happy until it's three to one."

"Three?" she said, closing her eyes. "I don't think I can do three."

I nuzzled her neck. "Of course you can. If you can do two, you can do three. You're young and you're multi-orgasmic."

"I don't think so," she said. "Two seems to be the most I can have in one encounter."

"You've just set me a challenge, Ms. Bennet," I said, enjoying the chance to try. "The kind a neurosurgeon like me can't resist."

I began nibbling at her neck again, unable to get enough of her smooth skin.

"Please, no," she said, gasping just a bit when I moved down to her nipples. I sucked one and she gasped and arched her back. They were still extremely sensitive from earlier. "I'm too sensitive."

I rose up briefly and frowned at her. "*Katherine...*" I kept my expression stern. "You signed. Is this truly a red-light matter?"

She blinked rapidly and shook her head. "It's just," she said, softly, "I'm so tender right now…"

"All the better to make you come again," I said. "Women are different from men, Katherine. You have a very minimal refractory period and can orgasm again almost immediately if you relax and let me take control. The way you *agreed* to…"

"What if I don't want to?"

"You gave control over your body to me. *I* want you to. I thought you understood that."

She sighed and closed her eyes, turning her head to the side.

I crawled up until I was directly over her, took her chin in my hand, and held her eyes with mine.

"What is it, Kate? Why are you resisting this?" I shook my head, surprised that she'd resist. "It's not like another orgasm is a bad thing."

She shook her head in return but said nothing.

"*Slave*," I said, my voice firm, "are you mine?"

She inhaled deeply. "Yes," she said, finally yielding. "*Master...*"

In the end, it turned out that Kate could come more than three times. In all, five. I made her come five times without stopping, using my fingers, tongue, and my once-more erect cock, to prove a point and reinforce that she wasn't to resist me, no matter what, unless what was happening was a red-light matter. Coming five times was not one.

By the time I was finished with her, she was almost incoherent, but lay with a satisfied smile on her face.

"I'm going to be sore tomorrow,'" she said, closing her eyes as I untied her hands.

"Good," I said and rubbed her wrists where she'd pulled at the leather tie. Then I lifted her up into a seated position in my lap and began massaging her shoulders. "I want you sore. I want you to remember that you came five times. That *I'm* the one to set limits for your body, not you. You're far too timid and fearful to do so. You're too inexperienced. You don't know yet what you're capable of sexually, Kate. Let me be the one to discover how far you can go. That's what a D/s relationship is all about."

"I'm so tired…" she said, her eyes closing. "I have to get home. I'll call a taxi…"

"Shh," I said, cradling her in my arms. "You'll stay here tonight. You need to recover. Just lie with me."

"If I'm not at home and—" she said, then hesitated. "And that person comes by, they may become suspicious."

"*Katherine*," I said, my voice firm, "when you're with me, I make the decisions. You're with me. I've decided you're staying the night."

She exhaled and then gave in, relaxing into my arms. "It's your neck, not mine…"

"It is." Then I laid her down on the bed and went to the bathroom, bringing back a warm washcloth that I used to wipe her off, starting at her face and then moving down over her body to her pussy, touching it gently to wipe away my come, the touch of the washcloth on her sensitive skin causing her to gasp just a bit.

I smiled, enjoying the thought that she was well-used.

"Does that please you?" she asked. "The thought I'm in pain?"

I stopped what I was doing and frowned. "Is it truly pain?

Or is it just discomfort from a very thorough and enjoyable fucking?" I waited for a moment, watching her. "Answer me, Katherine. Is it because you were well-fucked? Remember the rules…"

She was silent for a moment. "Yes, *Master*," she said finally, a bit of resistance in her voice.

"Yes, *what*?"

"Yes, Master," she said, her eyes closing. "It's because I'm well-fucked."

"Good *girl*," I said and kissed her.

"Can I ask why you call me a girl? I'm really not, you know. I'm almost twenty-five," she said while I continued to clean her. She opened her eyes. "A quarter century."

I considered while I provided her aftercare. The topic of how a Dom addressed his sub hadn't come up yet in any detail and it varied from Dom to Dom. Some called them "slave" while others called them "Little One" or by their name. The purpose of the scene was for each to assume a role and exchange power. Dominants did what they could and thought was necessary to reinforce the roles of dominance and submission. The name you called your sub could help in that process.

"I know you're a woman, Kate. You're an intelligent, passionate, caring woman. I respect you. I would never fuck a girl. The essence of a D/s relationship is power exchange between consenting adults. The submissive has to trust the Dominant enough to give over total control to him. In order for you to trust me, you have to *feel* that I truly am dominant in personality. That I can exert total control over you with confidence." I stopped my motions for a moment and turned to her to see her response.

"You sound like a professor giving a lecture."

"I *am* a professor."

"Of surgery…"

"Of surgery, but I could teach BDSM. I do give lectures

sometimes. You wanted to understand, Kate. You have to feel submissive for this to work. If you don't, you won't yield control to me. I have to use every weapon in my arsenal to ensure you feel it because that mind of yours is just too intelligent, too busy. When I call you "girl," that reinforces the difference between us. I'm thirty-seven, so I'm older than you. I'm more experienced. I'm more knowledgeable about sex. Most importantly, I'm able to control myself. Therefore, I'm able to control you. You can trust me to do so and you can just release yourself completely to feel whatever I decide you should feel."

I resumed cleaning her off, thinking about the whole Dom/sub relationship.

"Why are you doing this?" she said, curious. "I could clean myself off. Isn't this a servant's job? Shouldn't I be cleaning *you* off?"

I paused and caught her eye. "Are you in any kind of condition to wash me?" I smiled briefly. "You turn yourself over to me completely, Kate. You allow me to restrain you, elicit intense emotions in you, to make you feel strong passions and sensations, to use your body as I want to use it. You're my responsibility. My *complete* responsibility when we're together. Your body needs to be cleaned and tended. Your mind needs to be calmed and comforted. Doing so is my responsibility as well. Submissives can be very delicate emotionally after an intense scene. They need to be cared for. It's called *aftercare*. I enjoy doing it."

"So is our *scene* over now?" she asked, ever the student. "We're back to normal people?"

I stroked the cloth over her thighs. "I'd prefer that when you're here, we stay in scene. Usually, I don't have a sub stay overnight, but in this case, I don't think you should go home."

"Why don't you let them stay? Potatoes and gravy mixing with meat a bit too closely?"

I smiled at her metaphor, but kept my eyes focused on her body as I wiped her off. "Something like that."

"So, technically, I should still refer to you as Master."

I nodded. "I'll give you a bit of leeway since you're new." I threw the washcloth across the room into a laundry hamper and I knelt on the bed between her legs, my hands on my hips. "But next time, I expect perfect compliance with the terms of the contract or you'll get a spanking."

"Promise?" she said, a wicked expression in her eyes.

"Oh, *you*…" I laid on top of her, my face in her neck. "That's called topping from the bottom and deserves a spanking in and of itself. Or perhaps orgasm denial…"

"Yes, please, no more orgasms tonight!" she said, giggling.

I rose up above her, unable to hold back a smile. "Ms. Bennet, I can see you need a lesson in proper submissive *behavior*." I reached down between her thighs to touch her clit and she gasped, cringing away from me.

"No, please, Drake, *don't*…"

Then, to my surprise and shock, she bit her lip and turned her face away. I'd pushed too far with her. She was still too defiant, still too independent. She wasn't ready yet to completely submit as her saucy retorts showed.

"*Shh*," I said, rolling over and pulling her on top of me. I cupped her face in my hands, and wiped her tears away. "I *won't*. But don't tell me what to do and what not to do. Don't even tell me what you *want* unless I ask you. It's not your place, Kate," I said and then added, "*Katherine.*" I had to correct myself for I, too, had let myself slip.

She nodded. "I'm sorry *Master*."

I pulled her down so that her head rested on my shoulder, and stroked her back gently, one hand stroking her hair. We remained like that for some time.

Soon, she dozed in my arms and both of us fell asleep.

I woke sometime later, unaccustomed to having anyone in my bed when I was trying to sleep. In the five years since Maureen and I split, I had never once had a woman sleep over–not even with the few vanilla relationships I'd briefly had. I lay in bed and watched Kate, who slept facing me, one hand under her cheek. She looked so sweet and delicate–almost angelic–and at the same time, her lush body spoke of such pleasures. I had to stop myself from getting all emotional about having her there with me, in my bed. I felt a bit apprehensive about it, but at the same time, I didn't want her to go.

The night had been successful. I'd pleased her, her pleasure satisfied me, and we made a start at establishing a D/s relationship. I still had a lot of work ahead of me if I was to ever introduce anything more intense with her. These thoughts went through my mind as I lay awake. From long experience, I knew that if I was ever going to fall back to sleep, I'd have to get up and do something for at least half an hour so I went to the living room and picked up a guitar, plugged it into my amp and put on some headphones. I didn't want to wake Kate up. No need for both of us to be sleepless. I began to play the sheet music Kate had found earlier, a touch of sadness in me at the thought that my father was dead and that the hopes the two old friends had of growing old together would not come to be.

It was while I was playing that I felt Kate's hands rest on my shoulders. I stopped playing immediately and removed my headphones.

"You woke up."

She nodded, her arms wrapped around herself, naked and lovely standing there in front of me, the light coming in from the window highlighting the gold in her hair.

"You are a vision of loveliness in the moonlight."

She smiled, and although I expected her to cover herself, she didn't, and that pleased me. I wanted her to have no inhibitions with me. I wanted her to be completely relaxed with me.

"You couldn't sleep?" she said softly.

I shook my head and strummed the guitar, the sound faint because the headphones were still plugged in. "I woke up and my mind wouldn't stop. Sometimes playing helps."

"You still won't play for me?"

I exhaled heavily, not wanting to play for her, my reluctance to involve her too deeply in my life fighting with my desire to have her all to myself.

"No, it's okay," she said, but her voice betrayed her. It sounded hurt. "I understand. Potatoes and meat…"

Then I thought, what the fuck… This woman has just allowed me to tie her up and take complete control over her. I unplugged the headphones and started to play, and then I sang the lyrics, trying my best to shut off thoughts of what this meant for me and Kate.

The lyrics spoke of two old men sitting on a park bench like bookends, and I imagined my father and Ethan sitting in Central Park doing just that. It made my throat choke up a bit, but at the same time, I felt something deep inside my chest. I was with the daughter of my father's best friend. I was sure that if my father had ever met her, he would have loved her. Beautiful, smart, leaning to the left… My father would be a total sucker for her.

I finished and finally looked at Kate, wondering what she thought. Then, to my surprise, she took my face in her hands. She kissed me, her eyes wet.

"Thank you."

She left me sitting there as if she was too filled with emotion to stay. I put down my guitar, knowing better than to leave her alone at a moment like this. I went to the bathroom and saw her standing by the sink, a wet washcloth at her eyes. She was such an emotional person. That emotion was an amazing thing to me, for I knew I could control it and harness it to make our relationship all the more intense, but at the same time, I felt conflicted. Could what I gave her be enough for someone like Kate?

"Come back to bed," I said, my voice soft.

"Just give me a minute." Her voice was shaky with emotion, so I went behind her and slipped my arms around her, pulling her against my body. I said nothing, just rested my chin on the top of her head for a moment. Finally, I leaned down and kissed her shoulder before turning her around and embracing her.

"Sweet, *sweet Kate*..." I tilted her head up and looked in her eyes, wiping moisture from her cheek. "Why the tears?"

She shook her head, breathing in as if trying to get her emotions under control. "It's so beautiful and so sad," she said. "They were old friends with so much history. My *father*..." She swallowed back emotion. "I can't imagine losing my father."

I nodded. At one point in my life, I couldn't imagine it either, but then he was gone, his life snuffed out in a moment and I would never see him again.

I brushed her hair off her cheek, then led her back to the bedroom and pulled back the blanket, pointing to the bed. She crawled in and I followed her, spooning against her from behind, my arm around her waist.

"Close your eyes."

She snuggled down beside me, but I heard her breathing and knew she stayed awake for quite a while. Like me, she was probably thinking of two old men sitting on a bench in Central Park.

CHAPTER 25

KATE LEFT THE NEXT MORNING, insisting on taking a taxi and not letting me drive her to her apartment, her fear of this anonymous person hanging over her head.

I went to work, invigorated after our night together and morning pleasure. I would have liked to spend the day with Kate, but I had work to do and so I threw myself into my cases, shutting off everything but the work at hand. Knowing that Kate was mine now, that she'd signed the contract and that she wanted to explore D/s with me, removed any doubt about our relationship from my mind.

I was happy–actually happy—for the first time in a while, the sense that all was right with the world unfamiliar to me.

8th Avenue was our place and I would check my watch all day when it was our night together, excited to be meeting her there. Although I usually liked to be the one to arrive at my sub's apartment, with her waiting in proper submissive position—on her knees by her bed, naked, her eyes downcast, her hands behind her back—it didn't work out that way with Kate.

Instead, she would be the one to arrive after me for invariably, no matter how I tried to arrive later, I was perpetually early. It would be me who was waiting with bated breath, unable to hide my excitement when she walked up the stairs and through the door. Everything was backward from my usual routine with a sub. Indeed, there was no real routine anymore, and while I occasionally felt that it wasn't a good thing, I pushed that out of my mind and tried to enjoy what I had with her.

I had Kate all to myself. Willing, excited, open to me.

She'd text me when she arrived outside my building and then I'd stand at the door and listen to her feet on the creaky old stairs, two shots of Anisovaya in Yelena Kuznetsova's crystal glasses. We'd drink a toast to each other before falling into our respective roles. I'd take the glass from Kate's hand and place them both on the sideboard. I'd wrap my arms around her for a moment, giving her time to fall into sub mode with me, and I would transition into Dom mode. We'd experiment. I'd tie her up in different positions so she'd get used to the different kinds of bindings, ropes and spreader bars.

Everything was going along smoothly until the week that her period was due and she tried to avoid me. I stood at the doorway on a Sunday morning before she left, examining a wall calendar.

"I'm free Monday, Tuesday, Thursday, and Saturday this week," I said, because I had practice on Wednesday and a gig on Friday. "I hope you can make all four nights."

She shook her head and stood beside me, examining the calendar. "I'm due on Tuesday," she said, touching the date. "It will last until Friday. I can't make Saturday night because this person doesn't work that night. I guess we have to take a week's break."

No way. I was not going to take a week off from her. I shook my head. "I don't like that, Kate," I said, frowning. "Just because you have your period doesn't mean you can't come to me."

"I don't *think* so," she said, holding her hands up, stepping away from me. "I have bad cramps and on the day before and on the first day I'm what my father calls a hellcat."

"No, I still want you here. You said you had every Tuesday and Thursday for sure and one day on the weekend that you'd *always* be free, so I want you here then if I can't have you on Saturday. Monday as well. I have many techniques guaranteed to tame beasts, hellcats included."

"*Drake...*"

"*Katherine*," I said and pulled her against me. "You forget that I was married for five years to a woman who had periods. I'm also a doctor, in case you also forgot that fact. I even did an OB/GYN rotation and delivered babies, did C-sections, cut out uteruses. Why, I even had my whole hand and part of my arm inside a woman delivering a breech twin..."

She grimaced at that. "There's no reason to be together if we can't do things," she said, trying to wrestle free from me, but I held her tight, nibbling her neck playfully.

"What do you mean, we can't do things?" I said in mock affront. "We can *always* do things. Besides, a good orgasm will help your PMS and cramps."

"I could *never*," she said, making a face. "I'm way too uncomfortable. I can't imagine it."

"You can and you *will*," I said. "*Submission*, Katherine. It's what I want. I don't want to be away from you for so long."

"But it's *disgusting!* Haven't you heard about masturbation?"

"Why should I masturbate when I can have you? You are *such* a good Catholic girl despite being a socialist..." I reached down to her waist and tickled her.

"I'm *not* a socialist!" she said, laughing and squirming in my arms. "I'm not a good Catholic girl either. If I was, I'd still be a virgin and wouldn't let you tie me up and fuck me."

"And I'm so glad you're a bad Catholic girl, Kate," I said and laughed out loud. "If you weren't, I'd die of blue balls."

I chased her around the apartment, and she almost fell on

one of the small carpets that slipped beneath her feet when I cornered her. I caught her from behind and held her firmly.

"Now, no more arguments about it. I want you here on Tuesday and Thursday," I said, my voice firm, not to be deterred by her petty excuses. "I won't fuck you if you really don't want me to, if it really upsets you that much, but I *will* make you come and you will make *me* come. No more arguments."

Finally, she gave in and relaxed against me. "Oh, all right. But I don't have to enjoy it."

"Of course you'll enjoy it. Have I ever failed to make you enjoy what I do?"

She shook her head and then squinted at me. "I'll come by, but I can't promise you anything."

"I promise you that you'll be glad if you do. No regrets, Kate. No regrets."

She sighed and went through the door, but I stopped her before she closed it and kissed her quickly, squeezing her butt when I did.

"No arguments and no regrets."

Then she was gone and I was alone again until Tuesday.

Monday, I met Lara for lunch and found her in the back where she usually sat, looking impeccable. I ordered a BLT and an orange juice and took a seat across from her after our customary exchange of kisses.

"You're looking pretty happy," she said and glanced at me, a smile on her face.

"Have you been talking to Kate?"

She shook her head and forked her salad. "Not a word. How are things?"

"Things," I said and scooted my chair a bit closer to the table, "are going along swimmingly."

"Do tell."

I smiled. "I'm going really slowly with her," I said, thinking of our nights together. "I've restrained her using rope and cuffs and a few spreader bars. She seems to enjoy it."

"Good," Lara said and took a drink of her coffee. "I thought she was submissive. And I thought you two would get along well, considering you're both well-educated and come from well-off families."

"You didn't know we knew each other before hand, did you?" I said and frowned at her.

"What?" she said and made a mock face of affront. "Me? Do something as underhanded as that? Never." She laughed. "No, Drake. I had no idea you two knew each other. I was as surprised as you both were. It's just one of those happy coincidences that happen now and then."

I nodded, not sure if I really believed it, but if she did know, she wasn't going to tell me. I would have liked to push her a bit, but I'd known Lara for a long time. There was no way she'd give it up if she didn't want to. She was a defense lawyer and had a great poker face. Not to mention a will of steel.

We ate the rest of our lunch, talking about work and careers and holidays. Then it was time for me to get back to the hospital. I paid my bill and waited for her to do so as well.

"You really like this girl, don't you?" she said, her briefcase in hand, her eyes narrowed.

I considered. Yes. I did really like Kate.

"She spends the night," I said, offering Lara a piece of personal info I knew she was searching for.

She smiled and shook her head. "Drake Morgan…"

"Don't go getting all excited," I said quickly. "I don't like her leaving so late and taking a taxi home, and she won't let me drive her home in case this friend of hers sees us together. I'm protecting my reputation. That's all."

"Yeah, sure, Drake. Tell me another one."

"That's all, Lara," I said as firmly as I could.

But even I knew I was lying.

I kissed her cheek and was out the door before she could say anything more, but I found myself smiling at the same time.

ON TUESDAY, I took some time off in the afternoon so I could prepare for Kate's arrival and night with me. I'd been thinking all weekend what I could do to lighten the mood. I was determined to make her come while she was with me, even if she really wouldn't let me fuck her. First, I was going to get her a bit tipsy. Not too tipsy, because I wanted her responsive to me, but enough to relax her and loosen her inhibitions.

I was passing by Northern Cycle on my way home and saw a sign about used football and hockey equipment and that gave me an idea… She said her period made her a hellcat? I'd buy some football equipment as a joke and greet her at the door with it on. I wanted her to laugh, to relax and to have fun. I didn't want her dreading the evening and the experience so I stopped off and bought some shoulder, elbow and knee pads, an old helmet, and a cup and jock strap. I also stopped at a nearby liquor store and bought a good bottle of wine, hoping that it would both help with her cramps and relax her.

So it was with a lot of humor that I poured myself a shot of Anisovaya and put on the football equipment, waiting for her arrival sometime after seven. She texted me when she arrived and I stood in the doorway, grinning like an idiot, waiting for her to walk up the stairs and open the door.

"Oh my *God*," she said, covering her mouth with a hand, laughing.

"I thought I'd be prepared for a hellcat," I said, mumbling around the mouthpiece. I spit it out. "You don't look too hard to handle."

"You are so *bad*," she said, laughing as she removed her coat and boots.

I went to her and embraced her. It was awkward because of the bulky equipment, but by then I was laughing really hard, trying to kiss her but unable to because of the helmet. Finally, I just held her, enjoying the playful expression on her face and the fact she seemed completely disarmed by my stunt.

"You're not going to keep that on, are you?" she asked, and pulled at a shoulder pad that had come out of place.

"I don't *know*," I said, still laughing. "Kinda feels a bit kinky. You could get some pompoms. Shake your booty a bit…" I grinned, imagining her in a little cheerleader costume. "Maybe I'll keep them on just until I see how *hellish* you are."

"What's that?" she asked, pointing to the wine.

"A nice pinot noir," I said, a bit more in control. "Red wine is good for menstrual cramps. Helps stop the prostaglandins that cause your cramping." I leaned down but couldn't get close because of the face guard. "I'm going to get you good and drunk," I whispered, "and then I'm going to fuck you."

She stepped backwards, trying to escape my arms. "You said you wouldn't, Drake. I'm holding you to that."

I let her go and started to peel equipment off so that I was in my casual clothes, a white button down shirt opened at the neck and untucked, over a pair of faded jeans.

"I said I wouldn't if you really didn't *want* me to, but," I said, pulling her into my arms and putting on a fake German accent, "*Ve have vays to make you vant me to…*"

"You are a dirty, conniving *bastard*," she said and sidled away from me when I tried to prevent her escape. "I have a headache and can't drink wine."

"Just had a shower, so not dirty. My father was definitely married to my mother when I was conceived, so not a bastard. I am *not* conniving. I am *calculating*. I plan. I analyze a problem, breaking it down into its component parts, then I solve each problem so I can have the outcome that I want."

She finally escaped and ran away, but I chased her, lunging at her, grabbing her.

"I *want* to fuck you," I said. "As to your headache, an orgasm will help you with that."

"*Drake!*" she said, trying to avoid my grasp.

"*Kate*," I said, my tone chiding. "I said I want to *fuck* you. You're resistant because of out-dated sense of bodily modesty that is entirely inappropriate in a D/s relationship. I must break down your resistance. How better to do so than to get you good and drunk?"

"Why are you doing this?" she said, trying to keep me away, slapping my hands away only half-playfully. "Why are you pushing me?"

"That's what I *do*, Kate. You know this," I said, now serious. "You signed the agreement. There wasn't any clause that said you wouldn't fuck me when you had your period."

"I didn't think there *had* to be." She stood there, her eyes closed, her hands fisted. From the sound of her voice, I knew she was close to tears, despite how playful I was being.

"*Kate*," I said and put my arms around her, enveloping her in my embrace. "Just *trust* me…"

"You can't even go one week without sex?"

"There's no reason to," I said, keeping my voice soft, pressing my lips at her ear. "I don't *want* to go a week without fucking you. You wait. It will be so good for you. You'll have a nice orgasm and you'll feel so much better. I *promise*…"

"I won't be able to enjoy it."

"Let's have a bet," I said and pulled back, touching her bottom lip with my thumb. "You don't enjoy it, and I have to fuck you twice in your favorite position next time. You enjoy it and I get to fuck you twice any position I want."

"That sounds like a win-win for you," she said, smiling reluctantly. "No bets."

I laughed as I pulled her into the living room and made her sit on the couch while I poured us each a glass of wine.

"That's because you know you'll lose. How *are* you feeling? I mean your cramps?"

"I took some Tylenol. It doesn't do much."

"You need something different – ibuprofen's best." Then I motioned to her glass. "Drink that all down. You need the alcohol to dull your cramps."

She took a big gulp of wine as if she was hoping to get as drunk as possible as quickly as possible. "So you prefer old music," she said when she finished swallowing. I could tell she wasn't a big wine drinker from the way she squinted when she tasted it.

"Yes, there's more than enough great music from the sixties and early seventies," I said, amused by her nerves. I'd have to really try to calm her down. Loosen her up. "My dad was a collector and has thousands of albums."

"What's your absolute favorite piece of all time?"

"Drink it *all* down." I motioned to the glass again. "I want you silly drunk and giggling."

"You must have a favorite," she said, as if she was deliberately trying to distract me from the events of the evening.

I shook my head, refusing to let her take control. "Drink up. No more delaying, Kate."

She exhaled in frustration and drank down the rest of the glass of wine. "I'm a really cheap drunk," she said, smiling a bit. "I get drunk very quickly. No tolerance for alcohol."

"Good." I poured more wine into her empty glass. "Drink that down as well."

She took a sip. "You aren't drinking."

"This is just for show." I held the glass up. "I have to stay sober so I can have my way with you." I wagged my eyebrows.

"I don't want to do *this*," she said, pouting. "Why are you making me?"

"When we're in scene, it's not about what you want, *Katherine*. It's about what *I* want. I want *you*. *Tonight*. I've been hard all day waiting for you." I took her hand and placed it on my erection. She closed her eyes, but she squeezed me all the same.

"How can you stand to have sex with a woman when she's bleeding?"

"I'm a surgeon, Kate. A little blood doesn't scare me."

"It's gross."

"Oh, Ms. *Bennet*," I said, smiling and pressing her down so that her wine almost spilled. "You don't know what gross is. *You* could never be gross. You are an entirely delicious morsel of womanflesh and I can't wait to partake of your delights."

"You're going to make me spill," she said, trying hard to keep me distracted, but I wasn't going to let her gain the upper hand.

"Drink up." I took the glass and moved it and her hand closer to her mouth. "Drink it all."

She did, squinting once more. "You are so *bossy*."

"I *am*," I said and grinned, nuzzling her neck. "You love it." I couldn't wait to see her drunk. I wanted to see her lose control and be unable to fight me, or perhaps, not want to any longer.

"It'll be so messy," she said, closing her eyes as I pushed her sweater down and playfully bit her shoulder. "I'll be horrified."

"Kate," I said and took her chin in my hand. "Have you *ever* fucked during your period?"

She shook her head, her cheeks starting to get pink from the wine.

"No? Don't tell me how you'll feel. *I'll* tell you. You'll be orgasmic and won't notice the blood. In fact, think of the blood, what little there will be of it, as extra lube. I'm *big*. You're deliciously small and tight. I can use all the help I can get."

She sighed. "It really doesn't bother you?"

I grabbed her hand and held it against my erection once

more. "Does this feel as if it bothers me? Believe me, Kate. It *really* doesn't bother me."

"Is this a kink of yours?"

"No, it's not a kink. It's just not a deterrent." I poured even more wine into her glass and motioned for her to drink up. She complied without much hesitation.

"Oh, *fuck* it," she said, leaning back. "*Whatever*."

"Don't you *whatever* me, Ms. Bennet," I said, biting back a smile, "or I'll have to smack your round little ass."

She closed her eyes and smiled. "Promises, *promises*…"

I succeeded beyond my wildest dreams. Kate had enough wine so that she didn't care any longer. To keep her focused on her bodily sensations and not on any blood, I tied a blindfold around her eyes. She laughed as I ran a bath and tried to maneuver her into it without her falling and cracking her head. Then I washed her carefully, my fingers lingering on her clit, trying to arouse her. There was very little blood, and what little there was had no effect on my ability to enjoy myself.

She had a very intense orgasm while I fucked her from behind, my fingers on her clit. Even she admitted that she felt better afterwards. I didn't remove the blindfold until she was completely cleaned off. When I did, I kissed her warmly.

"See?" I said, running my thumb over her bottom lip. "That was good, wasn't it?"

She nodded. "I didn't call you Master once," she said, smiling, her words a bit slurred from the wine.

"You're drunk. I made allowances."

Kate went to the bathroom to fix herself up and then came out dressed in the black lace nightie I loved so much. I pulled her into the living room and put some music on the sound system. It was an old vinyl record from the sixties, of course, but rather than my usual Brit Invasion, I played something soft and mellow—something I thought would be more to her taste.

The Turtles, "You Showed Me." We sat together on the couch, her on my lap of course, her arms around my neck. She rested her head in the crook of my neck, and honestly, I didn't think I'd been happier in years.

"I should go home now," she said, yawning. "I'll call a taxi."

"You're not going home drunk," I said, shaking my head. "You'll stay here with me."

"I really shouldn't," she said, frowning. "What if…" She hesitated for a moment. "What if this *person* tries to come by my place and I'm not there?"

"Shh," I said and squeezed her. "No arguments. I bought some eggs and spinach and some nice feta cheese. We'll have what my dad called a 'hangover omelet' in the morning, to fight the one I know you're going to have."

She sighed and gave in. I kissed her cheek and then got up and put another album on the old turntable. One of my favorites, by a British artist who had acclaim among the critics but had never really won popular acclaim.

"Who is this?" she asked, tilting her head to the side.

"Nick Drake," I said. "This one's called "River Man." I like it because the guitar's in 5/4 time and in standard tuning. I play it with the band. My dad named me after him."

She listened for a moment and I realized that I was lucky in having Kate for a sub. She loved music. Maybe not my music in particular, but she appreciated it more than your average person.

"What's it about?"

"Can't say for sure," I said, examining the album cover. "He's dead and didn't say. From what I read, it's supposedly about Wordsworth's poem, 'The Idiot Boy,' which is about a mother with a mentally disabled son, but I think it's about Hesse's book, *Siddhartha*. It's really just the feel of the piece and the guitar I like."

"There are scratches," she said. "You don't mind? Don't they have re-mastered versions?"

I listened. It was impossible to avoid hearing the odd scratch or occasional hiss.

"Sure," I said but shook my head. "Real vinyl enthusiasts like the sound better. It has a certain quality that can't be caught in digital. I don't mind a few scratches to hear the original. This is a really rare album. I paid a lot for it."

"You don't like any modern music?"

I sat beside her, my arm around her shoulders. "I like some," I said. "But you're one to talk about liking old music. How old's Gorecki's piece?"

"Seventies."

"Touché," I said and smiled. "What do you like? Anything modern?"

She lifted one shoulder in a shrug, taking a small sip of wine. "Some. Mostly classical. Don't ask me why."

"Your absolute favorite piece of music ever? Besides Gorecki?"

She took in a deep breath. "Barber's 'Adagio.'"

"That sounds familiar. Where have I heard that?"

"It was in the movie *Platoon*. I saw it with my dad and it upset him so much. One of the few times I saw him with tears in his eyes."

"Oh, yes." I frowned for a moment, remembering that movie. Very realistic, according to one of my father's war buddies who went and then left before the end because he found it too upsetting. "I remember that movie. My father wouldn't go. Said the Hollywood capitalists were glorifying war or something." I said nothing for a moment, running my hand over her hair. "What else? What's next?"

"After Barber?" she said and frowned. "Not much better, I'm afraid. Music from *Master and Commander*. "Fantasia on a Theme by Thomas Tallis" by Vaughn Williams."

"I saw that. What piece?"

"The one that played during the scene when they have to cut the young man loose and let him drown."

I nodded. "I remember that." I said nothing for a moment, thinking of the music she loved. It was all sad, morose, funereal. "Gorecki. Barber. Williams. Awfully depressing music you like."

"It makes me actually *feel* something."

"Yes, but incredible sadness…"

"It's better to feel sadness than nothing at all."

I turned to her, surprised at this admission. "You don't feel anything unless it's sad?"

"Not for a long time. Not after my mother died."

I stared at her, taking her in, this woman beside me who was Kate, Katherine, so affected by her experiences. She was so sensitive. Part of my mind felt caution for someone with such a sensitive nature could be easily damaged by a careless word or deed. The other part of me relished her sensitive nature and guilelessness. She couldn't lie well. Her emotions were right there on her face and in her body. I could get so much out of her…

"You were ill after you returned from Africa."

She nodded, and I could tell she didn't want to talk about it by the way she avoided my eyes.

"Tell me."

She shook her head, forcing a smile I knew she didn't feel because it didn't reach her eyes, which remained haunted. "I didn't cry when she died," she said. "I felt nothing. It was like everything just shut off and I couldn't feel anything. My doctor said everyone grieves differently, but how could I not cry? I just went through the motions, day in and day out."

I squeezed her hand, trying to imagine a Kate who had shut down completely, turning off her emotions so she didn't have to feel anything at all.

"Then you went to Africa?"

She took a sip of wine as if trying to give herself courage. "Yes, I tried to keep busy. I think I was in denial. So I went to Africa even though I probably shouldn't have. I didn't cry until Mangaize. Then it was like I couldn't stop." She turned to me. "Why could I cry for complete strangers and not my mother?"

"You were crying for yourself."

That was it. She saw herself in those who were dying, who had lost children or parents, sisters or brothers.

She nodded and a look of recognition came over her face. "I was," she said, frowning. "I didn't think I deserved to feel sorry for myself. But those people in the camps? They deserved it."

We sat in silence for a while and I could feel the mood shift from happy drunk to sad and sober. "Sorry to be such a downer."

I shook my head quickly. "No," I said and smiled softly. "*Don't* be. I asked. Never apologize for your emotions."

She sighed and snuggled into my arms, finding comfort there, and in that moment, I knew I was in big trouble.

That Thursday night, as we lay in bed afterwards and I wiped Kate off with a warm, wet cloth, she asked about going to a fetish night.

"You want to go?" I asked, surprised and happy at the same time.

"Yes," she said, watching me as I cared for her. "When I read about them, I always wanted to go."

"Voyeuristic, are you?"

"Maybe. I don't really know yet. I *don't* think I'm an exhibitionist. The thought of people watching me makes me a bit queasy."

"I'll keep that in mind," I said, "but you have to know that people who host these events sometimes host play only parties where you have to do something."

"Like what? I don't want to have sex in front of people."

"We'd have to do *something*," I said and considered. "I might tie you up, blindfold you and demonstrate some bondage, or that kind of thing just so no one complained."

She cringed a bit, her shoulders hunching. "I don't *know*…"

"Let's play it by ear. There's a very private and exclusive pre-Christmas dungeon party in Yonkers I thought we could go to. Would you like to go? It's the Saturday before Christmas."

"Okay," she said but I sensed that as excited as she was to go, she was really reluctant about doing any kind of demonstration.

I kissed her. "Thank you. I want to take you. I have something special in mind for that night."

"What?"

I just smiled and shook my head. Then I finished wiping her off. After she finished her nightly tooth brushing and face washing, she came back to the bed. I pulled the covers over us, snuggling down against her from behind.

"What about you?" she asked. "Do you like to watch other people or have other people watch you?"

"I like to watch, yes. I can go either way when it comes to exhibitionism. I've done some tutorials and demonstrations of bondage and I can perform if I have to. I tend to like my sex private. I'll expect you to be dressed appropriately and I'll have to put a collar on you. We can do whatever you feel comfortable with."

"A collar?" She reached for her neck and then turned around in my arms so that she was facing me. I could barely see her face in the darkness, except for the contours of her cheeks and lips highlighted by the light from the window.

"Would you like that?" I said. "I'd have to make sure no one else tried to touch you or even approached you. I'm very possessive like that. I don't share my subs."

"I wouldn't want to have sex in front of people, though," she said, her hands on my chest, my arms wrapped around her. "I'm not into the whole poly scene. I'd like to watch what other people do, but I'm too shy to have people watch me fuck or have an orgasm. And I can't easily just fuck anyone."

"I *know*," I said and nuzzled her neck, playfully biting her shoulder. "I like that."

"You *do?* I thought you saw it as a failing in me." She glanced up at me, a confused expression on her face.

I felt a bit sheepish because I knew it was wholly self-serving. I wanted her to be eager to get in bed with me, but no one else. "I did, when I wanted you to fuck me that first time, but now, I see it as a definite plus. I don't want to think of you with anyone else…"

She smiled and kissed me, seemingly amused instead of insulted.

"But when we *do* go," I said, my voice chiding, "I'd expect you to remember to use the proper form of *address*…" I could barely hold back my grin. "If you don't in front of other Doms, I'd have no choice but to punish you."

Then she realized what I meant. "Oh. Sorry, Master. I've been very bad."

"That's all right," I said, biting my lip so I didn't smile. "I'll let it go tonight but I won't always be so tolerant."

"What *would* you do, Master?" she asked, tilting her head to the side. "If you had to punish me?"

"I'd bend you over my lap and spank you with my bare hand," I replied, imagining her over my knee, her nice round ass exposed. "And then I would have to fuck you, but it would be in private."

I knew she was curious about spanking, but at the same time, she was afraid to try it.

"I want to go, Master," she said, whispering. "I want you to have to spank me."

I pulled her against me, nuzzling her neck. "You are such a

bad girl to tempt me like that, Katherine. You've been very good. Except for the occasional lapse in your use of terminology, I've found no good reason to spank you. I like it that way. We have so little time together, I don't want to *have* to punish you, no matter how you might enjoy it."

She wrapped her arms around me, seemingly satisfied. Then, from out of the blue, she spoke. "You never told me much about the restraining order."

That surprised me. We hadn't spoken of it since the night we got back together after Nassau.

"For a reason, Kate. I don't like to talk about it. It was a mess."

She nodded and turned away, but I could tell she wasn't happy with the lack of discussion. I didn't like to think about that period of my life because it was very dark and I was a mess. However, she probably needed to know more, so I took in a deep breath and prepared myself to tell her more.

"Have I once hurt you in any way, intentionally? Or done something that scared you or made you upset?"

"No," she said, not meeting my eyes.

"Then please trust me that it had nothing to do with any kind of abuse."

She sighed and then, to my surprise, said nothing more about it. I was glad. Dwelling on the huge mistakes in my life was not something I tried to do too often.

We went to bed and she didn't push for more information, but I felt certain that it wasn't the last time she'd ask about it.

CHAPTER 26

I WAS WAITING for her when she arrived at the apartment on 8th Avenue on Saturday night, anticipating the fetish party. We didn't usually do Saturdays but Kate made an exception and so we had the night to ourselves without fear of her meddling friend.

She ran up the stairs, excitement on her face as she rounded the corner and I couldn't help but smile when I saw her so eager to go to the fetish club. I was in the middle of getting dressed when she arrived and was only in my leather jeans and belt, my feet and chest bare.

"There you are," I said, pulling her into my arms once I took her coat and hung it up. I rubbed my face in her hair, which smelled of Kate, her shampoo and perfume so familiar to me now that I craved the scent. "You smell so good."

She wrapped her arms around my waist, her hands sliding up my back and then down to cup my ass. I usually wasn't affectionate with my subs, and this was breaking the rules for her to be so forward, but in truth it was another thing about Kate that I craved. I loved it when she spontaneously showed me affection. I loved that she felt had rights to my body and considered it hers to touch and to enjoy.

"I think I really *really* like the pants," she said and ran her hands over my butt. "What are you wearing underneath?"

"Commando," I said, grinning against her neck. "I have to be ready to fuck you at the drop of a hat."

"Oh, *God*..." she said, gasping when my hands slipped under the hem of her dress to feel her naked pussy.

"Oh, God is *right*," I murmured against her neck. "I don't know if I can wait until later to fuck you, but I want to do it at the club."

She pulled away and looked at my face, in my eyes. "But not in front of anyone, right?"

"*Katherine*," I said, trying to sound authoritative even though I was certain that, by then, whatever authority I once had was gone. "We're in scene."

She inhaled deeply and nodded. "Forgive me, Master."

"Forgiven," I said, not that I was in the least upset, but I felt I had to give Kate what she wanted and needed—me, Dominant. "As if I could ever *not* forgive you." Then I frowned a bit. "As for what happens tonight, do you *trust* me? Do you trust me to know what you need and what you can handle?"

She looked up into my eyes. "Yes. Completely." I frowned and waited for her to use the proper form of address, smirking when her eyes finally widened. "Yes, Master."

"Good girl. I decide what happens tonight, not you. Your one out is to use the safe word."

"I never want to use it, Master," she said, frowning, her voice wavering.

"Neither do I," I replied. "Now, I see I'm going to have to wipe that frown off your face." I turned her around, tickling her from behind. She giggled and tried to wrestle out of my arms, but she was no match for me. When she was in near hysterics from my fingers, I let her go.

"Off to the bathroom," I said and smacked her on the ass. "I have something for you."

She mock-screamed and ran to the bathroom as I chased her, my hands reaching out. She stopped inside the bathroom and leaned against the vanity, waiting for me. I picked up the box holding the leather dress I bought for her during the day. It was a leather corset dress purchased from a leather shop that catered to Manhattan's leather and BDSM community. I took her measurements the last time we were together and told her I'd pick something out for her to wear.

"Take off your clothes."

She complied immediately, eager to try on whatever was in the box. I was busy unwrapping it and then I glanced up from the contents of the box and smiled when I saw her. "That's what I like to see." I went to her and pulled her into my embrace, kissing her neck and biting her shoulder just a bit, then stepped back. "I got you a very nice black number," I said. "But first, there's this." I reached into the box and pulled out a thick black leather collar that I'd selected as well. It was lined with felt on the inside and had a silver buckle and a padlock.

"My *collar*," she said, reaching up to feel her neck. She smiled and held up her hair so I could put it on.

"Wait," I said, holding up a hand. "There's more to it than just putting it on. This is symbolic, Katherine, of our relationship. It signifies that you're mine, completely and totally, when you wear it. Do you understand that? Completely and totally mine."

I held her gaze, trying to impart how serious and solemn this was.

"Yes, Master," she said, her voice a bit choked. "I understand."

"Good girl," I said and kissed her. "It means no hesitation from now on when you wear it. No questioning my decisions. No avoiding what I order you to do. You obey immediately and completely without thought or reservation. You only think of how to please me. If you don't submit fully and with pleasure to what I demand, you have to expect that I'll punish you. Up until now, we've been just playing a bit with D/s. This is serious now. Do you understand?"

"Yes, Master," she said a bit too quickly, eager to have me put it on.

I took her chin in my hands and caught her eye. "*Katherine*, I want you to focus. Tell me what this means. When I put this collar around your neck, what does it mean?"

She inhaled, blinking. I was really serious about this part and wanted her to take it seriously as well.

"It means I'm yours totally. I obey you completely without hesitation."

I narrowed my eyes at her because she still wasn't focusing.

"*Master*," she said, grimacing.

"Good girl. But it's more than just a symbol of possession. It means I've chosen you and you've chosen me. I'm offering this to you—being your Dom. You've accepted, with all that means. It means we're exclusive. People take collaring very seriously in the lifestyle. Do you understand how serious this is? It's not given lightly. It's not just for show."

She said nothing for a moment, her eyes holding mine. "Yes, Master."

I nodded, satisfied that she did understand. "Now turn around and hold up your hair."

She did and so I stepped closer, kissing her shoulder then wrapping the collar around her neck, watching in the mirror as I fastened the closure and secured the tiny padlock. I admired the thick, shiny black leather collar against her creamy skin. Then I held up the key.

"Slave," I said, my voice serious. "This key is mine, just as you are mine when you wear my collar. When I put this on you and close the lock, wherever we are, you must obey me immediately and fully. No hesitation, no complaints. If you do hesitate or complain or fail to comply, I must punish you. Do you understand?"

She nodded. "Yes, Master."

She examined herself in the mirror. The collar was shiny and thick, with soft grey felt to cushion the hard black leather.

"You look delicious, slave," I said. "I want to eat you. In fact, I think I will eat you before we go. But first, I'm going to dress you."

I slipped the black leather corset dress out of the box and Kate stepped into it. The skirt was short, barely covering the tops of her nylons. I tightened the corset with ties in the back, pulling them until the top fit more tightly, the boned bodice pushing up her breasts and squeezing them together.

"How's that feel?" I said, my dick hardening at the sight of her breasts pushed up beneath leather. I ran my fingers over the tops of her breasts spilling out over the cups.

"It's a bit tight," she said, adjusting her breasts against the leather.

"Can you breathe?"

She took in a breath. "Yes."

"Good. That's perfect. You look…" I said, eyeing her up and down. "*Delicious*." Then I reached into the box and pulled out a black lace garter belt and black fishnet stockings. "Put these on. Then I'm going to eat you."

She complied, pulling on the garter belt and then she sat on the edge of the tub and pulled on the stockings, one after the other. I knelt down and fastened each garter to the stockings. Before she could move, I forced her legs apart. She had to grip the back of the tub for support as I lifted one of her thighs over my shoulder.

She wedged the other foot against the wall, and when I kissed her, she almost jumped.

"Oh, God, Master, I don't know if this is a wise position…"

"Don't argue with me, slave. Tell me if you feel like you could lose your grip."

"Yes, Master," she said, closing her eyes as I began licking her naked pussy all over, my fingers spreading her open.

"I'm going to be very fast, Master," she said, her voice quivery. "I've been aroused all day."

I glanced up at her. "Good. Just remember to ask permission to come."

She nodded, gasping when I slipped a finger inside of her.

"Nice and wet," I said, then started licking her again, agonizingly slowly, before covering her with my mouth and sucking her inside. It didn't take long after I slipped several fingers inside of her and she was ready to come, her breathing rapid and her thighs shaking.

"Master, I'm ready…"

"You're what?"

"I'm going to…"

I stopped my motions, wanting her to work harder for her pleasure. "I'm not sure if you deserve it. I think I want to hear you beg."

"Please, Master. May I come now?"

I hesitated, making her wait. "I'll think about it."

Then, because I wanted to work her up several times so that she was really excited for our night at the fet party, I began licking her again, fucking her slowly with two fingers. Soon, she was gasping again, close once more.

"Master, I…"

I repeated this several times, and each time, her voice became more and more desperate, her thighs quaking and her breathing fast. The next time she asked if she could come, I pulled away.

"I don't think so. I think I'll leave you in need. Aroused. You'll be all the more aroused by what happens at the party."

She groaned in protest when I withdrew my fingers. I leaned over her, holding her in my arms and kissing her deeply.

We stood up, but her legs were shaky and I had to practically hold her up. I stroked my fingers through her hair.

"You'll be so ready later," I said, taking her hand and stroking it across my erection. "And so will I. Perhaps some of your inhibitions will be overcome."

I was hard as rock, my body ready, but I wanted to wait until the party, and perhaps, if she was loosened up enough, some almost-public sex, but I'd have to play it by ear. I didn't want to do anything to scare her away. I left her and slipped on a crisp white linen shirt, leaving it untucked, and then my socks and boots. Finally, I pulled a black tuxedo jacket over top.

We were ready to go.

Kate was extremely excited to go to the party and asked me a dozen questions on the drive to Yonkers.

"Will we wear masks?" she asked. "Master?" she added, catching herself.

"No need for this party," I said. "These people will be more afraid of you knowing them than you should be of them knowing you. These are some of the wealthiest and most powerful players. I'm already a member of the host's inner circle, but you'll have to sign a disclaimer, agreeing to keep private anything you see at the party, and not reveal any names to anyone. If you see anyone on the street, you'll ignore them unless you're in a social situation and it demands that you acknowledge them. This is to protect the people who attend, many of whom are very powerful people and could be harmed if word got out about their involvement in BDSM."

"What if someone knows me?" she said, her voice betraying her nervousness.

I reached out and touched her lips with a finger.

"Master," she said quickly. "Who is the owner? Would I know his name?"

I shook my head. "No. Just a very powerful banker with lots of money he made himself. He doesn't run in your father's old money circles. You might see his name on the Forbes 500 list, but not in the news. These people are very private."

"How did you meet him, Master?"

"Someone who knew him and knew me introduced us and I got an invite. After he watched me for a while, I was offered membership. Lara is a member as well. She may even be there tonight."

"Master, Lara will be mad that we're together."

I nodded. "I've smoothed things over with Lara."

"Are these all the kinky types from the one percent?"

I laughed at that but then reached over and touched her lips with a finger again. "Remember your manners, Katherine. You're being a bit lax because of excitement, but I can't be as lenient tonight as I usually am. If you disobey me in front of my very powerful and wealthy friends, I'll have to punish you."

"I'm sorry, Master. I'll do better."

"They're not all from the one percent. Some are there simply because they're good at what they do, kink-wise. Like Lara. She has several very powerful submissives, which is why she's invited. Men who run this country, but who like to be dominated in the bedroom."

We drove through a heavily wooded area in Yonkers to a mansion set high on a hill, surrounded by a security fence with remote control cameras spaced along the perimeter. A guard at the gate accepted my ID and checked my name on a list and then waved us through.

A valet opened Kate's door and helped her out. I went to her side and took her arm, handing the valet my keys. I led her up to the front door and into a luxurious foyer decorated in rich marble and mirrors, a huge crystal chandelier suspended from a vaulted ceiling in the center of the room. I pulled an invitation out of a pocket in my overcoat and handed it to a security guard dressed in a business suit, his head shaved and a wireless earphone in his ear. The guard examined it and then checked Kate out, eyeing her up and down.

"She's new, sir?"

I nodded.

"Sir, she'll have to sign," the guard said.

"Of course." I took Kate to a table where an old friend of mine sat presiding over the contracts. An older brunette dressed in a black corset and mini skirt, thigh-high stiletto boots, Mistress Innes was a Domme I knew through Lara.

"Master D," she said, making eye contact with me.

"Mistress Innes," I replied. "Good to see you again."

"You know the procedures. Your submissive will have to sign." She handed Kate a sheet of paper and a pen. "You can read it over there and sign. I'll get one of the Attendants to witness."

I led Kate to an ornate side table with a chair that had a tapestry seat. She sat and read over the document.

"Master," she whispered. "Is this legally binding?"

I nodded. "This is. It's a non-disclosure agreement. The Attendant is a notary public and can legally witness. You break the agreement's terms, you can be sued."

She signed and dated the document.

The Attendant was collared and dressed in leathers, his torso bare except for straps that crossed his chest. He wore a black leather hat and huge leather boots. Tattoos marked his chest and arms.

After he introduced himself, he turned to Kate. "You understand that you are now legally obliged to keep secret what you see here and the names and identities of those who you meet?"

She nodded. The Attendant signed in the appropriate spot and pointed to a room off the left. "You can leave your coats and overshoes in the coat check. Fetish wear is required. If you have none, you will be able to choose from what is in stock or else you'll have to leave."

I nodded and led Kate to the coat check. I removed her coat and handed it to the coat check girl.

"Thank you, sir," she said when she took Kate's coat. She hung it up and then accepted my overcoat and suit jacket and hung them up as well.

I pointed to Kate's feet. "Take those off," I said. Kate hesitated for a brief moment but then removed her boots.

"Master, what do I wear on my feet? I forgot shoes."

"Nothing. Submissives wear bare or stocking feet." She raised her eyebrows at that and I smiled. "It's psychological."

She nodded, staring down at her feet as if she wasn't all that happy with the rules, but she didn't resist.

The coat check submissive gave me four tiny tokens. "Sir, you're aware of the two drink per person maximum," she said. "Drinks are being served at the bar. The dungeon is downstairs, but there are stations set up around the main floor for demonstrations. There's dancing in the ballroom." She smiled at us and pointed to huge ornate double doors. "Have an enjoyable evening, sir."

"Thank you," I said and took Kate's hand, leading her through the doors and into another world.

We stood just inside and took in the scene. Perhaps fifty people stood around in small clusters, men and women dressed in leather and latex, some with collars on, various body parts exposed depending on their status as Dominant or submissive. Classical music played in the background from a small trio made up of a pianist, a violinist and a bass player. All wore fetish attire.

"These people are the movers and shakers," I said as I stood behind Kate, one arm around her, my hand resting on her hip. I wanted to show my possession of her to any onlookers. They'd know to approach me if they were interested in a scene with her or us, and of course, I'd politely decline.

I wasn't sharing Kate with anyone. I didn't mind other Doms looking at Kate. I was quite proud of having her as my own, but I couldn't tolerate the thought of anyone else touching her.

"I hope I don't see anyone I know through my father," she said.

I squeezed her from behind for she'd forgotten once more to use the proper form of address.

"*Katherine…*"

She stiffened in my arms. "Oh, sorry. *Master*. I'm just so nervous."

"I know," I said. "Let's get you a drink. I need you relaxed but still aware of the rules."

We went to the bar and I ordered two shots of vodka. We held them up and toasted each other as we always did and shot them back. I kissed her after she'd barely swallowed the vodka because I wanted to taste it on her tongue.

"This is going to be a great night," I said, excitement brewing in my chest.

We wandered around the main floor, and I introduced Kate to a couple of Doms I knew who where also there with their submissives. The greetings were short and although friendly, none of them were inclined to say much more than a hello. Everyone was here for the show. At various places on the main floor were the apparatus of kink, like the redesigned miniature pommel horse, a St. Andrew's Cross on the wall with manacles at the end of each of the arms. There were tables with whips and floggers, spray bottles and towels everywhere. It was like a gym or exercise room mixed with bondage gear set against an eighteenth century salon with ornate furniture and a huge marble hearth.

Kate shivered visibly. "Why do these people like this? All of this—domination, submission, pain and humiliation, Master?"

"*These* people, Katherine?" I said, my eyebrow cocked. "You happen to be one of *these* people now. Maybe you're not into pain or humiliation, but you're into submission. It's not illegal, so don't judge, Katherine. *Understand*."

I led Kate to a couch by a huge bay window and sat her down, while I remained standing in front of her.

"What's going on in that mind of yours, Ms. Bennet?"

"Master, I was just wondering why people are attracted to BDSM. Why you are. Why I am."

I sighed heavily. "In the end, does it matter? I've tried to understand why I am. Understanding why doesn't change things. I still want it."

"So you understand why, Master?"

I looked away, inhaling deeply. "Perhaps."

She didn't push for any answers and I was glad. I was tired of debates about why people were kinky. Freud tried to understand it, fascinated by sexual deviance. When I was really curious about my reasons, after Maureen left me and I met back up with Lara and trained as a Dom, I was sure it had something to do with my childhood and my sense of being betrayed by the women I loved after my mother left me, but now, as a successful, professional man, I didn't care why. I just wanted to enjoy.

She smiled at me, and as I looked at her face, so bright and beautiful and open, I felt warmth for her that surprised me in its depth, and I smiled back.

"I'm just glad to be here with you tonight, Master," she said, her voice low. "I'll do whatever you want me to do."

I reached down and took her hand, pulling her up and into my arms. "You make me very happy, slave."

I kissed her, my fingers threading through her hair, one hand on the small of her back, pulling her against me. She was so good, so warm, so open. I pulled away and brushed a lock of hair off her cheek. "But we're being observed. We have to do something public to merit participation in this evening. It also puts us at as much risk as others. It's the only way we'd be trusted to keep identities secret. I'd like to demonstrate an over-the-lap spanking of you in public, and then, I'd like to fuck you in private."

She blinked rapidly. I was sure she'd be pleased that finally, I'd finally spank her but she didn't look pleased at all. She looked a little reluctant, frowning. "I don't know if I like that…" she said, shaking her head. "You said you'd just tie me up, demonstrate bondage…"

I had to follow through with my threat to punish her for not obeying immediately and questioning my decisions or else the night would be totally wasted. "Katherine, are you refusing me?"

"It's just that it wasn't what I thought of when you promised me you'd spank me…" She glanced around at the people in the room, her cheeks red.

I grasped her hand and pulled her towards an empty spanking horse. I stood her in front of it, standing behind her, my hands on her shoulders.

"I'm giving you a choice, slave, which I wouldn't usually give a submissive. You can have a barehanded over-the-lap spanking in front of everyone over there," I said, pointing to a black leather cushioned divan in the corner, a couple of feet from the wall. "Or you can have a spanking using this spanking horse. Choose."

It took her only a moment to decide. "Over the knee, please, Master."

"Stay here." I went to an Attendant who stood on the sidelines, his arms crossed. We spoke for a moment and the Attendant nodded, giving me permission to use to the equipment. I returned and stood in front of Kate, my hands resting on her shoulders. I caught her eye, staring into hers, a frown on my face so I could drive home how serious this was.

"This slave has displeased me," I said, my voice rising so that anyone close could hear. "I'm considering what punishment I have to administer."

I could sense the shift in the air as several couples near us turned to watch.

I turned Kate around to face the small audience, my hands on her shoulders. "She's new and isn't yet quite as careful in her obedience as she should be. I have to keep reminding her not to hesitate or question my commands. Frequently, I have to remind her to use proper forms of address. I'm going to administer punishment for her failure to obey immediately and without question. Since she's new, and since we've never done this before, I have to go slow. I thought this would be a good time to demonstrate how to spank a novice submissive the first time. Over-the-lap."

Kate stiffened under my hands and I knew I had to play it very carefully or else I'd do more damage than good. There were a few appreciative nods from the onlookers, because they understood the importance of teaching a sub about obedience. Subs wanted to obey deep down, even if they forgot it every now and then.

I turned Kate around, my voice firm and loud enough for others to hear.

"The first thing to do with a novice submissive like this one is to acquaint her with the purpose of the act, telling her what she will experience. This will ensure she doesn't panic at any unfamiliar sensations and doesn't view it in the wrong way. You want your submissive to obey and to accept her punishment without protest, so going through each step first will help prevent that. Later, when she's more used to punishment, you can just carry it out without detailed explanation, quickly, to make a maximum affect on her state of mind, which isn't properly submissive. But the first time, a wise Master always explains what is going to happen. This isn't about pain. This is about obedience and reinforcing submission, demonstrating to her how she has given up her power entirely and is not permitted to protest or hesitate to obey an order unless it is to use the safe word."

I turned back to those watching. "A bare hand is good for over-the-lap spanking but you can also use an implement, such as a paddle or tawse—whatever works best given that you'll have only one hand available. The spanking horse is best if you want to use floggers or a tawse or riding crop, depending on your preferences. For this submissive, I'm going to use my bare hand, so over-the-lap is best."

I turned to her and pointed to the black leather divan. Now would be a test of my ability to deliver a proper spanking as punishment. Kate had been very bad with staying in scene and obeying without hesitation. I would never have allowed any other submissive of mine to get away with so much resistance. I did with Kate, and I knew that it would come back to haunt me if I didn't put an end to it soon. Now was as good a time as any.

"When I sit, you are to lay over my lap." I tilted her head up so that she had to look in my eyes. "Are you clear on what will happen, slave?"

She nodded, but said nothing—another example of her either not taking this seriously, or being unable to focus out of anxiety.

I turned to those watching, my eyebrows raised. A titter went through them when Kate had failed to use "Master" when responding.

"You can see I've been a bit too indulgent with this slave," I said, putting on a tired voice. "She needs to learn her lesson on how to properly address her Master, and how to submit to an order without question."

I turned back to her, frowning to show my dissatisfaction,

but then I started to doubt the wisdom of the whole thing. Would I drive her away if I actually gave her a proper punishment spanking? When she still didn't respond, I exhaled. "I said, are you clear on what will happen, slave?"

"Yes, Master," she said finally. "My apologies for not using proper form of address, Master."

I nodded. "Good girl."

I sat facing the group and pulled her down over my knee. When her skirt rose up to expose her bare buttocks, she stiffened.

"Master, my skirt…" She tried to reach back, but I held her firm, one hand on the small of her back. She was modest about her body, but she'd have to get over that if we were going to be regular participants at some of the more private parties.

"Did I ask for your opinion on what is happening, slave?"

"No, Master. I'm sorry." She went limp.

When I felt her submission, I removed my hand from her back. "Good girl," I said softly, then I took her hands in one of mine. With the other, I held her down, my hand on the small of her back. I turned to those gathered around us. "This submissive is not into pain, although she doesn't yet know her true limits. She has been pestering me to spank her so she'll know what to expect. I have to ensure she understands that this spanking is done to punish her, not to reward her curiosity or give her pleasure." I bent down to her. "Are you ready?"

"Yes, Master."

I turned back to the crowd. "The first time, let the submissive become familiar with the position. Don't rush things or you'll cause unnecessary panic. The Dominant's purpose is not to create fear and anger in the sub, but to reinforce the direction of power in the relationship, to teach her what is expected of her, and to help her become a better submissive. By losing all control in this way, the sub is reminded who has the power. Generally, any man is stronger than most women, especially in upper body strength. It should be fairly easy to restrain her and keep the struggling to a minimum. But a Master enjoys a bit of struggle. The pain from the spanking should be equal to the amount of pain necessary to make the point, but no more. This isn't about sensation play. This is punishment. Keep reinforcing that."

I pulled up her skirt to fully expose her buttocks. Kate gasped.

"*Master...*" she whispered, fear making her voice quaver.

"*Shh*," I said and rubbed one of her cheeks with my hand, wanting to calm her as much as possible.

After a moment, I spoke to the others. "This is virgin ass in every way. Never spanked properly. Never claimed. I aim to do both, but one thing at a time."

A murmur went through those who watched, and someone said, "Lucky you."

I chuckled. Every Dominant in the room knew what I meant. Claiming a woman completely and totally was the most satisfying thing for us. Being her first was, if you did it right, unmatched, for she would always measure others against her first. I wanted to be Kate's first, but I wasn't ready to imagine her with someone else.

"As I said, this particular sub is new to the lifestyle and has never been punished before, nor has she experienced a sensual spanking, or anal play or penetration. She has expressed her eagerness to be spanked several times and each time I have refused. I want her to understand that *I* choose when an act will be performed, whether sexual or punishment. She imagined I was just going to demonstrate some minor point of bondage tonight, but earlier, she questioned one of my commands and so I decided to use this opportunity to demonstrate how to properly punish a new sub who is not into pain."

I ran my hand over her ass, cupping each cheek, slipping my fingers between them. When I slid one finger inside of her, she tensed, and I knew this was a test to see if she could manage public sex. She didn't protest or struggle.

"This slave is very responsive sexually. She's aroused by this even though it conflicts with her self-image as a proper Catholic girl. I've enjoyed breaking down her barriers. This is just one more that I will cross."

I kept rubbing one ass cheek softly and then I bent over and spoke to her. "Now, slave, I'm going to spank you. I don't want you to protest or make a sound. Just take the punishment. You know the safe word. Remember what happens if you use it."

"Yes, Master," she whispered.

I spoke to the others. "The first time you spank a sub, do so just to let them know how it feels and to reinforce submission. The point will be made even if you stop long before you would in a normal session of punishment."

I struck her ass cheek with a loud smack, my palm hitting low on her buttock. She didn't resist or complain, and in fact, she relaxed, as if she was now relieved to have felt the first blow. I knew she thought she could take it, but she didn't realize that in a punishment spanking, the Dom was supposed to take her right the edge of her tolerance. No more, and no less. The strokes would get harder and more painful.

I smacked her harder this time and she tensed a bit in response, perhaps shocked that it hurt more than before. I rubbed her buttocks softly to soothe them, then slipped my fingers between her cheeks to test her arousal.

"She thinks she can handle this level of pain and is relaxing. You have to up the pain in order to find the amount that is just beyond her comfort level, both physically and psychologically. This is not a sensual spanking," I said, wanting to reinforce that to the observers and to Kate. "It's punishment and should hurt enough. *Just* enough, but not more. This is to make a point, to reinforce her submission. She should just give in and take it, and if you're lucky, she'll go into what is termed 'subspace.' You must watch a sub carefully to see if and at what point this happens. At that point, you have to rein yourself in a bit, because she won't feel the pain and you could hurt her beyond her tolerance, or even do permanent damage. A Master must be exceptionally attentive to his slave during such an encounter."

She tensed beneath my hand at that, and I knew she was starting to get worried again.

"My slave has just tensed in response to what I've said. Such is the danger of demonstrating a technique. The slave can undergo anticipatory arousal or anxiety. At that point, it's good to reassure her."

I bent down to her, my mouth next to her ear. "Do you trust me, Katherine?" I whispered.

She said nothing for a moment, so I stroked her hair, then down her back.

"Katherine, I won't do more than you can take. Do you trust me?"

Finally, she inhaled. "Yes, Master."

"Good girl," I said and began stroking her buttocks again, my fingers lingering between her cheeks, slipping down to her pussy.

"This slave is nervous, but also excited sexually. Some arousal, even when being punished, is inevitable simply because she is submitting and that is arousing to a submissive."

Then I smacked her buttock again, harder than ever, and I knew that this time, it would hurt. I administered several more blows, alternating between buttocks, several in a row, before I stroked each buttock softly.

"You can see her skin is very fair and fine. She's already getting quite a delicious blush to her nice little ass from the spanking. I'll have to be mindful of that. I don't want to draw blood, but a bit of warmth and tenderness will remind her of her punishment when she sits for the rest of the evening."

I spanked her several times, each a bit harder than the last.

She was doing very well, and I was proud that she was taking it and not complaining. After several more smacks, she let out a gasp so I stopped immediately and rubbed her ass tenderly. I leaned down and whispered in her ear.

"Have you learned your lesson, slave?"

"Yes," she said meekly, a sob in her voice.

"Yes, what?"

"Yes, Master," she gasped, crying now in earnest.

"Good," I said and bent down to kiss her buttocks, one after the other, resting my cheek against one. "Perhaps you'll be a bit more careful in your behavior when I give an order."

I sat her up and turned her face toward me. She tried to wipe away her tears and it was then I saw it. A split on her lip that welled up with blood.

"Oh, *Kate*," I said, shocked that she'd bit her lip so hard that it bled. "Your lip…"

CHAPTER 27

I TOUCHED her bottom lip and my finger came back bloody. Kate covered her eyes with her hands and cried quietly, no sound coming out of her mouth. I pulled her into my arms and kissed her shoulder, stroking her hair. I was angry that I hadn't been more attentive to how she was handling the degree of pain. I should have realized she was biting her lip and stopped her.

I pulled back, removed her hands from her eyes, and shook my head when I saw her face on. Tears filled her eyes and ran down her cheeks and her lip was bloody.

"I'm sorry," I said. "You were too strong and I went a bit too far, waiting for you to make a sound to indicate you'd reached your limit." I leaned in and kissed her, taking her bottom lip between mine, licking off her blood. Then I pressed her head to my shoulder and spoke to those who stood there watching.

"This slave was trying so hard not to use the safe word that she bit her own lip, drawing blood. Drawing blood is one of my hard limits and hers, so I inadvertently crossed it. This was a mistake on my part and is due to my failure to recognize how stubborn she is and what a high pain threshold she has. We're still getting to know each other. Don't let your position as Dominant or Master prevent you from apologizing when you recognize you've crossed a line or performed inexpertly. It's the only way to regain your slave's trust."

I pulled her back from my shoulder and wiped her cheeks with my fingers, filled with regret for what happened.

"I'm sorry," I said once more. "It won't happen again. I pressed her cheek once more against my shoulder and picked her up and carried her over to the Attendant. "Can you clean off the equipment for me?" I asked.

"Certainly, Master D. Do you need a private room?"

"Yes," I said. "Preferably one with a bathroom."

Kate kept her eyes closed, no doubt embarrassed by her show of tears in front of the others. I carried her up the central staircase to a second-floor bedroom. The room was grand, with thick carpets, rich brocade wallpaper, and an enormous bed. I took her into a small bathroom and sat her on the vanity. She grimaced and I knew her ass was sore from the spanking.

I ran some water and wet a washcloth with cold water, pressing it against her bottom lip for a moment.

"I'm fine," she said when I pulled the cloth away, a tiny bit of blood still on it. "Master."

"You're strong-willed," I said. "Stronger than I knew. I never wanted you to be scarred because of anything we did together, Kate. I never want to draw blood."

"Master, it's just a bit of skin I pulled off. It won't scar."

I pulled her into my arms, glad that she seemed unconcerned about the cut. She slipped her arms around my neck, her tears now stopped, a look of calm on her face. She was in that special state of mind after a spanking; calm, relaxed, almost dreamy.

I moved back and looked her in the eyes. "Do you want to go home now? Or do you want to stay? You've barely seen anything."

"Let's stay," she said, drawing in a deep breath. "If it pleases you, Master," she added quickly, making a face and tapping her head lightly with a fist. "I want to see the dungeon if you want to take me there."

"Are you sure?" I said, doubtful. "When we first met, I thought it would be good for your 'research' but now, I'm not so sure you'll enjoy it. Things can get pretty intense. There are people who *do* want to draw blood, Kate. There are people who do want to feel pain and administer pain. People will be fucking. It can be upsetting, if you're not used to it."

"Whatever you think, Master. I trust you to know what I should do."

I nodded, pleased that she was leaving the decision up to me. Despite my fuck-up with the spanking, she seemed to be more compliant and attentive.

"Maybe it would be good to go down there for a short while just so you can satisfy your curiosity. I may only go in a bit deep, but not to the really intense places."

"You're scaring me, Master."

"I don't intend to," I said. "Just want you to be prepared for what you'll see."

"I trust you, Master."

"I value your trust, Katherine," I said and I meant it completely. "I take your trust in me very seriously."

I kissed her softly and stroked her cheek with the backs of my fingers, touching her bottom lip. I pulled her off the vanity and took her back down to the main floor, walking through the people who gathered to watch various displays and demonstrations of technique. A few people nodded to me as we passed but didn't speak to me. We recognized each other, but weren't on speaking terms.

The atmosphere in the basement dungeon was decidedly different from that of the airy, light atmosphere on the main floor. Dark, old brick, with black painted walls, the space felt like a cave. Heavy bass-filled electronic music played in the background, its beat insistent.

The lighting was subdued and there were imitation torches on the walls, flickering with an eerie light. The basement was divided into room-like spaces. Each room was open to a central aisle. Inside each room was some kind of apparatus and people inside using it to inflict various forms of pain or pleasure on each other. People down here were all dressed—or undressed—for the atmosphere. Leather, latex, rubber. They wore and used chains, masks, ball gags, spreader bars. There were whips and floggers of every design on boards, and over the sound of the music came the unmistakable crackle of electricity.

"Electricity, Master?" Katherine asked softly, hesitantly.

"Yes," I said, my voice low. I squeezed her hand. "We won't go there."

We walked around a crowd watching a scene, threading through people who stood and watched, Doms with their subs on leashes, some kneeling at the Dom's feet, watching the events transpire inside the rooms.

In one room, a twenty-something male sub with short, spiky white-blond hair was standing in the center of the room, his hands bound to hooks in the ceiling, his legs spread with a spreader bar. His testicles were imprisoned in a cock and ball stockade and his Dominant struck him on the ass and back with a flogger. Dressed all in black leather, the Dom stood behind his sub, whispering something into the sub's ear every few strikes. The sub had a huge erection, obviously turned on by what was happening to him.

"…not allowed to come until I give you permission…" the Dominant said to his sub.

We stopped for a moment and I stood behind her. "Cock and ball torture," I whispered in her ear. "I can feel myself shrink just watching it."

I checked into one room and recognized Lara and her sub.

She was busy flogging her male submissive, who was bent over, his hands and feet in manacles.

"Master, that's Lara," Kate said to me.

"Shh," I whispered in her ear. "Remember your manners. She's in scene right now. Don't distract her. I said she might be here."

"Sorry, Master. That's Mistress Lara."

Kate watched her, fascinated. Lara's blonde hair was pulled back into a high ponytail. Her submissive wore only a leather jock strap and leather boots, a ball gag in his mouth. She stood behind him and lazily slapped his bare ass with the flogger. It was as if she couldn't really be bothered to flog him with any focus.

"Why does she look so bored?"

I stood behind Katherine, my arms around her waist, ignoring her lapse. "He's likely into humiliation as well as pain and submission. She's humiliating him by appearing as if she doesn't really care. It's what he likes and needs."

The sub's ass was getting progressively redder as she flogged him with a bit more gusto.

"You. Are. A. *Worm*," Lara said, her voice derisive, punctuating each stroke with a word. "You should be wriggling on the ground at my feet, *slave*."

Kate turned to me. "He likes that, Master?"

"Oh, yes," I said. "He's actually a very hot-shot fund manager by day, but in private, he likes to submit."

"She did that to you, Master?"

I smiled. "Yes. I never intended to use these kinds of techniques, but she wanted to see if there was a sadist in me—or a masochist. There wasn't."

As we watched, Lara bent over her sub and spoke to him, whispering in his ear. His ass was thoroughly red. Then she went around beside him and picked up a cane. She ran it over his ass, trailing it between his ass cheeks before striking him several times, leaving long streaks.

I could feel that Kate flinch with each strike of Lara's cane, so we left Lara's scene and went to another room where a man dressed in leather chaps was busy fucking a woman suspended from a hook in the ceiling, her hands in cuffs above her head, her feet in straps also attached to the ceiling. She wore a blindfold and had a ball-gag in her mouth.

Kate seemed fascinated with that scene, and watched, entranced, as the Dominant rammed into her, hard, his hands on her hips, pulling her to him with each thrust.

I stood behind her, one hand on her belly, the other wrapped around her and resting on her neck to measure her pulse and respirations. I needed to know what she responded to, and what she disliked.

"You *like* this scene," I whispered in her ear. "Your pulse just increased, your breathing is shallower. If I slipped my fingers between your lips, you'd be nice and wet. Do you want to try this one day?"

"Yes, Master," she said, her voice a bit shaky. "Except for the ball gag and the cane."

I squeezed her and she held my hands, which were now clasped around her waist. "What do you think of all this, Katherine?"

"I think that these people need each other, Master," she said. Then, after a moment, she turned to me. "I need *you*," she said quietly.

I bent down and kissed her neck. "I think it's time to go back upstairs," I said, my voice a bit husky.

"Yes, Master."

I took her back up the stairs and out of the darkness with its heavy scent of sweat and sex. We passed through the bright salon where couples stood and watched demonstrations of various techniques, and through the next room with darker lighting, where people danced to a VJ playing some Latin music. There was a video projected on a wall and a mirror ball spinning, casting the room in thousands of sparkles.

We stopped at the edge of the dance floor and I took Kate in my arms and started to dance, placing one of her hands on my hip and the other on my shoulder while I held her hips. We swayed together for a few moments, and she seemed to really enjoy dancing.

"Drake Morgan, MD," she said, smiling back at me. "I didn't know you could dance, Master."

"Oh, I have been known to cut a rug from time to time."

"Cut a rug?"

I laughed. "It's an old term for dance."

I led her around the dance floor for a few moments, smiling broadly. The next song was slow, and we danced close together, her arms around my neck, mine around her waist, her head on my shoulder, my face in her neck. The scent of her perfume, the warmth of her skin, the floral in her hair, and the soft swell of her breasts against my chest all conspired to give me a semi and I squeezed her closer for a moment, pressing my hips against her.

"Ms. Bennet, I think I want to fuck you now," I whispered in her ear.

"Yes, Master," she said in a breathless voice.

I took her hand and led her out of the ballroom and to the staircase, back to our bedroom. I pulled her over to the bed and threw her onto it. She laughed as she bounced. I climbed on top of her, smiling.

I was in no hurry. I rested on my hands above her, my eyes moving from her face lower to her breasts and belly. Then I bent down and kissed the tops of her breasts, which bulged out over the bodice of her leather dress.

"You look delectable."

I lay to the side of her and pulled the leather bodice down just a bit so that her nipples poked out over the edge. They puckered in the cool air. I began to suck and nibble them, and was rewarded with her arched back and closed eyes.

"Master," she said, writhing beneath my mouth. "Are you going to tie me up?"

"Shh," I replied and sucked one nipple into my mouth, my tongue circling the areola. She groaned and arched her back, pressing her breast into my face. I pulled away briefly. "A slave doesn't ask what her Master has planned. She just waits. But I think I'm going to just fuck you missionary style tonight."

She frowned.

"Don't do that," I said, touching her mouth. "Kate, you have to let me decide how I want to fuck you. It shouldn't be your concern. You're going to come one way or the other, so leave this up to me. Do you understand?"

She nodded and let her mouth fall open slightly. "Yes, Master. I'm sorry. I just thought…"

"When we're in scene, don't think of anything but pleasing me. If it pleases me to fuck you missionary style, it should please you to comply."

She inhaled deeply and closed her eyes. "Yes, Master. I apologize. I just can't help but be curious why. I thought at a BDSM party…"

How could I explain why I wanted to fuck Kate this way? I could have tied her up, blindfolded her, and treated her like an object for my pleasure, but she was more than that to me now.

"I like contrasts and appreciate irony, Kate. Downstairs, everyone's busy getting their kink on, and here we are, fucking like a pair of ordinary lovers."

She opened her eyes and stared into mine for a moment. "So this is an ironic fuck, Master?" she said, unable to keep a grin from starting.

I smiled widely at that. "*Very* ironic. How transgressive are we to fuck like this at this party? Now *shh* and spread your legs wide like a good vanilla girl."

I very deliberately and very slowly began to seduce her with my touch and my mouth and my words, whispering in her ear how much I wanted her, what I would do to her. I undressed her slowly, removing the dress and garter belt and hose, for although I loved the way they looked, I wanted her completely and totally naked.

I undressed as well and lay between her legs, fully naked, my erection pressed into her groin. I took my time, working her up with my fingers and my tongue, exploring every part of her body. I wanted her aching with need. Then I pulled her on top of me so that she lay with me between her thighs.

"Seduce *me* now," I said and closed my eyes. I wanted to feel her trying to arouse me.

She did, using her mouth and tongue and fingers, rubbing herself against me, shoving her breasts in my face, her hair trailing down my body as she placed a trail of kisses down my belly and began teasing me, breathing on me, slowly licking my cock all over before sucking the head into her mouth, her hands cupping my scrotum.

When I finally entered her, she was so ready, it took barely five slow thrusts with my fingers on her clit and she was groaning.

"Master, I'm going to…"

I didn't stop. I kept on thrusting, circling her clit with my thumb. Then, when I felt she was almost there, I lay on top of her, holding her face in my hands. "Say my name."

She tried, forcing her eyes open as her orgasm started, and I fucked her missionary style until she cried out "Drake" instead of "Master."

I came as well in a few strokes, ramming into her with each spasm, white hot pleasure blinding me. Then I collapsed onto her and panted in her ear for a moment, kissing her neck.

She smiled beneath me.

"So?" I said, raising my eyebrows and grinning like a fool. "How was vanilla ice cream without any chocolate sauce and whipped cream tonight? Good enough?"

"More than good enough, in case you didn't notice, Master."

I bent down and kissed her throat. I slipped out of her and quickly sat up between her thighs and spread her legs wide so I could watch my come drip out of her.

She covered her face, trying to hide her smile.

"What are you smiling about, Ms. Bennet?" I said in mock disapproval. "The fact I can't deny at least one of my kinks?"

She opened her hands and watched me enjoy myself with my artwork.

We were, at that moment, completely out of scene and I didn't care at all. The contract we had wasn't binding. We were both free to throw it out at any time and be whatever it was we wanted to be to each other.

At that moment, despite the fact I was totally off the reservation with Kate, I was more fulfilled than I had been in a very long time.

CHAPTER 28

THERE WERE ONLY a few times Kate was at 8th Avenue before me, despite how much I wished it was the opposite. The Monday before Christmas Eve, she was there waiting for me. She'd brought along a couple of strings of Christmas lights and some decorations.

"You're here," I said, smiling. "I was running a bit late in surgery."

"I'm here, breathlessly waiting for you," she said.

"Just the way I like you."

She smiled and helped me with my coat and packages. Then, she held her hands behind her back.

"What have you got there, Ms. Bennet?" I asked as I went to her, wanting to pull her into a hug. Before I could, she held up a sprig of mistletoe, grinning.

"Just this," she said. She tried to hold it high enough so that it was over my head but she was too petite. "I need stilts to get it over you."

"No stilts for you," I said and grabbed her, my arms slipping around her. "Too dangerous. Don't you know you're supposed to hold it over your *own* head? Not that I need any excuse to kiss you…"

I kissed her and soon, the mistletoe was forgotten. I grabbed her buttock with one hand and slipped the other under her skirt to feel her garters and naked pussy.

"*Mmm*," I said against her throat. "Slave, you are nice and wet."

She gasped when my fingers slipped inside of her. "You've got me trained like Pavlov's little submissive, Master."

I laughed at that and then pulled away. "Speaking of Russians, how about some Anisovaya?"

She nodded and went to the sideboard where the crystal glasses waited. We made a toast to each other.

While I nibbled her neck, she stroked her hands up my back. "I wish we could go somewhere to celebrate New Year's, Master."

I didn't say anything for a moment, trying to decide whether to tell her my plans or keep them as a surprise.

"We'll meet here during your time off. I have no surgeries for a week. I was thinking we could go to a special fetish party for New Year's," I said, knowing she would probably enjoy another visit to a dungeon. "This time, we'd have to wear masks so no one would recognize us. The party I have in mind is in Brooklyn. There'll be fewer people there that either of us might know compared to the one in Manhattan."

She smiled broadly and rewarded me with a kiss. "What are you doing tomorrow, Master?"

"I'll probably just stay around here. Play some music. You could sneak over if you can make an excuse to be alone for a couple of hours…"

She smiled. "I'll make sure. Will they dance at these fetish parties?"

"You liked dancing with me the other night, did you, Ms. Bennet?" I said, remembering how we had danced at the party.

"Yes," she said. "I did, Master."

I picked her up and swung her around my hip then I twirled her around before pulling her tightly against my body. "I did learn in high school," I said. "Although I haven't had much time to practice. I know a few moves..."

I went to the sound system and sorted through some records until I found an old mix with the right music.

"'Rock Around The Clock,'" I said, smiling. "Bill Hailey and the Comets."

I led her around the room, showing her how to do the Jitterbug, tripping a bit over the loose Persian carpets on the smooth hardwoods. I picked her up, lifted her up high, and then tried to swing her over my other hip, repeating my earlier move, but my foot caught on the carpet and I tripped just as she was coming down in a less-than-graceful arc. I fell backwards and we tumbled to the floor.

I tried to save us both from the fall by absorbing the force, my arm going back to stop us, but Kate fell a little too close to the sideboard with it's sharp corner, which struck her on the side of her head, right above her eye. By the time we came to rest on the floor, I realized something was wrong. She was on her back, her hands covering her eye.

"Oh, God, *Kate*," I said, and bent down to her. "You're hurt..."

I turned her face towards me using one hand, while I cradled my other hand against my body, and saw immediately that she needed attention. I left her lying on the floor, her hands touching her cheek. I went to my bathroom cabinet and rummaged around, searching for my first aid kit and some gauze and bandages.

"How are you?" I asked when I ran back with supplies. I pressed the bandage against her brow, examining her. "Did you black out at any time?"

"I don't think so. But I saw stars."

"Are you in pain? How many fingers can you see?" I held up a hand with three fingers.

"Three," she said. "My head really hurt for a minute, but now it just stings."

"Look at me, in my eyes," I said, and when she complied, I examined the cut. It was deep enough that it needed more than just a few butterfly bandages. I didn't have my emergency surgical kit at the apartment, so I'd have to take her to the hospital.

I exhaled. "*Goddammit*. I have to take you to the ER and get you stitched up. I don't have my bag here."

She smiled, despite everything. "You have one of those little black doctor bags?"

"Something like that," I said, but I wasn't smiling. "Damn, Kate. You're going to have to just come with me. We'll have to risk it. That cut is too deep for butterfly sutures."

"You're the neurosurgeon."

After I bandaged her up, we took the Mercedes to St. Luke's ER. It wasn't the nearest hospital, but Kate didn't want to go to Harlem because her friend worked there. I didn't want to go to NY Presbyterian because I had too many colleagues and associates who might recognize us. The ER nurses at St. Luke's had Kate in an examining room within a very few minutes of registering.

She sat on the gurney in the tiny space and I stood between her knees, examining her, brushing her hair back, feeling so bad that my two left feet resulted in harm. The young female physician entered and I stepped aside. She asked who I was and what happened. I related how we were dancing the Jitterbug. I told her that I was clumsy, and Kate fell and hit her head against a wooden table. She seemed upset that I spoke instead of Kate, but how could I explain that I needed to take control in such a situation? Not only was I a Dom, I was a surgeon. It was as natural as breathing to me.

The physician looked at Kate carefully while she repeated the story. Kate watched me and smiled while she told the story of her fall.

"He was a bit out of practice," she said. "Like twenty *years* out of practice."

"I'll be back in a bit to stitch that up," the attending ER doc said and left us alone.

I continued to examine Kate, cradling my injured hand, a tensor bandage on it. "I'm so *sorry*," I said. "I'm really not usually so clumsy." I grinned at her, trying to make light of things. "Kind of ruined the mood I was going for..."

Kate laughed and squeezed my good hand. "At least I was in the best hands. I mean, if you're going to fall and crack your head, who better than a neurosurgeon to look after you?"

The doctor came back in. "Can you excuse us, Dr. Morgan?" she said to me. "I'd like to speak with Kate alone for a moment."

I knew what that meant. She wanted to ensure the wound wasn't the result of domestic violence.

"Certainly." I leaned over and kissed Kate briefly where she sat on the examining table. "I'll be right back. You'll be fine."

She nodded. I stood outside the room, angry that I was being kicked out, but I had to remind myself that I would do the very same thing if I were confronted with the same scenario. Too many domestic violence incidents were described as the victim falling and hitting their head on a table or doorknob. We were trained to ask questions, however uncomfortable.

I went back a few minutes later and pushed the door open to check on Kate. I stood watching as the doc stitched Kate up, examining each stitch carefully, and holding Kate's hand on the other side of the gurney.

When she was done, Kate sat back up and the doc gave

instructions about aftercare. I felt somewhat insulted. I was a surgeon with a lot more experience than she had, but she was probably just dotting all her i's and crossing her t's. Finally, we left the hospital and went back to the apartment.

"You're staying here tonight," I said when we were back inside. I brought Kate a glass of milk instead of Anisovaya and motioned to the couch.

"No bondage tonight?" she said, sounding a bit disappointed. "No Anisovaya?"

"No alcohol for you, just in case. No bondage because of my wrist," I said, holding it up. "I'm useless. Not in fighting form and neither are you."

Kate sighed, and after I shot back my vodka and Kate drank her milk, we nestled on the couch.

I put on some Gordon Lightfoot, something my father played a great deal when I was a kid. There was a song in particular I wanted to play for her, although I felt a little foolish. It was pretty romantic and sentimental at the same time.

"What's this?" Kate asked.

"A Canadian musician, Gordon Lightfoot. One of my dad's favorites. He had every single album. He was a big fan of Canada, raving about their health care system and welfare safety net. He almost wanted to move there after the war, but he was accepted to Columbia and wanted to go study medicine."

"If he was such a socialist, why did he go to war?" Kate asked, frowning. "Couldn't he get an exemption?"

"He volunteered. He said if the poor black kids had to fight, the middle-class white kids should as well."

"That's what my dad said," Kate replied. "No wonder they were friends…"

I nodded. "He almost loved Canada as much as Mother Russia. We used to go to Northern Alberta every year on vacation and he'd do surgery up in the wilds. We'd fly in to these tiny communities and he'd donate his services. We'd always stop in Montréal and eat this absolutely horrible mess of french fries and gravy and cheese curds called poutine."

Kate smiled and snuggled against me and for a while, we said nothing, listening to the music. "What is this piece?" she asked finally.

"It's very appropriate," I said and went over to a stack of old albums. "This song is called 'Affair on 8th Avenue.'" I brought some sheet music over and handed it to her.

I sat back down while Kate examined the sheet music, reading the words that spoke of an affair between a couple who met at an apartment on 8th Avenue—just like us.

"It's beautiful. Can you play this?" she asked as she read it over.

"I can, but not with this wrist. I guess my hopes of playing with the band over the weekend are out."

"It's that bad?"

"I think I tore something. My whole arm hurts."

Kate snuggled against me. "So, what are we going to do?"

I shrugged, my good arm around her. "I don't know."

"I could *do* you," she said, her voice taking on suggestive tone. "You don't want me to just, you know, crawl on top? You wouldn't have to do anything…"

I leaned my head back, looking at her from the corner of my eye. "You're going to try to top me, are you?"

"It's not topping and you wouldn't be bottoming. It's just having sex. I'm a little aroused. I was really looking forward to tonight."

"Ms. Bennet, you're a horny little thing," I said, unable to keep a grin off my face, "but I just can't be safe with only one working hand and arm…"

"You don't have to restrain me."

She climbed onto my lap without me requesting it, but I

didn't fight. She leaned down and kissed me. I let her. Since that first night in Kate's apartment, I always signaled when our scene would start by embracing her, then kissing her. She had never made the first move.

At first, I didn't kiss her back, wanting to see what she would do and how far she would take it. When I didn't respond by taking over, she pulled away and looked in my eyes.

"You don't want me to fuck you?" she said, her voice a little hurt.

"Kate, I am never fucked," I said softly. "*I* fuck."

"But you're injured and can't manage," she said in protest. "I could do all the work. If it would make you feel better, you could always *order* me to."

"*Katherine…*" I eyed her, trying to decide whether to go with this or change direction. "Remember, we're always in scene at my place."

She sighed. "Drake, do I have to go home and resort to Big? I *need* you…" She kissed me now, and I could tell she was upset from the force of the kiss.

"I don't want you going home by yourself," I said when she pulled away. "I want you to stay here tonight."

"I want to lick you, and suck you, then I want to get on top and ride you. That wouldn't please you?"

"I thought you were uncomfortable taking the lead in sex, Kate," I said, wanting her to tell me how she felt. "That's why submission appeals to you."

She looked in my eyes. "I feel like I could do *anything* with you."

I smiled at that and ran my good hand up her back, my gaze moving over her body then back into her eyes. Usually, the idea of being passive didn't do anything for me, but Kate was so eager to please me…

"Convince me," I said, my body responding to the image of her riding me.

"I *need* you," she said. "I may see you only two or three times over a week but I want you *every* day and—"

I placed a finger over her lips. "I didn't mean with *words*…"

Then she understood and smiled. She crawled up a little bit closer to me, her arms around my neck, her groin pressed against mine. Her kiss started off soft and then deepened, her tongue finding mine. I tried to remain totally passive while she ground herself against me, pressing her breasts against my chest. When she pulled her sweater off, leaving her in only her lace bra and skirt, she pressed her beautiful breasts against my face and that did it. My dick had definitely overcome the fact that I wasn't in control. She pulled the fabric of her bra down to expose her breasts and squeezed them, tweaking her own nipples until they were hard. She closed her eyes and continued to touch herself, her lips parted.

It was a revelation to me. Watching her touch herself, trying to arouse me, wanting to take the lead, was delicious. I waited as long as I could and finally, I reached behind her with my good hand.

"Let me help you with that." I pulled her closer, my mouth covering one nipple. I took control, despite my injured hand. When she tried to initiate something, I took over. When she climbed on top of me as I lay naked on the bed, I directed her, telling her where to put her hands, how fast to move, when to kiss me. But she succeeded in getting me interested in the first place. I didn't tie her up, I didn't blindfold her, and I definitely didn't make her come four times before *I* did.

Kate came once and then I did, fucking her from behind, which didn't rely on my hand for anything.

She didn't call me Master once.

Afterwards, as we lay with our limbs entwined, the sheets wrapped up around us, Kate turned to me.

"You survived vanilla sex yet again."

I grinned. "It's all I ever used to do."

She said nothing for a moment and I knew her curious mind was working. "How did you start doing BDSM?"

I rubbed her back with my good hand, but didn't say anything.

"You don't want to talk about it?"

"Not really," I said. "Let's just say I recognized my Dominant side, then got some instruction—"

"From Lara," she offered.

"From Lara," I said.

"This was after your divorce?"

"Kate," I said, not really wanting to get into it at that moment. "I'm tired. I have to sleep…"

"I'm sorry," she said, her voice quiet. "This is hard for you. We're mixing up the food on your plate too much, right?"

"Shh," I said and shut the light off. Then I pulled closer, spooning against her the way I always did when it was time to sleep. I knew she wanted to talk, and I knew she wanted more from me, but at that moment, I was far too sleepy to comply. I closed my eyes and barely even thought about the night's events before drifting off to sleep.

CHAPTER 29

I WOKE in the middle of the night to find I was alone in bed. I frowned, for Kate was usually a deep sleeper and almost never got up for any reason. I felt the bed and it was cold—she'd been up for a while. I quickly left the bed and went to check out the bathroom, but the light was out and it was empty. With a bad feeling building in me, I went to the living room. She wasn't there either.

She'd left the apartment in the middle of the night.

I checked my watch. It was almost 5:30 and I'd be getting up for work soon anyway, so I sat down and sent her a text.

Why did you leave?

It took a while for her to respond.

I couldn't sleep. You were sleeping like a baby. I didn't want to wake you up so I just left.

I didn't accept her answer, of course. There was no reason to leave in the middle of the night. She was upset about something and I was going to find out what.

You can always wake me up. I wanted you to stay with me so I could watch over you, make sure you're all right. Kate, I'm a neurosurgeon. We get concerned with any kind of head injury. You should have stayed until I said you were okay to go home. Do you have a headache? Nausea?

She responded right away.

I'm fine. My mind just won't slow down. I have a deadline and am working on my article.

That still didn't satisfy me. There had to be something wrong. She was the woman who wanted a real relationship, and just when I think we're on the road in that direction, she leaves in the middle of the night. It didn't make sense.

You think too much. When you're with me, you don't have to think. That's what I'm for. But I suspect something's bothering you for you to leave without saying anything. Tell me what's the matter...

There was a pause before she responded.

Damn. If she had to think about it, it meant she wasn't happy.

Drake, I still have to think, even when I'm with you. I still have to think when I'm not with you.

You want the truth?

I didn't respond for some time. *Did* I want the truth? Instead of all the texts, I had to hear her voice so I could tell what her emotions were so I called her number. In truth, I wanted her there with me so I could touch her. She didn't answer my call, letting it go to voice mail.

Instead, she sent another text.

Drake, I don't like being shoved into a small box in the corner of your life.

I called again and again, but she continued to ignore me. Finally, I gave up and replied to her text.

You're not in a small box in the corner. In case you didn't realize it, you're in a very big and very central box in the middle of my life.

Another long, pregnant pause, which I took as a very bad sign.

I don't know if that's enough.

Fuck. Just *fuck*. This was going south far too fast. I had to go and see her, speak with her in person to stop this—whatever this was—from happening.

I'm coming over.

This time, she was quick to reply.

Don't. It's too much of a risk.

I said nothing and went to the bedroom to get dressed. While I was pulling on my jeans, my cell dinged. I picked it up and checked.

I'm not at my apartment any longer so don't come by. Don't risk it. We'll talk later. I just need to be alone for a while.

There was no way I believed that. It was way too early. The deli wouldn't be open and there was nowhere for her to go.

Being alone is the last thing you need, Kate. Meet me at 8th this morning. My surgical slate is empty the rest of the week because of the holidays.

There was a pause, during which time I kept dressing, then I went to the washroom to brush my teeth. When my cell dinged again, I checked it and there were three texts from her, two of them very long. I knew that they were bad news and my throat constricted as I read the first one.

Drake, this person knows that I was with you last night and thinks you've abused me. This person may tell my father no matter what I do. I want to warn you. I told her we broke up. We have to say goodbye for real, Drake. I can't take this any longer—this compartmentalization of my life. This pretending that we're not seeing each other, worrying that someone will find out and hurt you. I don't do compartmentalization, Drake. My life is a stew. I don't know anything different. I've tried it your way, but being just one part of your life isn't enough. The truth is that I could love you if I let myself. I can't do that because you don't do love. Lara told me that before we met and you made that abundantly clear to me.

You'll have no trouble finding another sub who wants to be a compartment in your life but that's not me. I'd only always want more and we'd have to end it, eventually. The longer we wait, the harder it will be. That first night, you said that someone would love me one day, and the truth is, despite how amazing the sex is with you, I realize I'd rather wait to find him than accept anything less. If you thought you could stop me from falling in love with you, you failed miserably. I can't accept what you can give. I deserve more.

Goodbye, Drake. I'm sorry, but this is the way it has to be for both our sakes.

I sat on my bed, my head in my hands and re-read the text over and over again.

Kate was right. She did deserve more than I planned to give her. She was an amazing woman with so much potential. Other Dominants would be ecstatic to have her as a sub and probably as a life partner. Could I give that to her?

Getting all mixed up emotionally with a woman, sub or otherwise, had been crossed off my to-do list for a long time. Kate had been filling up the cracks in my life since we started together, and I was happy—really happy—for the first time in a long time. Until I met Kate, I'd been content. Things were going well in my life. My practice, my band, the Foundation, the company... I had a few friends—Dave Mills, and a few fellow surgeons at NYP—with whom I had drinks now and then or played a game of racquetball at the club. Life was good.

My memories of my marriage were not so good—the times I'd spent lying in bed with my back turned to Maureen, the two of us distant for some reason, but me too busy to find out why or do anything about it. I didn't do emotional entanglements well. I was like my bastard of a father in that way.

I guess he taught me well.

My chest felt heavy as I looked at Kate's texts. A real man would "man up" and admit he wasn't up to the challenge and let her go and find someone who could give her what she needed. I couldn't give Maureen what she needed. I wouldn't let her go and that almost got me thrown in jail and nearly cost me my career. I couldn't do that to Kate, although every fiber of my being screamed that I had to go to her, prevent her from doing this—from breaking it off with me. I knew if I could get Kate alone, I could convince her to stay, but then I'd be doing exactly what I did to Maureen.

Blinking back tears, I texted her back.

You do deserve more.

Then I threw my phone on the floor and cradled my head in my hands. I'd fucked up another relationship. Allie had been disappointed with our relationship. She pushed things and I wouldn't give. Couldn't give. I couldn't make Kate happy, either. I couldn't give her what she needed and deserved. As much as I wanted her, some part of me held back from rushing over there to beg her to stay.

I lay on my bed, staring at the ceiling, feeling like a teenage boy who just lost his first girlfriend. I considered the two weeks I had off and what I would do without Kate in my life. The only thing I knew was that I couldn't bear to be at 8th Avenue for very much longer. I'd pack up my things and go back to my apartment in Chelsea. There were too many memories of Kate at 8th Avenue.

It was going to be a very long holiday.

CHAPTER 30

THE DAYS LEADING up to Christmas were perhaps the loneliest I had ever been.

I tried to keep busy with the Foundation, sitting at the desk in my office there and going over paperwork I'd been neglecting since I met Kate and started our affair. I tried catch up on work at the company, reading minutes of the recent Board meetings, looking at financial reports, looking at product development, but honestly, my heart just wasn't in it and I ended up reading the same paragraphs over and over again.

When I felt like eating, which wasn't often, I ate cereal and toast or grabbed something from the cooler at the coffee shop. I went through the motions of my life, not really engaged. I felt as if I had a personal storm cloud over my head, raining on my day and blocking out the sun.

On the day before Christmas, Ken called me and invited me to his family's house for Christmas dinner, knowing I was always alone on the holidays.

"If you're not spending the day with that new girl of yours, why not come to Mom's place? Everyone will be there—Chris and his family, and mine of course. Better yet, bring her with you, or is that too personal for you?"

"Thanks," I said. "I may drop by. Depends on whether I'm busy or not."

"How are things going with your girl anyway? You never speak about your love life."

I hesitated. I didn't want to tell him Kate and I had broken up because then I'd be subject to a round of questions and sympathy. But I didn't want to lie either.

"We broke up."

There was a pause on the other end. "Sorry to hear that, Drake. It sounded like she was a good thing."

I didn't say anything in response, my throat constricted.

"Look, come over to the house and eat some turkey," Ken said. "Then we can go to the pub and get drunk. I'll open the bar just for us two."

I thought about dinner with his family and couldn't imagine facing it.

"I don't know about dinner but the getting drunk part sounds good."

"You *are* in love, Drake, if you pass up Christmas dinner at my place. You always enjoy spending the holidays with us."

"I'll meet you at the pub at nine Christmas night."

"Okay, bro, but seriously. Mom will be hurt if you don't show. I'll tell her you have a broken heart and that'll excuse you —maybe. See you."

"See you. And thanks for calling."

I went to Ken's on Christmas Day anyway, unable to face being alone all day. As usual, the whole clan was at their place and it was almost standing-room only at the old brownstone in the Upper East Side. I kissed a lot of cheeks, ogled the new babies and toddlers, and sat with Ken and watched the kids playing with their toys around the Christmas tree—a real one with a top that reached the ceiling. Their home was always warm and inviting, with appetizers and a bar, plus punch for the adults and another for the kids. The table was huge, decorated with pinecones and fir branches, and the food was amazing. Mrs. O'Riley knew how to cook and put on a spread.

I never had Christmas like that when I was growing up and it was too appealing to pass up. I smiled so much my cheeks hurt, but I didn't feel it inside. Quite the opposite.

I helped carry dishes out of the dining room and into the kitchen after our meal was over and of course, Mrs. O'Riley cornered me and wouldn't let me leave without an interrogation about Kate.

"So, what's this I hear about you and your girl breaking up, Drake? Ken says you're in love and don't know it."

I forced a smile. "I'm fine, Mom."

"Your eyes aren't smiling. You don't fool me. You really liked this girl."

"I did. I *do*," I admitted. "We're just at two different places. She wants more and I can't give it. That's all."

"Listen to me," she said and wiped her hands on her apron. "You will regret it for the rest of your life if you don't try with her. Believe me. You always regret the ones who got away without giving them your best shot."

"The longer we'd stay together, the more it would hurt to end it, though," I replied, thinking of how much Maureen's leaving hurt.

"The more it hurts, the more you loved. Loving that much is a good thing, Drake. Don't give it up because you're afraid of hurting in the future. The future is a lie. Life is all about how you feel right now."

I shook my head. "I feel like I have a hole here," I said and pushed my fist in my gut, just below my sternum. For some reason, she brought out the truth in me in a way that other people couldn't.

"Don't let her get away then. Trust that," she said and poked me in the chest. "Not that." She pointed to my head. "Don't let her spend New Year's Eve alone."

I nodded. "I'll consider it, but she broke off with me and I don't think she'll want me back."

"Don't think. Feel. Listen to me," she said. "I know." She nodded and turned back to her sink full of dishes. I stood beside her and dried, and she didn't say another thing about Kate, leaving me to consider her words of wisdom.

ONCE THE PLACE was clean and all the dishes were done, I kissed Mrs. O'Riley on the cheek and left with Ken for the pub. He opened the back door and turned off the alarm. We had the place to ourselves. While he went behind the bar to get us a bottle of vodka, I went to the sound system and put on a mix CD of our musical influences.

We sat at the bar, him behind it and me on a stool.

"Pretend you're a customer and I'm your bartender. Tell me your troubles, man. I'm here to listen and get you drunk."

I exhaled heavily. "What do you want to know?"

"Tell me what happened with your girl. Like I said, I thought she was a good thing. You smiled when you spoke about her. You never did that before with your other girlfriends."

He poured us both a shot of vodka. We clinked shot glasses and then threw them back.

I sighed. "She was a very good thing. I wasn't good enough for her, I guess."

"What?" he said and frowned as he poured us another shot. "My mother would smack you for saying that. How could a single, attractive brain surgeon worth a cool billion dollars, who plays guitar no less, not be good enough?"

"She wanted more than I could give." It hurt to even admit it, but it was true, and if I couldn't tell Ken, who could I tell? It made me realize once more how truly empty my personal life was.

"You weren't in love with her?" Ken asked, his voice light.

I didn't say anything for a moment. "I *think* I was."

He shook his head and pointed to the shots. "If you were in love, you'd know it, Drake. There's no mistaking it. If you were in love with her, you'd feel gutted at the thought of not seeing her again. Gutted. Like you couldn't eat. Like the sun went under a cloud. That's what it feels like to lose someone you love."

I didn't let his words register. We did another shot and smacked the shot glasses on the bar top. He poured another.

"You sound like your mother."

"She's a wise lady. Now, drink up."

We did another shot and I felt warmth in my stomach, the alcohol lightening the mood. It was a good thing I had a full stomach from dinner or I'd start to feel it even more. After the fourth shot, though, even the turkey and stuffing and gravy couldn't keep the alcohol out of my bloodstream. I felt a little loose.

"I *did* love her," I said, nodding. "I *do*."

"There's my man."

That pretty much was the last thing I remember coherently. The rest of the night was spent singing songs from our repertoire. "Heart of Stone." "Paint it Black." I was relentless in finding every sad song on the Karaoke machine, Ken and I taking turns to sing our hearts out.

We took a taxi home at 3:00 a.m., and I didn't even care that I'd left my car at the pub. I'd get it in the morning. Ken helped me up into my bed and left me, taking the taxi to his own home.

I don't even remember my head hitting the pillow.

I SLEPT LATE the next day and did nothing, turning down an invite from Mrs. O'Riley to join the family for brunch at the pub. My head ached from the vodka and late night so I pretty much spent the day and evening in my pajamas watching action movies on pay TV channels.

I was on call on the days leading up to New Year's and had to go in to deal with a trauma, a brain injury resulting from a fall, and I was glad of it because it kept my mind off Kate. Then I got an email from Michael in Nairobi, asking me once again if I'd considered his offer to come to Kenya for six months, to teach a class and take on part of his caseload. I called him and we had a great talk, about his plans for the medical college and how he could really use me there.

I had promised him I'd come one day and help out, and now that Kate and I were over, I had nothing keeping me in Manhattan. I could handle the most pressing cases during the course of January and then head off to Kenya in February to start at the college in March. It seemed like a good idea, and would keep me moving forward. I needed something to make me feel less morose. I was making myself sick with how dispirited I'd been.

Going to Kenya might be enough of a distraction to keep me from drowning in self-pity. Kate hadn't contacted me and was obviously moving on.

THE DAY before New Year's Eve, I was at NYP checking on a patient I'd worked on the night before. Lara called me while I was sitting in my office, reading the man's file.

"What's up?" she said. "I haven't heard from you for a while."

I took in a breath. "Not much. I'm probably going to Kenya in February. A colleague—a mentor—has invited me to teach at the medical college and take on a caseload."

"What?" she said, her voice shocked. "And you were planning on telling me when? The day before you left? Jesus, Drake..."

"I'm telling you now."

"What about Kate? You given up on her?"

"Other way around," I said, not wanting to rehash things about Kate, my gut knotting at even the mention of her name.

"She's in love with you, so I think you're wrong about that."

"No, I think it's you who's wrong. She broke off with me before Christmas. I haven't heard from her since."

"You big dumb...*man*," Lara said, as if trying to find the right insult. "She's in love with you."

"She ended it," I said in exasperation.

"She's in love with you and I have proof."

"What do you mean?" I frowned, a surge of something very much like hope in my chest.

"Just wait," she said and I heard her fumble around for a moment, the sound of something clattering. "Listen to this..."

I listened and heard faint voices—Kate and Lara speaking. I tried to hear what they were saying, but had a hard time making it out.

Lara spoke first, her voice firm and to the point. *"You broke up with Drake? Why? I thought you said things were good."*

Kate responded: *"The sex part was great. Better than anything I could ever imagine, Lara. This is just too much risk for Drake. I could never stand to live with myself if he was hurt because of me, because of my greed for him. But even more, I just can't do only sex. I'm not cut out for it. He doesn't want more. Considering all the shit he could get into because of me, I had to just make a clean break."*

"It's probably for the best."

"You understand."

"I do understand," Lara said. "This is my fault. The reason I chose Drake for you was precisely because he wasn't interested in anything long-term. I thought that was what you wanted as well. You know, just doing interviews, learning about the lifestyle. That's what you said to me…"

"I know I did. I did say that. I meant it at the time. But Drake is so much more…" She didn't say anything for a moment. "I think I could fall in love with him. All I know is that it isn't enough anymore."

"Nothing like a new Dom to wash away the taste of the old one. Listen," Lara said. "I can hook you up with a Dom who's looking for a life partner, if you'd like. Not every Dom is like Drake. Some want a relationship. Why don't you come to a fetish night with me? You could come under my protection and I could introduce you to a few Doms I know. Only the ones who are looking for a relationship beyond play. I already have someone in mind. His name is Steve. He's closer to your age. He's even in the arts. He does copy editing for a publisher. He's kinkier than Drake, but not a sadist. I know you're not into pain."

I wanted to shout – *What the fuck, Lara!* but kept my mouth shut, wanting to hear Kate's response.

"I can't meet with anyone else, Lara," Kate said, barely speaking loud enough to hear her. "I can't even think of it."

"You were alone for what—a year before Drake? Don't you want someone else?"

"I want Drake. I can't have him. Not the way I really want him."

"Well, I offered," Lara said as if that was that. "I still think you should come to a fetish night with me. There are lifestyle partners and there are lifetime partners. It is possible to meet someone who wants D/s and a real relationship. You won't find another man who will satisfy your submissive side outside of the lifestyle, Kate."

"Maybe I'll just go with my friend to India and become a nun, working at Mother Theresa's hospice."

Lara laughed out loud at that. "Yeah, sure Kate. If you liked Drake as much as you claim, you'll never be able to go back to normal again."

"That's hopeful."

"Look, it's hard enough to find compatible lifestyle partners, let alone someone who you could be with in a permanent relationship. If that's what you really want, you have to get out there and meet people."

"It's too soon. I can't imagine it. I only want Drake."

The recording ended. "There," Lara said. "Does that convince you?"

I considered, all the while desperately tamping down the sensation that was growing in me that I couldn't describe. I didn't want to label it *hope* in case there was none.

"She didn't say she was in love with me," I said, frowning. "Only that she thought she could. There's a difference."

"Oh, for God's sake, the two of you are head cases," Lara said, exasperated. "She's in love with you, Drake. You're in love with her. Go fucking propose to her, you dolt…"

"She ended it…" I said weakly.

"To protect you."

I sighed, shaking my head, unable to process everything I'd heard and what Lara said. "I don't know. I told Michael I would probably go to Nairobi for at least six months, maybe a year."

"Take Kate with you. From what I understand, she's pretty much an "I Love Africa" kind of person. The two of you are like two sides of the same coin."

"I have to go," I said, overwhelmed, the conflicting feelings too much for one telephone conversation.

"Seriously, Drake. Listen to me. I've never been wrong

before about two people. I knew you two were perfect for each other the day I met her."

I hung up, shutting everything down, not feeling anything because it was too confusing. I liked things neat and tidy and in control. I felt on the verge of being out of control and it was not my thing.

I SENT AN EMAIL TO MICHAEL, formally accepting his offer and then I sent one to Ethan, letting him know that I had done so and would be leaving NYP for a year. He called me shortly after, wishing me the best.

"I'll miss you, son," he said, his voice warm. "You have to do what you think is best."

"I do," I said, wishing he'd try to talk me out of it, but if he knew anything about Kate and how she felt, he said nothing. I think that's why I emailed him—hoping he'd protest and try to talk me out of it. But he didn't.

I hung up and opened a particularly difficult case, trying to lose myself in its demands.

ON NEW YEAR'S EVE DAY, I was at home, lying on the couch and listening to the most depressing music I could find on the sound system when my cell rang. I picked it up and saw that it was Elaine.

I sat up, alarmed. Something must have happened to Kate for Elaine to be calling me.

"What's the matter, Elaine? Is everything okay with Kate?"

"Drake, I hope you don't think I'm meddling, and Ethan would kill me if he knew I was calling, but we talked about this and both of us agree. Ethan wouldn't call you but I can't stand to see Kate so upset. She's a real mess. She told me you two broke up, and I don't know the exact details, but she said she was in love with you. I wanted you to know before you left."

"She said that?" I said, a feeling of something bordering on a roar building in me. "She actually said she was in love with me?"

"Those were her exact words. She said she fell in love with you. That you were so much more than she imagined."

I said nothing for a moment, my eyes closed, wondering what the hell Kate was doing. Was she protecting me once more from her meddling friend?

"Thanks for calling, Elaine. I mean it."

"You're only too welcome. I hope things work out for the best if you go to Nairobi."

We hung up and I sat and rubbed my head, squinting, gritting my teeth, trying not to over-react to the news that Kate actually said she was in love with me.

I knew then what I had to do. I had to go to Ethan and confess.

I CALLED Ethan and asked if I could come by and speak with him. He was only too glad to welcome me into his office when I arrived, after a servant had taken my coat and scarf. There were a few cleaners in the apartment, vacuuming and dusting, and several people were in the kitchen unloading boxes of alcohol and food, so it looked as if there was some event planned.

"Come in, my boy. Sit down."

I did, exhaling and wondering whether to use the short speech I composed in my mind to Ethan, pleading my case, which I had practiced on my way over. Now, it seemed too rehearsed, so I came right out with it.

"Ethan, I'm in love with Kate."

He nodded, his face poker straight. "Go on."

"I think she's in love with me, but she broke it off because she's being blackmailed by some friend."

"Blackmailed?" he said and leaned back in his chair. "Why would anyone blackmail Kate about your relationship?"

I sat forward, my eyes not meeting his. "I'm involved in…" I said and stopped, not knowing the best way to put things. "I have certain preferences…" I said, but even that sounded stupid. "I'm into kink."

There. I put it in the most blunt terms I could think of.

"*Kink*?" Ethan said, his hands folded in front of his face. "Like what? Whipping? Torture?"

I shook my head vigorously. "No, no pain," I said quickly. "I'm into what's called Dominance and submission. It's power exchange. It's when a couple play certain roles—"

"You mean BDSM?"

I glanced up at his face.

"I'm not a spring chicken, Drake," he said, and it looked as if he was trying not to laugh, pressing his lips together. "I've been around the block a few times. You're into the BD part of BDSM. Am I right?"

"Bondage and dominance, yes," I said, relaxing just a bit that at least he knew what it was and I didn't have to go into any details. "No pain. No humiliation."

He shrugged. "What two adults do in the privacy of the bedroom is none of my business," he said. "In fact, I don't really want to know. You can understand why."

"I know, and believe me, this is terribly awkward for me, but this friend threatened to tell you. To tell my employer at NYP. They also threatened to tell NYP about a temporary restraining order my ex took out on me."

"What?" he said and sat forward, frowning. "They threatened to tell NYP about the restraining order?"

"You knew?"

He shook his head. "Nigel told me about you a while ago. I

knew about Nigel because he got into trouble back when I was a defense lawyer and I helped him out. Someone tried to blackmail him. I also know about the restraining order. I learned of it when I did some sleuthing. Your dad asked me to keep an eye on you, and, well, I have ways of getting information that the usual person on the street doesn't."

I didn't know what to think about that. Nigel didn't like me. He thought I wasn't good enough for Kate.

"Nigel's the one who told you?"

Ethan nodded. "So why are you here?"

"I wanted you to know about me so it couldn't be used against me, but I understand completely if you never want me to see Kate again."

Ethan shook his head. "Look. I personally don't give a rat's ass what people do in the privacy of their own bedroom. For some reason I can't think of off the top of my head, Kate seems to have a preference for a dominant man and you're a helluva lot better than some jackass who doesn't know what the Sam hell he's doing, like that flyboy she had the sense to get rid of."

I closed my eyes and took in a deep breath. "You don't care that I'm involved in kink?"

"If I cared about your proclivities, I would have kicked you out on your ass in October. I've known about you for quite some time. Nigel told me soon after your father died. I told him I was taking you under my wing, and he let me know when I said I wanted you and Kate to meet. Look, Drake," Ethan said and leaned forward. "I know you young kids think we old fogies know nothing about anything, but I don't care what bedroom games people play in the privacy of their own homes, for God's sake. I've played a few of my own. You have to in order to keep a marriage alive, and I was married to the same woman for twenty-one years…"

"I don't know what to say," I said, sitting back, at a total loss for words.

"Don't say anything. Go home and put on you best suit and come back for New Year's Eve dinner with us. Kate will be happy. If you love her as you say you do, don't waste any more time. Tell her. Life's too short and the biggest regret I have is that I didn't tell Kate's mother that I loved her more often. Don't make the same mistake."

In that moment, I knew I wouldn't.

I shook Ethan's hand, a sensation of relief and happiness filling me that made me want to hug him, but I restrained myself, not sure that Ethan would want me blubbering on his shoulder. I went home, Ethan's words bouncing around in my head, my heart rate speeding at the prospect of being with Kate and telling her how I felt. I picked up the box with the choker in it that I planned on giving Kate for Christmas and was determined to give it to her tonight if she accepted me back and agreed to come to Kenya with me.

With that thought firmly in mind, I showered and dressed. Before I left, I grabbed Yelena Kuznetzova's shot glasses and made it back to Ethan's in record time, my heart in my throat.

Hoping…

I ARRIVED at the building and parked my car in the guest parking area and made my way up to Ethan's penthouse, more nervous than I had ever been but also more hopeful that things might work out with Kate. I tried to squash my excitement but I could barely keep it under control. I stood at the door and took in a deep breath, blowing it out in an attempt to calm myself.

I rang the buzzer and was admitted, taking the elevator to Ethan's floor. One of the serving people answered the door and invited me in. She took my coat and scarf and I went immediately into the living room. There, behind the bar, was Kate. My heart skipped a beat when I saw her. She wore the black lace dress that she wore that first night I met her and she looked...*beautiful.*

I waited and finally, she glanced up from the bottles and glasses and saw me. I smiled and held out Yelena Kuznetzova's shot glasses.

"I brought these along just in case you didn't have anything quite so special." I placed them on the bar and smiled at her.

For her part, Kate looked shocked, her face pale, her mouth open. She put the bottle on the counter and stepped back, leaning against the wall. She actually closed her eyes and took in a deep breath. I went behind the bar and took her in my arms and practically had to hold her up. I took her chin in my hand and she finally opened her eyes, which were filled with tears.

Oh, Katherine...

"Drake, you can't *do* this to me," she said, biting back a sob. "This is cruel."

"You're the one who left. You can't do this to *me*." Then I kissed her, squeezing her body against mine. She didn't stop me so I kissed her more deeply. When I pulled away, I held her face in my hands, wiping her tears away with my fingers.

"Why are you here?" she said, her voice a whisper. "You're leaving. I don't want to see you..."

"Your father told me you'd be here tonight. He told me that if I was going away, I should come over and say goodbye."

"This is torture."

I smiled, bursting to tell her that everything was all right, unable to stop grinning like an idiot. "Kate, your father *knows.* He gave me a dressing down, telling me that he already knew about the restraining order. About my 'proclivities' as he called them. He's known all along."

"He *knows?*" Her eyes widened.

I nodded. "He's been watching me for years, monitoring me for my father. He knew about the restraining order. He knew about the BDSM through Nigel."

I led her to the couch in the living room and sat with my arm around her, touching her bottom lip, brushing a strand of hair off her cheek.

"He and Nigel go back a long way. I guess Nigel faced some blackmail over his sexuality years ago when your dad was still a defense lawyer and your dad advised him. Nigel told him about me after he saw me at a fetish night."

"That's why Nigel was looking at you that way the night of my father's campaign fundraiser…"

"Yeah. He told me that I'd better not ever hurt you or he'd have my balls. I had no idea he'd told your father."

"My father *knows* you're a Dom?"

I laughed ruefully. "Who would ever have believed it? He knows even more about me than my own dad did."

"And he *approves* of you as my boyfriend…" She shook her head. "I don't understand. I thought he'd be horrified."

"So did I but I guess not. He said," and I put on a mock voice that sounded gravelly like Ethan, "*'For some reason I can't think of off the top of my head, Kate seems to have a preference for a dominant man and you're a helluva lot better than some jackass who doesn't know what the Sam hell he's doing, like that flyboy she had the sense to get rid of.'*"

She covered her mouth, tears filling her eyes. "He said *that?*"

"His *exact* words."

She closed her eyes and leaned against me. "But you left NY Presbyterian. You're going to Africa…"

I pulled back and looked in her eyes. "I figured that if I did, I could lay low for a year and return when all this blew over. I talked to the head of the college and we agreed that I'd take a year leave of absence. I've been meaning to go to Africa and do a longer stint. Teach a class at the college in Nairobi."

She shook her head. "So you came to say goodbye."

I took her face in my hands again. "I *came*," I said, taking in a deep breath, "to say that I've developed a taste for potatoes and gravy and meat all on the same fork." I stared into her eyes, my chest feeling like it could explode. "Lara played a recording of you telling her you thought you could love me. She even tried to entice you to meet another Dom and you refused, saying you wanted me. That *almost* made me reconsider leaving, but *could* isn't *does*."

I moved closer. "When Elaine called me this afternoon and told me that you said you *had* fallen in love with me, I realized that I would never meet anyone like you again in my life. So perfect for me in every way. And I think I'm good for you, too. I think I could make you happy."

I leaned down and kissed her tenderly.

"I couldn't stand it. I couldn't lose you," I said, "so I came over and spoke with your father while you were sleeping, perfectly willing to accept what ever he said I should do. He admitted to knowing about me all this time and said that if I had feelings for you, I shouldn't leave without telling you. Then he sent me home to change and I came back as quickly as I could so we could talk and I could confess my feelings for you."

Kate said nothing, her eyes searching mine, biting her lip.

"Ms. Bennet," I said and shook my head. "Kate, I *love* you. I never, *ever* want to be separated from you again."

She was still speechless, and seemed to be holding her breath.

"Kate," I said, smiling at the expression on her face. "Your face is getting red. You should *breathe* now."

She burst out crying, covering her face with her hands. I wrapped my arms around her, her face in the crook of my neck. I pulled a handkerchief out of a pocket and gave it to her so she could wipe her eyes, rocking her back and forth. Then I tilted her head up and kissed her.

"But you're leaving…" she repeated.

"I want you to come with me."

She shook her head. "Africa was so hard for me."

I brushed hair off her cheek. "Not where we'll be. Kenya is so beautiful, Kate. Where I'll work, it's so full of hope and promise. You'll love it. The wildlife is spectacular. You could work on your art, your photography, write…"

"I haven't finished my MA."

"You can take a leave of absence. When we come back, you could finish it."

"What would I go as? Your submissive?"

"As my *love*," I said, filled with emotion. "As the woman I can't live without. And, when we wanted it, and needed it, as my submissive."

She sighed, her eyes still brimming, and leaned against me, her face in the crook of my neck.

When a guest arrived at the front door, I took Kate's hand and led her to the bathroom, closing the door behind us. I lifted her up onto the vanity while I rifled through the drawers in search of a washcloth, which I ran under cold water. I held it to her eyes, which were red from crying, her nose pink and a bit swollen. I leaned against her, resting between her thighs, and stared into her eyes.

"I look a mess," she said and slipped off the vanity. She opened a drawer and took out some makeup. "You don't have to stay with me for this," she said and applied foundation to cover up her red nose.

I sat on the bathtub and watched her in the mirror. "I forgot how much I love watching a woman dress and put on her face," I said. "It's so intimate."

"You used to like it?"

I smiled. "When I was married. I used to watch her in the morning before she went to work."

"What did she do?"

"A nurse—of course. Who else do doctors spend so much time with? We worked together at NYP. If the nurses have a bad opinion of me, it's because of the divorce. It split them into two camps—those who still liked me and those who hated me because of the split."

"Sorry to hear that. It's hard to stay neutral in a divorce."

Kate finished her makeup and turned around, leaned against the vanity and watched me. I knew she probably wanted to hear more about my failed marriage, so as much as I hated speaking about it, I did for her sake.

"I thought I'd never make the same mistake as my father, but I made every single one. He neglected my mother. He was so busy with his business and with his charity and his music that she finally gave up and left him."

"She didn't keep in contact with you?"

I shook my head. "My dad won custody. He had a really great *lawyer*..."

"Who?" she said, her eyes widening. "My father?"

I nodded. "Yep. Your father was working in Family Court then and advised my dad. My dad was just really starting to make money and was able to hire nannies and housekeepers to look after me. The judge thought I'd have a better life with my dad even if it meant I was kept away from my mother. She left and went back to California where her family was, remarried, and that was it. My father never remarried."

"I'm so sorry, Drake," she said, her voice warm and sympathetic. "To grow up without a mother..."

I shrugged. "It explains a lot, really."

She nodded, but didn't say anything else.

I stood up and went to her, putting my arms around her. "I've learned the hard way. Now, enough reminiscing. I want to have a nice evening with you now that we can. Your father wants us to come out with him to dance, but I pointed to my arm and used it as an excuse. I said I wanted to ring in the New Year with you alone. He thought that was probably a better idea, considering..."

"I can't believe he accepted that you're into BDSM…"

I shook my head, smiling. "He said *'I don't care what bedroom games people play in the privacy of their own homes, for God's sake. I've played a few of my own. You have to in order to keep a marriage alive, and I was married to the same woman for twenty one-years…*"

"Bedroom games," she said, smiling back. Then she closed her eyes and leaned against me, her arms slipping around my waist. "Do you suppose he's a bit of a Dom himself?"

"I wonder…" I said. "Sly old bastard, if so. Still, it must be hard for a father to think of his beloved daughter being sexual."

"And vice versa. But, as long as he thinks of it as bedroom games, that's okay by me."

"Seriously, Kate," I said. "I'm pretty tame when it comes to Doms. A lightweight. He said he did his research."

"You're just right for me."

I smiled at that. "I think so."

"I *know* so."

I kissed her and while it started out affectionate, it became passionate quickly, my hands slipping down to the hem of her dress to search for garters, which she hadn't worn.

"No garters?"

"I was too sad to wear them."

"Do you have them here?"

She nodded, a smile starting on her face. "I packed up my things and kind of moved back for a while."

"Go put them on with nothing on underneath."

"Are you serious? At my parents' New Year's Eve dinner?"

"*Please*," I said, grinning. "I didn't get a present from you and I'm feeling all deprived. Consider it your present to me."

She left the bathroom and I went to the living room to wait, enjoying the thought that she'd be bare beneath her dress.

She returned in a few moments and stood at the entry to the living room. I was at the bar where I was speaking with the bartender, who was pouring some Anisovaya into my shot glasses. I took them and turned to Kate, a leer starting on my face when I thought of her wearing her stockings and garters and nothing else.

I went to where she stood by the fireplace and handed her one of the glasses.

"*Za vas, moya lyubov*," I said. "To you, *my love*."

She said nothing, covering her mouth with a hand, smiling through tears.

We shot the Anisovaya back and then I leaned in and kissed her immediately, wanting to taste the anise on her lips and tongue.

"With you looking like that," I said, stepping back to examine her up and down, "and knowing what's underneath that dress? I don't know if I can wait until later. We may have to sneak off in between courses for a quickie."

"You haven't given me a present yet either," she said, a grin spreading on her own face. "Maybe you could use me the way I've always wanted—a fast fuck in the broom closet that leaves me panting, in need of you. Later, you could take your time and satisfy me… Maybe pour some of that Anisovaya over me and lick it off…"

I pulled her against me. "You *are* a kinky little thing, Ms. Bennet. You're going to make me very uncomfortable if you keep up with that teasing mind of yours and then I'll be embarrassed in front of your father's guests because of the tent in my pants. But maybe later, after dessert when there's a lull in things before we get into liqueurs, I'll tug at my ear and you'll go into the bathroom off your bedroom and wait for me. I may just have a nice *big* present for you…"

She closed her eyes, and it pleased me that my words had such an effect on her. That was my Katherine—so responsive. How could I not love her passionately?

After a round of cocktails and some light conversation with

various guests, Ethan joined us, a huge smile on his beefy face, his boisterous gravelly voice indicating he was happy to see us standing together. I stayed with Kate the entire time and did my best to speak with everyone, although my mind was occupied with being alone with her. She never left my side, and together, we talked to whoever came by to greet us.

Nigel arrived with his partner and I was curious to see how Ethan would respond but Ethan smiled and shook Brian's hand and that was it. As soon as Nigel saw Kate, he came right over, introducing Brian to us both. After we said our hellos, Elaine came by and pulled Brian away for a moment to show him some artwork.

Nigel leaned in to Kate and whispered something in her ear. It could have made me a bit mad but I was too ecstatic to let anything bother me.

Then Nigel laid a hand on my shoulder. "I already had my little talk with Drake about you," Nigel said, referring to our little talk at Ethan's fundraiser, "so I won't say anything more."

I smiled, biting back a snide comment.

"Quit being my big brother, Nigel," Kate said, pointing a finger at him.

"Someone has to be. Heath seems too busy with his own children."

Then Nigel leaned down and kissed Kate on the cheek. "Happy New Year, Kate." Then he left us and went to where Brian and Elaine stood, admiring a piece of art.

Kate sighed and turned to me. I put my arm around her shoulder. "What did he say to you that night?" she asked, leaning against me.

"He just told me if I ever hurt a hair on your head, he'd have me thrashed soundly."

We laughed at that. Mostly, we spoke to each other, and I took every opportunity to whisper in her ear, telling her what I wanted to do to her if we did get a chance to meet in the bathroom later.

"Ms. Bennet, I want to slip my hand down under your dress and feel you. Are you already wet for me? I bet you are, you *vixen*..."

"Shh, *Drake*," she said, her cheeks pink, but she couldn't stop smiling.

We sat together at the table as we had that first night at Ethan's fundraising dinner, but this time she paid me constant attention and I couldn't keep my eyes off her, barely acknowledging the rest of the guests, even Ethan himself. Luckily, people seemed to let us be, so we could enjoy each other.

Once dinner was over and the servers took away our dessert plates, Ethan announced that we'd take our after dinner drinks in the living room. Ethan spoke to me about the dance afterwards, and I took the opportunity to tug on my ear so Kate would know I wanted her to go to the bathroom. She glanced away quickly, as if embarrassed, but then she stood up. "Please excuse me."

She left the dining room just as people started to filter out and make their way to the living room. I lagged behind for a few moments, making small talk with Elaine before sneaking down the hall to the front entrance closet, where I removed the gift I'd brought for Kate. I slipped it into my trousers as a joke and opened the door to the bathroom. I went inside, closed the door and leaned against it.

"I have something for you, Ms. *Bennet*."

"You do?"

"In my pants," I said, wanting her to think I meant my erection. "Come and see for yourself. I need you to take it out. It's very uncomfortable."

She obeyed like a good submissive and came to me, opening my suit jacket and running her fingers over my groin. She frowned and opened my fly before reaching in to find a long black velvet jewelry case.

"*Drake…*" She opened it to reveal a black velvet choker with a single teardrop diamond in a white-gold setting.

"I had it made specially for you back before all this happened," I said, taking it out of the case. "I thought a black velvet choker would substitute pretty well for your leather collar and would be more appropriate to wear at special events like tonight." I went behind her and slipped the choker around her neck, fastening it, my eyes meeting hers in the mirror.

She covered her mouth, tears in her eyes.

I adjusted the choker so that the diamond fell in the hollow at the base of her throat, watching in the mirror. "*Beautiful…*" I whispered in her ear, for she was beautiful. I pushed her forward so that she leaned over the vanity facing the mirror. I lifted up her dress, groaning when my hands slid over the garters. Then I gave her another Christmas present.

I *tried* to give it to her just the way she asked.

I really tried but I couldn't stand not seeing her fulfilled.

I was greedy like that.

CHAPTER 31

PACKING up Kate's apartment gave me the opportunity to get to know her a bit better. As we sorted through her possessions, deciding which items to put in storage, throw out or take with us, I learned more about who and what she was. It made me love her even more.

We sorted through her artwork, taking down the framed pictures and stacking them against the wall. I stood at the sound system, hooking my iPhone into it and selecting a song to play.

"What's this?" she said, when I played something new I'd heard and immediately liked, despite it being contemporary.

"It's 'Please Don't Go' by Barcelona."

Kate listened for a moment. "Sounds awfully sad for you."

"I listened to this a lot during those days between Christmas and New Years."

Kate smiled, and turned back to the pictures. I went and stood beside her.

"I want to keep all of these," she said, tilting her head to the side to examine one, "but none of them have to come with us."

"I want this one to come," I said, pointing to the pencil drawing of the knight and his lady.

"You like that one?"

I nodded. "That was me when you met me."

"Really?" Kate turned to me, a frown on her face. "I thought you said it was about me and how I couldn't have sex without intimacy because I wanted to feel like a good girl."

I shook my head and pulled her against me, my arms slipping around her waist. "I can rationalize anything," I said and kissed her neck. "I was trying so hard to keep everything separated, my emotions under control."

She took my hands in hers. "Why? I don't understand. I *wanted* to fall in love. It's a loveless relationship I couldn't imagine."

I exhaled. How to explain? "When my marriage failed and I was given that restraining order, it was as if I had failed as a man." I thought back to that time. "Kate, I was like Flyboy. I was the asshole who didn't know what I was doing. I had to face up to who and what I was. I had to keep myself under complete control. Whatever the reason, I tried to keep you under control, confined to one spot, my emotions restrained. Luckily, I failed miserably."

"I thought you had me quite well under control. I submitted completely and willingly. If it hadn't been for Dawn, you might have had your wish. She kind of forced things."

"Like I said, luckily."

"Do you really feel that way?" Kate asked. "If she hadn't, we might have been happy in a simple D/s relationship and none of this would have happened."

"I was already in love with you, just in denial."

"Already?"

I kissed her neck, my hands moving up under her left breast. "I think I fell in love with you at the concert. No, I *know* I fell in love with you then."

She turned around in my arms, her hands on my chest, and looked me in the eyes. "Why the concert? That was so soon after we met. You hardly knew me."

I shook my head slowly. "You don't understand. I'd heard your father speak about you for years. Katherine the beautiful, the brilliant, the humanitarian, the sweetheart who cried when she listened to music."

"He told you that? You knew that when we went to the concert?"

I nodded, feeling a bit guilty. "That's why I had to be there with you."

"But you left when I asked you to."

"Yes, but I hid and watched you. I had to see you, see if what he said was true."

She turned back around and stared at the drawing of the knight and lady.

"I asked someone who met you what you looked like," I said. "He was sniffing around you, another hungry dog like me, and he said you had these huge green eyes and long dark hair. Fair skin like your late mother. How petite you were but with lush breasts and curvy hips. I think I was a bit in love with you before I even met you. I kept hoping your father would bring you to a function, but he never did, as if he was protecting you. I should have known it was you when I saw you in the hallway at your father's apartment, and then I was so close to you in the bedroom, but I was distracted by your garters."

Kate leaned back against me, squeezing my hands in hers. "Those garters were my undoing."

"No, it was the heels. The heels did it. They're responsible for everything, so as much as I hated Dawn, she made you wear them and I could kiss her for it."

I thought about Kate's former best friend, who wanted to break us up. Kate finally told me the whole story during our reunion night as we lay considering how close we came to breaking up for good. As much as Dawn tried to come between us, in the end, she only succeeded in pushing us closer together.

"You bumped into me and practically fell into my arms at the bar because of them, and you did fall in the alley because of them, and then you were in my arms when I carried you to the bed. You were so lovely and desirable with your cut knees and ripped nylons, your scraped hands and those damn garters. It brought out the doctor in me and the Dom all at the same time. Even before I knew you were her, I was a goner. Not a chance in hell."

I nuzzled the back of her neck.

"Her?"

"The beloved *Katherine*. The daughter of my second father. He was so proud of you. But he would never bring you anywhere, as if you were this princess who was too good for the rest of us. He was the kind of father I felt would never let a man anywhere near you unless he was top notch. I was so damn curious about you but you were like this mythical creature."

She was a mythical creature to me back before I met her.

"I feel like such an idiot," Kate said. "I thought my father disapproved of me. That he thought I was a lightweight compared to Heath and that's why he never invited me to join him."

"He didn't invite you to join him because he was sensitive about your problems after Africa. He wanted to give you time. My father died soon after your return and that's when your father and I really started to be friends. When I asked about you, he said to me that a daughter embodied a father's hopes and dreams. He said he wished for you the kind of man he wanted to be to his own wife—someone who would love you forever, deeply, passionately, and be devoted to you. Someone who would allow you to be who you were, and respect you for it, but who would help bring out the best in you."

"That's so sweet," she said softly.

"That's why I didn't ask you out after we met, despite wanting to. I didn't think I'd be able to be that man."

She turned around again and hugged me, her arms slipping around my waist. I ran my hands over her hair.

"He talked about your trip to Africa. He talked about your thesis. About your position at the school newspaper. I knew you'd be amazing before I ever met you. Like I said, a goner." I smiled, remembering how I wanted to meet Kate for so long. "And then I met you at the fundraiser and you were the girl with the luscious tits and garters and you were Katherine. I wanted to know you so badly. I wanted so badly to be with you despite knowing it was probably impossible for us to be together, given what I was. I thought your father would hate me if he knew…"

She smiled and ran her fingers through my hair. "He loves you like another son."

"And then," I said, pulling her closer. "Then a miracle happened and you were this little subbie, pretending to be a researcher who wanted to meet a Dom and learn about BDSM. You were this sweet little thing Lara wanted me to mentor because she thought you wanted this for real and I was the best teacher she knew. *God*, Kate… You can't understand how I felt when I saw you at the café and realized it was you."

"I was so mortified."

"I was *ecstatic*. There you were, this woman I'd always wondered about, this delicious little morsel of womanflesh I couldn't wait to eat, and you wanted a Dom. It was like I'd won the lottery. Found the pot of gold at the end of the rainbow."

"I felt like a silly girl in above her head, mortified that you knew I was interested in kink."

"I felt like the luckiest man alive." I pulled her closer. "I knew I'd have the battle of my life with you, keeping things under control, but it was a battle I just couldn't turn away from, no matter what."

She stared at me. "My dad talked about you, too. He used to talk about your father. Liam the crazy man, his best friend from 'Nam. A wild sonofabitch. A crazy idealistic socialist. He talked about Liam's son—this brilliant young neurosurgeon who spent time in Africa doing delicate surgeries for free. Donating hospital equipment. A man's man. Solid. Strong. Intelligent. Professional. In control. You sounded like a dream, a fantasy. If it wasn't for the fact you were a Republican, I would have wanted to meet you."

"I told you none of that matters when we fuck." I grinned. "Do you suppose he was matchmaking even then? Before we ever met?"

"He was!" she said and laughed. "I realized it the night of his first campaign fundraiser. He knew you were a Dom and yet he was pushing us together. He thought I needed someone like you."

"He did."

"I do." She pulled me down and kissed me and I felt a stab of emotion in my chest.

"My father would've loved you, too," I said when I pulled away. "I think he'd especially love the thought that you're Ethan's daughter."

"I remember the moment I fell in love with you," Kate said, cupping my cheek. "It was that night on 8th Avenue when you played that song for me. Hearing you play and sing that song, knowing it was from my father to yours and that it meant so much to you. It was as if you were letting me in. Letting go of all the control and dominance and confidence to see right into your heart and I just *fell*."

We embraced, our arms around each other, the bright sun of the clear January day streaming in from the bare windows.

"You know," I said, looking around the apartment, "I always felt deprived after that first night…"

"What do you mean?"

"I never *did* get to fuck you here. If I recall correctly, I walked out of here that night with a boner."

"That was entirely your choice," she said, grinning. "You could have done me. Why didn't you?"

"I didn't want you to think that I would use you like that."

"You still won't, even though it's a fantasy of mine. Even on New Year's Eve, you made me come."

"No, that was just you being far too hot," I said, grinning now, too.

"One of these days, I want you to just fuck me until you come, leaving me panting and desperate for you."

"Why on *earth* would I want you not to come? I said that for psychological purposes because I knew it turned you on. But I wouldn't enjoy myself unless you did."

"Chivalry is not dead with you, Drake Morgan."

"I don't want to leave this apartment without at least christening it," I said, pressing my hips against her. "I want my last memory of this place to be a good one."

Then I kissed her, my mouth finding hers, pulling her up and into my arms. "Let's fuck missionary-style on the bed. It's still here."

"Missionary style?" she said, running her hands up under my shirt. "Again? Where's your imagination?"

"It's the middle of the day," I said. "I want to see you naked beneath me in the full light so I can watch you come." I took her hand, dragging her into the bedroom and throwing her across the bed. Then, I lay on top of her.

"We're having a lot more plain old vanilla sex since New Year's Eve," she said. "I hope you're not losing your taste for D/s and bondage."

"No fear of that," I said, one hand slipping beneath her

sweater to cup her breast. "I love that you're such an eager student. I want to see how far I can take you. I'm always going to be a Dom, Kate. I'm always going to want to have control, but I don't need to use it any longer as a shield to keep things in their proper place."

"Meat, potatoes, and gravy touching each other?"

"My plate is thoroughly mixed up now," I said, smiling. "There's no chance of keeping things compartmentalized any longer. You're in each part of my life and I'm in yours." When she pulled me down for another kiss, I closed my eyes, unable to think of life without her.

Everything was mixed up now and I couldn't imagine it any other way.

THE END

S. E. LUND'S NEWSLETTER

Sign up for S. E. Lund's newsletter and get updates on her releases, sales and even free eBooks!

http://eepurl.com/1Wcz5

Unsubscribe whenever you want – your email will never be shared!

ALSO BY S. E. LUND:

Contemporary Erotic Romance
THE UNRESTRAINED SERIES
The Agreement: Book 1
The Commitment: Book 2
Unrestrained: Book 3
Unbreakable: Book 4

Forever After: Book 5
Everlasting: Book 6 (Coming September 2017!)

∽

THE DRAKE SERIES (The Unrestrained Series from Drake's Point of View)
Drake Restrained
Drake Unwound
Drake Unbound

∽

Military Romance / Romantic Suspense
THE BAD BOY SERIES
Bad Boy Saint: Book 1
Bad Boy Sinner: Book 2
Bad Boy Soldier: Book 3
Bad Boy Savior: Book 4 (C0ming in July 2017)

∽

Paranormal Romance
THE DOMINION SERIES
Dominion: Book 1 in the Dominion Series
Ascension: Book 2 in the Dominion Series
Retribution: Book 3 in the Dominion Series
Resurrection: Book 4 in the Dominion Series
Redemption: Book 5 in the Dominion Series

∽

Coming in 2017
Prince of the City: The Vampire's Pet Part One

Printed in Great Britain
by Amazon